THE AGE OF CHIVALRY —AND VIOLENCE...

Elizabethan England and the war with Spain.
Plots, counterplots and secret couriers.
Romance ashore and the Armada battles at
sea. The whole color-filled panorama of the
momentous 16th Century, its heroes and
heroines, its explorers Sir Francis Drake and
Sir John Hawkins, the mighty King Philip
of Spain, the rival queens of England
and Scotland, Elizabeth and Mary.

And a swashbuckling young English nobleman, George Fitzwilliam, the Iron Cavalier,
who outwitted and skewered his enemies,
tempestuously courted the beautiful Anne
Crofts, and tried to serve two Crowns
at the same time . . .

Donald Barr Chidsey, the master
of richly-textured adventure and romance,
has written his most high-spirited
and exciting novel.

"GRADE-A HISTORICAL FICTION . . ."
—*Miami Herald*

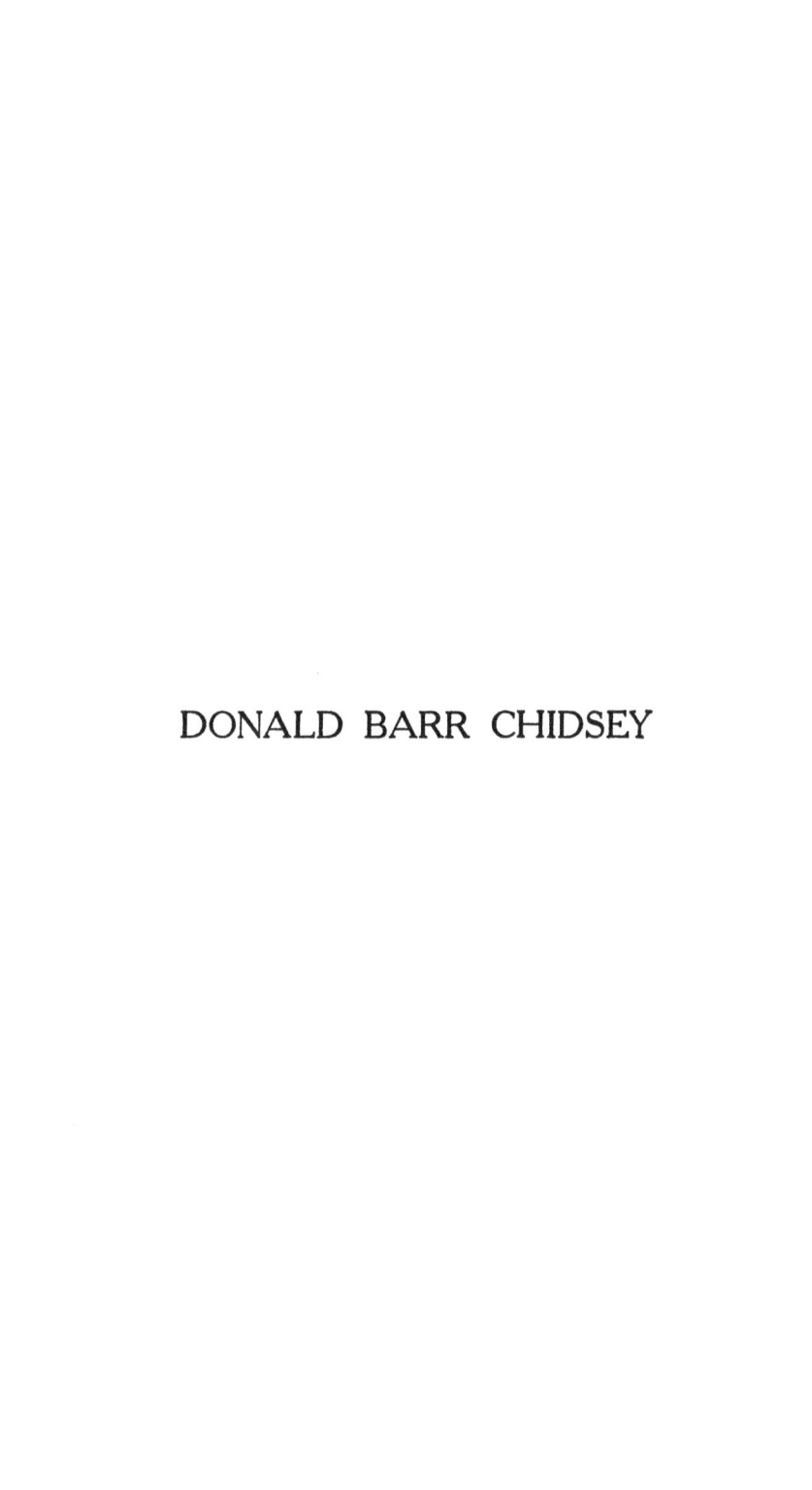

DONALD BARR CHIDSEY

THE
IRON
CAVALIER

(Original title: RELUCTANT CAVALIER)

WILDSIDE PRESS

TO
JOHN CLARK CHIDSEY

The Iron Cavalier ⚜

1

Come with Clean Hands

GEORGE FITZWILLIAM KICKED OFF HIS SLIPPERS, leaned back in his chair, put his feet on a window sill, and wriggled his toes.

As one just released from three years in their most noisome cells, he was unlikely to love Spaniards. But—give the Devil his due. They did know how to dress! And his Aunt Jane had done him well at one of the best tailors in Madrid. George was a prince in appearance.

The slippers, cork-soled, were bright blue with black bows.

The hose, twilled sarsenet, crimson in color, yellow-clocked, fitted with never a wrinkle, reaching to his buttocks.

The sword, silver-hilted, like its companion-piece, the dagger, was Toledo; and the hangers and cross-straps were Cordovan.

The doublet, black silk slashed with silver, was picadilled at its base, ruffled at the cuffs, and had a waist that was girlish, its tightness emphasized by the bombast above and by huge shoulder welts. The ruff was short, stiff with starch, bright yellow.

George's beard, until lately Visigothic, had been trimmed almost to the point of invisibility. There was a pearl in the lobe of his left ear; perfume at his armpits; and on his head a high-crowned, narrow-brimmed velvet bonnet.

"So you have actually met King Philip," snorted Master Hawkins.

"Aye."

George still was smiling, a fond bemused smile. He did not like Plymouth, a noisy town; but it was good to be back in England.

"And—did you spread your tail when you bowed?"

George frowned. In this year of Our Lord 1571 each unpropertied person, no matter what his blood, must have a protector. This was in the nature of things, and George did not chafe against it. His own older brother had inherited so little that even for him life would be a struggle: indeed, William Fitzwilliam had been obliged to go to Ireland as deputy lord lieutenant. George knew that he himself would have to be somebody's "man," and John Hawkins,

7

though a commoner, was not unkindly. George might have hoped for some post more exalted, since he was connected on his mother's side with the Dormers and the Sidneys, on his father's with John Russell; but there were many cousins and nephews to be cared for, and Hawkins at least was prosperous, a pusher. The trouble was, John Hawkins could not seem to forget George Fitzwilliam's family. It was *he* who, defensively, obliquely, yet unmistakably, sometimes made sarcastic references, as now, to the difference in their respective stations. *He,* not George, resented it.

"Did I do anything amiss?" George asked mildly.

"Oh, you did well. But—your aunt couldn't get the other prisoners out?"

"Couldn't or wouldn't. Me, I think it was a trick to win some concession from you. Which," George added grimly, "it certainly did."

"And the king believed it?"

"Aye, once I'd told him that you fretted and you'd turn over to him every ship you commanded when the Spanish invasion came, provided the captives from New Spain were freed *and* provided all your mariners' back pay was furnished."

"I had prepared him. I'd already approached his ambassador in London, who's utterly gullible."

"So is Philip. He might be perplexed by your persistence in trying to free those men, but that you should seek to recoup your money losses—that seemed natural to him."

Hawkins liked this young man and valued him, but he suspected he would never understand him.

"*My* persistence?" he said softly. "It was *you* who was ready to move Heaven and Hell if it would get those nineteen men out of jail. It was *you* who returned to Spain with my false offer of a fleet sell-out, though surely you don't fancy that sort of work?"

George said nothing, staring out the window.

"This is praiseworthy, Fitzwilliam, but it's puzzling too. *You're* out. Why should you spend so much time and trouble—yes, and run such risks—for *them*? Every one is a man of low degree. Oh, I grant that in the eyes of God we are all equal! But you can't pretend that those mariners are men to your own taste?"

George regarded his silken toes for a moment. When he spoke it was low.

"After you've lain in the same lousy straw with men for months on end, and shared the same pail with them, and

8

swatted the same damned cockroaches, rank doesn't seem to make much difference."

"You're not about to say that you *love* these men?"

"Yes," George said carefully. "Yes, I think I love them."

John Hawkins opened his mouth to laugh, but his servant hadn't stirred; and after a while John Hawkins closed his mouth, having given forth no sound. Embarrassed, he harrumphed.

"Of couse King Philip had heard of me?"

"Of course. But he pointed out that he was being asked to take the word of a pirate—"

"A pirate!"

"—as, in his view, sir, you are. I of course drew myself like a man that had been buffeted, and I cried that my master was honorable."

Hawkins grunted with indignation.

"There at least you did not need to lie to him. You, uh, you mislike the rest of it, Fitzwilliam?"

"Aye. Falsehood always has stunk in my nostrils. And it's no joy to call yourself a traitor's go-between. Even though you know better."

"As you do. All I'm working for is the release of those prisoners. Nor do I sally forth on my own. I consulted Burghley first."

"Who?"

"Master secretary Cecil. Sir William. The queen's first minister. He was elevated while you were away. Lord Burghley now."

"I see."

Again George wriggled his toes, glorying in his apparel, watching Plymouth, smelling the air of England. It was almost too good to be true. But the others who had been captured with him at San Juan de Ulua: they must be rescued. There had been forty-one of them, including George, in Mexico. There had been thirty-three when they were shipped across the sea to Seville. There had been nineteen when at last George was able to get a message to his aunt, the former Jane Dormer, presently duchess of Feria. He wondered how many there were now. Whatever the number, they would be lying in clothes that crawled, praying for death, cursing the sturdiness that had caused them to survive.

"And—then?" Hawkins persisted.

"King Philip said he would consider your offer if I got from his 'sister of Scotland,' as he called her, a letter vouch-

9

ing for your *bona fides*. He would write me an introduction to her. Such honor!"

"What would Mary Stuart know about me?"

"Nothing. You're here, and she is a prisoner at Sheffield."

"A guest, you mean."

"I doubt that Philip's English could encompass that distinction. He did ask me if you had ever met, and I was obliged to say no. But the letter he gave me is harmless."

"How do you know?"

"Why, I opened it and read it."

"You— The seal looks solid."

"I used steam. It wasn't hard. And my hands were clean."

"But then—"

"True, there's something written in the margin."

"Ah?"

"You don't see it at first. You must heat the paper. Then it comes out a watery brown, for a little while. I can guess what was used for ink. Any prisoner could. Yet it might have been lemon juice, the effect is similar. They have many lemons in Spain."

"Did you memorize the message in the margin?"

"Of course."

George brought his legs down. Gangling, lazy, he rose. He crossed to John Hawkins' writing desk.

"Here—"

EXTCUVCVKOXVUEKCOUK3OGV4ORCTVKCCPCIGPFXOUKPV.

Hawkins' eyes popped like tennis balls.

"It's some sort of cipher!"

"An easy one. I cracked it on the way back."

John Hawkins was a solid, stolid man, a merchant not easy to sway. He was in his middle thirties, well past the hot emotions of youth, and had but lately served a term as lord mayor of Plymouth. Though a great gambler, his daring proverbial, his seamanship celebrated, in person he was staid, a man whose eyes never flashed, who seldom raised his voice, a man as firmly foundationed as this his square stone house in Kinterbury Street. Now, however, he was trembling, and his face gleamed with perspiration.

"Do you know what this means, man? We must make for Burghley!"

George stared at him in amazement.

"I had hoped to ride to Sir John Crofts' place."

10

"To see Anne? She's still alive. And she knows that you are, too."

"But, sir, I haven't seen her in three years."

"She's not married, if that's what you mean. She can't afford it."

George sighed.

"Neither can I—yet."

"Hurry! We're going to London!"

John Hawkins rang for a servant to bring his boots, to saddle horses. George never had seen him in such a state. A mite awed, despite himself, George retrieved his pantouffles, strapped on his sword-and-dagger.

"And when I meet this new baron, what should I tell him?"

"Why, the truth!"

George sighed again.

"That at least will be a change," he said.

2

Read Me This Riddle

GEORGE HATED THE SEA; and understandably he hated seaports even more, since if their stink was much the same as that of any ship—bilge and tar, sour beer and stale vomit —it was multiplied and intensified, and the water bobbed garbage; while the air, what with horses and carts, tuns, levers, and hucksters, was loud with sounds to split the ear.

Once Plymouth was behind them, George expanded, looking right and left, laughing, sometimes singing:

> *"In Sherwood lived stout Robin Hood,*
> *An archer great—none greater.*
> *His bow and shafts were sure and good,*
> *Yet Cupid's are much better."*

That part of England, the south, is lovely in any season, but it is especially lovely in May. Three weeks earlier, when he first returned from Spain, George had been given no chance to get away from the cacophony that was Plymouth. He had been shoved off on the next ship with instructions to take an offer to his majesty Philip, by grace of God king of Castile, king of Leon, king of Aragon, of the Two Sicilies, Jerusalem, Granada, Toledo, Valencia, Galicia, Sardinia,

11

Cordova, Navarre, Corsica, Murcia, Jaen, Algarve, Algeciras, Gibraltar, the Canary Islands, the East and West Indies, and all the islands and continents of the Ocean, a small, rickety, squinting man with a mean mind and the soul of a clerk, who was also, incidentally, archduke of Austria, duke of Burgundy, duke of Brabant, duke of Milan, count of Hapsburg, count of Flanders, count of Tyrol, count of Barcelona, lord of Biscay, lord of Molina. . . . This, the greatest emperor in the world—one with a mouse's squeal for a voice, and small suspicious eyes—had listened to the glib young ambassador and seemingly had swallowed the fabrication. Now George was back, inhaling England.

> *"Robin could shoot at many a hart and miss;*
> *Cupid at first could hit a heart of his."*

He had no wish to think, only to glory in being alive—much as when he was released from prison and lay on his back, eyes closed, drinking the sunshine through every pore.

Not that there was much sunshine on the east road out of Plymouth. It rained or threatened rain most of the time. George didn't care. This was *clean* rain forsooth, good rain!

He reproached himself for his happiness. Those poor lads still lay, far below the street level, in Seville. He wondered how they were, and whether they still clung to a belief that somehow he would save them. He hoped so, for he meant to. He wondered in particular about Ellis Waters, that seamed, acidulous little prisoner with whom George had shared a leg-iron chain three feet long for more than a year. You got to know a man mighty well in those circumstances. Ellis was a feltmonger's son, illiterate, runty, short of temper too, a boy in age but with mean eyes and the face of an evil monkey. In fact, except in the matter of clothes he much resembled his gracious majesty Philip II, by grace of God king of Castile, king of Leon, etc., etc. Even his fellow mariners looked down upon Ellis Waters. Yet George Fitzwilliam had come to love him and he prayed for him a moment, there on the road. Silently, without moving his lips, he prayed for them all, that they might be delivered out of Hell.

They quit the sea, turning north, and then all the world was not gray but green. Drift-lanes led to the village fields, cowslip and larkspur thick at their edges. Among the fern in the glades hares leapt and flies buzzed, and now and then, abruptly, would come the screech of a woodpecker. The houses smelled of fresh thatch, the woods of mint and acorn.

White-painted stiles were jostled by gillyflower and love-lies-a-bleeding. All the while the cuckoo called. And everywhere, making a mingle-mangle of fields and lanes alike, were the hedgerows. The dear hedgerows! George believed that it was them that he'd missed the most.

It was hard to keep his somber thoughts, and hard not to sing, and soon, impulsively, like any lark, he was at it again.

> "Hey, jolly Robin!
> Ho, jolly Robin!
> Hey, jolly, jolly Robin,
> Love finds out me
> As well as thee
> To follow me to the green wood."

His companion was not so gay. Essentially a man of the sea, John Hawkins was not an imposing sight as he sat the stolid shaggy Hungarian. He was very old, nearly forty. Yet he was dogged. He resented every pause, no matter what its purpose; and on the late afternoon of the second day they reached London Bridge.

George sagged with weariness—his muscles, made soft by those years in prison, pleaded for a rest—and he would have sought an inn. To his amazement, John Hawkins command-ed that they continue, not drawing rein until they reached Cecil House in the Strand, where the bodyservants were dis-missed, while George and Master Hawkins entered, George being struck by the deference shown his paunchy, glum companion.

The place was vast, a palace; yet in a matter of minutes they were ushered into the presence of the queen's first councilor, the most hated man, as he was the most feared, in all the realm.

Burghley harrumphed, nodding; then thoughtfully spat.

"Aye, Hawkins, your courier arrived about noon. So this is the one who will meet Scotland? Sit down, both of you."

George's first thought, an irreverent one, was that his lord-ship need fear no pun upon his title. He was not burly. Ra-ther, though large, he showed flabbiness, and appeared to have sunk into his bones. He was very old, even older than Hawkins. His ruff was stubby, his doublet and gown and flat cap rich but severe. He wore a massive gold chain around his neck, but no gems. The chain might have been a symbol of office—perhaps a yoke.

This man's eyes, a wishywashy blue, were exceedingly

intelligent; and on occasion they could harden. Mostly he kept them cast down. But when he raised them, to look directly at the person he was addressing, it caused a shiver to pass up the back of that person's neck and head.

Burghley never smiled, and he looked as though he had been born grave.

He sat with his back to a window through which, over his shoulder, they could see in the failing afternoon light London's main thoroughfare, the Thames. They could hear the cries of wherrymen and bargemen, the bumping of tilt boats, the squeal of tholepins, creak of oars, a tintinnabulant sound that was blurred and seemed far away.

Burghley spat again. Without looking up, he said quietly to the servant who had admitted the callers:

"Close that door, and don't let anybody come near."

By following Burghley's own example and not looking up as he spoke, George found that it was possible to avoid the disconcerting directness of that stare. But he didn't enjoy keeping his head down. It did not become him.

"Why did you open this message?"

"Because I was bored and had nothing else to do. Also because the thing looked strange. Why should a crowned monarch send to an imprisoned exile a request for information about an admiral who has proposed to sell his country's principal war fleet? And do this, mind you, by means of a messenger he professed to esteem a pirate?"

"Did I not understand Master Hawkins here to say that you are kin to the duchess of Feria?"

"Yes, my lord. My aunt, Jane Dormer, was a maid-in-waiting on the late queen, Mary."

"Bloody Mary!"

Elizabeth's minister said this with a vehemence as unexpected in so mild-seeming a man as the roar of a lion would have been from the throat of a rabbit.

"The same, lord. And when Philip of Spain came to this land to wed her—Queen Mary, I mean—he had with him the count de Feria—a count then, not a duke. They met, and they became affianced, and after Feria had returned to Spain he sent for her to come and marry him. That was in '59, before the present queen had ascended to the throne."

"Whom God bless," muttered John Hawkins.

"My aunt traveled in state, as became her fiancé's position," George went on, "and I was a page in her suite. My relatives thought it would be a way for me to become acquainted with the Continent, with no cost to them. For my

14

aunt, being afraid of the sea, went through France—very slowly. I picked up some French then, my lord. And later I was a part of her household in Madrid for more than two years. So I have Spanish as well."

"But who was it taught you that steam will loosen wax? I never would have known that this"—and Burghley tapped the letter—"had been tampered with."

"I think nobody, sir. Certainly I can't *remember* anybody ever telling me that. But I'd noticed that steam undid things, usually. It was worth trying. And it worked."

"Why, so it did. And the message? You memorized that?"

"Not word for word, no. It didn't seem worth the trouble. It was in French, and went something like this—"

Burgley, having heard, belched.

"Now the marginal note What made you seek for that with heat?"

George shrugged.

"Prisoners are forever hiding things. It's natural. You get very cunning when you haven't anything else to do. And you look for secreted things, for you have plenty of time."

"That message I trust you've remembered exactly?"

"Oh, in truth. Here—"

George wrote. In the dusk, bent over, Lord Burghley peered at what he had made.

"You believe you have broken the cipher?"

"My lord, I'm sure I have. It falls right into place. First, it was a question of what language it would be in. French? But Latin was conceivable. You'll notice there are several *X*'s *and V*'s, and once they come together, *XV*. Those could be Roman numerals. They could also be letters in any European language. And there are at least two Arabic figures —a *3* and, three spaces away, a *4*. Each of those is followed by an *O*, which could be either the letter or the zero. Assuming that each is the figure—which seems a good way to start—that means that there are two letters, *G* and *V*, between two figures, *30* and *40*. In that case the word between them would probably be 'and.' Now that happens to be a two-letter word in both Latin and French, and exactly the same, 'et,' as you probably know, sir."

"Yes, I do know."

"So if we say that *G* represents *E* while *V* represents *T*, then it's easy to see that we have a simple transpositional cipher, the kind they call a Julius Caesar's, because each of those letters is two spaces in the alphabet behind the one it's supposed to represent. The Latin and the French al-

15

phabets are the same, you know, sir. They only have twenty-four letters instead of twenty-six, like ours. They're missing the *W* and the *Y*."

"I know that too," said Lord Burghley.

"So it turns out to be Latin after all. It makes sense in Latin."

Poor though the light was, Lord Burghley performed an astonishing feat of concentration. He read off the entire message without a miss.

"Exactly," said George. "Breaking it into letters, in a logical way, you get *CURA STATIM UT SCIAM SI 30 ET 40 PARATI AD AGENDUM SINT.*"

"That is correct," said Lord Burghley.

George, fearing embarrassment, was hoping that his lordship would translate for a puzzled John Hawkins; but when Burghley showed no inclination to do so (perhaps being unable to conceive of a person who was unacquainted with Latin), George diffidently explained.

"It means 'Take care at once that I know whether thirty and forty are ready to act.' "

"It does," bumbled Burghley. "It means exactly that."

The room was quite dark now. The eyes of William Cecil, baron of Burghley, glowed like live coals. Nobody stirred.

"And who," Hawkins asked at last, "are thirty and forty?"

"Cipher names for conspirators, probably, although I don't know," answered Burghley. "The ones I suspect are in high places, and I must step with care. First we shall see what our linguistic young friend here learns for us at Sheffield."

"I had hoped to visit in Northampton—"

"You will go to Sheffield Castle. You will meet Mary, Queen of the Scots. You cannot refuse this, Master Fitzwilliam, for unless I am mistaken—and I'm no alarmist—the safety of the throne, the very future of England, may hang upon what you learn."

"Yes, sir."

"You should be warned that you are about to encounter an extraordinary person. Mary Stuart has been called the most beautiful woman in the world. And she's no fool. I can vouch for that! I met her myself a few months ago, and—well, I am more than twice your age, Fitzwilliam, but I have never been the same since. You understand?"

"I don't believe so, sir."

"You'll learn," promised Burghley.

3

A Wash and a Wet

THE INNS OF ENGLAND—so visitors from the Continent said—were the finest in the world. Some were sumptuous, and could put up two hundred travelers, more or less. They were expertly staffed—kitchen, court, stables, taproom. They were handsomely furnished. Their food and wines were fabulous, their rooms ducal. They changed sheets with every guest.

The Continentals must have confined their wanderings to the larger highways: the Dover road, up from the Channel; the Chester road, which went by way of Barnet, St. Albans, Dunstable, Lichfield, Stony Stratford, Coventry; the Bristol road, Reading, Marlborough, Chippenham; the Carlisle road south from the town by way of Lancaster, Wigan, Warrington, and Newcastle-under-Lyme, to join the Chester road at Lichfield (a busy intersection;) and of course the Great North Road. It is unlikely that they strayed along lesser routes. They would hardly have kept their enthusiasm if they had.

It was the Great North Road that George Fitzwilliam followed for as far as he conveniently could, quitting it at Biggleswade, where he turned west toward Bedford. It was then that he met the mudholes.

Had he planned to go directly to Sheffield, as he'd been ordered to do, he would have stayed on the Great North Road at least as far as Retford. But the queen of Scots could wait. George would not ride half the length of the kingdom without stopping at Okeland Manor to see Anne Crofts. She was not married, Hawkins had said. Good!

It was right in the middle of Northamptonshire, where the road forked—one part going due north toward Market Harborough, Ashby-de-la-Zouch, and Sheffield, and the other, a mere track branching westward to the left, in the direction of Rugby—that there was situated a Crossed Keys.

The grander hostelries were proud of their signs, important accessories since so few of the wayfarers could read. Some of these, men whispered, had cost as much as thirty-five or even forty pounds. However, the sign at the Crossed Keys in Northampton was not such a one. The fee for its painting might have been a jug of wine, paid in advance. That sign swung despondently, at a crazy an-

17

gle, before a structure badly in need of paint and at first glance deserted. The Crossed Eyes was the neighborhood name for this inn.

Nevertheless, since he was so near to Okeland Manor, George decided to pause for a wash and a wet.

He dismounted, noting that no one offered to hold his horse. There were two living things in sight: a fleabitten dog all but asleep, which lacked even the energy to bark, and a saturnine green-aproned scarecrow who stood in the doorway and must have been the boniface, though his countenance belied this title.

The Chinese have a saying that he whom it hurts to smile never should open a shop. Mine host at the Crossed Keys might have heeded this. Acid-eyed, dour in the droop of his mouth, he was a stranger to George, himself not a stranger to the Crossed Keys. This was not a posting stage and never had paid well: it might have changed hands several times since George Fitzwilliam sailed for America.

"You seek lodgment?"

"At this hour? No, only a yard of ale and a chunk of cheese. Banbury. And water."

"There's the trough over there."

It was a change from the over-exuberance of the usual tub-of-butter host; but it irked George, who watered and walked his own horse, then washed face and hands, the proprietor having disappeared into the shadows of the ordinary.

A lone horseman was coming up the road, coming from the south, approaching the point of the fork where George stood. George wondered at this, for even in broad daylight men usually coursed the back roads in bands. However, George did not stand gawping, for it was his belief that a man who travels alone should mind his own business—or at least should appear to do so.

He loosened the saddle girth, and patted and thanked the horse. Here was no racer! John Hawkins, to the city born and bred, might risk thousands of pounds in maritime gambles on the far side of the world, but he could be uncommonly close, a pinchpenny, in matters near at hand. To him a horse was primarily a pack animal; and he could see no sense in paying the demanded extra fourpence a day for one that could be spurred to ten miles an hour. Yet this mare was what couriers called a good continuer: she had heart and was strong. So George congratulated her.

The cheese was excellent, though the bread, made of rye, was coarse, cretaceous, and the ale was flat.

18

The boniface, his eyes squinched half-shut in disapproval, his lips twisted as though he held a mouthful of citron juice, watched from the far side of the room, saying never a word. There did not appear to be another person in the inn; and when the court doorway suddenly was darkened it gave both of them a start.

"Your worship?" said the innkeeper uninvitingly.

The newcomer was very large and filled the doorway. Though they could not distinguish his features, the light being behind him, each instantly took him for a foreigner.

"A jack of wine, and some of that cheese our friend here is eating. It looks good."

The speech was accented. An Italian? When they could see him better his beard, trimmed high, would seem to confirm this. His clothes, dark, all but funereal, were neither rich nor drab. The two most remarkable things about him, aside from his great size, were his manner and his rapier.

Your large and powerfully muscled man is seldom truculent, since he knows no need to be. It is the small one, the runt, who shows too ready to fight. Yet about this giant in the Crossed Keys—and this despite the fact that he kept his voice low, his movements lazy—George Fitzwilliam read an inbuilt belligerency, a tenseness always near the snapping-point. It was not simply a superabundance of vitality, though he did have that. It was training. It was the result of deliberate habit, professionalism. The man was a bravo. He was a hired bully.

The sword went with him. It was a Spanish rapier, the longest George ever had seen, with a steel bellguard and long steel outcurved quillions. The hilt like the scabbard was plain, but sturdy. George of course could not see the blade itself, but he had no doubt that it was Toledo of a temper to compare with his own.

There weren't many such blades in England, where indeed there were not many men who knew how to use the rapier, a new weapon imported from Spain, double-edged, dangerous with both cut and thrust, which made it possible to attack and defend at the same time. The broadsword, together with a tiny dishpan-lid buckler held at arm's length, still was the favorite weapon among men of all ranks excepting those fine-feathered ones who spent much time at court; the rapier was esteemed new-fangled, over-fashionable, even effeminate, and no blade for a true-born Englishman. George, most of his life, had taken the rapier for granted—in Madrid, when he served as a page for his Aunt Jane, he had been a pupil of the illustrious Luis

19

Pacheco de Narvaez himself, and his lessons in fence had been as stringently supervised as those in dancing—but he knew that this was not the case with the majority of his fellow countrymen.

Now, what was a bird of ill omen like this doing in the middle of sleepy Northamptonshire, so far from any court or port?

"The wine, aye," said the innkeeper, who appeared to take a delight in being the bearer of bad news, "but not the cheese. That wedge the gentle over there eats happens to be the last bit of Banbury in the house."

George's dagger, which he had been using, was on the trencher before him. Without hesitation he cut the Banbury in half.

"Please take this," he said. "There's more than I need anyway."

The stranger hooked a foot behind a stool and jerked it to the other side of the table from George—since the boniface showed no readiness to do this for him—and when he sat down he was reading George intently.

"*Muchas gracias, vuestra merced,*" he said.

George nodded.

"*De nada.*"

"I knew you were Spanish," went on the other, "from your clothes."

"You are very perceptive."

"Whereabouts in Spain did your mercy live?"

George waved vaguely.

"About half the time in the Duke de Feria's palace, the other half of the time in one of the Archbishop of Seville's deepest dungeons. They were equally objectionable. Too confining."

He gave his companion no chance to comment on this, but rose, nodding an apology, and paid the shot. He went outside.

Before George had so much as retightened his saddle girth, the big man was by his side.

"I wasn't very hungry," he explained, "and with only a few hours of light left to get to an acceptable stop we'd better push it, eh?"

"We?"

"Why, your worship is riding north. I saw you ahead of me, down the road there. You're making for Leicester, I take it?"

George said nothing.

"Or further, Sheffield, perhaps?"

George mounted.

"Your suggestion has many merits," he said, "but I am taking this turnoff to the west, see? Good afternoon."

A little along the track that led to Okeland, on the pretext of seeking something in his saddlebag, he sneaked a look behind him. The bravo still was standing there, fists on hips, feet spread wide, as he stared after George Fitzwilliam.

George rubbered out his lips, and shook his head.

"Something tells me that I'll see that man again."

4

Beware Jezebel!

As ONE WHO HAD BEEN BITTEN by a thousand bugs George Fitzwilliam knew many minor sensitivities. Since his release he could never seem to wash enough, and he bathed his whole body, not simply hands and face. He might do this every week, even two or three times a week. It was an obsession. But he did it gingerly, as though he feared that his flesh would still smart.

Also, he seldom rode forth without a loo, or half-mask. He wore this not, like so many, to advertise his gentility—his word could do that—but to protect the upper part of his face. His beard, trig though it now was, could guard chin and lips and lower cheek; but the fashion was for extremely short head hair, and George's new velvet bonnet in the latest mode had a curled brim that was no more than a decoration, so that unless he wore this vizard, the upper part of his face—paled and softened in the years of darkness, dampness, and fetid air—would be exposed to sunlight, and dust, fog, rain. This, then, was part of his usual traveling costume, and he was not miffed when he rode through a village where the yokels guffawed, jeering at him as a lady. George would only grin, and wave to them.

He had, however, forgotten about this mask, so natural a part of him had it come to seem, when he crested a rise and came into sight of Okeland.

Sunlight goldplated the landscape—one of hills, aimless lanes, meadows slightly askew, and a sleepiness that seemed deep-seated. The manor house was new, a simple, two-story, bar-shaped building built of oak and local limestone, a cream color shading into tawny, yet it appeared to have been settled there snugly for a long while. It

21

was not as well windowed as Sir John Crofts would have wished, for glass was expensive, yet such panes as there were glittered brightly. But there was no sign of movement behind them. No one walked the garden. The outbuildings—dairy, dovecote, chickenhouse, stable, cowshed, cider mill—were utterly still. Hazed by the sun, murmurous of bees, sprinkled with birdsong, here was a scene that might have entoiled any poetically minded person from the city. It struck horror to George Fitzwilliam.

Was this the peace of an English countryside—or was it the silence of danger? Had the place been visited? The thousands of masterless rascals who infested the roads of England—the rogues and foists, the Abrahams, the jarkmen, hookers, fraters, whipjacks, dummerers—were desperate persons. The average wayfarer had lost an ear or the end of his nose, or had been branded on the face, to testify that he was an "habitual." Governmental patience would go no further. The next time he was caught he would infallibly be hanged. Knowing this, he was not prone to tame treatment of such as might fall into his hands in out-of-the-way places. Moreover, these rovers always were hungry, even ravenous. Had such a pack . . . ?

Sir John Crofts, as his record in Ireland could attest, was a stout fighting man. But he was only one, and his staff was small.

The thought was an icy hand that squeezed George Fitzwilliam's heart so that he came to a halt. The mare, that good continuer, was willing enough.

George closed his eyes, shook his head, muttered a prayer, then looked again.

Now here indeed was an act of enchantment, for the spell was lifted. Okeland—still for perhaps no more than three beats of a butterfly's wing—suddenly came to life.

There was a rustling flutter at the dovecote; a scullery boy, whistling, crossed the court; somebody opened a window and shook out a duster; a cock, neck outstretched, wattles flopping, started to chase a hen around the chicken run; sensing George for the first time, and ashamed of having been caught asleep, an unseen hound began to bark furiously.

And George saw coming toward him, not twenty feet away, Anne Crofts.

She had not seen him, for she was walking with her head low in thought, making, George supposed, for the strawberry patch behind him. A small woman, compact, round-armed, tow-headed, this afternoon she was also bare-headed, a shocking circumstance. Not only did she wear no sort of cap, but her honey-colored hair was innocent of flowers, lace, jewelry. This, together with her plain puce-colored homespun kirtle, her unwired hips, and a petticoat so short that it showed her feet and even at times her ankles, elsewhere would have suggested a peasant.

She was slightly below George, walking an upgrade, and despite the averted head her body moved at a brisk pace, arms swinging, hips aroll, while her breasts, not braced by buskery, jogged.

With a small glad cry, George dismounted directly before her. She looked up, startled.

"Pray what is it you seek?"

"Why, recognition first, my chuck," he cried, snatching off the mask, "and then mayhap a cousinly buss, eh?"

"George!"

The kiss was much more than familiar, and a dozen persons in the manor might have seen them on the hillside, and probably did. George reflected, as he held her, patting her, petting her, upon the difference between women of the English countryside and women of Spain or the Spanish colonies he had known. Yet it was good to have Anne again; she must have been twenty, but she was still lovely, especially since the sight of George had taken the cockiness out of her. She clung to him, sobbing with relief.

"They said thou wert dead, but I never did believe it. Then Master Hawkins rode here, and told us that thou wert coming back."

"John Hawkins himself?"

"Oh, aye."

Who would have thought it of that grumpy old man, so squeamish in saddle? He had not told George this, simply mentioning that he had notified Sir John and Mistress Anne. Even if he'd come only from London, where he had an office now, it was full seventy miles; and from Plymouth town it must be more than twice that. George was touched. He resolved to be a better servant in future.

"That was more than a month ago. I'd never believed, before, that thou wert dead, but *then*—I began to believe it."

"I live," George said simply, "though there were times I wished I didn't. But that's past. I would have come instanter upon landing in England, but they sent me back to Spain. Didn't grant me a chance to catch my breath."

"It must have been a most important mission."

23

"It was," he said cautiously, as he disentangled himself. "Now, how fares thy father?"

The master of Okeland himself answered this question by his arrival, a bit out of breath, from the direction of the house. Sir John was smallish and weather-bitten. An old warrior, he made no show of courtliness. His chest was thin, his face too. He was a notably handsome man, with a graying beard, the nose of an intelligent hawk, and eyes large, dark blue, very expressive—Anne's own eyes.

George felt sorry for Sir John Crofts. As they rushed into each other's arms, whooping their delight, he had caught a glint of gladness in the knight's eyes, a glint he knew had been caused by the sight of his, George's, brave new clothes.

Sir John was anything but greedy, mean of spirit. But he was human; and his road had been a rocky one. A widower, almost landless, he had lost both of his sons, one in Ireland, the other in the Low Countries, and was left with a daughter, so much younger than the dead lads, something indeed of an afterthought, and two aged cantankerous maiden sisters who were dependent upon him.

He adored his daughter. Nothing could have made him so happy as to see her wed where her heart was. And when a young man returns from America in such costly garb, any father might be permitted his instant of wild hope.

"Nay, sir," George laughed as they finished their embrace. "I'm as poor as ever. Aunt Jane Dormer bought me these rags."

"We'd heard that Hawkins heaped it high—till the Spaniards broke their pledge at Ulua. And then he limped home with nothing. But *thou* art back, there's the main thing! Come along. A mug of ale, and then I'll show thee around."

Bored with country life, delighted to have a man to talk with, Sir John prattled on as he led the way to the house. The path was narrow and they passed in single file, Anne in the middle, George last, frankly studying the figure of the woman before him.

For she *was* a woman, and this jolted George. He could not remember a time when he had not meant to marry Anne Crofts. Three years had done a great deal so that she was no longer the wiry wench he'd once climbed trees with, and anticipation tingled him now. Perhaps he should have been ashamed of this feeling; but he wasn't.

A peasant? Oh, no. She was rather a fine healthy animal, despite her smallness. And if those hips and buttocks he looked at, being without whalebone, were somewhat wider

24

and more protuberant than a fine lady of the court would have deemed proper, at least there was no waddle about them. They didn't flap. Here was a woman who, without being smudged by it, belonged to the land. Here, when they could marry, they'd live. George was somewhat shocked by the lack of a bonnet or even a cap, which seemed to him carrying country liberty too far, but the free-swinging body pleased him. You wouldn't see anything like that at court. But Anne was too honest, too straightforward for the court anyway, no woman's paradise at best, since a jealous female, seated on the throne, ruled it. It was bad enough, George reflected, to see men making their knees callous from groveling, slapping smiles upon their mouths as readily as they might slap masks upon their eyes—

> "Cog, lie, flatter, and face:
> Four ways at Court to win your grace."

—but for a woman, it would be Hell. No matter what happened, George thought, Anne must stay here. She belonged to Okeland.

"Here we are, lad."

George was disappointed by what he saw at the house. Sir John pattered of breeding a rag of colts, of marling and skuttling and the difficulty of hiring sarclers these days; but as George was led through the screens, the spicery, the maltery, the dry and the wet larders, the pewter room, the "warm room" where hams and bacon were being smoked, he shook his head. That garden wall, he had noted, not mentioning it, still was not built. And precious little else, as far as he could see, had been done. Sir John might boast of his boldness in trying an innovation from Holland, the planting-out of turnips in open fields; he might splutter about the poor return from flax and saffron, as he might gloat over the high price of wool; but the fact remained, undeniable, that in the three years since George had been here, not a single painted cloth had been added to the walls of Okeland and hardly another piece of furniture, while the staff, as gathered for food, looked definitely smaller. "But I clack on! *Thou* careth nothing about the saffron crop!"

George did care about it. But he was embarrassed; and just at that moment, at table, he would have preferred to look at Anne Crofts. She was ravishing in a yellow kirtle, white cutwork forepart, a dark blue gown open down the

25

front, and below her bodice the scarlet taffeta stomacher he had brought her from London town. But to see her he would have been obliged to lean far over the table and peer past her two elderly aunts like any gawping fool, while to talk to her he would have had to shout.

The Croftses did not have feudal pretensions. The one real meal of the day, dinner, which started in the middle of the afternoon, they ate in the great-hall with all their servants, to the number of about thirty, excepting those in the kitchen and scullery and those who fetched the food. But all tables, connected, were on the same level, while the food and wine at one end was the same as that at the other. The family and George were the only ones seated above the "salt," a silver cellar that had belonged to Sir John's mother; but it was mere covention because everybody was seated on the same side, since this made it so much easier for the serving men. This was the reason George was not vouchsafed a stare at Anne in her surprisingly wide farthingale, her waist a wasp's, her face now pale as that of any court lady. Perhaps it was just as well.

The food was sound—pigeons, spitchcocked eels, a pastry of fallow deer, carrots, radishes, cabbage, sugar meats, rock samphires, and gallons of perry and of wine—but the noise was such that a man couldn't have heard himself think.

Later, the cloths and crumbs were cleared away, the boards and trestles too, and only Aunt Helen and Aunt Sylvia and Sir John and Anne were left to share the hall with George. There was no fire, and it was too early to light a candle, but the shadows were long across the ceiling, and the rushes, which must have been recently changed, smelled clean and green on the floor. Then George could and did feast his eyes upon Anne.

There were many questions to be answered. He was not eager to talk about his imprisonment, which had been unspeakably dull, and it was needful for him to avoid mention of why he had so soon been sent back to Spain—they would hardly have credited it of Hawkins anyway, and George himself was none too proud of his own part—but he saw no reason to conceal his present mission. He told them, then, that he was carrying a message from King Philip to the Strange Guest.

"*Jezebel!*"

Sir John, ordinarily so mild a man, sat now on the edge of his X-chair, his fists clenched, eyes aflame.

George spread apologetic palms.

"Well, there are all sorts of stories—"

"George, thou'lt meet her? Thou'lt go into her very presence?"

"Why, I suppose so."

The aunts, blurred shadows now, were still. Nor did Anne stir in the failing light as she spoke. She was looking away from George, which was not like this forthright girl. Her lips did not tremble, but her voice did.

"They— They say she's beautiful."

George shrugged.

"I hadn't heard that."

Now she did look at him, not reproachfully but with a hurt astonishment, while he cursed himself for having lied yet again—and so thoughtlessly, so senselessly. He tried to toss it out of his own mind, telling himself that he'd only spoken figuratively, that he had meant that he hadn't hitherto *thought about* Mary Stuart's beauty, of which, like everybody else, he had *heard*. But there was no escape from that harpoon, Anne's stare.

"The Devil can take any form," Sir John cried, "but he remains the Devil all the same."

George glanced at him. George was no stranger to the severer forms of puritanism; but he never could go with the passion it inspired. God knew, George had no love for the Inquisition! But back here in England, where men were more moderate, he knew no need for such choler. He had learned, however, not to argue.

"Steel thyself, lad. They do say that Shrewsbury's got guts of stone, and no heart at all. But steel thyself, dost hear?"

"Aye," said George.

"Aye," murmured Anne in the dusk. "Aye, do that."

He could not see her face for the shadows, but he sensed her perturbation. Was this because she feared for her father's spleen, or was it because of the nature of George's errand? It was amazing what a difference the naming of Mary Stuart's name had made in that darkening hall. Damn that queen! Why hadn't she stayed in Scotland? Even the aunts, customarily garrulous, refrained from stir, sidewise eyeing their brother in fear. Anne sat breathless. It was as though Satan himself had entered this hall, where the air grew cold, musty, close.

Only with an effort did Sir John recover his composure, reminding himself that it was no time for the vehement expression of religious thought. He asked George if he was weary.

George had been in saddle since sunup, and he welcomed an excuse to retire. Yet he was troubled as he rose. And a little later, in a borrowed nightrail, he drifted into Sir John Crofts's chamber.

The knight was in bed but not asleep. He had whuffed out his candle, and there was only a drizzle of moonlight at the window.

"I'll be calling on thy daughter for a sweet-dreams kiss," George explained.

"Well, don't take all night to do it."

There was no corridor upstairs at Okeland, where there were doorways but not doors, the various bedrooms opening into one another like the links of a chain, the master's being in the middle.

Anne, also in a nightrail, was seated on her bed, a narrow one, untestered, scarcely more than a pallet. Her arms were around her legs, her knees pushed her chin, and she had been looking out her arrowslit of a window at the moon.

Though she must have expected him, and surely as a cousin it was his right and almost his obligation to claim a buss, when George entered she held close over her breast the folds of the nightrail. It was as though she had been startled by the entrance of a stranger. She had never done this before, but always had taken George for granted. She was tense, too, when he kissed her.

He sat by her side.

"Art fearful, chuck?"

"They say many things of that woman."

He held her tight. She was so small and soft! He had come such a long way for this!

And suddenly, again, he was afraid—for her, for them. It was absurd; but he had not shaken off that earlier wing-brushing fear he had felt when he saw Okeland for the first time in three years, a fear, baseless of course, that the place was under a spell, caught up in mysterious unseen toils. Here in the very middle of England he was more frightened than ever he had been in the Indies. Here in his own cousin's house, with his arms around his beloved on a calm and quiet moonlight night, he had to battle panic.

So he held her, hard. Even in this dim room she might read his face, and he wouldn't release her until he had won control of himself. Then he tried to laugh, a sound that sagged.

"I'm off with the dawn, dearest," he whispered. "I may not be able to stop on my way back to London—'tis a

28

matter of what message I carry, if any. It may be a week, weeks."

"They say she's a sorceress."

Now he really did laugh.

"Nay, chuck, I've not outlasted prison and schemed my way back here only to be dizzied by a French witch's brew."

"George, if she tries to—"

"Besides, here's a headier draft. Give me that mouth again."

She was submissive, but no more than that. The muscles of her arms and shoulders, his hands felt, were taut, tight. George had a conviction that she was struggling against tears as a moment before he himself had struggled with his panic; and he believed that she would break down and weep the moment he left.

He rose, uneasy, sorry that he had come.

"Good night, chuck," he whispered. "God— God be with you."

And he went out.

When he passed through the master's chambers there was no sound from the bed. Was Sir John asleep? George thought not. But if asleep, as if awake, no doubt the knight was plagued by a dream of the queen of Scots. George sighed. He went to bed.

5

Fifty Men a Whistle Away

RAIN FELL SULLENLY out of a sky that was the color of a rat's back.

The freshets of spring long since had been abated, and the Don ran clear and low, refusing to fill yet at the same time failing to drain the most of Sheffield Castle, where the scuma, which stank, was darkly iridescent.

George had been made to give up his horse at the barbican, a rather perfunctory outwork made of fine-grained bluish-gray stone, so he crossed the bridge on foot, his boots aclack. Two men with mauls were banging the massive lift-chains to knock off the rust. They were methodical like machines, like figures on a clock, and the clangor they set up rang throughout that web of walls and buildings, while the rust flew in red-brown flakes from each impact, littering the bridge.

The gate tower itself was high, thick, square, rimmed by

a crenelated parapet. It was gloomy under there, giving George a feeling of immense weight that strove to press down upon him. The gates were open, but hurdles had been set up so that every entrant had to pass through a small space in the middle, where two halberdiers stood. Overhead, slitted into the second story of this tower, the portcullis was suspended on unseen cables. Though it must have weighed several tons, it was so delicately hung that it swayed in the breeze. George, looking up as he passed beneath its sharp spikes, fairly scurried like a rabbit. One of the halberdiers snickered.

A captain, cuirassed, laconic, examined the letter from Lord Burghley. He hmmmed portentously.

"It looks genuine."

"Damn it, man, it *is* genuine! D'ye think I'd ride this far with a forgery?"

"Many of the papers presented here are not what they pretend to be," was the captain's comment. "And many of the men who present 'em too."

The halberdier snickered again, and the officer gave him a spine-straightening glance.

"Come, enough of this," cried George, exasperated. "Take me to her majesty of Scotland."

"Things aren't done that directly at Sheffield," the captain warned him. "You," to the other halberdier, the one who had not laughed, "escort this man to the offices of master secretary Bateman."

"The queen's secretary?" George asked.

"The earl's. You're yet a long way from the queen."

The drawbridge led to the southern face of the castle, so that George had ridden right for it, not seeing a need to circle the place first. In consequence he had little conception of its size. There were towers, a grim dirty gray, wet now with rain but no doubt damp even through sunny hours. There was the barbican and the great gatehouse. This much he had glimpsed.

When he started across the outer court, following the halberdier, George saw with wonder that he was in a place of immensity, a city in itself. The pavement was flagstone, and it stretched far. There were hawkers, some with tents pitched against the wall, others strolling. There were off-duty guardsmen, gentles, children, villagers. There was a farrier's forge, an armory, a shambles. There was even a tavern, an ale shop of sorts, ramshackle, rickety, but crowded; and somebody was singing in there.

> *"The abbot of Burton he brewed good ale*
> *On Fridays, when they fasted.*
> *But the abbot never tasted his own*
> *As long as his neighbor's lasted."*

At the gate of the inner bailey they were halted, and during the time when the guardsman dickered with somebody inside, George, against the wall out of the rain, idly contemplated that guardsman's weapon. Most persons, he supposed, thought of the halberd as decorative only, a symbol of power. It was much more than that. Despite its old-fashioned and even medieval aspect, it was ideal for the keeping back of crowds, he'd been told; and he could readily believe that. The axe-like edge of this one, so near to George's face, was fully two feet long, and as bright as a beacon, as sharp as a razor. Nobody in his right mind would get close to that edge. The shaft was heavy, necessarily, the thickness of a midget's wrist; yet George had heard that some halberdiers, burly men for the most part and unlikely to be swift in pursuit, could throw their weapon as accurately as a Spaniard his knife: they could cut a cat in half at fifty yards whilst running, or shear off the lower part of a fugitive's leg.

"Very well, sir. This way."

The inner bailey was smaller as it was quieter, and to judge from the facings of some of the buildings even had about it a certain air of elegance. But it was austere elegance. There was no joy here, nor ever had been.

The donjon keep dominated this yard, which indeed had been built around it, a great square shaggy tower made of brownish stone different from the other buildings, much older. Today it was a relic, and not a remarkably picturesque one, used perhaps as a storehouse if it was used at all, kept for sentiment's sake, or, more likely, because it would be too much trouble to tear down. This was the original stronghold, the first fort, and it might have been reared in the days of the Conquest.

The other buildings, set in a square, formed the inner wall, which was also the outer wall on the north and east, the sides of the Don and the Sheaf. They were less martial, but they were hardly more attractive. They all looked the same to George; yet the halberdier without pause went to a certain door, which he opened.

"A visitor to the guest from Scotland."

"Come in, come in. She hasn't had many these days."

31

John Bateman was the perfect secretary. He could always keep track of things, his beard was scrawny; his chin was long and thin, a pump handle. His gown was long, trailing the floor. His mouth twitched absently. He squinted. The table at which he labored was piled with papers, all of them neatly arranged. The pen he put down was immaculate, and his inkhorn gleamed with oil. Carved into the legs of the table, into the back of the chair in which he sat, and into the keystone of the fireplace, untinctured but clear, were the Talbot arms—argent, a hound courant proper.

He did not look up from the sheet he had just signed and was sanding, nor did he ask George to sit. He put the paper away with one hand, with the other reaching for Lord Burghley's letter. He perused this letter swiftly but with care, rubbering out his lips.

"It really is Cecil's handwriting," he murmured.

"Did you expect it to be the Sultan of Turkey's?"

Bored, yet conscientious, Bateman reached for the message to Mary; and George, without thinking, passed him this, which Bateman immediately began to open, tearing the seal.

"See here, that's for the queen!"

"She'll see it, in time."

"My orders were—"

"Here you take orders from the earl of Shrewsbury."

"God rot it, man! I'll not stand and—"

George stepped forward, instinctively reaching for his sword. But he had forgotten the guardsman, who lowered his halberd. There were no snorts, there was no bluster. The blade itself stopped George, speaking loud words. It shone a few scant inches from George's eyes; and it was bright, seemingly alert, like a live thing.

Bateman looked up for the first time.

"Guard, this man's armed. How dare you bring him that way! Take his sword and dagger to your officer, and then bring that officer to me."

Resistance would have been fatal. There were fifty men a whistle away. George shrugged, submitting.

"But I want a receipt for it," he grumbled.

The truth is, he was uneasy without that sword. Never a ruffler, not one to cry "Lug it out!" at any slight provocation, he nevertheless valued his Toledo as a true companion, and without it he stood naked, vulnerable.

Bateman was reading King Philip's letter. He appeared to find it in no way extraordinary, and clearly he didn't seek

32

any cipher or secret writing. At last he nodded, and proceeded to leave the room.

"Wait here," he directed George over a shoulder.

Soon the captain of the guard came, an unhappy man; and for some time he and George Fitzwilliam stood before the paperstrewn table, trying to refrain from looking at one another.

"Very well, Fitzwilliam. His lordship will receive you. This way. You," to the captain, "wait for me."

George Talbot, sixth earl of Shrewsbury, knight of the Garter, lord-lieutenant of York, Derby, and Nottingham, master of Sheffield Castle and Sheffield Lodge, of Worksop, Wellneck, Bolsover, Tutbury, Wingfield, Handsworth, and Rufford, and through his wife also of Chatsworth and Hardwick, was a short man with a long silky beard and harassed eyes. His doublet was rich, if somber. Like his secretary he made no move to invite George to sit. Yet there was nothing of arrogance about the man. His voice was low, and somewhat fretful.

"You have asked for an audience. Ordinarily this would not be permitted. Scotland's majesty is not in the best of health, and we are obliged to keep her from overstraining herself."

"I'm sure of that."

"My Lord Burghley's letter makes it otherwise. Why is it you wish this personal interview, may I ask?"

George told him:

"Those men suffer. This I can swear to from the bottom of my heart. For three years they have been starving. Any morning they might be dragged before the Inquisition and sentenced to be burned alive—what's left of 'em. And yet, what have they done? Even pirates should not be treated like that. But they're not pirates."

Shrewsbury, head low, was studying him through frizzy eyebrows.

"You believe that if you explain this to Mary Stuart she will grant you a letter commending Hawkins to her cousin of Spain?"

"I believe so, sir, yes."

"What cares Philip for Master Hawkins anyway?"

George did not answer.

"I see. Well, my Lord Burghley hath his own affairs to arrange. The least we can do here is accommodate him whenever we can. So I have asked Scotland for this interview. It will take some time to prepare. She wishes to receive in state, of course."

33

"Me?"

"Even you."

The secretary meanwhile had resealed King Philip's message, and this he placed before his master. George noted that the remolding of the seal was not an expert job, as his own had been. He hoped that Queen Mary wouldn't notice.

Conceivably she was used to broken seals. Of one thing he was sure: Nobody had applied heat to this letter.

"Do you speak French, Fitzwilliam?"

"Not well."

"Italian?"

"None at all. Does the Queen speak Spanish?"

"I think a little. But she'd be rusty in it. It would be best to stick to English. Only—remember to say the words slowly."

"I see."

"And now you may wash and have some wine. Bateman will send for you. I'll require a little preparing myself. For of course I'll have to present you. Can't do that without a tail, eh?"

"Could I—Could I have my sword and dagger back, sir?"

"Certainly not. Not until you are ready to leave the castle."

Two hours later George was summoned.

Brushed, kempt, he thought he looked well; but he would hardly shine in this company. Lord Shrewsbury now wore an oyster-white silk doublet slashed with silver lace and set with three rows of crystal buttons. His sky-blue hose, too, were silken, as indeed was his manner. There was a velvet bonnet on his head, set with a blue plume caught up with an aigrette of sapphires and diamonds. There was a gold chain around his neck, a huge pearl at his right ear, while his fingers glistened with rings.

He was attended by six gentlemen, one of them master secretary Bateman, each almost as flamboyant as his lordship himself. George noted that they all had swords.

These attendants, neatly in line—while George trailed like a shackled prisoner—followed Shrewsbury by a few steps as the little procession moved out of that building, across the inner court, and to one of the tallest of the towers, the door of which was flanked by guardsmen. This, George was told, was called the Scroll Tower, nobody knew why. It overlooked both the Don and the Sheaf, as well as Shrewsbury Park beyond, and the Lodge; and it might have been

34

the least barnlike part of the castle. The queen of Scots had her throne room on the ground floor, George learned, opening directly off the court. She and her close attendants lived upstairs.

The master of the household, an ascetic Scot in a long cinnamon-colored robe, appeared briefly at the door. He shook his head, and backed away.

"My lady has decided upon another shade of garter ribbon," Bateman ventured under his breath.

"That will do," Lord Shrewsbury said.

Fortunately—for there was no antechamber save this the yard, and it still rained—the wait was not a long one. The master of the household reappeared, to throw open the doors. Shrewsbury and his attendants marched in. George, by instruction, remained outside. The doors were closed again.

George had seen nothing, but he could hear well enough.

"Your majesty!"

"My lord, it is always heartlifting to see you."

The voice was low, limpid, perfectly clear, a somewhat throaty voice with a hint of laughter in it. Even separated from its possessor, that voice was thrilling. George leaned forward, forgetting the rain. It was as though he held a bowl in which he sought to catch every clear sweet syllable.

"Are you amazed to find me alive? The food I'm served has had a curious tang of late. Are you poisoning me, my lord?"

"God forbid!"

'Yes. It would be awkward for my dear cousin Elizabeth of England if I was found dead, wouldn't it?"

"Your grace jests."

"Being still able to, praise the saints. No—what brings you here this afternoon, my lord of Shrewsbury?"

"A visitor from Plymouth, who bears a message to you from his most catholic majesty Philip of Spain."

"Ah?"

"This young man is a servant of Master John Hawkins, and he would help to free some of Hawkins' men who are within Spain's danger."

" 'Awkins? Who is that?"

"A mariner, ma'am. And merchant. He hath been lord mayor of Plymouth. He is admiral of the royal West Channel fleet."

"I see. And the messenger?"

"Nay, I never viewed him before, nor heard of him. But he comes with an authentic letter from my Lord Burghley."

The voice said, warmly, "Why, have him up then, Shrewsbury. Have him up."

The master of the castle called: *"George Fitzwilliam."*

The doors were flung open.

George took a deep breath, and walked in.

6

More Beautiful than Heaven

He KNEW ONLY HER. The hall, the persons in it, were a smear on either side, but Mary Stuart directly before him was real, more beautiful than Heaven. He had uncovered before crossing the threshold, and this was as well, for thereafter he was in a daze, and as he walked toward the throne, toward the queen, he was unacquainted with anything else: had there been a gaping hole in the floor he would have fallen in; had there been a stool he would have tripped over it.

Somehow he got there, to the very foot of the dais. He went to one knee.

"Your majesty."

Even as his eyes turned to the floor they were still full of Mary of Scotland.

He would always see her. He knew this; he would never be the same again. God's providence had done this. Or the Devil. It didn't make much difference just then. Helpless, on one knee, head bowed, he collected his impressions of Mary.

She was tall, lithe. She wore black, turned over with scarlet, and a goffered white ruff. An ivory fan hung from her waist at one side, a gold filigreed pomander on the other. Her hands, startlingly white, were folded in her lap. The cap she wore, like the rest of her clothes, was extremely simple, a flat thing of black silk with a white rutching that served to broaden an already broad forehead as well as to accentuate the heart-shape of the face.

The features of that face were delicate and small, even the longish nose being fragile. The chin was tiny, the base of the heart. The mouth too was small, and it had been grave when George glimpsed it, though surely a smile would come swiftly to it and perhaps as swiftly go, like cat's-paws caused by wind upon the surface of a pond. This was no conventional beauty! The hair was dark but not black—

chestnut, he thought. It was wavy, but unfrilled, and obviously her own. The eyes, small, though oddly penetrating, were set wide apart. George could not have told their color: yellow-brown perhaps, or burnt sienna, or even hazel, or somewhat reddish. The upper lids were heavy, and shone a faint blue. The brows were thin and set far apart.

"It was kind of you to come, Master Fitzwilliam." Her voice was clear water purling over clean round shining stones. "Please rise."

He rose, appearing, he hoped, outwardly unrubbed. He sucked his breath when he saw her again in the flesh, so near at hand, gazing at him. His bonnet was in his right hand, properly held over his heart. His left hand felt for the hilt of his sword, which it couldn't find.

Then the queen smiled. It was not a swift passing flashing surface smile, such as George had envisioned whilst kneeling. Rather it was slow to come, slower still to go away. It made her mouth look larger, and George noted that there was no dimple on the chin. That smile could hardly have been called regal. It came close to being a grin.

"You feel lost without your tuck?"

"Ma'am, what is a man without a sword?"

"They are not supposed to be men when they're admitted into my presence. Decorticated conies, I think. But—you are different."

He bowed, not knowing what else to do.

"My Lord Shrewsbury says that you have a tale of English mariners unjustly held by my cousin of Spain?"

He bowed again.

She spoke English slowly, picking her words, having trouble with her aspirants. It was a slightly nasal accent, and she tended to stress the last syllable of any given word, which made for a somewhat singsong effect. It didn't matter. With that liquid voice she could as well have been talking Chinese. The words themselves were unimportant.

"I know nothing about this, Master Fitzwilliam. But I can be enlightened. I am interested in the welfare of all prisoners anywhere, since I am a prisoner myself."

If this was intended to produce a stir it failed. Nobody so much as shifted his feet. George was becoming aware of the chamber in which he stood, and which he now knew to be small for a throne room, with a ceiling comparatively low, from which was hung a many-prismed chandelier, one of the few pretentious pieces there. The carpet was, appropriately, red; and the somewhat skimpy windows were decorated with red velvet. In addition to the queen herself

37

and George, the two halberdiers at the door, the master of the household, and Shrewsbury and his six attendants, there were only about twenty persons in the room, male and female, all of them obviously part of Mary's suite. The master of the household necessarily carried a sword; but none of the other men behind Mary did.

The throne itself was a handsome high-backed chair of some dark wood, upholstered with crimson damask and raised by three short steps from the level of the floor. Above it was a state canopy of cramoisy woven with gold thread in the arms of France and those of Scotland, the arms of England being prudently omitted, though Mary Stuart, in the eyes of thousands, had a better claim to the English throne than did the woman who sat there, Elizabeth Tudor. There was also a motto of some sort on that cloth of state, something French. George could not keep his eyes away from the queen long enough to read it.

Seemingly unmindful of the bungled seal, she broke open Philip's letter, which she read carefully, nodding a bit. Her lips did not move as she read.

"I had not been told," she said slowly, when she had finished, "that you are a nephew of the duchess of Feria."

"Save for the good offices of my aunt, ma'am, I should be lying in a lousy dungeon right now, along with those others."

"Ah, yes. Tell me about them."

More than once it had been suggested to George Fitzwilliam that he should have been a courtier. He was told that his eloquence was unstrained, persuasive. "You *look* honest, George," a friend once said, "and that's a diplomat's chief need." Yet George disliked the life and would have none of it, excepting when, on occasions like this he felt a moral obligation to help someone.

They assured him afterward that though he did talk too fast, on the whole he gave Mary Stuart an excellent account of the third Hawkins trading voyage to the New World and the bloody end it came to at San Juan de Ulua. He could recall to memory very little of that talk. They were to tell him that he went into particulars, giving the Hawkins argument, as it was his duty to do; but he was to remember none of this. All he knew at the time was Mary Stuart.

When he had finished she leaned forward to ask him questions, and she listened carefully to the answers.

To his mind, she did this for two reasons. In the first place, she had not been too sure of what he said, though

38

reluctant to admit as much. She had watched him carefully; it was the expression that interested her, the light in the eyes, rather than the words. She would interpret the man himself, and only incidentally the tale he had to tell. She was used to being lied to, anyway.

In the second place, she was lonesome. It brought a lump to George's throat to realize that he was providing pleasure for her with what would ordinarily have been a routine request, a matter to be disposed of, one way or the other, in a few minutes; and she was purposely prolonging the interview. She *enjoyed* the talk with him, every second of it! She hated to have it end!

For three years, since she fled over the border from the rebel Scots led by her own brother yammering at her heels, Mary Stuart had been the captive of her cousin, Queen Elizabeth, the woman upon whose mercy, pledged in advance, she had thrown herself. That confinement, galling to a person of her active mind and ambition, of late had become severe. George had seen this for himself. He'd been told, bluntly, that if it had not been for a letter from Lord Burghley, a most urgent letter, he would not have been admitted into the presence of Mary Stuart, that "guest" about whom the net was being pulled tighter and tighter every day.

George answered each question with care. He told her a great deal about New Spain, a great deal too about the Spanish court and especially about his aunt, matters that, truly, had no bearing upon the case of the imprisoned sailors.

Two or three times Shrewsbury, behind him, coughed. Several men back there stirred restlessly. They should be reprimanded! Didn't they know that they stood before royalty? How dared they to—

For his own part, George Fitzwilliam could have gone on talking all afternoon. But even Mary Stuart, though grateful for the break in the boredom, knew that she must keep bright the fiction of her power. She thanked George, giving him another smile.

"Come to my chambers in an hour's time, and my secretary will give you a letter of reply. Also, I think, a gift for your aunt. It has been kind of you to come."

She glanced at the master of the household, who thudded the floor with his staff.

Queen Mary rose. The others fell to their knees. And then she was gone.

George said little at dinner. He would have preferred to

take that meal in the great-hall, where the noise and confusion might serve to hide his feelings, but he could scarcely refuse when the earl of Shrewsbury asked him to dine with him *en famille*. It was an honor, true, but it was also an ordeal. Even the presence of the hatchet-faced countess, the celebrated Bess of Hardwick, surely the most married woman of the time—Shrewsbury was her fourth husband—did not lift George from his thoughts of what had just passed. He tried to be polite, but undeniably he was vague, and he excused himself as early as he could.

The Scroll Tower consisted of four stories, of which the throne room was on the ground level, the next above was largely offices, while the third, George had been told, housed the nearer servants and attendants, and the queen herself lived on the top story. It was upon the third landing that George met a slim dark-haired lad who appeared to have been waiting for him.

"Are you the secretary?"

The other blushed.

"Oh, no. I'm a page. Anthony Babington, sir, at your service."

"At yours, sir."

"The secretary will be out in a moment."

They stood awhile, George studying his companion sidewise.

"You have been in her majesty's service long?" he asked at last.

"Two months, sir."

"You like it?"

Young Babington seemed astonished, and shook his head as though not sure whether he'd heard right.

"Why—Why, it's paradise!"

George looked around.

"A rather grubby paradise, I'd say."

"Oh, no, sir! Not when *she's* here!"

"I see."

"I wonder if you really do, sir. You met her highness for an hour, but can you imagine what it would be like to see her every day?"

George said nothing.

"A kinder, sweeter person never walked the face of this earth. No matter the castle! It's a privilege to serve her. It would be a privilege in a pigsty."

"I see. An angel. The others feel that way too?"

"Why, of course. Everybody who knows her loves her."

40

"And yet—there are those who say she's an adulterer, a murderer, a traitor, the personification of evil."

"Damn you, if you—"

"Tut, boy! I didn't say *I* thought that. But others do."

"Then they don't know her. Why, for that lady, sir, I swear, I'd let myself be torn to pieces, limb from limb!"

"Let's hope you never have to."

The door was opened, and the secretary, Rollett called them in. He handed George a letter not dissimilar in appearance to the one George had brought, though sealed with the Stuart arms rather than those of Hapsburg. He had probably been doing a bit of last-minute tampering. The place smelled of snuffed candles.

"Her highness has been pleased to vouch for the dependability of John Hawkins of Plymouth."

Whom she'd never even heard of a few hours ago, was George's thought.

"She, uh, she said something about a package?" he ventured.

"She will bring it personally. Ah, here she is—"

Mary Stuart came down a circular staircase, as the three men sank to their knees. She was wearing dark blue, an informal garb, somewhat fleecy; and there was a flimsy silk scarf, bright yellow in color, about her neck. In her hands she carried a small prayer book, leather with gold stampings, which she opened.

"You must give this to your aunt when you go back to Mádrid. Tell her that I often think of her. See, I have written in it."

Absit nobis gloriari nisi in cruce Domini nostri Jesu Christi. Maria R.

George took the book, closed it, put it into his purse. He had not raised his head and could not see her face, only the ends of the yellow scarf.

And now there appeared before his eyes her hands holding two large ruby earrings. They were perfectly matched, each the shape of a tear drop, the clasp being gold.

" 'Tis the fashion among you men to wear but one of these at a time. When you pass through London again, then, I charge you to leave one with the Spanish ambassador, Don Gerau de Spies, as a token of my esteem."

"And—the other, ma'am?"

"Why, the other, Master Fitzwilliam, I had hoped that

41

you yourself would accept as an unworthy memento of our talk today."

"Majesty!"

"Wear it sometimes and think of this poor caged bird. But not often! You are too long and strong to have many sad thoughts. And now—farewell. God speed you."

She held out her hand, palm down. For an instant George could not believe what he saw; he had never hoped for this. The ruby was riches enough, but—her own hand! Tears scalded his eyes and he sobbed, all unashamed, as he seized the hand in both of his own and reverently kissed it.

Then the queen was going, up and around, around and up, until the staircase itself disappeared into the gloomy shadow of the Scroll Tower.

Half an hour later George Fitzwilliam left Sheffield. He had been offered hospitality, but he was too nervous to remain. Besides, he wished to be alone, without conversation. He reckoned that he could make the inn at Grantham, reputedly a good one, before full darkness.

He walked over the drawbridge, and the heavy wet planks plunked stodgily under his feet. At the barbican he was obliged to pay a tester for the care of his horse, which annoyed him, for the animal hadn't even been fed. He cursed fervently, yet the guardsman beamed.

The rain was relentless—small vindictive drops, slanting angrily.

"You're the last one, sir," the guardsman called. "She'll go up now."

"I could tell you *what* she might go up," George retorted.

Fifty yards away he reined, and turned. His heart felt like a cold crabapple. There was a banging behind his eyes. And he wondered whether he would ever be able to swallow again.

Signals were shouted. The guardsman scampered across the draw to the gatehouse. A windlass in the second floor of the house began to squeal; then another. The big-linked iron chains trembled, growing taut. Very slowly, lurching like a great bear, the bridge rose. The links clanked as they were drawn in, one after another. The bridge shuddered, rainwater dripping from its bottom. Inexorably, noisily, the chains pulled it up, until with a thud that seemed to shake the very earth it fell into its destined position as a part of the castle wall. Thereafter it was motionless, the rain lashing it in vain.

George heard a huge oaken balk being shoved into place. Sheffield Castle was closed.

42

Higher up, much higher, and further back, at one of the top windows of the Scroll Tower there fluttered a long, bright yellow scarf.

7

In the Dark of the Night

HE HAD MISCALCULATED. Sheffield to Grantham proved a good forty-odd miles, and it was several hours after sunset when he clattered into the innyard. Even so, there was an ostler to take his mount—and take it in such a fashion that George knew the beast would be well cared for. This was no Crossed Keys.

Though George sagged with weariness, his mind was awake. And now he felt like talking. He nodded to the sign.

"That's no bag of nails."

" 'Twasn't once, your worship. I can remember the old one. Master Blake bought it cheap. But he never did like it. Thought it wasn't decent, you might say."

"Decent?"

"Well, it showed a fat man without hardly a stitch of clothing on, except where there had to be, if your worship knows what I mean?"

"I think I do."

"He had some vegetables over his head, and he was holding a mug. That's the part Master Blake *did* like about it. Thought that might egg on guests to buy more beer. But then, there was all that skin . . ."

"I'm beginning to understand."

"The Bacchanals was what it was called then, sir. But these country people around here, they couldn't say that right. They kept calling it Bag o' Nails, and pretty soon that's what everybody called it, even Master Blake himself. And then the paint partly peeled off, and two-three years ago Master Blake got a man to touch it up a bit."

"Yes."

"And Master Blake, he said to that man: 'See if you can make it come out less naked.' So the painter—oh, he was yare, that one!—he made it into a sort of bag. To go with what everybody had been calling the place anyway. The vegetables that had been on the man's head, they got to look like drawstrings, see? And the belly, that was the bulge of the bag itself. He didn't do the whole job. Master Blake wouldn't pay him enough. Still, it shows better'n it did

43

afore. And when you look at it sort of sideways, squinting, it *does* seem sort of like a bag of nails, don't you think, sir?"

"Very interesting," said George. "And now, d'ye suppose I could have a bird and a bottle? Not to mention a bed?"

"Sure to, your worship. Here comes Master Blake right now."

This boniface might have been stingy when he dickered with an itinerant artist, nor was his appearance impressive, for in looks he reminded George of poor squinched little Ellis Waters deep in the archbishop of Seville's dungeons; but he did know how to treat a guest. Within minutes George found himself installed in a large clean room overlooking the yard on one side, the Great North Road on the other. Without undue fuss he was provided with everything he asked for. The night was chill, so a fire was lighted. A chicken for picking and a tankard of ale were produced as though by magic. So too was a tub of water, miraculously warm. Master Blake did not even complain when George asked for two extra candles, though doubtless he made a mental note to put these down on the bill.

Tired as he was, and late though the hour, George yearned for that bath. Even more fervently he yearned to work open Mary Stuart's message to her "cousin of Spain." This latter it was not his business to do; and Burghley might resent it. George did not care. He must know whether the queen of Scots was plotting against the peace of the realm of England, the very life of Queen Elizabeth. George did not believe that Mary was a conspirator—not a woman so sweet and lovely, so beguilingly frank! If the margined cipher had been read, and if it was being answered in kind, it must be the work of the secretary, Rollett.

This was the way George fretted; and despite the excellence of the service he was wishing that Master Blake and his so-efficient lackeys would get it over with and be gone. George did not fail to thank them, yet he shooed them out like geese.

He had already in part undressed, and had sipped the ale and nibbled the bird; but not until he was alone did he drain the stein, which was light, made of latten, and after filling some of this with warm water from the tub, placed it on a rack made of his dagger and the rung of a stool, bunching just beneath it three lighted candles. This was the reason he had asked for the extra candles. The fireplace would have been uncertain.

The saying is that a watched pot never boils. George tried *not* to watch. He went out to the jakes. In his room again, he stripped. He washed thoroughly, determinedly; but

44

this act brought little relief. Garbed only in canions and cod-piece, he strode the floor, striving to keep his gaze from the heated container in which water scarcely had begun to simmer.

He fetched forth his wallet, and from it took the little book of devotions. It was a rich thing, expensively bound, showy; and he noticed for the first time that it was in Latin. He did not try to read it. All he was concerned with was the inscription, *"Absit nobis gloriari—"* The hand was exquisite, the letters cobweb-thin, delicately formed, but regular, and without flourishes. *"Maria R."* He could see her still.

George and Hawkins had not been entirely uncommunicative in the course of that ride from Plymouth to London, nor had Burghley been mum at the meeting in his room overlooking the River Thames. George knew the situation in general. He knew—his common sense might have told him anyway—that it was to England's advantage to play Spain and France off against one another, at the same time keeping an eye on that small boisterous country just beyond the postern gate to the north, the back door, Scotland. The weaker the government in Scotland, the better for England. As for France and Spain, England could not face either alone, since each was so much larger, richer, more populous. Those two must be kept, if possible, at each other's throats. In no other way could England survive.

So it was Elizabeth's policy to blow hot and cold, now this way, now that; and at the moment, as George knew, she was smiling toward France, the country where the queen of Scots had lived for so many years—she was indeed its dowager queen—and from which aid for the royal Scottish cause normally might be expected. But Elizabeth was countering this danger with a flirtation of her own with the duc D'Anjou, younger brother of the French king, whom she intimated she might marry. D'Anjou was a misshapen, pock-marked midget, twenty years Elizabeth's junior; but this didn't stop her. Elizabeth's antics, not perhaps as silly as they looked, were serving to keep assistance from the imprisoned queen of Scots, at the same time scaring Spain.

Did Mary Stuart know this, or sense it, and was she planning to strike back by means of an alliance with Spain? Burghley believed that. So did Hawkins, as well he might; though Hawkins' chief interest, as it was that of his servant, George Fitzwilliam, was the release of those mariners in the archbishop of Seville's dungeons. Philip had snapped with telling avidity at the bait Hawkins held before him, agreeing

45

almost without hesitation to pay the price the seeming traitor sought. But—who was *30* and who *40?* Were these English noblemen of incalculable power who might co-operate with Spanish landing forces? Why, otherwise, would Philip be asking Mary Stuart in secret, for affirmation of their treason? Or was he asking *her?* Could it have been Rollett, or somebody else in that pathetic household, that phantom "court"?

The water sang a small song, but there was only the veriest wisp of steam, not nearly enough. Yet more was forming.

"Sssh-blup!"

George put away the devotional. He fished out the ruby earrings. These were striking, perfectly matched, large. It would be a pity to separate them. He hung one in the lobe of his left ear, which had been pierced. He strode back and forth, wishing that he had a mirror. He went to one of the windows, and tried to catch sight of himself in a panel of glass.

He saw that the rain had ceased, the Great North Road being bathed in the thinnest of moonlight. Nobody stirred out there. The inn was utterly silent.

This must have been near midnight, but George knew that he would not sleep until he had learned about that letter.

More steam was forming in the stein. It swirled languorously.

"Blup! Bl-u-u-up!"

His sword had been hung over the back of a chair. He unsheathed it. In guard position, he made sundry passes at air. He must have looked ridiculous; but there was nobody to watch.

George got out of breath easily these days. He was soft, after that long confinement. He should renew his fencing lessons, he told himself. There were places in or near London —Ruffian Hall in West Smithfield, La Belle Sauvage on Ludgate, the Curtain, the Grey Friars, the Bull.

He sheathed, panting.

A man was dismounting. He was very large, with bulky shoulders. He was calling in a low carressive voice for the ostler. Somehow that voice, like the form, was familiar.

But George's interest was elsewhere; for at that moment he knew that the water in the tankard was boiling.

He turned away from the window.

He worked slowly on the seal, restraining an impulse to tear it. This must have taken him a quarter of an hour.

The message was conventional enough, written in French,

the same spiderweb hand as that in the book of devotions.

Trembling, George took it to the fireplace, where he held it up, moving it back and forth.

Gradually, in the left margin, brownish letters appeared. When he held the paper back to cool, these letters went away. But he had memorized them.

He restored the letter to its envelope, which with great care he resealed. He found he was sobbing.

The message was simple: *YTCKOGPV*. By use of the same cipher, this because "vraiment," French for "truly." It could only be an answer to the other margined message, which likewise had been written in the invisible ink, an answer to the question about the dependability of *30* and *40*.

And the hand was the hand of Mary Stuart.

Nature was kind that night. George soon fell asleep. Not until he was about to take the road again, well after dawn, did he think to ask about the late arrival, who, he learned, already had departed. For George remembered who it was —that light-moving hulk, that low taunting voice.

It was the bravo of the Crossed Keys.

8
Who Would Rise High

IT WAS TWO DAYS LATER.

William Cecil, Lord Burghley, rolled the ruby back and forth on his palm, grunting approval.

"It might bring twenty marks."

"I wouldn't sell it for a hundred!"

Burghley looked up, his rheumy eyes atremble. He was a shaky man anyway, continually quaking, and one who suffered from many ailments—gout, headaches, indigestion. The wonder was, what with all his fussiness, that he could be so incisive in affairs of state.

Now he shoved the gaud back across the table.

"There is no ill in accepting gifts. 'Tis a courier's prerogative. I'll fadge with that. But mind, lad, that you wear this only on your ear, not on your heart."

They were in Cannon Row, an obscure Burghley residence, more a house of work than anything else, filled with clerks, secretaries, copyists, couriers, rather than with place seekers. There was no distracting view of the Thames from Cannon Row, where all was business.

My lord sorted his papers, already serried in rigid neatness.

"Now let's start it all over again, at the beginning, eh?"

George sighed. He saw why they called this man "her majesty's housewife." Elizabeth's first minister liked everything to be on paper, preferably put there by himself. Specifically, he appeared to make two sheets, or lists, of each interview, situation, argument. On one would be the cons; on the other the pros. The report at an end, Lord Burghley would balance these, one in each hand, much as if he were estimating their actual weights. Everything on both sheets, to be sure, was duly numbered, lettered, indexed.

He had already done this once in the case of George Fitzwilliam's account of his mission to Sheffield; and now, as a check, he proposed to do it again.

Burghley heard George's sigh.

"Many lives may be at stake," he said. "The very safety of the realm may be involved. We mustn't skip it lightly."

Resigned, George went over the whole thing again, omitting nothing of what he had seen, heard, felt or even smelled at Sheffield Castle, though he gave no detail of his journey, coming or going, this not being properly a part of his report. As before, he was amazed at the keenness of Burghley's questions, which were few but astute. My lord, for his part, appeared well satisfied with the account; nor did he exhibit any astonishment at the proof of Mary's duplicity. He only shrugged.

"I have the greatest admiration for that queen and lady," he told George. "But—she plays the game as she found it."

"She wouldn't be human if she didn't hate to be cooped."

"Perhaps a queen is not expected to be human."

"Elizabeth isn't, then?"

Burghley made no reply.

"She called herself a caged bird," George pursued, working himself into a small frenzy of defense. "Can you scold a caged bird for beating the bars with its wings?"

Burghley harrumphed.

"It's not my intent to enter a judgment of Mary Stuart. Let's be back to the queen's business. When you went to Don Gerau's did he receive you personally?"

"Oh, yes. Kept me waiting about an hour, that's all."

"Not long for a Spaniard. They think it enhances their importance, somehow. Now—did he make any mention of Master Hawkins' offer to sell out the fleet to Spain?"

"No."

"Did you?"

"No."

"Do you think he *would* have brought that up, if you'd baited him?"

"Mayhap. I'd say he's a fool."

"He is. And the earring would have impressed him. He's probably at his writing desk this very minute, praising you to his king. That letter will go to Spain on the same vessel that takes you, the hoy at Deptford."

"Speaking of that hoy, sir—"

"It will wait," he said dryly. "Simply make you sure that the project doesn't quail, at sea."

"If I ever get to sea. Those men rotting in prison—"

"They too can wait a little. Now, when you went to the Spanish embassy, and later when you came away, were you followed?"

George shook a puzzled head.

"Was I attended, you mean? Why, no. I have no servant, sir."

"No, no! I mean did a spy watch you."

"Why should a spy do that?"

"Why not? You're a spy yourself."

George knew this, but he did not like to hear it said, and he winced.

"You set spies on spies, then?"

"Of course. Everybody does. And other spies to spy on *them*. And so on."

"And when they report I assume that they all contradict one another."

"Oh, they do, aye."

"Then which one do you believe?"

Burghley spread pudgy hands.

"That's diplomacy, the selection. It isn't pricing like a merchant, or counting like a clerk. It's—Well, it's an art."

"I think it's one I don't like. Lies, always lies!"

"Sometimes there can be a great good come out of lies, if they're properly valued."

"I'd prefer to leave that to God."

"Don't be saucy, young man."

"I'm sorry, sir."

"Round-aboutness too can have its uses, though it *look* mean enough. Have you ever heard that he who would get to a high place must use a winding stair?"

Again George winced. The memory of his last view of Mary Stuart as she climbed that spiral staircase in the Scroll Tower was fresh, even raw; and it stung.

"As for diplomacy, you'll need every bit of that at your

49

command when you go on the errand I'm about to send you on."

"An errand? But see here, my lord, that boat at Dept-ford—"

"It will not sail without you. Meanwhile, my coach awaits to take you to a certain person who'd question you about the guest at Sheffield. And let me warn you—"

"What person would be of such stature to keep those mariners waiting even one more hour in a Spanish prison, sirrah?"

"Would you esteem the queen of England to be of such stature?"

"The queen!"

"Go to, lad. You have looked upon the lady of Scotland, and that lady's cousin, who happens to be at Greenwich right now, is eternally curious about her. She will ask you many questions."

"About Mary Stuart's politics?"

"About Mary Stuart's looks. Confine yourself to that subject, pray. *She* surely will. There's no need to bring up the real reason for your journey, or its result. The queen's highness will know as much of that as she wishes, in good time. Just now it might fluster her."

"My lord, I meant to ask it before: have you learned yet who *30* is and *40?*"

"No. We thought at first that they were Mary Stuart herself and the Spanish ambassador, Don Gerau. But your own marginal messages have made it clear that they're English noblemen. This will go high, lad. We must be sure of ourselves before we strike."

"But you *will* strike?"

"Of course. By the time you return from Madrid I hope to have *30* and *40,* whoever they are, safe in the Tower. I make for that pile myself, this very morning. There is a young man named Bailey, arrested at Dover when he came back from the Low Countries. His papers tell us something, but methinks the boy himself can tell more—such as who those numbers represent. La Gehenna should persuade him."

George shuddered. There were many stories of the horrible things that happened in that little low-ceilinged room in London Tower where La Gehenna, the rack, was maintained. Torture was not a customary practice of the English government, but when it was used it was used with a vengeance. And this same William Cecil, baron of Burghley, who was waggling a schoolmasterish forefinger at George right now, supervised those questionings. He was a man who did

50

thoroughly whatever he took to be his duty. He was known as the most learned rose fancier in the kingdom; and just as he would lean with appreciation and solicitous care over a rosebush, so would he lean over some poor pale screaming sweating prisoner caught up with leather straps. In the one case he would prune tenderly, and clip; in the other he would whisper edged questions, or else instruct a remorseless rackmaster to put on more pressure. He would do each task as well as the other, for he was a conscientious and highly capable old man.

Burghley came around from behind his table, put a hand on George Fitzwilliam's shoulder, and in a burst of graciousness conducted George all the way out into Cannon Row and the coach.

"Don't think of Charles Bailey," he advised. "He'll be unhappy, aye. But—so will you."

There rose from out of my lord something that was almost a chuckle—a grisly sound, in the circumstances.

"You may be wishing in a little while that you could change places with him, Master Fitzwilliam. But—courage! And good luck! You'll need both."

9

Straw-Colored

G EORGE HAD NEVER BEFORE been in a coach, and it frightened him. The device had been brought from the Continent, like so many so-called luxuries, and perhaps this accounted for its popularity: there must have been twenty of them in London alone, and almost as many more throughout the rest of the country. In God's name, *why?* Well, the expense might have been one attraction. The man who could maintain a carriage was the kind of man who wished always to be shouting, "See how rich I am!" Burghley of course kept one because in his governmental capacity he could do no less: foreign ambassadors expected this.

Save that it would keep out the rain—and as luck would have it this was a sunny morning, the first in more than a week—George could see no advantage to the vehicle. Any horse, even some nag begnawn with the botts, sped with spavins, would be quicker, cleaner, and incalculably more comfortable. The coach creaked; it was slow, drafty, dirty, dark; it proceeded on its lumbrous way in a series of spine-jolting bumps. From time to time it stopped altogether; and when it started forward again it jerked.

Worst of all were the onlookers. My Lord Burghley's professionally inspired extravagance did not extend so far as the hiring of a whiffler, or clearer-away, that long-armed one who strode ahead of a coach making a path for it by the use, when needed, of a bum-walloper or paddle. Some such *fonctionnaire*, George was sure, would have been provided anywhere on the Continent, where, indeed, there would be less need for him, since Continental crowds never had the naughtiness to peer into carriages, an English affectation.

London streets were narrow, so that even a whiffler might have been unable to keep the inquisitive crowds from eddying back. The windows of the coach were wide, and protected only by linen curtains, which were pushed back again and again by persons who stared jeeringly, or laughingly, or fiercely, at the poor bruised occupant. George could do nothing to stop them; and in truth he was afraid of many, for he could not know when one would appear, or on which side, and because the light was behind them he could not see clearly, getting only a flash of eyes, sometimes of teeth. Shouting at them did no good. They'd reply with smut. And George could not possibly have drawn his sword in that space.

It must be misery, he thought, to be a great man.

Fortunately the ride was not a long one, for they went not to Greenwich but only to Pudding Stairs, where George transferred to a boat.

Here was a sensible way to travel! The craft was royal, but not one of the state barges, which would have drawn attention. It was a small wherry, canopied, steady, and smooth. Excepting the royal badges on the sleeves of the boatmen— a point few watermen noted—there was nothing to connect this craft with any palace. But it went fast. The men who drove it were experts, and *they* at least were aware of the badges they sported, so that they had no hesitancy about bumping other boats, shearing oars, or threatening to; nor did they as much as turn their heads when some of their tactics brought profanity.

Profanity in fact was everywhere, as was blasphemy and garbage. The Thames, George reflected, as he leaned back against the cushions provided for him, was no dream stream, as once it had seemed from a window of Cecil House, Westminster. It was noisy and malodorous. When they passed the Fleet George wished that he had a pomander, and he did hold a sleeve beneath his nose, for the stink was such as to

52

bring tears to the eyes of a cutthroat. Something, George told himself, should be done about the Fleet.

For the rest, he enjoyed every minute of the trip. St. Paul's loomed enormous, a rambling gigantic pile, òne of the wonders of the western world. Behind it, higher, the bishop of Ely's palace, lately made over to Christopher Hatton, whose dancing the queen so admired, showed aloof, remote, lovely, the center of a celebrated rose garden.

Then the Bridge. Only four of the twenty arches were open to traffic, and through these, in the middle, the current was wicked, a cataract. Timorous passengers might bypass the Bridge, getting out, climbing over, and hiring another boat. George, however, had confidence in the royal wherry; and it took him through with a rush, spray flying.

On the south bank the fields were green, and the tower of St. Mary Overy made a mark against the horizon. Then too there was the bishop of Winchester's sprawling palace. Why did bishops need such large buildings in which to live?

On the city side he watched Queenhithe and Billingsgate slide past with their massed quays and wharves, churches, warehouses.

Far back were many steeples—St. Botolph's, the Minories, others.

The Tower. There was a city in itself, a glum one, with the cannons and cranes that lined its wharf, with the louring watergate, Traitor's Gate, and the pepperpot turrets, the scaffold on the hill . . .

Then St. Katherine's Hospital.

And at last, glorious multi-windowed Greenwich.

At the palace water steps the chief boatman passed some word to a porter, who in turn sent somebody for the gentleman porter, while George, watched like a felon, stretched his legs. The gentleman porter was long in coming, though loud with apologies when he did arrive. He guided George into the palace proper, up one corridor, down another, and at last into a room on which he shut the door.

It was not much of a room. There was but one window, which looked out on a wall. There were no mats or even rushes. The ceiling was low, the room itself small. There was little light, and no furniture.

In this place George, to the best of his calculations—he never heard a clock strike—spent about an hour.

He got fidgety. He walked back and forth. He listened and could hear little but footsteps, the closing of doors, the creak of stairs, mumbly voices.

One thing he did need; and that was what in a fancy

53

household like this would be called mincingly, the *domicilium necessarium.*

It might be breaking a royal engagement, but nature must be considered, as well as kings and queens.

Angry, his mind made up, he started for the door.

It was flung open from the outside, and a tiny straw-colored old woman burst in. Gawping at George, she came to a halt.

He made a leg. Likely he did this well, for he'd been trained in such bendings at Madrid, and he was a supple man.

He was quick, too, and lithe, in conversation.

"Mistress, it tells me you're seeking the same spot that I was about to seek. Let be! Wherever it is, 'tis not here."

This lady did not glitter, yet there was a certain brightness about her. Her hair, for instance. Her eyebrows and eyelashes alike were thin and washy, neutral, against the faded yellow-brown wash of her freckled face; but the hair of her head was a flaming red: clearly it was a wig, and just now askew. Her yellow gown, though rich enough, was hardly eye-grabbing; but at her waist hung a small mirror that George noticed was backed with diamonds, while from her wrist dangled an ivory fan, its handle made up of a gold ring that flared with sapphires. Brighter, and even harder, were her eyes. They were very small suspicious eyes, dark blue, with a purplish gleam.

"Ballocks! I seek no such chamber. What I seek is one Fitzwilliam, a lout who's never learned to kneel before his monarch."

"Majesty!"

She might have gloried over his abasement, but she had no time for this. She rapped the side of his jaw with her fan. It was no accolade, and certainly no love-tap. It hurt.

"Hulk, look up to me."

He looked up.

"You find me beautiful?"

George paused. He had heard many times that no flattery was too fulsome for Elizabeth Tudor, who reveled in it, though she pretended to disbelieve it. But—this would be difficult. He swallowed.

"You're too near," she said crisply.

"It is like being too near the sun, that burns us all," he whispered.

"Stand up, and back away a bit."

Glad to get off his knees, George was equally glad to retreat. The queen of England was flat-chested, though there was little else to be guessed about her figure. From behind, George supposed, if she didn't move she might have been mistaken for a girl of fourteen. Or twelve. But those eyes, that creased mouth, bloodless, folded like a priest's, and the wrinkles and freckles, were not easily outstared.

"Well, lad?"

George spread his palms.

"Ma'am, nobody in my family, so far as I know, ever was blind."

"That's not answering my question."

It was best not to look at her, and the convention that her beauty dazzled excused George from doing so. You lie best when you don't look directly at the person you are lying to.

"I had been told about England, and I've read many a sonnet in praise of her. But now I know that I should say like Sheba to King Solomon that I hadn't heard half of it."

Elizabeth slipped the fan into the palm of her other hand. George thought that she might strike his face with it as he deserved, after such a clumsy compliment. But she allowed the fan to swing.

"You've looked upon another royal lady this week, Master Fitzwilliam."

It wasn't a question, rather a charge.

George inclined his head.

"You found her, too, to be fair?"

"She is—not ugly, ma'am."

"How does she compare with me, in appearance?"

George did not squirm, for he had expected the question. He shrugged, eyes still downcast.

"She is—taller."

"Clod, I know that! But is she too tall for real beauty?"

"Who am I, ma'am, to know what real beauty is in woman?"

"You're male!"

This accusation, being incontestable, George surveyed the queen surreptitiously, estimating her height and weight.

She jiggled, harsh, not prepared for prevarication.

"Well, sir?"

She bit off her syllables the way a seamstress snaps off thread. Her unmammary front rose and fell. And her eyes flared.

"As your highness has so perspicaciously pointed out, I am a man. Aye. And no man wishes his love to be taller than himself, or even as tall, which tends to make her *look* taller. I am graced in this respect, ma'am, for as you see I have height, as the late Lord Darnley did—"

55

He paused, but got no response.

"Yet an ideal of beauty should not be framed for selfish reasons. And I should say, and indeed I always have said, ma'am, that the truly beautiful woman is a *small* woman."

"And *how* small, prithee?"

"Ah, well, I should say a whit under five feet. Possibly four feet nine inches, ma'am."

She did not show overjoyed, seemed thoughtful rather; and George wondered whether he had misgauged. Flustered, he resumed.

"Such a woman, such a paragon, must be able of course to carry herself with preciseness. She must be slim. She must be slender."

"Has Mary Stuart been putting on weight?"

She leaned forward from the waist, fairly shooting the words with saliva, so that George started. But he spread his hands again.

"Highness, the light was not good, and my mind was on many other things, and—"

"Ballocks! I'll get nothing from thee. For months I've been striving to learn how my cousin of Scotland fares. But can I? Nay! You're all courtiers, every one! All liars!"

There was a rap on the door, and voices called anxiously.

"Your grace?"

She turned her head, scowling, her profile a hawk's.

"Nay, another moment. I'm safe. Nobody's assassinating me."

She jabbed her fan at George.

"Come, come, clod. At least bob me out."

She lifted her mirror, examined her face, patted her hair, while George Fitzwilliam went half around her, and dropped to both knees, and opened the door.

There was a welling murmur of relief, and pantouffles scuffed as many men went low.

Elizabeth of England leaned over George a little as she swept past, and she tapped him with her fan, whispering.

"You turn to the left, clod. It's the last door down."

Twenty minutes later, having thanked and slipped a fee to the gentleman porter, George strode down to where the sherry waited.

He had been only mildly out of ease, and never would have changed places with poor Charles Bailey, as Burghley had suggested.

Bailey? Was he having his joints torn slowly apart because

of him, George Fitzwilliam? Would many others so suffer?
Would Mary Stuart?

"The woman's right," he muttered as he stepped into the
boat. "She's right. We're all liars."

"Your worship?"

George threw himself upon the cushions.

"Deptford."

10
Parade of the Scarecrows

SOME CAME STUMBLING, three had to be carried, all of
them sobbed, blinking when they emerged into the glare of
the sun, which bit them and caused them to whimper.
How they had lived this long nobody knew. The *muertos de
hambre* they were called, the walking corpses.

A few did not even seem to be certain of George as he
faced them, embraced them. They swayed, mumbling. He
slapped a smile on his mouth.

"Horace! ... John! ... Little Perry, thou'rt looking pert
today!"

"Ah, ah, Master Fitzwilliam!"

"It's all right now. You're all going back to England."

It would have been impolite to peer, yet he did seek Ellis
Waters. But there were only eighteen scarecrows here, not
nineteen.

"God praise you, Master Fitzwilliam. Another month
and we'd all have been stiff. Aye, another week. One went
only last night."

George kept grinning, but his heart thudded.

"He was the little nasty one you was chained to, sir."

"Ellis? He wasn't nasty," George cried. "He was—unsure
of himself."

"He all but fell apart when they lifted him. We watched.
We thought a leg would come off, or an arm. Gawd-a-
mercy, how he stank!"

"Now, now, don't we all?"

"Ellis was brittle," George conceded.

Then as though at a signal they wept. They sat down
and rocked against one another.

Coughing, his eyes bitten with tears, George rose and he
spread his arms.

"But—*you* lived! Thank God!"

Only the Spaniards failed to weep. Spaniards, George had

57

noted, do not weep easily—or laugh easily either. Your don was exact, stolid, punctilious, but not emotional. On this occasion the governor of the prison, together with a clerk and two assistants, also three ecclesiastical personages, waited, stone-faced, the clerk methodically checking off each name as it was called and causing the wretches to sign their releases or else to make marks opposite their names, while the governor himself, ceremoniously but without a touch of graciousness, handed to each a coin.

For they were rewarded. The pressure brought upon the court by George's aunt's husband, a duke, and George's own appearance and convincing mendacity, had had their effect. A benign Spanish government would not push these men back into the world without a penny. To each, then, was given an eight-piece, or piece-of-eight, a gold coin sometimes called a dollar, worth about four shillings eight pence in English money. It was not bad pay for three years. Clutching this coin, each miscreant no doubt could go a long way toward forgetting the past.

The mariners made much of these pieces-of-eight, becoming hysterical, as though sudden liberation had gone to their heads like a hot sun.

George had provided asses for the short trip to the river; for though there was only negligible luggage—their pitifully few sleazy belongings they could hold in their hands—he had sensed that some would be unable to walk. Asses were cheaper than horses, and he had used the difference from his expense purse to buy unguents, ointments, balm, and wine. Asses were easier to mount, gentler to ride. The archbishop's office had provided a squad of foot soldiers, lest citizens be tempted to set upon and maul the departing heretics; but these were not needed, for the Spaniards encountered on the way had nothing but scorn for the *muertos de hambre*, these dead men who somehow moved, yet who giggled and whooped while they held up eight-pieces, crowing about the farms they would buy with them, and the beer, and the doublets, when they got back to God's country.

This magpie cackling continued even on the hoy, on the trip down the Guadalquivir, when the men washed most of the time. George, who had taken care to provide extra water, noted that they washed as he himself had done when first out of prison—eagerly yet with frightened hands, afraid of hurting their flesh. But they loved it; and they sang and gloated, and they asked George questions, praising him, thanking him.

58

It disconcerted George to be hailed a hero. Again and again he explained that the release was the doing of John Hawkins, whose agent he was; but they had known already, learning when George first got out of prison more than a month ago, that it was his relationship to the duchess de Feria that made the difference and they had all known his thoughtfulness, his kindness.

George did not tell them of the weeks of planning, the days of waiting in anterooms, the hours of tortuous, ingenious falsehood. He made no mention of the colossal trick by means of which he had talked King Philip into releasing these wretches at last. Nor did he name the queen of Scots; nor the final touch—his thought, not that of Hawkins (and George was appalled at his own cunning)—the last-minute demand that Philip not only set the mariners free but also grant to John Hawkins a written pardon for all his "piracies" in Caribbean waters and along the Main. This demand had made the whole thing seem real to King Philip, a man not noted for his imagination, and he had gone further, giving George not only the pardon but also a writ of ennoblement, a writ that, as far as George could make out, created John Hawkins if not a grandee at least a minor hidalgo. Don John, forsooth! This paper too reposed in George Fitzwilliam's pocket.

But George did not tell them of this. For one thing, he was not proud of his own part in it. For another, they wouldn't have believed it anyway.

They stopped briefly at Canlúcar de Barrameda, at the mouth of the river, for more water and for fresh fruits, then they stood out in the open sea, with a fair breeze and a blue sky, for the roll home.

This was when the gambling broke out.

The hoy was a large one, as such unexciting vessels went, not fit for a run to the New World but a dependable coaster. The men were huddled in the waist, where they would be least in the way. Dropping down the Guadalquivir there had been a great deal of handling to be done—resetting of canvas, running out and taking in of preventers, walking of the whipstaff—and the castles fore and aft were scenes of much activity. Though every one of the passengers was himself a seaman, they took no part in the management of the hoy: they were too busy enjoying themselves, swapping gossip and questioning George.

The hoy was a Hawkins property, out of Plymouth town, and George's orders, as was but proper, came direct from the owner. He had been told to arrange for the release of these nineteen men on any reasonable terms he could get, to provide them with food, beer, clothing, and whatever medical attention they might need, and to get them out of Spain as quickly as possible. This immediate departure, indeed, had proved to be something the Spaniards themselves insisted upon, for they feared to have heretics loose in their streets, less they pollute some of the faithful. The prisoners for their part were more than willing to get right out. As for the men who handled the hoy, none of them was granted so much as a minute of shore leave. Nor would they have taken it if it had been granted, for the Holy Office was known for its habit of picking up stray English sailors, who never were seen again.

George took it to be his obligation to stay with the nineteen men until they had got used to life outside. This was also his preference. Though every one was his inferior, they were his friends, his companions in suffering. Moreover, their faith in him was touching. When he rose to a place where he could afford a body servant, as he hoped soon to do, he would pick one from such a group as this—loyal men, easy laughers, independent, rough, bawdy, and exceedingly hard to kill.

When one of them drew forth a pair of dice he had doubtless fashioned from bones throughout interminable days of rasping against a rough cell wall, and the eight-pieces clacked on the deck while the men eagerly called their bets, it never even occurred to George Fitzwilliam to object.

Not so the captain.

The captain was a young man, known to George slightly— he had been at San Juan de Ulua, commanding one of Hawkins' smaller vessels, *Judith*, in which he'd escaped— and not favorably. This fellow was a relative of John Hawkins, a second or third cousin, George believed. He was one of the "new men," assiduously on the make, edgy, irascible, efficient, undeviating. Likely enough he was annoyed to be commanding a mere coaster, however well found, as an interim appointment: for that very reason he would be the more touchy on the subject of his dignity.

The captain had been on the poop all the way down the river, a busy man. Now, having supped, he came to the waist.

"Stop this ungodliness!"

His small, intense, light blue eyes flashed. His curly tight red beard glistened. He was stocky, and had all the arrogance of the short; he scarcely came to George's shoulder, though they were of about the same age, twenty-two.

"This is not the Sabbath," George pointed out mildly, for he knew the man to be a hot gospeler, the son of a preaching Puritan, and it was in his experience that such men put a disproportionate importance on the Second and the Fourth commandments. You might raid, rob, even rape, you might covet whatever you felt like coveting, and bear false witness, and even kill, even commit adultery, yet still have some chance of forgiveness, but if at anytime you so much as glanced at a graven image, or if on the Day of the Lord you spat on the floor or kissed your wife or picked a flower, then surely were you doomed to everlasting torment.

"Sabbath or any other day, I'll have no such devilish practices aboard my ship!"

They glared at one another. Never friends, they were also rivals, in a sense. The captain was a godson of Francis Russell, the earl of Bedford's heir, and George was Francis Russell's cousin.

"Captain Drake, my orders were to tend these men's material wants, which I take it includes their recreation after long confinement. And I see nothing dangerous in dice."

"Master Fitzwilliam, I have orders from a Higher Source to tend their souls. And I do."

"They are under my command."

"They are on my ship."

Here was your "new man": one who insisted, with vehemence, that the skipper of any vessel should be more, much more, than a glorified sailing master, a skilled laborer hired only to handle that ship, not to fight it or to direct its course. He believed that off soundings a captain should be supreme, a small king, regardless of the rank, position, or ability of anybody else aboard. He believed that the time was past when a ship's commanding officer could be treated with no more respect than a coachman or a mule driver and he was damned well going to prove it.

George thought fast. In the privacy of a cabin he would have argued, resisted. But the thing was out in the open, and prestige was involved. From what George knew of this particular skipper he was quite capable of clapping all nineteen men into irons for the rest of the voyage to Plymouth. Hawkins might reprimand him for such an act—though he might just conceivably uphold him, for Hawkins himself was essentially a man of the sea—but that would not do the nineteen passengers any good.

And those passengers were in George's thoughts. He could climb down from his dignity, he decided, for their sake.

"I'm glad that you have come, captain," he said affably,

61

taking a new tack, ignoring the other's bristle. "The men and I were just saying that we should have a proper service to thank the Lord for delivering us from the forces of the antichrist, even as long ago he delivered Israel from the Amalekites. And we wondered if you would have the goodness to read to us."

"I'll get my Book," muttered Francis Drake, obviously pleased.

He read well. He rolled the periods, like any shaven priest, with scarcely a hint of Devonshire drawl.

". . . for Achan, the son of Carmi, the son of Zabdi, the son of Zerah, of the tribe of Judah, took the excommunicate thing: wherefore the wrath of the Lord was kindled . . ."

George did note, however, that the captain seldom glanced at the open book before him. When he turned a page he would do so with a portentous flip that seemed to have nothing to do with the message. It could not be the light which though failing still was sound. George decided that the captain wasn't really reading at all: he was reciting from memory.

"And Joshua sent men from Jericho to Ai, which is beside Beth-aven, on the east side of Beth-el, and spake unto them, saying 'Go up and view the country.' "

When he was finished—and it was a passionate finish, appropriately dramatic—they all knelt in prayer. Afterward the men thanked the captain, who having already supped and now seeing that all was well aloft and alow, went to his cabin to sleep.

The dice were immediately re-produced, and the game continued until the middle of the night, when one man had won all nineteen eight-pieces.

"A diplomat, eh?" George muttered to himself as he stretched out on a sack of straw. "A damned hypocrite!"

Yet the men had been happy on their first day of freedom, as he knew from the snores all around him; and if his methods were devious, at least he *had* done his duty.

11

One White Hand

NOT FROM SMACKS AND CRUMSTERS spoken on the way, nor from bumboats in the Catwater, nor yet from waterfront busybodies, did George Fitzwilliam learn what had happened in high political circles during his absence. Not until two nights after the landing, while the released prisoners were being given a banquet in the Guildhall, did this come to his ears. Nor even then was it publicly announced. George heard it at the raised table he shared with sundry prominent county men, substantial men, Grenvilles, Raleighs, Gilberts, and of course a few Hawkinses. John Hawkins himself, who had been on his way to London when he heard of the return of his hoy and who had immediately come back, told George; and what he said was confirmed by others.

The rest of the banqueters were having too good a time to worry about international intrigue or the succession to the throne. The men from the dungeons, the guests of honor, already had been so stuffed by wellwishers that they could scarcely see; but their thirst was unimpaired. Under cover of the clamor, the more serious feasters could cluck their tongues and shake their heads.

"The duke's been arrested."

Only Norfolk could be meant, for there was no other duke in England. The earl marshal, head of the house of Howard, Elizabeth's richest and most powerful subject, who was also, alas, one of the most pusillanimous, had tasted the Tower some months before, when there was reason to believe he was in secret correspondence with the prisoner of Sheffield, and that these two thought of marriage, of an uprising in the north, war, the deposition of Elizabeth. At that time he had stoutly denied—as had Mary Queen of Scots—any such plan. The duke had been released. But he was back again.

"He was *30?*" George whispered.

"He was *40.* Lord Lumley, his brother-in-law, was *30.*"

"It couldn't have been *all* my doing?"

"No. Bailey confessed. Not readily, I believe. They had to work on him several days."

"And—Mary Stuart?"

Hawkins shrugged.

"She's still alive. That much I do know. But if you ask me, she's lost her last chance."

"She is not likely to stop struggling."

"Without a head she could hardly fuss. Chickens do—but not for long."

Dully, making bread crumbs, his wine untasted, George idly heard the lower-level boisterousness. Some of the men down there were singing:

"There was a wily lad met with a bonnie lass.
Such pretty sport they had, but I wot not what it was."

63

Mary of Scotland and the duke, acting together, had sent an emissary to Alva, the Spanish regent in the Low Countries; to the pope; to Philip II himself. The proposal this man carried involved invasion, assassination. And he had recently reported by letter to Mary Stuart, a letter that had been watched for, intercepted, and because of previous experience, readily deciphered.

"The duke will go first," Hawkins predicted in that suave undertone so out of place here. "They say the queen's majesty balks at the thought of signing her cousin's death warrant. A queen shouldn't kill a queen, lest that prove her mortal. And Mary Stuart after all is an anointed monarch. But she'll be cooped up much tighter."

> *"He wooed her for a kiss, she plainly said him no.*
> *'I pray,' quoth he. 'Nay, nay,' quoth she,*
> *'I pray you let me go.' "*

George sighed.

"Well, I did see Mary, anyway. The first time and the last."

"I wouldn't be too sure of that."

"Eh?"

"It's my thought that Burghley will send for thee. What better informer than an attractive young man who would thank Mary for her letter to Philip and report that the men are free? She might say things to such an one she would never say to Shrewsbury, and at a time when it's urgent to study how she feels—and how much she knows."

"I hope you're wrong," George muttered.

Yet Hawkins was right, as so often. The very next day there came from London a command that when Master Fitzwilliam returned—for my Lord Burghley could not have heard of the return when he wrote this letter—he should be kept on call at Plymouth, "like a foyer page" in George's own bitter description.

No explanation was given, none being needed. It was George's duty to obey Hawkins, Hawkins' duty to obey Burghley, who in turn obeyed the queen. This was government, this was life.

George had many friends in Plymouth, yet he did not like the town with its bustle and bang, its prevailing smell of brine, bilge, and tar, its ceaseless talk of trade. Was there nothing else to life but money? Plymouth faced the sea, as did the people of Plymouth, and the sea was something George felt it impossible to view in a romantic light. Oh, it

64

was natural enough for some landlubber to thrill at the sight of a ship coming in past Rame Head, all sails snowy in the sun, the wake a dance of delight. George knew that, up close, the canvas was anything but snowy, the wake, blotched with garbage, no needlepoint. George had sailed; and he knew the putrid food, the sour-tasting ale. He knew the ulcers and vomiting, the dysentery, the boils, the intolerable itch of scurvy. He preferred to turn his back upon the sea. The countryside of England was his love. Cut rye was *clean;* perry mill was *clean;* but no quay ever was.

Feeling that way, perforce he remained in the port for more than a month—a precious late-summer month too, when the countryside would have been at its best—with no more arduous labor than acknowledging again and again, whilst deprecating them, the thanks and praises of the mariners he had helped to raise up out of a dungeon, not to mention those of their relatives and friends. And even when at last he was summoned to London, it was only to loiter in that capital for another month before being ushered into the presence of an overworked Lord Burghley.

George's orders were simple, suspiciously so. After all this delay, to no apparent purpose, he was to ride to Sheffield posthaste, stopping nowhere, sleeping as briefly as possible. He was supplied with money generously, as well as a let-pass issued by the lords in council, which would assure him of the best horses. He was given also a letter to Lord Shrewsbury from, Lord Burghley, requesting that George be admitted into the presence of Mary of Scotland for the purpose of thanking her for her assistance in freeing the sailors at Seville. He was to do this, noting her answer, noting everything. If she asked him to carry a message he was to accept it: as a representative of Lord Burghley he would not be searched.

All this was irksome to one who might have spent the summer and early autumn with the Croftses in rustic Northampton, so that George was scowling when at last he set forth on the Great North Road. But at least nothing had been said about hurrying *back,* and he was determined that Okeland would not go unvisited.

Sheffield Castle was grim and glum as before, my Lord Shrewsbury querulous. Shrewsbury was a conscientious man of no notable imagination, a man harassed by worrisome details of wealth, harassed too by an unamiable wife, and now in addition saddled with the care of an expensive royal guest who might yet prove to be the death of him. For if the unmarried Elizabeth were killed, almost certainly this "guest"

65

at Sheffield would be elevated to the throne, in which case Lord Shrewsbury's head would be one of the first to fall. George sensed that Shrewsbury now was annoyed not at George himself, a mere tool, but at Burghley. Shrewsbury must have known that his charge corresponded with persons in England, Scotland, France, Spain, Italy, the Low Countries. He must have worked hard to stop this traffic. And what else could Master Fitzwilliam's visit mean? My lord was not so naive as to suppose that a personable and wellborn courier would be sent half the length of England to render formal thanks that could have been expressed as well in a letter. What, then, was Burghley up to? Shrewsbury was hurt, and he was also sore.

Nevertheless he made arrangements for an audience. These arrangements took longer than the previous time.

The atmosphere of Sheffield Castle, though it was not changed in any radical way, had tightened. The soldiers were like soldiers on the eve of battle, hushed, full of thought. The servants were stony, scared, excrutiatingly exact. The very doors of the massy pile closed with a more ominous thud; the very walls gleamed with an icier wetness.

Mary Stuart herself, just at first, seemed the only unchanged thing. Erect, radiant, she greeted George with a smile. It was not the smile of a politician, but that of a friend. She was glad to see him. She gave him her hand, which he thankfully kissed.

When his heart had slowed to a more normal quap, however, George Fitzwilliam was quick to see that even Mary Stuart had changed—and for the worse. It was but a few months since George's first visit, yet she looked years older. She wore rust-colored sarsenet trimmed with a great deal of gold lace, and wore it well; but her mouth was tighter, her eyes harder. She greeted George from a standing position, but soon afterward she sat down, and it seemed to him that she sat with difficulty, as though her side hurt.

The royal cloth where her arms were emblazoned hung above her head as rich as before, but it was badly out of press, and George divined that it had not been used since his other visit. For the first time he could make out the motto: *En ma fin est mon commencement.* Now what did that mean? George translated it as "In my end is my beginning," but he could have been wrong, for his French wobbled.

There were twelve or fourteen persons behind the throne, not half the number he had seen before.

The queen of Scots asked George about his health and about that of the duke and duchess of Feria and of "our dear cousin of Spain," Philip II. She remembered to ask about Master 'Awkins, to whom she sent gracious regards. George bowed.

She seemed distraught, keeping her mind upon her duties only by an effort of will. Shrewsbury had told George that she had not been notified officially of the arrest of Norfolk, the man she meant to marry and her last hope; but he doubted not, Shrewsbury said, that she knew. George was inclined to agree. She was lost, this lovely lady. She had no chance. Yet he believed that it would be hard to overestimate her courage.

She asked about the fashions in Seville, in Madrid. George had no enthusiasm here.

"Drab, ma'am. Not like London or Paris."

"Alas, I have never seen London."

"They're mostly black in Spain, and they haven't any—any *swirl*. The men, yes. But not the women."

There was a pause, which Mary Stuart broke by asking George if he would like to see her pets, always assuming that my Lord Shrewsbury gave his agreement—or did my lord fear that she might smuggle something out in a grain of birdseed?

Shrewsbury gave permission, though it was clear that he was not pleased. Mary Stuart rose. They all knelt.

She lifted George.

"You come with me, eh? The way is narrow, and I'd have you right behind me lest I slip."

He remembered Burghley's remark that one who aspires to a high place must use a winding stair. It was so again. Four flights they climbed, to the roof of the Scroll Tower. Mary Stuart went first, George, by request, immediately behind her. She did not talk. The dogged Lord Shrewsbury was close after George, being the third in this upspiraling procession, and if the queen of Scots had said anything he would have heard it and noted it. Besides, no doubt she needed her breath. She was panting when they reached the top.

"I spend many hours here, when there's no rain. It rests my eyes after so much needlework. For I age, Master Fitzwilliam, I age."

"No," George objected. "You never will."

She acknowledged this with her small smile-grin, crinkling the corners of her eyes. Her Tudor relation at Greenwich, George reflected, would have simpered.

Most of the pets were birds. They were in gilded cages with silken covers to protect them from sunlight or showers.

"Like me," said her majesty of Scotland and the Isles. The cages were presently on the parapet, but at night as in times of bad weather, she told him, they were placed under the overhang of the parapet, protecting them from the elements.

There were turtle-doves and Barbary fowls, canary-birds and parakeets, and many a small, brightly plumaged bird that George had never before seen. The lady had names for them all.

There were also several small dogs of uncertain breed. And there was a pair of rabbits. She told George she kept five cats in her bedchamber. They wouldn't consent to mix with the other pets.

"So you see, I am not unbearably lonesome. Yet it is good to have you come here, Master Fitzwilliam."

The chat and the animals appeared to brighten her, and she was humming as she led the way down to the throne room.

She commented upon George's earring, which he vowed he would always wear.

An attendant had brought a casket, and for a moment George feared he might be gifted again. It would have unsettled him. But Mary had other plans.

"Master Fitzwilliam, I know little of the geography of this realm. When you return to London do you go through any part of Northampton?"

"This time, aye. I'll visit friends there."

"Ah? Do you know, perhaps, a young gentleman named Weddell—Terence Weddell?"

"Slightly, ma'am. He lives near the people I shall visit. Only a few miles away."

"What good chance! He attended me once, when I was in happier circumstances, in Scotland. That was so long ago . . . and I could not be sure that he was still alive."

"So far as I know he is."

"Tomorrow would be his birthday. D'ye suppose you could take this to him, Master Fitzwilliam, as a small token of my admiration? And tell him that I have not forgotten?"

She lifted from the casket an enameled miniature.

"My Lord Shrewsbury will have to poke and pound it, of course, to make sure that there is no billet-doux. But you could arrange for that."

She held it out, and George came nearer, kneeling.

"Think you it looks like me, Master Fitzwilliam?"

"Nay," he muttered.

"The artist never saw me."

"Anyone who had would know that."

68

"And yet, in certain lights...Look at it this way."

She turned the gaud, holding it low, so that George leaned even further forward. He could feel her breath upon his neck. He saw her left hand move.

Some who stood behind the throne might have seen that hand. None before the throne, save only George, could have done so.

There was a piece of paper, folded many times, scarcely more than a pill held together by sealing-wax.

"And if you would give this to Don Gerau in London? Simply a matter of convenience. By the time Shrewsbury got it translated and made fourteen copies—"

"Of course, ma'am."

She tucked the thing into a pleat of his canions, a sleight that might have been done by a magician.

"Yet if you think this might cause trouble—"

"Ma'am, I'm honored to serve you."

"I thought so too," she said in a louder voice, leaning back. "I am glad that we agree."

George rose, stepping back, holding the miniature, which he would turn over to his host for examination. But almost immediately, with the rest, he was on his knees again; for the queen had risen.

She gave him her hand.

"And now we have to thank you again—"

The audience was over.

12

Visitors

AUTUMN WAS COMING EASILY. The leaves had not changed, and would not change with dramatic suddenness but hesitantly, quietly. The rain when George rode south was warm, the air soporific.

Though commanding no such mounts as he could had he returned by way of the Great North Road with its posting stations, George made good time, pushing it. And he had got off to an early start.

In part his thoughts were of Anne Crofts and her father, for George, an orphan, already looked upon Okeland as half a home, and he was sick of wandering the world. But in part too those thoughts were of Terence Weddell.

George scarcely knew him, a quiet young man, something of a student. There were two startling things about

69

Mary of Scotland should remember Weddell's birthday after him, in George's presentinterest, however. One was that all those years and should ask George whether he planned to ride back through Northampton—not the usual route from Sheffield to London. The other was that Weddell was said to be a papist.

The request might have been coincidence. Mary Stuart could be ignorant of the English terrain; and though she was esteemed a learned woman, trained to reign, for obvious reasons she would not have had much chance to study maps while under the jailorship of George Talbot, sixth earl of Shrewsbury. Also, she was allowed few guests. She had little choice in the matter of messengers, but must try what she could.

Was Weddell's religion, assuming that he *was* a papist, something connected with Mary Stuart's request?

Until recently Catholics in England had not been persecuted. The *official* assertion in this regarded was that nobody ever was proceeded against because of his religion, but only if his political standing or political potentialities might imperil the throne; and if his churchly connections forced seditious thoughts upon him, and seditious duties, that was his ill luck. George admitted to himself that from what he had seen and heard of the rest of the world England was, in sober truth, wonderfully tolerant.

Several things had happened lately, however, and all more or less at once, to throttle this rule of moderation.

The papal bull excommunicating Queen Elizabeth and calling upon Catholics to refuse to recognize her authority had been published. The first of a flood of zealous young English priests, Jesuits coached at Douai, dedicated men, eager for martyrdom, had been smuggled back into the land of their birth, where, though outlaws, they were making themselves felt. And finally—though in point of time this was first—Mary Queen of Scots had appeared in England, where she was retained as an embarrassing "guest." Mary was a Roman Catholic, and a convinced one, devout. Even if it could be supposed that she would accept Elizabeth's treatment without demur, she still, inevitably, would be made a rallying-point for the discontented, especially among Catholics, who could not be expected to accept Henry VIII's divorce, Elizabeth's legitimacy, and who, hence, thought Mary the rightful queen of England.

Until lately the only strong anti-Catholic feeling was among the more rabid puritans, who were clustered in the cities, the seaports. For whatever reason, Protestantism and commerce—or as some put it, Protestantism and piracy—

70

seemèd entwined. As George saw it, the average English-man, until stirred from the outside, did not give a hoot. He only asked to be left alone. But the average Englishman *had* been stirred. Now was intolerance making its way in-land? Was even sleepy Northampton to be fouled?

Burghley's servant, like Caesar's wife, should be above suspicion. As Mary had known, George was not searched after the audience. Yet Shrewsbury asked him many prob-ing questions; and it was only by a display of his new-found talent for prevarication that George Fitzwilliam emerged scatheless from that interview.

In the trinket my lord had shown only a perfunctory in-terest. Mary Stuart's devotion to her attendants, like her prodigality, were well known, making her a contrast to the distrustful, scolding, pennypinching Elizabeth. Though shab-bily provided for just now, Mary of Scotland still owned the duchy of Tuscany, on paper at least. Reports had it that her income, some £12,000 a year, was being systematical-ly looted by her French friends; but there was a great deal left; and what there was, and more, Mary spent.

Weddell Lodge was small, curiously trim, not a working farmhouse but a gentleman's residence: the farmer or farm-ers, George surmised, lived elsewhere. It was about three miles from Okeland.

There was a handsome pair of gates, an avenue of lime trees, very formal, after which the house, though it was modern and well kept and gleamed with windows, came as an anticlimax.

There appeared to be nobody about, and George was reminded of his visit to Okeland early in the summer, when the trance-like stillness that overhung the place had fright-ened him. As on the previous occasion the lull was broken when a dog awoke to its responsibilities and began to bark.

By then George was no more than a hundred feet from the house, the door of which stood open. He did not see the dog, which might have been chained in the rear, but he did see a white face—a man's face, he thought—appear briefly at one of the downstairs windows, then vanish; and he heard a low scuffle of feet.

George was unruffled, and at the moment uninterested, it being his hope to fulfill this assignment swiftly and be on his way to Anne. He dismounted. For a moment he feared that he'd have to tether his own horse, but soon a groom scuttled around a corner of the house, making for him with bumbled apologies. This fellow, like the dog back there, had been asleep.

"Master Weddell?"

71

"Uh, yes, your honor. He's here."

"Well, *where* is he?"

"Why, he —Maybe if your worship was to come around back—"

George frowned.

"I am not concerned with the kitchens," he said coldly. "Show me to your master."

"Uh, why, if—Well, there he be now, sir."

Terence Weddell stood in the open doorway. He smiled. He extended a hand.

"Master Fitzwilliam! This is an unexpected pleasure. Come in, sir, come in."

They had met but once, and then briefly, and not here. Before setting out for the West Indies, and hopeful that he might return rich, George had examined a piece of property Weddell had for sale, property that adjoined Okeland, to which farm it would have been a convenient and probably lucrative addition. The land proved rich and well watered, and the price was low. Weddell did not seem immersed in his farming. Had George come back from America with his fortune made he would have bought it, an acquisition that would justify his marriage to Anne and partnership with Sir John Crofts, even though Sir John could not put up a cash dowry. Since he had returned without so much as a tester, George thought no more of Terence Weddell, whose very name he had forgotten until Mary Stuart mentioned it.

Now he met a different man, not a man of business. Weddell was somewhat short, and he was slim, though wiry, with a merry eye. His face and hands were pale, not suggestive of a squire. His shoulders were stooped. He was older than George, yet still less than thirty.

He clattered politenesses as he conducted George through the screens, past a dark wooden staircase unexpectedly baronial, and into a library that took the guest's breath away.

In the screens, fleetingly, from a corner of his eye, George thought he glimpsed what might have been an expunged light. This was low against the dark side of the stair, the bottom of a piece of oak paneling. At the same time George fancied that he sniffed a whuffed-out candle, which was odd in a bright hall at that hour of the afternoon.

The library caused him to forget these impressions for a moment. It was not large, but it contained many books, possibly a hundred of them, more than George ever before had seen in one place. He strolled about, glancing at the backs of some of these books, which seemed to be about geography, travel, navigation.

72

But there was more than books in that library. Besides a table, two chairs, and two goblets half filled with wine, there was distinctly, unmistakably, an aura of recent occupation.

"You've had a visitor?" George asked casually, nodding at the wine goblets. "I hope I'm not interrupting anything?"

"No, no! That was earlier. Most unusual. *Two* visitors in one day. I don't ordinarily get that many in a month."

"It is quiet out here," George conceded. "That's one reason why I hope to move into the neighborhood sometime."

"You'd be a welcome addition, I can tell you. Here— let me get you some wine."

Weddell left for another part of the house.

George went out into the screens and knelt by the side of the stair at the panel where he might have seen light. There was no light now, but he believed that he could smell candlewick.

He put an ear against the paneling. There was a faint mumble; also a sound, very thin, that could have been rosary beads.

He returned to the library.

He was examining some of the books when his host returned: Digges' *Tectonicon, A treatyse of the newe India* by Sebastian Munster, Dee's *Astronomicall and Logisticall Rules,* Cunningham's *Cosmographical Glasse,* Cortes' *The Arte of Navigation,* as translated by Richard Eden, and of course the *Decades of the newe worlde* by Peter Martyr of Angleria, another Eden translation.

They raised their goblets, and Weddell, always courteous, asked George if he cared to propose a toast.

"To Mary Stuart, queen of Scotland," said George.

Weddell all but spilled his wine. He looked flustered, then frightened, and at last puzzled.

"A most estimable lady," he said. "I once attended her as a page, in Scotland. But—why did you name her?"

George produced the miniature.

"Because I have just come from her presence, and she sends this as a gift for your birthday."

The effect upon Weddell was astonishing. Tears leapt to his eyes. He seized the miniature, and passionately, again and again, kissed it. He shook George's hand, in a trembling voice thanking him.

"She never did forget a birthday or a friend. Forgive the outburst, Master Fitzwilliam, but you've brought up the memory of an angel. Every one who ever attended her feels that way."

George nodded, for he understood. He mentioned young

73

Babington. Did Weddell know Anthony Babington of De-thick? Weddell didn't.

"He feels the same way," George said simply.

Weddell, greatly moved, stalked the room, windmilling his arms.

"Here she is, but a few shires away. I've written her, offering my services, for such as they might be worth. But I doubt that the letter reached her."

"Not likely."

"Certainly it did no good."

"It might have revealed your tendencies to the person who did read it."

"I don't care! Is it a sin to adore a mortal woman as though she were a saint? I'll keep the peace, I'll obey the law, but no one need legislate against my love of Mary Stuart! And if that be treason, by God, then rack me!"

George liked this man and would have talked longer, but he was keen to be off. He nodded to the half-finished wine.

"You referred to another visitor? Do you get many strangers here?"

Weddell's eyes flickered ever so briefly toward the screens. George did not acknowledge this.

"No. And that's a curious thing. This man came only about an hour ago, and he didn't belong to these parts. Truth is, he looked Italian."

George's heart grew small and tight.

"Dark clothes?" he asked. "Very big? Black beard, cut high? And a monstrous long rapier?"

"That's the one. You know him?"

"I've met him. Why was he here?"

"He asked the way to Okeland. There are no real roads around this country, as you know, only lanes, and—"

"I must go. Excuse me, my friend. And many thanks for the drink."

"D'ye think he's dangerous? Perhaps I'd best sword up and go along with you?"

"No. You stay and keep company for that priest under the stair. He must be uncomfortable in such a small space."

13

Die Well, You Fool!

Soon AFTER, slightly asweat, George strode into the great-hall at Okeland, to face three persons.

Anne stood on one side, Sir John on the other, while be-

74

tween them, very much at home, smirking, seated upon a stool, his legs this way and that, was the bravo of the Crossed Keys.

There was no subservience about his bravo now. He showed pleased, sure of himself. He did not rise, but with a sleepy smile extended a hand toward George, the palm up.

"Master Courier, you have a message, eh? Give it to me."

George flared. It was only by a shuddering effort of will that he kept himself quiet.

"We'll talk about that later," he said coldly, and went to Sir John, whom he embraced.

"How long has this lout been here?" he whispered.

"Half an hour. He said he knew thee, so we offered him wine."

"Which he drank?"

"No."

"Probably feared that there was poison in it. That's the kind he is. Tell me, have you seen anything French about him—in his effects maybe?"

"French? Why, no. He looks Italian to me."

"He is. But I think he might be in French pay."

"I see. A spy. So that they can disclaim him, if needs be?"

"Aye."

"*Is* he a spy, then? Should I kill him, George?"

"He might be somewhat hard to kill, sir. I think he's a professional sword-fighter."

"There will be trouble?"

"Probably. But not here."

Mostly this was done in small tight swift whispers as they embraced. Yet the Italian was alert, watching them. In another moment he might have broken in; but George stepped back, smiling, at the same time signaling with his eyes that Sir John should engage the man in talk.

George then went to Anne.

She was frightened. He knew this instantly, even before he had kissed her. Her shoulders trembled, and her hands were tight on George's forearms. Still, she managed a smile. And her kiss was warm.

Since they were cousins it was expected that George would kiss her, and the visitor must have known this—if he knew anything at all about English customs. The kiss this time was prolonged only a bit beyond what etiquette called for.

But George held her a little while afterward, smiling fondly upon the small slight freckles at the top of her cheeks.

75

"I said," the man from outside put in, "that I'd have that message."

"So you did," George said carelessly.

He put an arm across Anne's shoulders and led her to a bink, on which they sat side by side, very close.

"Art—Art safe?" she murmured.

"Nobody's safe, just here. Now tell me," he asked of her, "hast noted anything French about this fellow? Anything he carried or used?"

"Well, he opened his wallet. He can read. He wasn't sure of thy name, and he read it out."

"And there were other papers in the wallet?"

"Oh, yes. And they were in French. I don't know much French, but I know enough to be sure of that."

"Official-looking papers?"

"Aye. Tape, sealing-wax, all the rest."

George nodded, staring at the Italian, who by this time was confronted by a determinedly polite Sir John Crofts.

Yes, he would be a French agent. George had been told there were many such on the fringes of the French court, where the queen mother, the power behind the throne, smooth and serpentine Catherine de' Medici, herself an Italian, had many uses for them, all underhanded. They would be especially bold just now in England, where arrangements for the d'Anjou match, together with the need to prevent Paris from moving to the aid of Mary Stuart, had put France in the ascendant, Spain in shadow.

George's Spanish clothes, his association with Hawkins, their visit to Cecil House, George's two trips to Spain, all had conspired to bring about in the mind of Giuseppe here —for George had so named the man to himself—the conviction that George was a Spanish spy. When George turned off the Great North Road at Biggleswade, on the first visit to Sheffield, Giuseppe had followed him, had overtaken him at the Crossed Keys, and, no doubt thinking this a brilliant stroke, had accosted him in Spanish, and received a Spanish response. Surely the man had made inquiries about George afterward, learning of his overnight stay at Okeland. Then he had trailed George all the way to Sheffield Castle and back.

Had he followed George too to the London home of Don Gerau de Spies? This was possible, even probable. And now, after the second visit to Sheffield, Giuseppe must have felt sure that George was carrying something of significance. If Giuseppe could get that piece of paper he might gain much credit and even some gold. On the highway he may have hesitated to use such a direct approach, but here in an out-of-the-way place like Okeland he thought it safe. Here, immediate might could count. Giuseppe, sure of his own strength and skill and speed, also of the length of his rapier, had assumed that he'd meet with no resistance. The reporting of so delicate a matter to the lord lieutenant of the shire or even to the sheriff was not likely. By that time anyway Giuseppe would be back in London, where he could sue for the protection of the French ambassador, a man nobody dared to offend just now.

In other words, Giuseppe knew just what he was about to do.

Yet he looked puzzled. No memory of manners impelled him to pay heed to the remarks of his host. He was worried about George, whose offhandedness might mask some subtle scheme. Crooked himself, Giuseppe searched for crookedness in others. Was George playing for time? Did George expect friends? The Italian shifted uneasily.

"I'm sorry I attracted this toad," George said to Anne. "Forgive me."

"George, art thou—"

"Diplomacy, my chuck, my dear. I've been walking a path that is not always straight, and sometimes the way is mud. Like now."

He patted her knee, and tilted her face up and kissed her. She asked: "Will there be trouble?"

"Probably," he replied as he had replied to her father, "but not here."

He looked around. It was outrageous that violence should even be thought of in the comfortable, homely, familiar great-hall of Okeland. What was that damned foreign pimp doing here anyway? Who did he think he was, to invade the home of an English gentleman?

In any event, this was not a good place for a fight. The light was poor. The ceiling was well out of reach, but a couple of suspended coronas for candles would have hindered high strokes, and the rushes below, fresh, green, would make for slippy footing.

George was only surveying the scene, as any swordsman might. He didn't mean to engage with blades. Fighting was not for him. Fighting was only for fools, or for those who were concerned.

But was he concerned? At least Giuseppe was between him and the door of the screens. True, George knew every inch of this house, and he might flee to the kitchens and from there out into the barn or the stables, where he could

77

graciously permit himself to be hunted down like a rat. No. He shook his head.

Anne shivered under his arm. He smiled a little when he realized that she was anxiously watching him. Giuseppe was watching him too. And so, though he strove not to, was Sir John Crofts.

George could have made everything quiet by handing over the message. He didn't know what it contained, and did not care. But he refused to give it up. This was not out of loyalty to Hawkins, to Burghley, or even to Mary of Scotland.

"Thou'rt thinking of *her?*" Anne accused, as abruptly as though the name of Mary Stuart had been written on a large sign.

"No," George said.

And he was honest here. His pause had been brought about by something quite different—a distaste of taking orders from a strutting foreigner, right here in the middle of England. Bugger diplomacy! His betters George would heed, when he had to; but a man can get tired of being pushed about.

"Darling, what wilt thou do, then?"

"Something shameful, my sweet. I'm going to run away. Scurry off like a coward. You must steel yourself for this."

"And leave us—"

"That lout won't linger. It will draw him away. I have something in my purse he seeks. Anyway, countryfolk like thee and thy father, people without court connections, they aren't for this hulking brute. Buss me again, my sweet—and trust me."

He rose languidly. He started to stroll toward the screens.

Giuseppe was up at the instant, his hand near the hilt of his sword, his eyebrows low.

George made Sir John a bow.

"I must ask your indulgence, sir. I'm about to liver-heart."

Then he spun on his heel and ran outside.

George had not seen the Italian's horse and supposed that it had been led around to the stables. His own horse he had left, saddled and untethered, just outside of the door. It was tired, the poor beast, having traveled hard, yet George reckoned that it could take him to sanctuary before Giuseppe could saddle and pursue.

As he mounted and dug spurs into an animal that deserved a rest, he heard Giuseppe bellow.

Unexpectedly, there was a thud of hooves; and George looked back to see that the Italian, now mounted, was chasing him. Giuseppe was not the dimwit he looked. He had anticipated a flight and had left his own horse saddled.

It would not be a long chase. It couldn't be. The Italian's was by far the better horse and, in addition, was less tired.

By assiduous spurring George reached the Crossed Keys. It was as dreary and drab as before. There was no one in sight around the inn itself and nobody on the road leading north to Ashby-de-la-Zouch, south to Wellingborough.

George, although not sure what to do next, didn't pause, but his horse did. Blind with fatigue, outraged, the animal stepped into a hole and with a squeal fell forward.

Giuseppe could have cut him down dead. He didn't. Instead he dismounted. He might have been reluctant to murder a man before an inn, even though there were no witnesses. Conceivably too it never occurred to him that George would resist. He had drawn, and now he moved forward, not with the wary cat-steps of a fencer but rapidly, carelessly, his point advanced.

"Hand me the letter. Nay, I don't want your money."

"It's just as well you don't," George said.

He slipped under the other's point, which however still threatened George's face, and, afraid to lunge, flicked his edge against the Italian's elbow. He sprang back.

Giuseppe roared with rage and pain.

"Porco cane!"

He charged, fully in guard position now, his sword-arm straight.

"Ti faccio a pezzi!"

It was a ferocious attack, yet not wild. George retreated before it, stepping a little right, a little left, as he fell back, not consenting to move his own steel. George wasn't flustered. He would not risk a riposte until he had studied this man's style, but he saw no reason to let Giuseppe learn the nature of his favorite parry, his instinctive one, the one he used when hard-pressed or excited. Every swordsman had such a parry, of course, and his opponent's work was half done when he learned it. George gave no clue.

It was a curious duel, and a brilliant one. It merited more appreciative spectators than two tired horses and perhaps, somewhere in the depths of his dingy inn, the boniface. It was such rapier play as seldom is seen.

The Italian, especially after suffering the first cut, might have been expected to resort to all manner of stampings

79

and blade-beatings, snorts and violent flourishes meant to intimidate George. He was that way in everything else—his walk, his talk, and clothes. But when he wielded a sword he was another man, all efficiency and concentration. Gone was the rant, the rodomontade cast off like a cloak. After that first explosion he never made an unnecessary move. He was alert, but he saved his wind.

Each knew, each sensed, as only a swordsman can, that he was meeting a master.

They took their fighting seriously, these two.

If there had been a spectator, just at first, and if he was unlearned in the art of fence, he might have supposed that those two were afraid of one another. It was never well to start in a hurry—let the other fellow do that. Yet neither did it pay to prolong a duel. Once you had sized up your man and decided upon the best attack, go right in and finish the affair. Posing was for beginners—and for popinjays. When men faced one another with bare steel there were too many accidents possible, too many slips that could occur, to make safe even an extra second of combat. "Playing with" an antagonist, "cat-and-mousing it," not only was cruel: it could be damned dangerous.

The Italian was the first to disengage. Warily, making his point move in small circles, he began to feel the air with his weapon as a climber might feel for crevices in a slick high wall.

George raised his guard a trifle.

Giuseppe advanced. George fell back, making no movement with his sword. Giuseppe advanced further, using small, very fast steps. Again George retreated, having refused to parry.

But now George's left foot felt stones. It would not do to retreat among them. So he stood his ground, and even pressed forward a little, his point menacing the other's eyes. Giuseppe permitted this, seemingly intent upon learning something about George's reach and speed of disentanglement.

Suddenly the bravo undercut George's blade and throwing his own point out of line, swept upwards with a high guard attack, a smash that was more like saber play than a *passe* with rapiers. Its unexpectedness almost caused it to succeed. George's blade was lifted, all but wrenched from his hand, and the Italian struck for the top of the head.

Unable to protect himself with his weapon in that instant, George darted back. Giuseppe, having missed, also sprang back. George had been given no time for a counterattack.

Thereafter each allowed the other plenty of room.

Giuseppe crouched. Accepting this invitation, George attacked high. By arching his body and going up on his toes in order to offset a possible riposte, he got his point to the top of the bravo's right shoulder.

It was not much of a wound, not painful. Perhaps the Italian never even felt it.

For a little while, still not panting, they regarded one another. Such was the intensity of their study that they looked not slaughterous at all, but merely preoccupied. Neither showed any sheen of sweat.

Abruptly, as though at a signal and by mutual agreement, each attacked.

They needed to know more about one another, and they were willing to risk a few cuts to learn, though neither went in full-length. Sparks flew. It must have *looked* sensational, that exploration. Yet neither man was ready to kill.

Had there been a watcher he would think that George came off second-best from that flurry, for the bravo had pinked him three times—twice in the right forearm, once in the right elbow. But these touches were trifling. There was little blood.

In fact it was George who profited from the feeling-out, or so he believed. For he thought that he had found a flaw in Giuseppe's defense.

When they did withdraw, simultaneously and even ceremoniously, stepping back, again it was as though at a signal, perfectly in accord, in time, as though they were treading the figures of some intricate dance—a pavane or a galliard.

Stolid to see, motionless, George recast his strategy.

Here in the Italian was a fencer who could lunge and parry with the speed of light. His reflexes were exquisite. In the middle line of engagement he was never at a loss: the uninitiated might have said of him that he had a wonderful wrist, though in truth all the muscles of the arm were involved, as well as most of those of the whole body. He could fight well in the high line too, and in the low line. But . . .

When he shifted from high line to low, or back again, Giuseppe was the slightest bit slow. In a less finished performer this would have gone unnoticed. It was because his swordsmanship was so sound that Giuseppe's one weakness —if it was a weakness—stood out.

There were three possible reasons, George reflected as he steadied himself for a kill.

81

One was that the bravo's knees were not the supple joints that his elbows were. A touch of rheumatism? Perhaps that sunbirthed frame had found England's climate hard to bear.

The second was that Giuseppe's tallness and great length of limb caused him to favor the middle line, where reach counts most, over the high and low lines of engagement, which he could have neglected.

The third possible explanation was that this dark bully was *not* slow, ordinarily, in getting into and out of the low-line position. He might have been acting this for the purpose of causing George to plan the very attack he now was planning. In that case George would catch a counter that might kill him.

It was a risk he meant to take.

He went in.

He used a long arm, as the saying is, his elbow scarcely bent, blade high. He kept his point dancing, licking in and out. He was raising it more and more, getting up on his toes, beginning to arch his body, all the while moving forward.

The bravo might think that George, having touched him from this position, was about to try the same trick twice. In that case he would counter not for the drawn-in body but for the face or the neck.

George stopped. He took no step either ahead or back, but simply bent his knees.

Giuseppe was lunging, high. George made no move to parry, for he had been prepared for this.

The Italian's sword slithered right over the top of George's head.

All of Giuseppe's right side, from the armpit down, was exposed in that split-second. It was enough. George did not even need to lunge. Giuseppe, coming in, spitted himself.

He fell forward, caroming off George's left shoulder as George started to straighten, all but knocking George down.

George jerked his sword out. It was wet halfway to the hilt.

The Italian flopped like a great fish, arms flung out. He clung to his sword. The only thing about him to move was his throat, which throbbed as great thick gouts of blood gushed out of his mouth.

Whatever else he might have done in the past, he died well, that brute. He died as a man should.

Gingerly—for the flies, attracted by the sweet sickish odor of blood, already were beginning to gather—George got down on one knee and unfastened the Italian's wallet.

Yes, he was in French pay. And the French ambassador would clamor for the punishment of his assailant. George's Spanish connection and his recent trip to Seville would tell against him. Burghley would do whatever was possible, but Burghley would be perilously embarrassed and might forswear him. The very best that George could expect was a long term in prison. More prison! And they might well rack him. Or hang him. Or both.

He looked up the road, down the road. Not a sight, not a sound. Nor did anything move along the lane that led past Okeland to Rugby. The inn too was still, though George was convinced that somebody in there stared.

His horse lay on the ground, panting heavily, perhaps not crippled but certainly exhausted. The Italian's horse too was tired. George was more than fifty miles from London. He might ride to the Great North Road, where, with the order of the lords-in-council to support him, he could command fresh mounts. He might push it all night into London, and throw himself upon the mercy of Lord Burghley. But the hue and cry would be raised behind him, and the sheriff's men too might have strong horses. George could easily be traced through the posting stations. Burghley might be out of town. And then, there was the letter.

The shadows were long, the west red. Soon it would be dark.

So still was the scene that when a sparrow landed on the small of the bravo's back, and cocked its head at George, George all but jumped. Jerkily the sparrow looked around; and when it saw nothing of interest, it flew away.

George looked again at the papers he had taken from the wallet, noting with a wry smile that the dead man's name was not Giuseppe but Antonio, Antonio Salvo.

He felt suddenly doused with shame, standing there with those papers in his hand. To kill a man in fair fight was one thing. To rifle a corpse was quite another. Impulsively George knelt again, and he replaced the wallet. What if they did find it? The thing to do was keep them from finding *him*.

He rose, and sheathed, and brushed his knees. He fetched a sigh. Head low, shoulders hunched, he started to run along the land that led to Rugby. But he did not go as far as Okeland. Instead, about halfway there, he swerved to the right and made across a field of cut hay to a wood. There, very tired and beginning to be afraid, he lay on the ground and waited for night to fall.

83

14

It Was Hot in the Hole

AGAIN IT WAS A CASE of the watched pot. Would this crepuscular lull never end? What was there that made daylight cling so stubbornly?

Fear, which had come suddenly just before he entered the wood, was violent and undeniable, like nausea; it did in fact almost make him sick. Worse, it wouldn't let him rest; and tired though he was, all his muscles aching, he could not lie still on the leaves but must be up and prowling, peering cautiously now out of this part of the wood, now out of that.

The scene he surveyed was one of peace. Here and there in the distance a workman trudged in from a field and a few columns of smoke wobbled lazily against the reddened sky.

No tocsin rang. No courier, bent low in saddle, spread the hue and cry. There was nothing to indicate that a little while ago a man had been slain.

True, Antonio Salvo would not be known in these parts. It might be several days before the French ambassador, hearing of his agent's death, would pound a table and demand arrests. Yet even out here, a district seemingly so remote from international plot and counterplot, the rich doublet of Antonio, his long sword, his horse, also his foreign aspect, should cause a stir. Yet no sheriff's men were in evidence.

The wood was small, largely clear of underbrush, a neat round park rather than part of a forest. It occupied high land, as land in that part of England went, and from its perimeter George could examine all the surrounding territory.

It was not a wood favored by charcoal makers, because of its size. Neither was it an oak wood, which would have brought swineherds to pasture their charges among the acorns. As he soon saw, George had the place to himself.

Yet he walked around and around, peering out from time to time like some hunted animal.

Darkness came at last, but even then George waited for some time before he slipped out of the deeper darkness of the wood. He did not turn toward Okeland, although that had been his original thought. It would be easy to learn of his friendship with the Croftses, even supposing that nobody had seen him visit there today. Sir John and Anne surely would be questioned, among the first. They were not likely to lie, seeing no reason to. Nor would either of them have *made* a good liar, George believed, if he induced them to shelter him. It was better not to put that strain upon them.

The moon had not yet risen, and it was truly dark by the time he set forth from the wood. Nevertheless he moved from cover to cover, as careful as a stalking cat, tree to hedgerow, hedgerow to ditch, ditch to tree. And when he heard horsemen he fell flat and wrapped his head with his arms.

From the sounds there were two of them. They never spoke. They were walking their horses fast, and George sensed that except for the uncertainty of the ground on a dark night they would have urged them to a gallop. He heard the creak of their straps. Then they were gone—in the direction of Okeland.

It was some time before George rose.

Scurrying now, scuttling, bent low, he made for Weddell Lodge. He had already seen the light.

It was not customary in the country for men to stay up after dark. In the instance of Terence Weddell there were two possible explanations. He might be reading, or—he might have visitors.

The dog barked as George approached. Damn that animal! But though the turf was broken—he could smell its clean freshness—no steed was tethered there now.

George went boldly to the door and knocked.

The balk was thrown almost immediately, as though somebody inside had been waiting, and the door was opened without challenge.

"You're back sooner'n I thought, sir. If you—"

George stepped in, pushing aside a stumpy gnarled gnomelike man he hardly saw. He went to the right side of the stair and rapped with his knuckles.

"Is he still in there?"

The little man wore Weddell's cognizance on his sleeve. Clearly a servant. The way he stooped, his head cocked, and the way he squinted in that dim corridor made him seem somehow subterranean. He should have been inside a mountain. Yet he was not servile, and his voice boomed, startlingly loud.

"What the Devil are you doing here?"

George pounded the panel again.

"I'm your next guest," he announced. "That is, if the reverend father has been whisked away, as I suspect. Open this up."

Whether the little man had glimpsed George that afternoon, or for some other reason knew or could guess who he

85

was, George did not learn. But he hesitated only an instant, keenly studying George. Then, pressing a place down near the floor, he lifted the panel out.

"There you are, sir. Since you insist. 'Tis no palace."

George was dismayed by what he saw. He had expected at least a little room in which to move around; but the closet or hole—whatever it should be called—at first glance seemed impossibly cramped. Could any man get in there? It was no more than a padded space about six feet long, possibly two feet square. It might have been a coffin, tipped up at one end; for it was at a forty-five degree angle, following the slant of the steps.

George caught up a quick breath and wriggled in. He went right side first, which meant that his sword had to follow him. He had some trouble getting the sword in.

"They don't usually carry 'em," the dwarf offered. "I'll warrant it's been through somebody lately?"

"You warrant too much," George said coldly. "Now I want you to report me to your master as soon as he comes back."

"Aye, that I'll do, sir."

"Close the door."

There was no clack, no thud, or even a scraping sound. It was as simple as though somebody had blown out a candle.

George knew an instant of panic, but it was only an instant. Firmly and more than once he told himself that he could have no *logical* fear. Weddell, whatever he might think of the visit, would not give his guest away. The very fact that he had such a closet, clearly designed for priests, meant that he was part of a conspiracy to protect those outlaws. Such a man if nabbed would be hanged. Terence Weddell knew that. So, assuredly, did the dwarf, whom George now heard moving away.

It was hot in the hole, though the night was chill. He crossed his arms on his chest, having some trouble in doing so, and he muttered a short earnest prayer made up for the occasion. He refused to let himself twist or push. In the darkness, grimly he grinned.

He might have been half asleep when the knocking came. It was very loud. He thought at first that someone with a heavy fist was pounding on the panel beside his head.

He heard the dwarf, muttering to himself, fumble with the latch, swing open the door.

There were bootsteps, heavy, ominous.

"Where's your master?"

"Riding around his fields. He does that to clear his head, when he's been studying too hard."

"First time I've ever known Terence Weddell to take any interest in his fields, day or night."

The men were very near. There might have been four or five of them. George could hear their hangers and cross-straps creak. He could hear them breathe. Again and again they passed within inches of the place where he lay, the servant pattering after them like an importunate child.

He should have been a stage player, that servant. He made no try to keep the men away from the panel, and his voice was a whine.

The men went to the library. Probably they were afraid to range much farther without a warrant and in the absence of the owner. When they came back they stopped again by the slat of wood that blocked off George Fitzwilliam.

What were they doing there? Were they staring at that panel? Would they reach down and push it?

"Have you seen anybody go past here tonight, or heard anybody?"

"Tonight? Certainly not. Nobody ever comes here."

"You've been awake?"

"Of course. I have to wait up to unlatch the door for the master when he comes back from his ride. Who—Who is this person you're talking about? What kind of horse does he ride?"

"He'd be on foot. He hasn't got a horse, as far as we know. But he's got a sword, and it's a long one. He killed a man with it this afternoon at the Crossed Keys. He might kill another if he thought he was about to be caught. You'd best not open this door again tonight unless you're mortally sure it's your master."

"Oh, I won't! I won't, truly! And—thank you!"

The latch fell into place, and in a little while George heard them ride away. He sighed with relief and slumped a little lower.

Next thing he knew there was light slamming against his eyes, and Terence Weddell stood there.

"Here, let me help you—"

It was well that he did. George was indescribably stiff. "Forgive me," he muttered. "D'ye have anything to eat?"

"Come into the library. It's safe just now."

Watchful, much quieter, the dwarf trailed them.

George was smiling a little, but Weddell was frankly worried, as they sat down, facing one another.

"I don't understand. Are—Are you—"

87

"I'm not of your ring, no. Nor am I a member of your church. But I *did* come direct from Mary Stuart."

"And how did you know about the panel?"

"Guessed it. Sensed it. And when you went out to fetch wine this afternoon, I put my ear up against it, and I heard somebody clicking rosary beads. The rest wasn't hard. This must be simply an overnight stop. There wouldn't be a large enough congregation to justify the risk of a longer stay. So I assumed that you would be moving his reverence tonight. And I came."

"Here's your food."

George was feeling better. He ate deliberately and well, seldom looking up to smile, though he could feel Weddell's eyes upon him.

At last Weddell said carefully: "There was a man killed before the Crossed Keys late this afternoon."

"I know."

"He was the one who stopped here to ask the way to Okeland."

"Yes. He was a French spy."

"And—you?"

George opened his wallet and drew out the small balled missive that had been sneaked into a slit of his canions.

"You know her escutcheon? Mary Stuart herself handed this to me, and I shall take it to Don Gerau de Spies in London, if I ever get back there alive."

He did not say that he would take it by way of Lord Burghley.

"I believe you," Weddell said quietly. "I have no choice anyway."

"That's true. Now could I have writing materials, please?"

"Sir John?"

"And his daughter. I'd like to reassure them."

"No."

"*Eh?*"

Weddell still was pale, despite the light of the library fire that played upon his thin thoughtful face. But he shook his head.

"Your wish to tell them does you credit. But if I carry your message or if my servant does, they'll know where you are. I don't say that they'd betray you! But there could be a slip."

"How?"

"Crofts has servants too, remember. I'm not equipped here to put up a fugitive for more than one or two nights. It may be much longer than that before I can make arrangements to pass you along. And if there's a slip—any slip at all!—it might mean the lives of many, many devout persons all across the land."

"Yes . . ."

"So you see how it is? As soon as possible I will make arrangements for you to tell them you're safe. Meanwhile it would be all right for you to sleep on a trundle-bed in my room, except of course at such times as there's somebody nearby. Tonight I don't think we'd better trust it."

"I'll survive in the hole."

"Many a man has."

"I am sure of it."

"But you don't want to go back there right now. You're not tired enough to fall asleep. What about a game of chess instead?"

George Fitzwilliam put his feet up on the table.

"I'm not much good at chess," he confessed. "Let's just talk about something that interests us both much more. Let's talk about Mary Queen of Scots."

15

Stay Away from Windows

ONE OF THE REASONS George preferred land to sea, the country to the city, was that he loved to live well, enjoying good clothes, good wine, company. The many months afloat in appallingly overcrowded ships, the years in a Spanish prison, had only sharpened his fondness for life's material amenities. And yet, though the routine at Weddell offered these things in abundance, days there dragged with a more pronounced bumpiness than any he had endured whilst cruising off the Main or lying in the grip of the Inquisition at Seville.

Terence Weddell treated him well. Not the trundle but the master's own magnificent four-poster was George's for sleeping. He was allowed full liberty of the library. Cider and perry, hippocras, metheglin, alicant, claret, charneco, and sherris sack were his for the asking, served too in silver goblets. Weddell's valet de chambre, the gnome Sylvestre, the only servant George ever saw inside of the house, waited upon George with skill, combing his hair, trimming his beard, perfuming his doublet, starching his ruff, and washing and mending his clothes. Weddell's cook, a wizard George was never to meet, must have spent all his waking hours in

89

the concoction of marchpane and sugar meats, gingerbread, biscuits, candied eringo, and pastries of red deer and fallow deer, coney and goose, squirrel and swan.

Weddell himself was away in the daytime—riding off alone, returning alone, disinclined to talk about his business. But at night he was at George's service, and an accomplished host he made. Weddell's keenness to play chess had blabbed of his ability: he was much too good a player for George Fitzwilliam. But at mumchance, as indeed at all games of cards, they were evenly matched, while at the pastime George himself had first proposed, the discussion of Mary Stuart, they were one. A few times they fenced; but Weddell was as inferior to George in this as George was inferior to him in chess. Some nights they had music. Weddell played a cittern very well, Sylvestre was an adept at the curtal, and George could acquit himself tolerably well on a recorder. They sang too—"Fond Youth is a Bubble," "On Going to My Naked Bed," "Never Weather-Beaten Sail," "Green Sleeves"—the dwarf taking the counter-tenor, George the bass.

Nevertheless the month was the longest in George's life. There was not a pinch of danger to spice it. Though he was taught how to work the panel and the priest-hole was always at his disposal, George had recourse to it only a few times, and never for long. At first the sheriff's men and a little later some queen's men from London came calling at Weddell Lodge, but they seemed satisfied with the explanation the squire gave and did not ask to be permitted to search either house or grounds.

Of other callers there were few. Nonetheless it was advisable that George stay away from windows.

In the country even more than in the city, a man's wealth might be gauged by the number of windows he had in his house. All over England, and whether or not they could afford it, men were smashing holes in their gloomy old houses, admitting light and air, putting up costly glass panes. Weddell Lodge was modest in size, but it did boast a great many windows, having been built since the beginning of the fashion.

Fortunately the ones in the library were high. "I had 'em cut that way so's I wouldn't be distracted from my books on a beautiful day," Weddell explained. George himself spent a great deal of time over the books, out of boredom studying the art of navigation, the proper drawing of loxodromes, the handling and reporting of ring-dials, astrolabes, nocturnals, cross-staffs, and geographical planispheres.

There were many reasons why George remained at Weddell Lodge so long, but the first of these—the question of where he should go if he *did* leave—was enough in itself. George had no home, no headquarters. His mother and father were dead, his godfather as well, while his brother, Sir William, presently the head of the house, was in Ireland. His master, John Hawkins, was either in Plymouth or in London. *His* master, and truly George's, Lord Burghley, George thought best not to mention; but Burghley would be among the first to learn of the death of Salvo, and it was likely that he would guess who had brought this about.

It was an agony to George to reflect upon the fact that Okeland was but a few miles distant, almost within sight of Weddell Lodge, yet he was not permitted to communicate with the Croftses. Here Terence Weddell, in many matters easygoing, was firm. When the questioning parties had ceased to come, Terence Weddell spent a good part of each day away, arranging stopping-places for George. Weddell would refuse to release him until a whole chain of such places had been staked out, so that George would be far away from the Lodge if caught. This took time. In no circumstances, Weddell made clear, would Okeland be one of those places, nor might George pause there even briefly in passing. Okeland was too near. Weddell liked Anne and her father— who, as George happened to know, liked him—but he pointed out that Sir John was, well, perhaps a bit puritanical in his views. George glumly agreed. He remembered the rage the very mention of Mary Stuart's name had brought about. Sir John was not a hot gospeler—no, not like that detestable little Captain Drake who had read to the released prisoners Joshua's instructions to his lieutenants—but beyond dispute a man of stern religious principles.

Once the first ado had subsided George wrote a letter to John Hawkins in which he made no mention of Salvo but hinted mysteriously at some cause for delay and in effect asked for orders. He signed it with his own name and addressed it to Hawkins at his London house. At the same time he entrusted to Weddell for delivery to the Spanish ambassador at London Mary Stuart's smuggled note; for he had read this and resealed it, and knew that it was harmless, a tester of a potential new outlet.

How these messages were carried and by whom, George never learned. He could only hope at the time that they would get to their respective destinations.

He wished now that he had done the whole thing otherwise. It was not in his nature, ordinarily, to cry over spilt milk. But perhaps he had too much time on his hands. He should either have given Antonio the message, or else he should have fought that bravo right there at Okeland, with Sir John Crofts as witness. Anne's father wasn't rich and he had no political connections, but he was a man of unimpeachable honor, and his testimony would have acquitted George at once. Instead, George had ignominiously bolted. What did Sir John think of that? What did Anne think?

Then one morning—a morning filled with rowdy-dowdy sunshine and birdsong and the buzz of bees—George was about to cross the entrance hall when he saw that the door was open. He should have jumped away, like a thief who fears detection, for this was the practice at Weddell Lodge. But he looked out—and saw Anne.

She was alone. She had tethered her horse by the gate and was walking up the alley of lime, slapping her knee with a riding rod.

Once again she was bare-headed, for she was daring that way; and the sun fleered from her honey-colored hair. The tilt of her chin, the set of her shoulders, and the way she walked, thrilled him. He gave a cry—never before had he wanted her so much—and started through the door.

He was hauled back, yanked as unceremoniously as if he were a sack of rye. Sylvestre, though so short, was strong.

"You fool," he whispered.

George flung him off.

"Now this is too much, by God! Nobody's going to—"

"Get into that closet!"

It was as though a rabbit had transformed itself into a dragon. The little man meant it. All fire and fury, though he was fond of George, he would have slashed. His first thought was for his master.

George, who had started to draw his own dagger, clacked this back. He nodded.

"You're right," he muttered.

In agony, he snatched a glimpse of Anne, who came on. It was as though he gulped her with his eyes. Then he folded himself into the priest's hole, and Sylvestre closed the panel.

As though set off by the clicking of that clasp, hot suspicion struck the back of George's eyes. He started to sit up and was slammed back by a bump against his head.

Why was Anne coming here?

There might be a hundred reasons. Weddell Manor was not properly a farm in the working sense that Okeland was, but the two were contiguous, and many homely everyday articles might well be exchanged between them. One of the hands or Sir John himself would seem a more convenient runner of such errands, but the hands might have been busy, while the knight's feeling about papistry was so strong that he might have feared to find himself in Terence Weddell's presence. Again, Anne could merely be dropping over for a visit. Where was the harm in that?

Nonetheless George writhed. Perspiration broke out all over him. Never before in the course of an immurement—save for the first terrible instant—had he known a touch of fright. But now he verged on panic. He had all he could do to keep his fists from pounding the panel.

However, he forced himself to lie perfectly still; and he was able to hear every word, for Weddell had come out of the library and he and the visitor stood only inches away.

"Mistress Crofts! An unexpected pleasure! Will you have some cherries? A mug of cider?"

"Thank you, no; I have so much to do. I came to ask you about Master Fitzwilliam."

"Nothing's been heard of him?"

"Nothing."

There was a pause and George, though an inch of oak intervened, could all but feel the piercing intensity of Anne's eyes. They must be making Terence Weddell uneasy.

"He knows the country well, of course, and he must have learned that the man he killed had French connections. So it's best to lie low, very low indeed."

"He knew of Salvo's French connections before he fought. He didn't want to fight. He tried to run away."

"Run away? George Fitzwilliam?"

"Aye. It was best. He's not the fool he sometimes looks."

There was another pause, which Anne broke abruptly:

"Master Weddell, the sheriff's men and the queen's men must have visited this house, right after the duel?"

"Oh, yes, they were here. They searched the place."

"And found nothing?"

"There was nothing to find."

"And you told them that you hadn't seen George Fitzwilliam that night?"

"I told them that, yes."

"Was it true?"

"Why, of course it's true!"

"Master Weddell, did you also tell them that George Fitzwilliam had visited you that very afternoon, just before he killed Salvo at the Crossed Keys?"

George could not hear Weddell's gasp, but he suspected it. Anne, he reasoned, had not been idle. She'd combed the countryside in search of information, and no doubt she had come upon some peasant who remembered having seen Master Fitzwilliam ride up to Weddell Lodge that fateful afternoon. There was no reason why she shouldn't; there had been nothing furtive about the visit.

"No, I did not tell them that. Their questions were sharp enough as it was. It is the custom these days to press down hard upon persons of my religious belief, no matter what the issue or how far removed from any church. If the sheriff's men were to learn that Fitzwilliam was here that afternoon they'd tear the house to pieces. They'd welcome such an excuse."

"Yet I can't help thinking that George Fitzwilliam is somewhere near here, somewhere very near, right now."

"What makes you think so?"

"His horse was tired, and he left it behind. He couldn't have gone far on foot. There's no real forest around here, only small woods that can easily be searched. He must have ducked into some house before the chase was fully up, before the hue and cry. But why hadn't he reached me with at least a word? We're betrothed, you know."

"I hadn't known that."

"Oh, no banns have been posted, and he hasn't given me a ring, but that's only because he hasn't had the time. George is very busy these days—getting into trouble."

Again there was some silence, and George was convinced that Anne had put a hand upon Weddell's arm and was looking up at him, appealing to him. George wriggled, pettishly.

"If he should chance to visit here, Master Weddell, or if you hear aught of him, please tell me, won't you?"

"I shall surely do that, Mistress Crofts."

"He may be avoiding me for fear of implicating me. He —He's foolish that way. He has old-fashioned ideas of chivalry."

"I see."

"But make no mistake about it, Master Weddell, I love that man. If it would spare him a single unhappy moment I'd let myself be thrown into a fiery furnace, like Shadrach and Meshach and Abednego. No, I won't have any cherries or cider, but thanks again. I must off."

George heard them move toward the door and pause.

"By the way,"—Anne's voice was fainter but still distinct —"*why* did George stop here that afternoon?"

Weddell never hesitated. No doubt it was his policy, as well as a personal preference, to tell the truth whenever possible.

"He had just come from Sheffield, from Queen Mary. It

was my birthday and she'd remembered it, being graciousness in all her parts. You must know that I was a page in
her household once, in happier days, at Holyrood. So she
took the opportunity to send me her miniature, by Master
Fitzwilliam."

"I see ... And this is it?"

"Aye. I keep it next my heart. Perhaps I too have old-
fashioned ideas about chivalry."

"Does she reallly look like that, Master Weddell?"

"Not a bit. She's lovelier. Much lovelier."

"You and George must have discussed her. What does *he*
think of her beauty?"

"Ma'am, I couldn't know. He did not seem interested in
the subject, so we didn't talk about it."

George hugged himself, chuckling without a sound, and
when Sylvestre opened the panel a moment later, he was all
grin.

"Your honor, I'm sorry I was so urgent."

"You were absolutely right, Sylvestre. I lost my head."

Terence Weddell was thoughtful as he returned from the
doorway.

"She didn't believe me, that last thing I told her."

"Of course not."

"You know, Fitzwilliam, you're a very lucky man. I had
never really met Mistress Crofts before today, never in-
formally."

"You like her?"

"Let's put it this way: I think you have more reason than
ever for keeping away from windows. Now, what about a
game of chess?"

When a week later the answer to George's letter arrived
—George, clapped into the priest's hole, never did see the
message—it was from London, and from Burghley, being
indeed in the baron's own hand. Burghley, like George,
had eschewed ciphers but wrote with a careful vagueness,
making no mention of the law, the duel, Salvo, the French
ambassador, Mary Stuart, or anybody else excepting only
George's master, John Hawkins.

Hawkins, the letter informed, was on his way to Plymouth, where George was instructed to rejoin him. Every
precaution should be taken. What would happen if George
was nabbed—whether these two would dare to come to his
defense—the letter did not say. Neither did it say specifically
what was planned for George when he got to Plymouth,
though there was an implication that it might be another
assignment to the New World.

Even after the letter had been received and even though

George had no preparation to make, it was three days before Weddell would permit a departure. Arrangements had to be made for his reception in some house a short night's ride to the south. Also, there was the matter of the moon. On the night in question it would not rise until near midnight, when assuredly no one would be abroad. Terence Weddell had taken everything into consideration.

The parting touched them both. George was not in the least amazed when Terence Weddell guided him to the lane that led to the Crossed Keys, being careful on the way to avoid Okeland or any rise from which Okeland could have been seen; but he was shaken by the force of his own emotion.

"Go to the inn. 'Tis closed now, but there will be a man lurking in the yard. Somebody you've never seen before. Trust him utterly."

He extended a hand George could scarcely see. But George leaned past that, his throat tight, and they kissed like cousins, embracing one another. Each was sobbing.

"God bless you, Fitzwilliam!"

"Amen."

"God lead you safe out of this!"

"Amen."

Weddell, who knew every inch of the country thereabouts, rode quickly away. Despite the dark, the lane was easy to follow.

George sat silent for a moment.

The way was dappled with gently wavering starshine. A breeze soughed, and above and on either side of the lane a few leaves rustled peevishly. Somewhere low there was a guarded scurry of small feet, perhaps a fox. The thunk of Weddell's steed had long since ceased.

George turned back toward Okeland.

16

Oh, Wait for Me!

ALL GEORGE MEANT TO DO was look at the house. He had no thought of betraying his friend's confidence by rousing the Croftses. He would look a moment from afar, that was all.

But when he saw a blur of white nightrail at the window he knew to be Anne's, his head was caught up. It was too much, and he rode right across the garden.

The window was old-fashioned, without glass. Anne stood alone, immersed in her private thoughts. She had been

96

weeping, George thought, though he couldn't be sure.

How he loved her! And must he always be hurting her, always riding away? Was it his doom to skulk like an outlaw, shying from the company of decent, normal people? If only this were home, thought George, who had no home. If only he could dismount and go inside for a kiss and a good night's sleep! He sighed.

Directly under the window, he rose upright in the stirrups.

"My chuck—"

She started and leaned out, staring wildly.

"George!"

She knew him from his voice; it was too dark for her to have seen his face.

"Sh-sh!"

"I'll come down!"

"No! And thou must not tell Sir John!"

She would have been obliged to pass through her father's bedroom to get to the stair, as he knew.

"I'm off, my sweeting. I may be gone for a long while. But I'll come back. Wait for me."

She leaned out even farther, extending a hand. He could not reach it. He climbed to the horse's back and stood in saddle, and then he could reach the hand.

Her hair fell, a cascade of perfume, all around him. He kissed it. He kissed her hand.

"But—why? *Why?*"

"Sh-sh! 'Tis too long a tale for here."

"It hath something to do with that French woman!"

This he could not deny, so he only kissed her hand again. It was some time before he ventured to speak.

"My sweet, you must believe me when I say that I ran from that Italian only because I thought—"

She brushed this aside with the swift impatient gesture of one who walks into a cobweb in the dark. She was not interested in tickle points of niceness in masculine honor. She was interested in Mary Stuart.

"George, you love her!"

It was well that she couldn't see his face.

"I love *thee*," he said quietly. "If it would spare thee a single unhappy moment I would let myself be thrown into a fiery furnace like Shadrach and Meshach and Abednego."

He heard her gasp and instantly realized what a foolish thing he had done. He was no psalmsinger like her father, and it would not ordinarily be natural for him to make an Old Testament allusion. The truth is, the phrase had stuck in his memory ever since—crouched in that priest's hole— he had heard Anne Crofts utter it of him more than a

97

week ago. It had come forth by itself, unbidden, blurted out, and it startled Anne.

George knew better than to protest. She was not easily duped, and she'd have time to think it over later. He squeezed her hand so hard that it must have hurt.

"Darling," he whispered, "thou must tell nobody! Not thine aunts, not thy father! Promise me!"

"Oh, I promise."

Once again, she was not interested. She was not thinking of Terence Weddell and the possibility that his head was in a noose. She thought only that George had told her he loved her.

He slithered down into saddle, and his feet found the stirrups.

"I'll come back," he repeated. "Wait for me."

"George!"

"Wait for me."

He tugged at his rein and rode off.

The manner in which George was passed along was miraculous. The organization astounded and delighted him, and sometimes it frightened him. Everything had been thought of; and he could not help wondering whether London, Burghley, the government of the realm, the queen, could have commanded so neat a performance. There was no house at which he was not expected, no groom who took his horse without appearing to know why. Nobody asked his name, or whether he had any title (he was sometimes addressed as "Father," and he never corrected this), or presumed to make any mention of where he might be going or on what manner of mission.

The houses were good, many of them palatial. The grooms were expert. The hosts, like the hostesses, quite clearly were of fine or even exalted blood. The food was excellent, as was the wine. Repeatedly he was offered money, an offer he declined. His horse, readied the night after his arrival or three or four nights later, invariably was in prime condition. Some of the holes in which he had to sleep were tight, yet none was as cramped as the one at Weddell Lodge; and the padding, the sheets, the pillows, were silken, like the mien of those who bedded and waked him.

All he lacked was exercise. He still was obliged to avoid windows; and his rides at night were short ones, customarily with a guide who insisted upon silence and no gallop. George feared that he was growing fat.

It was an extraordinary experience, and it vastly increased

his respect for Terence Weddell and for the English Catholic party; but in itself it answered no question, settled no dispute. They might have been from another world, those gracious persons who wined and dined him, passing him along. They spoke English, they *were* English, yet they were more alien to George Fitzwilliam than had been the colonists of New Spain.

When at last he came to the end of the chain a bit north of Plymouth, he realized that though he had been handled by charming persons, he didn't know a single name. It had been planned that way.

Plymouth itself he entered on foot. Not masked, for that would have drawn attention to himself, but wrapped in a long dark loose cloak that hid his Spanish costume.

He made his way swiftly and without the slightest trouble to the Hawkins house. It was this trip that he had feared. He knew so many persons in Plymouth, where so many more knew him! It would have been awkward if some relative of one of the released prisoners had spotted him and pounced upon him with glad grateful cries.

The Hawkins house was in Kinterbury Street in the southwestern part of Plymouth, a neighborhood he knew well. He was surprised to see that it was lighted, for this must have been two hours after sunset.

George noted with a grin that since his visit there had been carved into and painted on both gate posts the newly granted Hawkins arms: sable, on a point wavy a lion passant or; in chief three bezants. Ex-Major John, who grew paunchy, was doing himself well as a gentleman. But in all truth, a soul saw ever so many newly-granted escutcheons in the seaports, for they were fairly slubbered over with these. And all fancy, complicated. The molet of the Veres, the Percy crescent, the simple Crofts chevron, the lozenge of the Fitzwilliams, were not for these "new men."

There was a holdup at the door, the only hitch in the trip from Weddell Lodge, but when George raised his voice he was admitted. John Hawkins appeared, clad in cramoisy.

"*George!*"

"Sh-sh! Is that permissible?"

"Go to, lad. I don't have a servant I can't trust. You'll wash?"

"Truth is, your worship, I'm abnormally clean at the moment. But—where do I go?"

"Why, to bed, if you wish."

"Let be! We'll wade no further into that. Where do I go

tomorrow, your worship? You have some oversea enterprise making up?"

"Well asked. I have. The admiral himself is here, by good chance. You'll meet him. Come."

"America again?" George faltered.

"America again. Till this blows over. 'Tis needful that I win back some of the losses, you understand?"

"Oh, clearly. So we—pirate?"

"Tut, lad. You'll be assigned to the admiral, and you'll watch after my affairs. All's ready. We shall have to smuggle you aboard, but smuggling you're used to by now, eh?"

"Aye."

"At this moment, a person who has in any way offended France is not a person to banquet, I can tell you. You know that there's a warrant out for your arrest on a charge of murder?"

"Those who have entertained me made no mention of a warrant, but I could guess as much."

"Aye."

"And so I must go far away?"

"Aye. And for a long time."

"Ah, well. Where's this admiral you mentioned?"

"Why, in the next room. Kin of mine. Come."

John Hawkins was kindly, and he had embraced George in a manner that left no doubt as to his relief and pleasure. Yet that "Come" stuck in George's craw.

Hawkins put an arm across George's shoulders. He led George into his solar. And the admiral rose, nodding curtly.

George bowed.

"So we will smite the Amalekites together?"

"You will smite the Amalekites as I direct," replied Francis Drake.

17

Delicate, Dangerous Too

THE JUNGLE WAS A MAW, implacable, pitiless, in color so dark a green that it was almost black. Sunlight smashed upon the water, as dazzling as diamonds; but the shore shone with a dull cold wet gleam that made George think of Sheffield.

The men of the *Pascha*, like those of the *Swan* anchored nearby, were in frolicsome mood, what with fresh water and fresh fruits. They did not dare to dice or play cards, since any such activity was forbidden, but they fished up-roariously, and now and then one would try a crossbow shot at a gull. The gulls were bewildered, never before having seen sea vessels. Their necks were far-stretched and they screeched querulously as they circled. They were not good meat, being bitter, and it was against regulations to waste quarrels or arrows on them; but a certain amount of lenity can be allowed when you have just crossed an ocean.

None of these sounds did the jungle reflect. Rather it swallowed them, leaving no echo.

Not only was there no surf, there were not even small love-patting wavelets, for the very water seemed stricken with awe when it approached that somber beach.

Nowhere along the Main or among the West Indies, or in New Spain, or even at an earlier stop off the coast of Portuguese Guinea, had George Fitzwilliam seen so menacing, so dark a shore.

" 'Tis a little more than twenty miles, you say?"

"Aye. You should make it by Wednesday afternoon."

"Two days to travel *that* distance?"

"When you have stepped on land," Francis Drake said, "I think you will see what I mean."

Thoughtful, they went to the captain's cabin, a pretentious place paneled in oak, with high closets that housed the captain's extraordinary collection of fine bright clothes and his plate—real silver, each piece engraved as was everything else there with the Drake device: argent, a wyvern with tail nowed gules. The captain knew nothing of heraldry—probably couldn't have told a flasque from a flanch or a cross engrailed from a cross urdee—but he was fascinated by this wyvern, or dragon, that he so fondly believed to have been a grant to his ancestors, and he had planted it in every place he could find.

George was familiar with the cabin, where he spent a great deal of time, though he had never been comfortable there. While he was experienced in sailing, as a gentle it would not have behooved him to haul a sheet or help at the capstan. And on the same vessel with Francis Drake—who, whatever he might not have been, was a great mariner—it would have been presumptuous to make any suggestion about the condition or employment of spritsails, clew-garnets, leechlines, forebowlines, falls, swifters, preventers, bonnets. Consequently his duties aboard the *Pascha* were largely clerical. Besides being the representative of John

101

Hawkins, the heaviest adventurer in this voyage, he had become a sort of secretary to Francis Drake.

Drake needed one. As George had divined in the hoy out of Seville, this cousin of John Hawkins could not read. Or rather, he read very slowly, awkwardly, uncertainly. Most of his reading had been in the Bible, which George sometimes thought the man must know by heart, not by memory which is a different thing, but by heart. But he did have other books in that splendid cabin, most of them about discovery, travel, geography, and of course navigation. Drake was extravagantly sensitive about this near-illiteracy of his, which he would not confess even to George, and often he had George read to him on the plea that his own eyes were tired. Always George pretended to believe this.

They did not like one another, these two, but they got along well enough.

Yet not even George Fitzwilliam with a secretarial exemption would have ventured to enter the captain's cabin unless he was, as now, in the captain's company or unless he had been invited. This was a stern rule. Drake, George suspected, feared being surprised in the act of strutting in his fancy clothes or perhaps with knotted brow and moving lips struggling over a letter.

So George was astonished when he found the cabin occupied.

There was only one man, but what a man! He was huge, a giant, veritably a Goliath of Gath. He was also black—not tan, or the color of chocolate, but black. He was naked to the waist, and the muscles of his magnificent shoulders and arms rippled.

"This is Diego. He is a Cimarron."

"Oh?"

George had heard of them. Members of an African tribe noted for its ferocity, brought over to New Spain as slaves, they had broken loose and taken to the hills—the word meant hill-people—where they ran wild. Understandably, they hated the Spaniards by whom they were treated like beasts to be shot on sight. But they were tough. Without arms or equipment of any kind, they kept up the struggle and pressed it. There weren't many of them, but they were cunning, fierce.

"I did a favor for Diego a few years back," Francis Drake reported. "I believe in his gratitude. He says he will guide one of my men to Nombre de Dios. At least, I *think* that's what he said. Suppose you talk to him?"

Drake's plan was plain enough, if a breath-catcher.

Twice a year, treasures in gold and silver and pearls were shipped down the west coast of Mexico and up the coast of Peru to the far side, the South Sea side, of this isthmus of Darien to a city called Panama. From thence they were sent by muleback across the isthmus to the town of Nombre de Dios on the Atlantic side, near the mouth of the Chagres. At about the same time a *flota* or treasure-fleet was on its way to Nombre de Dios from Cartagena. When these two met for a week or so twice a year, Nombre de Dios, which othertimes must have been a sleepy village, would teem with life. From there the combined fleets would move to San Juan de Ulua, the Atlantic port of Mexico and the port of George Fitzwilliam's capture, where they would join still another treasure fleet. Under very heavy escort they would start for Spain itself.

There would have been no sanity in trying to attack the various treasure fleets, separately or together. There were not enough ships and fighting men in England and France combined to make a dent in the Spanish navy.

Drake's plan was to sack Nombre de Dios while the Mexican-Peruvian treasure was there waiting to be loaded. It was as simple as that. The odds in man power would be heavily on the side of the Spaniards, but surprise might turn the trick. After all, what reason had the authorities to suppose that there was an Englishman within three thousand miles?

But now, it appeared, something had gone wrong.

Diego's Castilian left much to be desired, and it was interspersed with outlandish words that had no meaning for George, but the black was a naturally expressive man, and in time George had the story.

The regulars were bad enough; they would more than come from Panama with reinforcements of one hundred and fifty crack regulars and some cannons. Not because anybody dreamed that Drake was in this part of the world! Rather it was because of the Cimarrons, whose raids had been very bold.

The regulars were bad enough; they would more than double the size of the Nombre de Dios garrison. But the cannons might be worse. As nearly as George could get it from Diego, there were six of those big guns—the black of course knew no technical details as to bore, tonnage, etc.— and they had been or were being mounted on a hill on the east side of the bay.

It was not likely that these cannons would prevent a

landing. But they could cut off retreat. If they were properly mounted, and manned with even a minimum of skill, they could blow the poor little *Pascha* and the poor little *Swan* out of the water.

"Um-m. Yes, that's what I thought he said."

Was Drake inhuman? Anybody else would have dropped the plan, perilous to the point of foolhardiness in the first place. Francis Drake seemed never even to have considered quitting; an obstacle to him was simply something to be pushed aside.

The only doubt in Drake's mind, George believed, pertained to his selection of a man to sneak into Nombre de Dios from the land side, from the jungle, and make a preliminary survey. George, unmarried, his face darkened by the sun, wearing Spanish clothes, speaking Spanish, was a logical choice. George, though not powerful, had powerful connections, and Drake might have been pondering whether he should risk the loss of a man like that.

" 'Twill be fraught with peril, you understand, Fitzwilliam?"

"There seems little doubt of that."

"Your first move should be to find out about those cannons. Then, where are the reinforcements housed? And where is the treasure—in the cabildo or in the governor's palace? If you know this when we land, if you meet us with this, 'twill help enormously."

"You'll invade anyway?"

"Of course."

Might the admiral of this small expedition also be influenced by the fact that George could prove an embarrassing passenger on the return if the raid was not a success? Given treasure, nothing else was needed. "Who ever heard of being a pirate for a million pounds?" Drake once had asked his secretary. And he hadn't been jesting—he never did that. If, on the other hand, something went wrong, so that the expedition's investment did not pay dividends, or some unlooked-for international events should cause France to lose favor at the Enblish court, necessitating a switch to Spain, then this voyage wold be discountenanced, and the recruiting of a fugitive from justice would prove one more count against Master Drake. But if George was killed—

George had not been asked to volunteer for this assignment, but he decided to act as if he had.

"I'll go," he said, "providing I get two extra parts in the share-out."

This was a stipulation Francis Drake could see. It made

the whole thing clear to him, as John Hawkins' offer to sell out the Channel fleet had suddenly become clear to King Philip when Hawkins demanded that he be paid. So far from resenting the request, Drake welcomed it. That would make the whole business legitimate in his eyes.

"You are entitled to that. Write it, and I'll sign it."

While George wrote, Drake ignored Diego and scowled at the shore through a port.

"The men must not learn about those reinforcements. I think it would be best if you go right away."

"Yes."

"But you will need God's help, Fitzwilliam."

"Don't we all need that?"

"This is different. If you're taken it will mean more than death. It will mean an exceedingly *prolonged* death."

George smiled.

"You think that if when I'm screaming under their red-hot pincers I tell them how I got there, 'twould be a warm reception you'd meet, eh?"

"It would be the end of England's hope for empire," Francis Drake said gravely. "For each of us would be hanged, and after that the queen's majesty would permit no man to sail west. Should we give up half the world for fear, Fitzwilliam?"

"Have I said anything about fear?"

Francis Drake got to his knees.

"I think we should pray," he pronounced.

Embarrassed, yet rather touched, George got down beside him. He clasped his hands, closed his eyes.

Drake prayed at some length.

Diego watched them, wondering what they were doing.

When at last they rose, George tightened his sword-belt and grinned at Diego who grinned back, all teeth.

"Shall we be getting on our way?" George asked.

18

Through Hell with an Angel

SHIPS, he supposed, were the most malodorous conveyances ever devised by mankind. Yet it was true that if you could stay on deck you got fresh air. The voyage just finished, combined with the easy living in rural England, George hoped, had stiffened a frame made slack by months in prison. When he stepped ashore he felt ready for any physical ordeal.

It was amazing how quickly the jungle took away that confidence.

The blood might have been drained out of him and warm soapy water substituted. It was as though the walls of his lungs came together, striving to stick to one another. His joints moved grittily. His skin itched with sweat.

It was extremely hot and close, and he kept his mouth open even when he was not moving. He panted.

It was extremely dark too. Entering that jungle was like being swallowed up by the speluncar gloom of a cave. From time to time they came upon what might have been called a clearing, a break in the vines and spiked creepers, the branches and boughs, the roots, the hanging moss, so that they could move a few steps without pushing something aside or cutting something down; but there was never any clearing in the roof that blocked the sky, and not so much as a javelin of sunlight found its way to where they were. Until his eyes adjusted, George could not even see his own feet.

More difficult still to see, even when his eyes *had* accustomed themselves to that Stygian darkness, was Diego's back.

The Cimarron went ahead, bent like a hound on scent. It almost seemed as if he snuffed the ground. Certainly there was no path or trail. Yet he never hesitated. He carried a weapon strange to George Fitzwilliam, a scimitarlike broadsword with no point, and he used this to hack vegetation, to carve a tunnel through the undergrowth. Yet even when thus engaged, Diego moved faster than George, who, from time to time touched by panic at the prospect of being lost, shouted for a stop. Diego was polite, but puzzled. He couldn't understand how anybody could be so slow.

Twenty miles? It might have been a hundred! Since there was no sun there were no hours, and night was the same as day. They never slept in the stretched-out, proper sense. Whenever they stopped for a little while, George just collapsed, careless of whether he dropped on mud or in a pool of scummy water. Diego would hunker down, his forearms on his widespread knees. As far as George could see, Diego never did close his eyes, which gleamed in the dimness as did his teeth when he smiled.

At these times, George dreamed in a kaleidoscopic fashion. The images were jerky, flighty; he might have been suffering from a touch of fever. Lying in that primeval ooze, George would see Milton in the days before the death of his father. (The seat was a ruin now, his brother's property.) He saw the Anne Crofts of childhood, and the Anne of today, with her grave gray-blue eyes and the smile that came so quickly but went quickly too, leaving her face as serious as before. He saw the prison at Tenochtitlán, also the dungeons beneath the palace of the archbishop of Seville ... The audience hall at the Escorial, so depressing in its grandeur . . . The look on Guy Harris' face when they led him out to be burned alive in the marketplace . . . The Thames as seen through a certain window at Cecil House ... The majesty of Scotland being brave beneath a shabby cloth of state ... That saucy sparrow that had landed on Antonio Salvo's back ...

When Diego apologetically shook him, and he struggled to his feet again, the images disappeared as abruptly as though washed off a slate. When he walked, slogged rather, George thought about nothing at all.

It was always George who called the halt, Diego who called for the resumption of the journey. Diego in some mysterious manner kept track of time. He maintained a schedule. Though he smiled, he was insistent when he signaled that it was time to take up the trudge.

They saw no human being nor any evidence of such—footprints, the charred remains of a fire. Nor did they hear anything that might indicate human life. It was not probable that sound would reach them anyway. The air was too wet, sopping up each syllable they spoke, and multitudes of insects swarmed around their heads, humming loudly. Diego paid no attention to these insects, which he called *mosquitos,* but George Fitzwilliam was tormented by them.

Once they saw a snake. Diego had just shaken George, who opened his eyes to find himself staring at the thing. It was slender, sleek, five or six feet long. Its back was composed of pale green, pink-edged triangles that glowed as though from an inner light. Its head was small, and shaped like the head of an arrow. At its throat, as George saw when the snake lifted itself to stare at him, was a bright yellow bib.

"Barba amarilla," said Diego.

"Poisonous?"

"O, mucho, señor. Mucho muchísimo."

Yet though the big Negro held in his hand the chopping weapon he called a *machete,* he made not the slightest movement toward the snake, which soon slithered away. One of his gods, perhaps? George shivered, yet at the next stopping-place he slumped to the ground again without hesitation.

They had plunged in, but they crept out. There was nothing dramatic about their emergence from the jungle. As much as he could be considered conscious of anything, George for some time had been aware that they were going downhill. Gradually the roof of foliage lightened, and there was even a spear of sunlight now and then. They began to come upon small glades or clearings, in each of which a column of that same sunlight, very sharp to the eyes, stood upright. Diego went around these places.

Once they saw the sea, far off, and that was a heartlifting glimpse.

They found a path, or rather the path appeared to find them, quietly sidling out of nowhere to slip without fuss beneath their feet. It was not much of a path and didn't seem to be leading anywhere. Nevertheless Diego trod it with caution. He kept further ahead of George than he had done in the jungle, and his machete was held high, ready for action. Every now and then he would stop a moment to listen.

At one of those stops Diego turned. He went back to George and knelt, and with hands as big as hams, yet unexpectedly gentle, he smoothed George's canions and base hose, brushed his boots, flicked bits of foliage from his sleeve.

Diego wasn't even sweating, wasn't even breathing hard.

From the position of the sun and the direction of the sea vouchsafed by that one glance, George took it that this was mid-morning. They had traveled all afternoon and all night, and now they must be near Nombre de Dios. Diego could go no further; that much was clear. He would be killed like a mad dog by the first Spaniards he met.

The big Cimarron was smiling, yet at the same time there was a glint of moisture in his eye. He bobbed, nodding. He leaned over and rubbed his nose against George's nose, first on one side, then on the other. He stepped back, beaming.

"Thank you, Diego. *Gracias*. You've been an angel."

George took the savage's hand and shook it. Diego looked alarmed, shying like a pricked horse. But he grinned again, sure that George had meant him no harm and in his queer way was only trying to express gratitude.

It was the first time anybody ever had shaken hands with Diego.

He bobbed again. Then he disappeared.

There could be no other word for it. Big as he was, he seemed to have vanished like a wisp of smoke. At one instant Diego was there, at the next he was gone.

George waited a moment, thinking that Diego might come back, wishing that he would. He looked around; he felt hideously alone and more than a mite frightened. He swallowed, and marched up the path.

108

He came to a trail. It could hardly be called a road, but it was clearly marked, and straight. It went toward Nombre de Dios on the right, toward the South Sea on the other side.

George paused. A boy passed, whistling. A *recua* or mule train passed—perhaps thirty beasts, all heavily laden, and half a dozen drivers. There was also a considerable clump of foot soldiers, who outnumbered the drivers, and obviously had been assigned to protect the train from Cimarrons. The soldiers looked cross, but the muleteers were bright, and they all smiled at George, three of them lifting their hats.

He made no acknowledgment. It was not the part of a minor grandee to smirk at mule drivers: a salute would have brought suspicion upon him.

He waited a little longer, now knowing what to expect. Nothing happened. Yet the trail was a well-traveled one, trampled by many feet, human and other, and stippled with the droppings of many mules.

At last he turned to the right, and in a little while he came to the south gate, the Panama Gate, of Nombre de Dios.

There was activity here—some sort of squabble between the soldiers and the muleteers, while the animals themselves, half asleep, resigned to the lack of grass, stood to one side.

The only other person in sight was a sentry, who sat under an umbrella, and who showed no interest in the spat, being concerned with keeping flies off his face.

One of the muleteers appealed to George to intervene, but George scornfully refused even to acknowledge the request and walked past, toward the gate.

The sentry never looked up.

George was in Nombre de Dios.

He drew a deep breath.

19

When in Doubt, Be Haughty

THE POLICY OF ALOOFNESS could prove a sound one. Nombre de Dios was a small town, just now seriously overcrowded. It had a holiday air. Informality was the watchword; and more than once George was hailed by men who would have made his acquaintance. It was always men; he never saw any women. If there were women in Nombre de Dios they were kept indoors, as was the Spanish custom in the Old World.

George made no reply to these breezy salutations. He was Señor Stiff-Neck. In Spain he would not have feared for his Spanish, but here in America there might be local expressions, an ignorance of which would set him apart. Besides, when in Darien, he told himself, do as the dons do.

His first thought was for a wet and a wash, also some food. The town was filled with strangers, many newly arrived, and whether they had come by sea from Cartagena, by boat down the Chagres, or on foot or muleback across the Panama Trail, they would be dirty, thirsty, hungry. It was an innkeeper's night.

There were three ordinaries along the beach, and he picked the least dingy. He took a place near the middle of the table, an act of seeming sociability that his manner soon belied, for he spoke to no one save in monosyllables, though he listened assiduously. There was much to hear.

The food was hot and spicy: yams soaked in molasses; a salmagundi made up in part of eggs, liquor, nutmeg, garlic, leeks, and cinnamon; a lettuce salad; and a creamed white meat of delicate flavor somewhat resembling breast of swan, though sweeter (not until later did George learn that this was iguana, a particularly repulsive lizard). The wine, a Canary, was excellent. George ate a great deal and drank as much as he dared. He loitered over the meal, for men were coming and going all the time, and they were loquacious.

There was no fumbling for money. The shillings and pence had been cleaned out of George's purse, and now he carried reals, escudos, castellanos.

When at last he quit the ordinary all weariness had gone. He felt an exhilarating sense of destiny. His position thrilled him. He was supposed to be seeking his fortune, not just risking his neck, but he believed that he would have volunteered for this errand even if Captain Drake had not agreed to grant those two extra parts of the share-out. Undeniably it made a man feel good, in his chest and clear up and down his back, to realize that he was alone in the midst of so many enemies. How he longed to tell these cocky colonists that there was an Englishman among them, that their hold upon the New World no longer would be complete! But he walked on, picking his teeth, saying nothing.

When Drake came at dawn they would learn.

George already had gathered that the town was in a state of twitchiness, fearful of attack. But this was because of the Cimarrons, who were stronger than ever and multiplying at a high rate. They had recently thrown themselves against Nombre de Dios and came within an ace of taking it. No one would have been left alive if they had succeeded. This was the reason for the reinforcements from Panama, which as Diego had reported numbered a hundred and fifty men and officers. These were quartered with the regular garrison of eighty men in a long wooden barracks near the Panama Gate at the far end of the town from the beach. In addition, no fewer than nine royal *recuas* had arrived in Nombre de Dios within the past week, and by regulation each of these was accompanied by fifteen soldiers to protect them against the Cimarrons. Many of those soldiers might still be in town. Surely there had been private *recaus* too, such as the one George saw. And it could be assumed that every male civilian was armed.

Drake would have seventy-odd seamen.

Nombre de Dios was not hard to survey. It was a square, the sea being its northern side. The three land sides were walled, a mud wall, thick, fifteen or sixteen feet high, with no rampart but some temporary plank hoardings. Since the Cimarrons did not have boats of any kind, not even the most primitive dugout, no fear was felt from the sea side. There was no palisade. The customs house was not slitted for crossbows, nor did it show strong in itself. There was a battery of four small brass pieces, more ornamental than fierce; they were probably intended only for saluting purposes. The new battery, on the hill to the east, should be his first point of inquiry, George decided.

Half an hour later, still chewing his toothpick, he was there. Nobody had turned a head. He had gone unchallenged at the east gate.

He saw right away that Drake would not have to send a squad to spike these guns, six iron eleven-pounders, for they had not been mounted on their trunnions. There was a small but strong magazine, and a long rack of ball, guarded like the guns themselves by a lugubrious pikeman. Nobody else was around.

George divined that the task of mounting these guns had been postponed in favor of erecting the hoardings on the wall, attack from one of the land sides being thought the immediate threat. Or again, it could be that the machines needed for mounting the pieces were being used on the bench for loading treasure. Whatever the reason, many hours of work must be done before these cannons could boom.

The pikeman looked hopefully at George, though he did not venture to speak first. George nodded affably, Señor

111

Stiff-Neck forgotten.

"Get lonely, lad?"

"Now, that it does, sir. There's times I all but wish somebody would storm the town. But—not them Cimarrons!"

"Nasty fighters, are they?" George said, adding: "I'm new here."

"Oh, terrible fighters! The saints only know what we'll do about 'em if they ever get guns. It's bad enough when they're only using sticks and stones and their bare hands."

George, bemused, looked down over the town and bay, toys from here, bright figures on the shore, the high-castled ships, the sloops with their masts waving, the pert yellow-and-pink houses. He smiled.

"Who else but the Cimarrons are likely to strike?"

"Well, there're the French, sir. They might, some say. They're pirates, you know. Hug-o-nots. They're heretics, aye, but at least they're *men.*"

"The English?"

"What English, sir?"

"Well, there *are* English, aren't there?"

"Eh, I suppose so. But they'd stay home. They'd never come this far. They'd be afeared to. Ha-ha. Imagine the English here!"

"Ha-ha," muttered George Fitzwilliam. "Well, it's been a pleasant chat. *Hasta la vista, amigo.*"

"May the saints walk with you, sir."

George drifted back to the town, still unaccosted. His problem was not how to get the information Captain Drake sought—that would be absurdly easy—but how to get it without showing too busy or, contrariwise, too casual.

First he walked all over the town, fixing it in his mind. This was not difficult. Few of the streets were of any importance from a military point of view. The broadest—Avenida de la Something-or-Other—bisected Nombre de Dios neatly, running up a slight slope from the middle of the beach, the place where the brass pieces were, to the plaza, which was in almost the exact center of town. Beyond that, in a somewhat less wide form, it continued to the Panama Gate. The soldiers, stationed near the gate, would come down that avenue. Drake and his men would ascend it. Yes.

The treasure was stored in two buildings: the governor's palace, a low stone structure about seventy-five feet long, which made up the east side of the plaza; and the cabildo, a much stronger-looking pile about halfway down the Avenida, between the plaza and the customs house. Each of these buildings was full. Each was well guarded.

The only thing George was unable to learn—for he feared to .probe too far—was which one contained the better part of the treasure and which the overflow.

His inspection over, George found himself faced with a predicament nobody had anticipated. What would he do with himself while waiting?

It was about half past four. Drake and the Devonshire men were not due for twelve hours.

He was tired. Though he walked a razor's edge, and with the lightnings playing about his feet, he could not help but fetch a yawn. His heart beat fast, yet he could hardly keep his eyes open.

It was in this condition that he started to look for a place to sleep. In less than an hour he knew that he would not find it. Not even a bed shared with two or three others was available. Not even two chairs pushed together, or the top of a table. Nombre de Dios was crammed. He would be obliged to stay out-of-doors.

This would not have unsettled him—most of the buildings were arcaded, so he would have protection against rain—but for one thing. What about his clothes? Aunt Jane's bounty had been well used. For all the mud and spiked creepers of the jungle, for all his sweat, and the days at sea, days of salt air and sun, George Fitzwilliam still was the most richly dressed man in the streets of Nombre de Dios. It would never do for such a one to sleep under an arcade, or on the beach.

Hungry again, he went into a tavern and ate a large supper, washing this down with wine. He brought there a small leather bottle of rum, a spirituous drink made from sugar cane. He did not like rum, but it had a stronger smell than wine, and George thought that if interrogated he could feign stupor.

He lingered as long as he dared. Then he roamed the streets for a little while, until he saw that he was alone.

There were many places to sleep if he didn't mind stone, something not likely to disconcert an old prisoner. He should think of two things: where he would be most useful when the alarm was sounded and where he would be the least conspicuous meanwhile.

The waterfront near the brass cannons would be the nearest spot, and it might prove—what with the sand—the least adamantine. On the other hand, the plaza probably would be crowded with such as him—though it was not likely that any of the others would be wearing such silk. And the plaza, after all, was not far from the beach, and the way was downhill. He chose the plaza.

As he had expected, there were others there, already asleep. Their snoring was loud in the dimness of the arcades, and they were curled up sideways on sleazy blankets, their sombreros over their faces.

George picked a secluded spot, sat down, and leaned back against the wall.

He purposely sat that way so that he wouldn't fall asleep. It did no good.

Two men were shaking him, and he knew instantly, even before he opened his gummy eyes, that it was not dawn. Yet he knew he had been sleeping for a long while. He was very stiff.

He mumbled something, feeling for his purse. The coins still were there. These men weren't petty thieves. Groggy, George lifted his head.

They were soldiers.

"You must come with us, señor," one of them said.

He waggled his head. He managed a hiccup, and sank back.

But they were persistent. They shook him again.

"Señor, the captain of the guard—"

From what he had seen of the moon George reckoned that the time was at least two hours short of sunrise. Much could happen in two hours. If he wasn't down there on the beach when the Devonshire boys came tumbling ashore, how would they know that they didn't have to smash the east gate and climb the hill to the dismounted eleven-pounder. How would they know where the treasure was?

"Señor, it isn't right that you should—"

And if the raid was made without him, he would be left in captivity, sure to meet an investigation. It was not pleasant to think what might be done to him then.

He shook his head again. When in doubt, be haughty.

"Go away."

They started to lift him to his feet. He got up, but he pushed the soldiers off.

"Pudendos," he screamed *"Puta madres!"*

In the darkness somebody giggled.

A coin? A handful of coins? But since these men had not already robbed him they could be believed to be honest guardsmen. There *were* such things. His luck! He straightened his ruff, snorting.

"Señor, the captain of the—"

114

"Mierda!"

George drew.

They could have encircled him, one on each side. They could have yelled. But they paused, irresolute.

Then from the beach at the bottom of the Avenida came a shout.

"Fitzwilliam! Where are you?"

George smiled at the two soldiers, for whom he felt sorry. Sleepers were sitting up. Somebody came running from the direction of the customs house, his voice a shattering screech.

"Piratas! Los Piratas!"

George moved his point coaxingly back and forth.

"You would fight?" he asked.

The sword was long.

"Piratas!"

The soldiers did a sensible thing. They turned and ran, back toward the Panama Gate.

And George ran the other way, down the hill to the customs house.

20

A Few Feet Away

HALFWAY DOWN THE SLOPE he met the watchman running up, a swagbellied stumpy man, rufous of countenance, who kept yelling *"Los piratas!"* The watchman stopped, his eyes bugging out, when George lifted his sword. His lips moved as he muttered a prayer; he thought he was about to die.

George hit him only with the flat, over the left ear, a blow that sent the man spinning. Without any pause, George ran on.

But the damage had been done. Heads were popping up at windows. Back by the Panama Gate where the two soldiers had given the alarm, a drum rolled, trumpets blared.

In the light of a leprous moon intermittently besmogged by clouds, the men on the beach were a motley lot, hissing in whispers as they toiled. They were making boats fast, resetting their helmets, passing out arms, or spiking the touchholes of the brass saluting pieces, while others, grasping mauls, were knocking away the supports of the platform on which those pieces had been emplaced.

Breathless, unable to shout but seeking the admiral, George running down the slope forgot that his sword was naked in his hand, forgot too the Spanish apparel. He was

115

astounded when two men leapt out of the shadows, their swords and targets high.

He dropped to one knee, leaning backward, and parried the first stroke, but with no time for a riposte. The second man, stooping, he touched on the kneecap, producing a squeal of pain.

"Ye fools!" he cried.

"Master Fitzwilliam!"

They were John Oxenham, an adventurer, and stout Tom Moone, the company's carpenter. They were in agony over their mistake, though they could scarcely be blamed. George had appeared so suddenly, so swiftly, in his Spanish clothes, with his sword . . .

"No matter now! Where's the admiral?"

Suddenly Drake was with them, asking questions. George gasped out his report in a few words. He told Drake that he could forget that battery of eleven-pounders. The treasure was in two buildings, but the one on the plaza should be broached first, since whoever held the plaza held the town, and the man who struck from the sea would be covering his own line of retreat. This latter point was important, as they both knew. The raid would depend for its success largely upon surprise, confusion, speed. The loot would be heavy.

"But, 'tis not dawn!"

"I started 'em early, Fitzwilliam. They twitched. There was no more to do while we lay behind that island out there, and they fell to fretting about the Spaniards. So I declared it was dawn, and we moved."

"Thank Christ you did!"

"Fitzwilliam, watch your language! I'll have no profanity in my command!"

There was no time for further reprimand. The admiral did not bustle, and though he was giving orders in a swift stream he seldom raised his voice.

"Keep to me," he told George. "We'll be making all the clamor we can, and it might be hard to talk."

The party had been broken into two groups, about equal in numbers, each containing a drummer and a trumpeter, boys. One group was in charge of the admiral, the other of his brother John, captain of the *Swan.*

Some men already were armed. Weapons were being passed to others. These were pikes and fire pikes, swords and targets, partisans, longbows, even some muskets and calivers. George's heart sank when he saw them, so inferior to the Spanish arms. Longbows! Why did England's armies drag?

The Devonshire boys were not atwitter, dancing on their toes; nor yet were they making last-minute practical preparations, as soldiers should. They were nervous. They were even frightened.

It was no way in which to leap into a lion's mouth.

Drake gave these feelings little chance to ferment. "When trouble threatens, keep the boys busy," was an old skipper's adage; and the admiral, with some reason, seemed to think that it would work on land as well.

"We'll storm the square from two directions. I'd make it three, if I could spare the men. Now how—"

George was ready.

"Along the beach until the second tavern. It has the sign of a pig before it," he told John Oxenham, who was to share command of the flanking group with the admiral's brother. "Turn left just past that. It's a wide street, like this one, and it goes up. Four-five hundred yards you come to a church on the right. Turn *left* there."

"Aye."

"That's well, off with ye," cried Francis Drake. "Trumpeter, drummer, strike up. And you others, all of you, *cheer, sing*. I don't care what it is, but make a noise. Now—come along."

He started up the slope at a trot, George behind him.

From the questions called by residents who were barricading their windows, George could deduce that, despite the "piratas" cry, most of them believed that the town was being assailed by Cimarrons. Nobody appeared in the street itself. The visitors didn't see a soul until they burst into the plaza, on the far side of which the Spanish soldiery was lined up to meet them.

Then there was an instant that appeared to last a year.

George could not help but admire the spirit of men who in the middle of the night could tumble out of their bunks and into their uniforms, gather their gear in perfect condition, array themselves as neatly as though on parade, and await an unknown enemy—all in a matter of minutes. Most of them were arquebusiers, with a few pikemen to protect them after misfires. Their weapons were supported, and obviously loaded, an elaborate process that must somehow have been done on the run between barracks and the plaza. Their matches were lit, the serpentines cocked.

This was the Spanish infantry, the best in the world.

Impassive, they waited.

There was an order. Then came the volley, one great roar, a terrible explosion that reddened the square. Chips of stone flew, chunks of plaster dribbled down to the pave-

117

ment. The trumpeter, who had been standing alongside Drake after they had stopped at the entrance of the plaza, went right over backward, a Catherine wheel. Drake—as though some powerful person had pushed him in the chest —was slammed back against George, who in turn was pushed against a wall.

"You're hit!"

"Sh-sh! I'm all right. *Bows!*"

Many were fired. Some Spaniards fell. But this was not Agincourt, not Crécy. The arquebusiers started to reload, while pikemen stepped forward to protect them.

"*Pikes!*"

They got there in time to prevent a reloading, a second volley. The arquebusiers were obliged to fall back, carrying their equipment. The Spanish pikemen, though outnumbered now, clearly were prepared to stand—until they heard the drum and trumpet together with the shouts of men from the west, their left. Then their officer, not knowing how many invaders he had to contend with, wisely ordered his pikemen to fall back. This they did in perfect order, still covering the arquebusiers.

Drake asked: "Which is it?"

George pointed to the governor's house.

From somewhere a battering-ram was produced. It was a thirty-foot trunk of chestnut, each side studded with spikes of ash. It had not been built here. It had been brought. Even before he left England, Francis Drake was preparing to break down treasure-house doors.

The men who had hauled this ram up the slope were too winded to swing it at first, but Oxenham's party now burst into the plaza, and there were plenty of volunteers. George himself, forgetting his heritage, took a spike. So did Francis Drake, just before him.

"Better let me look at that leg, sir," George said.

"Sh-sh-sh!"

Thunk the thing went. *Thunk ... Thunk ...*

The door fell.

They poured inside. The first of them, though he was limping badly, was Francis Drake.

"The cellars," George called.

There was another door, but their shoulders took care of that. Then they stormed into the cellar.

It was only one room, albeit an enormous one, perhaps seventy-five to eighty feet long, fifteen feet wide, twelve feet high. And it was filled almost to the ceiling, almost to the last square inch of floor space, with one pile of crisscrossed metal bars.

The ingots flared like white fire in the light of the torches. Hundreds of tons. An emperor's ransom.

"Silver," cried the admiral in a tone of disgust. "Leave it here. Too heavy. Fitzwilliam, where's that other building?"

Amazingly, he was obeyed. Not one of them ever had seen anything like the heaped fortune in the cellar of the governor's house at Nombre de Dios, and nobody but Francis Drake ever could have dreamed of such a mass. Yet they turned their backs upon it.

There was no further fighting in the plaza; and the fallen Spaniards, four in number, already had been stripped, while friends were carrying the trumpeter's body down the slope to the boats. Still no face appeared at a window. The Devonshire boys might have had the town to themselves.

But they knew better. Eyes were watching them, mouths reporting their arrangement to a rally of regulars by the Panama Gate. Soon the Spaniards would know the weakness of this invading force and would stamp it out like a cockroach.

Keep the boys busy. The admiral unhesitatingly commanded that the ram be taken halfway down the slope to the cabildo, the front door of which should be smashed. Meanwhile he told off a rear guard to wait in the plaza, with orders not to battle but to return fire only when fired upon and then fall away.

Drake stood leaning against a wall of the governor's house, nursing his wound, but his voice was clear and sure, his eyes flashed, his very whiskers appeared to bristle. The man was not playacting. He *believed*. The Lord had so ordained it.

But when Drake walked off it was with a wrenching limp, and George, who followed close behind him, noticed that blood pumped out of his left boot at each step.

The cabildo was a tougher nut to crack than the governor's house. Its walls were thick, its oak door triply bolted with iron. Moreover, it was more difficult to swing the ram. Unlike the plaza, which was level and floored with flagstone, the Avenida was paved only with jagged stones. The footing was treacherous. Because of the slope, the men on one side of the ram were higher than those on the other. Worse, they had barely started to hit when the heavens, as though at a signal, opened up. None of the boys from Devonshire had known such a rainstorm. It was a cloudburst. It came down in sheets, pounding them, all but forcing them to their knees. Lightning flared and thunder banged, shuddering the town.

Francis Drake sloshed among his men, screaming encouragement.

119

It did little good to reason that this rain meant wetted matches on both sides. Not a musket, caliver, or arquebus could be fired now. But man for man, pike for pike, sword for sword, the Spaniards were greater; and as time passed, their organization was improving. Soon it would be light.

Men came running down the street from the plaza, yelling that the Spaniards had returned in overwhelming numbers. They were lost to decency, those deserters. George, Oxenham, John Drake, a few others, tried to stop them or even to drive them back with the flat of the sword. It was no use. In that torrential rain they slipped past, down to the shore to the boats.

Then the men who held the ram dropped it.

Drake shook his fists at them, and even above the thunder his voice could be heard.

"I bring ye halfway across the world! I bring ye within a few feet of the heaped-up treasures of America! And you— you—"

He pitched forward on his face and was still.

The Spaniards gave them a farewell salute, some time after they'd pushed out into the bay, from one of the small brass cannons they had managed to remount, but whether this was done as a chivalrous gesture or in derision or merely as a token pursuit was never known.

The rain had ceased. The sky to the east was streaked with dawn.

Many of the men rowing back were worried about the admiral, and tender after tender approached the moses boat of the *Pascha,* in the sternsheets of which sat George Fitzwilliam with the admiral's head in his lap.

"Is he— Is he dead?"

"He's not dead," George would reply, looking down at the taut small red face. "He'll never die, this man."

21

This Was the Blackest Time

PIRACY WAS A YOUNG MAN'S GAME. The admiral himself, at twenty-eight, was the oldest member of his band, many of which were in their teens. Their powers of recovery were prodigious. In truth they had not been much hurt of body—

the trumpeter killed, Francis Drake with a nasty wound in the groin, Tom Moone's kneecap, an assortment of bruises and flesh cuts—and the damage was largely in confidence, in morale. They'd been beaten, and they knew it. They had quaked and quavered and had run. Now their chance was past. It was known that they were off the coast of Darien and every post would be warned, every ship's master. They had not pressed their boldness, and they might as well go home and admit it.

For all that, the excitement of the unforgettable morning, the weather, the fresh sea breeze where they lay at anchor in the lee of a little island bunched with clean-smelling pines, and perhaps most of all the fish they caught, the fruit they picked, the fresh water they drew, combined to make them talkative again. But they would fall silent whenever they chanced to glance at the door of the cabin where Francis Drake lay, for they dreaded the time when he would come forth to flay them.

Yet the commander-in-chief, as his secretary already knew, was not disgusted with their performance at Nombre de Dios.

"Fighting comes natural to some men, I suppose, but most of 'em have to learn. Soldiers are taught, but nobody ever expected sailors to fight. They're just laborers. They're supposed to take the real fighters, the soldiers, from one place to another—that's all."

"Well, I'll not huck with that. Now, your bandage—"

"Let be. 'Tis good enough. I tell ye, Fitzwilliam, they will show up all right, those lads out there, once they come to know that a don's mortal."

"They behaved well enough that night. The dons, I mean."

"They did. They have courage, and equipment, and good training. But we have—God."

"Um-m-m."

"D'ye doubt it, Fitzwilliam?"

"Certainly not. But even with God's help we couldn't get that treasure back here now. It's on the way to Spain."

"There'll be another along in half a year."

"You'd come back, sir?"

"No, I wouldn't be able to raise the money. No, we're going to stay here."

"For *six months?*"

"Longer, if need be. We'll not go home until the voyage has been made."

"But—*six months!* What will we do all that time?"

"Well, to start I thought we might attack Cartagena."

It was the capital of the Spanish Main, the strongest city in the New World, and George did not take this announcement seriously, supposing as he did that it was intended only for circulation among the men for purposes of enheartenment. Yet a few days later, when Drake was able to hobble about, they made a course for Cartagena.

To storm such a place with the force they had would have been suicide, but they did pounce upon one unsuspecting vessel loaded with supplies and guarded only by a single aged watchman who told them that all the others had gone ashore to fight about a woman. The next day, despite all the fury from the shore, they cut out a larger ship even more richly stocked. They tacked all that day just out of gunshot, easily fighting off attempts of small craft to board them. They took two coasters putting in from Nombre de Dios; and one of these bore official dispatches informing the governor-general at Cartagena that the pirate El Draque was loose somewhere along the coast. Alas, the poor governor knew it well!

They withdrew, on their own terms, with several well-found vessels, a large number of prisoners, all of them willing to talk, and vast supplies of food and gunpowder. It was not a history-making exploit, but it stimulated them. They had cocked a snook at the king of Spain, they'd snapped their fingers under his very nose, and they felt good when they sailed away, singing.

"You watch them next time," said Francis Drake. "It'll be another case of the sword of the Lord and of Gideon."

"Had it occurred to you, sir," George asked slowly, "that what we have just done was an act of war?"

"I'll take the responsibility for that. If you had any qualms about the justice of our cause you shouldn't have come."

"I was given no choice."

"And I," he said bitterly, "was given no choice about taking you."

"I wonder how the lawyers would handle it," George mused.

"Certainly you have not acted as a *hostis humani generis,* nor yet with *animo furandi.*"

Himself unlearned, Drake always was rasped when anybody quoted Latin. He thought it was done to shame him.

"Spain is our natural enemy!"

"Yet England has not officially declared war on her. Or at least, not at the time we sailed."

122

For the months previous to their sailing, George, although cooped aboard the *Pascha* and not even allowed on deck except after dark, had been kept informed of political events in London. John Hawkins had seen to that. George knew about the duke of Norfolk's trial and conviction and knew too that the queen hesitated to sign the death warrant of her most exalted subject. He knew that Don Gerau de Spies had been called before the privy council, told that his treasonous connection with Mary Stuart would no longer be tolerated, and ordered to leave the kingdom forthwith. He knew that both houses of Parliament as well as the whole convocation of bishops had petitioned Elizabeth to have Mary Stuart executed. He knew that Alva's atrocities in the Low Countries had brought hatred of the don to a new pitch of intensity so that volunteers were pouring into Holland and Zealand to fight for the rebels, even without pay. He knew too that Spanish soldiery in Ireland had done anything but increase Whitehall's love for Madrid. And then, just a few days before the often postponed sailing itself, Queen Elizabeth at last made up her mind and signed her name, so that on a rainy morning on Tower Hill the duke of Norfolk's head rolled. All the same, as George had just pointed out, there had been no actual declaration of war.

"Spain is papistical!"

"So is France. So are all of the Italian states and most of the ones in Germany. We can't fight the whole world."

"Fitzwilliam, you split hairs."

"An old academic custom."

"I was wronged, I appealed to my government for redress, and redress was not forthcoming. By the law of nations, that gives me the right to collect as best I can."

"Provided your monarch has assented. Has she?"

Drake did not answer. Not even with his own confidential secretary should a man discuss such a matter. Conceivably Drake himself didn't know. Conceivably he was taking the word of John Hawkins, Sir William Wynter, and the others who had adventured in this voyage. *They* knew!

George himself believed that the queen had been aware of the purpose of this expedition and quite possibly had invested in it under another name. But he also believed that if the political situation dictated, Elizabeth would unblushingly deny everything and make scapegoats of Drake and his men.

"Home is the place for the timid," averred Francis Drake,

somewhat sententiously. "He who'd cross the sea should have a heart for anything."

Quietly: "Did I cower at Nombre de Dios?"

"Forgive me!"

The admiral did not like George any more than George liked him, but they respected one another. And Drake knew George's value.

"Only mind you this," he added. "Tickle points of law won't decide it. We'll not be adjudged pirates if this voyage is made. The only way for us to be hanged is to go back empty-handed."

They sailed along the Main for some weeks, picking up all sorts of small prizes. There was no resistance, since until this time it had never occurred to the Spaniards to arm against any outsider. The prisoners were puzzled but grateful for the good treatment. Drake never held any of them for ransom or as hostages, but put them down as soon as he conveniently could. There was nothing bloodthirsty about this corsair, who seldom even punished his own men, though he kept strict discipline. He was avaricious, but not stupidly so. He took whatever he could carry, but he did not wantonly destroy that which he could not take.

This was too good, this cruise, to last. In a few months the rains came, and a terrible time set in. Food rotted, men sickened, the beer turned sour. The dons, alive at last to their danger, stayed in harbor, save when they sailed forth in specially built galleys to raid and destroy the magazines Drake had established up and down the Darien coast.

Drake changed boats as other men might change shirts. The *Swan*, which drew too much for his purposes, was stripped and scuttled, and the *Pascha* was marked to go. He was using Spanish vessels now, small, shallow-drafted, speedy.

In addition to the magazines, Drake's men had built on the shore of Port Pheasant—their secret harbor—a blockhouse they called Fort Diego after the devoted Cimarron, who had rejoined them with a sizable following.

The Cimarrons brought word that the *flota* from Cartagena was putting in at Nombre de Dios, which meant that the treasure-laden mule trains soon would be starting across the isthmus. To strike again at Nombre de Dios would have been the height of folly. The Spanish authorities had learned their lesson, and undoubtedly that battery on the east hill had been mounted and manned. To waylay the *recuas* somewhere in the jungle in the middle of the isthmus would hardly be wise. From the nature of the terrain there, they could not hope to get many muleloads in one place, and once the alarm was out a retreat might be difficult. Besides, the authorities would be most on their guard along the jungle trails, for those were the favorite lurking places of the Cimarrons, men who cared not a whit about gold and pearls but who dearly loved to slaughter Spaniards. The boldest possible strike, and therefore the best, would be just outside of the gates of Panama itself, when the *recuas* had barely started.

Accordingly, on Shrove Tuesday, February 3 of that year 1573, the English set forth. Eighteen men out of the original seventy-three were all that were available for this back-breaking trek. The others had died of wounds or of sickness, or were left behind to protect the escape route. However, a large force of Cimarrons went with them.

Those black men had noses like panthers. Time after time when the little party was near some Spanish outpost they would literally smell out a sentry, locating him exactly. They smelled the matches of the Spanish firelocks, they explained. They could sneak up on such a man and kill him with their bare hands before he could utter a sound. They did not believe in prisoners.

For days, for weeks, Drake and his men struggled through some of the worst country in the world. They viewed the great southern ocean, the first Englishmen who ever had. They descended upon the coastal plain, the *llano*, enduring a merciless heat as they crept, sometimes for miles on their hands and knees, closer and closer to the fabled city of Panama. Then they had a stroke of bad luck. An overexcited sailor who did not wait for the signal caused their presence to be betrayed so that instead of the princely treasure that had been within their grasp they got only a few armfuls of bar silver. They retreated to the interior, to Venta Cruz at the navigable head of the Chagres, a town they stormed and took and pillaged. With negligible loot and against unspeakable hardships, they fought their way back to Port Pheasant.

This was the blackest time. The Spaniards had been alerted against them; the *recuas* would be heavily guarded. And these weary fleabitten men, most of them shoeless now, many of them sick, could not be expected even under the leadership of Francis Drake to hang onto that pestiferous coast for another half year.

It was George who proposed that they all make the same trip he and Diego had made from the mouth of the Rio Francisco, twenty-odd miles through dense jungle, to the Panama Gate of Nombre de Dios. George argued that this was the one place where an attack upon the *recuas* would not be expected. Fairly within sight of their goal,

125

the soldiers and the muleteers would relax their vigilance. Since it was open plain there for some distance from the cover of the jungle, they would believe that any small attacking force surely would already have been seen and routed by the now large garrison in Nombre de Dios.

"God knows I don't want to make that trip again," George said, "but if Diego will guide us I'll carry my share."

This time the bag was unbelievable: three *recuas*, all royal, one of fifty mules, two of seventy mules each. There was a fight of course, but it was quickly won. There was a counterattack, an energetic pursuit. They were forced to leave behind an estimated fifteen tons of silver, which they hid in land-crab holes and shallow brooks. But they won through, staggering under the weight of pearls and gold, rich men, every one.

The *Pascha* had a rotten bottom now and was too slow for them, so they gave her to some prisoners. They sailed home with an all-Spanish fleet, good boats, fast. They did it in twenty-three days from the Cape of Florida to Scilly, a record.

The voyage had been made.

22

I'll Never Go Away Again

THE HOUSE IN KINTERBURY STREET WAS SOLID, substantial. It knew none of the damp and rottenness of the tropics. Winds couldn't shake it, suns bleach its walls, nor rain rip away the tiles of its roof. Whatever might be their shortcomings, these "new men," when they built, built to last. The walking lion and three bezants—all appropriately yellow, the hue of gold, upon a black background—had been carved or sewn, painted or etched, into every place where room could be made for them. Otherwise the house was without ostentation, being a structure to live in.

This was August, the windows were open and George Fitzwilliam's feet were on one of the sills. He wriggled his toes—tipped back in his chair, grunting, as he had the day he returned from the Spanish prison.

No crowd surged outside. Much fuss had been made at their arrival the previous day, but none of it was official. They had not been summoned to London. No plans for a banquet were announced. They had not even been greeted by the lord mayor. Indeed, after the first burst of joy, embarrassment set in; and far from being hailed as heroes, they were being treated somewhat furtively. The crewmen had been loosed upon the town and were throwing their money away with shouts. But the admiral together with John Oxenham, Ellis Hixom, and sundry other officers and gentles, had been *sneaked* into this house in Kinterbury Street, where John Hawkins greeted them with a wry smile.

The others were made uneasy by this, but George Fitzwilliam was too happy to be home to care. He was thinking of Anne.

The share-out, held on the way back, had taken George's breath away. Even after the adventurers had been accounted for, the part that remained for the officers and men was stupendous. Because of his charge from Hawkins, and through Hawkins from certain other investors, the share-out had meant a great deal of work for George Fitzwilliam; but it was gratifying to see in his own figures, especially with those two extra shares, how rich he was.

Hawkins wiped sweat from his face, though it was not a hot day.

"So there it is," he said. "You'll hear the whole tale elsewhere. And it's grisly enough, I can tell you!"

Somebody asked: "And this happened a few months after we sailed?"

"Aye. Last August. A year ago. Matter of fact, it was St. Bartholomew's Day. That's when it *started* anyway. The duke of Guise's varlets pounced upon Coligny when he was crippled in bed and couldn't defend himself. They hacked him to pieces, threw him out of a window, and cut off his head. Gallant men!"

For all his insouciance, George shivered. He could not forget that Mary of Scotland was half a Guise.

"That *started* it, as I say. Paris went mad. So did all the rest of France, catching it like fever. Mobs coursed the streets of every city and town, killing all the Protestants they could lay hands on—and not only killing them but slashing them to pieces. Men, women, children, everything, even pet cats and dogs and birds. They say it took weeks to scrub off the blood. From the pavement, I mean," Hawkins added bitterly. "It'll never be scrubbed off history."

They were silent for a while, flabbergasted to come back from savage America and hear this tale. Why, even the Cimarrons would never have behaved like that! There was nothing so beastly, they supposed, as a "civilized" man when he went mad.

"They came pouring over by every sort of boat, poor stricken souls! England was inundated with 'em. And what they said about the butchery would make your veins freeze. Everywhere you went you saw Huguenots, still in a panic, starting at every small sound, with the memory of hell in their eyes, Ugh!"

He paused, as though to apologize for his eloquence. Hawkins was normally not an eloquent man. Again he wiped his face.

"But what has all this got to do with us?" asked Hixom, who was not quick-witted.

Hawkins looked long at him, unblinking, expressionless, like some huge owl.

" 'Tis an axiom," Hawkins made known, "that England must cling to France or Spain, one or the other, for we're too weak to stand alone. That's simple, isn't it?"

"Well, I suppose so."

"A little while ago it was France. Spain waxed too strong. France was nearer. She should be placated lest she back Mary Stuart. So nothing was too good for our friends across the Channel. The queen even hinted that she might take the French king's brother, that little hop-toad D'Alençon, for her mate. France could do no wrong—then."

He looked at George.

"That was the moment you elected to skewer a French spy."

"*I* didn't elect it. *He* did."

"No matter. That was why you had to depart. And from what Captain Drake tells me, it was a good thing for us that you did. But things have changed now, and nobody cares who killed a French agent. You need have no further worry on that score, lad. I took care of it last month. The warrant hath been quashed."

He belched thoughtfully.

"Aye, now 'tis the other way 'round," he went on. "The D'Alençon match is off, France is out of favor, we're sending men and ships and arms to help the Huguenots. Even the exigencies of politics couldn't make us stomach such a shambles as that. And Alva in the Low Countries and Philip in Spain are taking advantage of this change of course. Naturally. We don't truly fawn on them, but we do favor 'em. Now it's *Spain* that can do no wrong. And what d'ye think Spain will say about your exploits?"

This time there was a considerable silence, for even Ellis Hixom saw the point. They shifted uncomfortably—all but George, who smiled out of the window, still thinking about Anne Crofts.

"If we asked the law—"

Hawkins shook a heavy head.

"There's no legal or non-legal here. The queen's majesty must do what she can for the defense of her realm, and if that means hanging a man she knows to be innocent— or even a dozen such men—why, then she must do so."

"You really think they might make us pirates?" asked Hixom.

" 'Tis possible, yes. The least they would do to placate the Escorial, to soothe the ruffled feathers of our dear cousin Philip, the very *least* would be to strip away all the treasure you've won— and hand it back to Spain."

He rose, sighing. He had hated to tell them that. For all the beauty of the day, and the glorious success of the expedition, it was a topsy-turvy world they faced. It was a world in which any man might have a hard time making an honest living.

"The lord mayor won't send word of your return until tomorrow. He's promised me that. And the messenger will lag. But—there could be other messengers, faster ones. I think that within a few days somebody will be riding here from London, and your presence will be demanded in an order we can't ignore. I'd suggest a disappearance. Things were turned upside down while you struggled on the far side of the sea. In another year or so, if you can stay hidden that long, they may be reversed all over again. And then you could come back."

Francis Drake nodded soberly. He had worked and mucked, saved and slaved, and fought with fury for more than a year and a half, taking a tremendous gamble. And now that he'd won, he had lost. Because of something agreed upon over a conference table he was to be treated henceforth as a criminal. If he wished to keep his loot, he must fly. He must hide.

"The Lord's will be done," he muttered. "I'm to Ireland. It's a place for kites, not hawks. But nobody asks questions there."

"A good plan, Frank. And—you others?"

"The Low Countries for me," Hixom said promptly. "No matter what they might say at Whitehall there's always room for a man who is willing to fight. And somehow I've got to be like those blacks we marched with: I've got to enjoy killing Spaniards."

"For me, America again," John Oxenham said. "It'll be hard to raise the money, since now it turns out that we are all thieves. But I'll do it somehow."

"They'll hang you if they nab you," Drake warned.

"I'd rather be hanged by a foreigner than by my own countrymen."

George rose, smoothing back his doublet. Plymouth was no

Madrid, but in the circumstances he had done well for himself with his new riches. He wore lugged boots, purple silk hose, an oyster-colored taffeta doublet trimmed with galloon and crystal buttons, a high-cocked black velvet bonnet with an ostrich plume. The bonnet was French, which assumedly would be out of fashion now, but he fancied it all the same. He drew a velvet rose-colored mandilion across his shoulders, and lifted a gold-filigreed pomander to his nose.

"And you, Fitzwilliam? Holland?"

"America again?"

"Ireland with me?"

George shook his head.

"I'm making for Northampton," he said.

Two days later, after riding hard, and no longer affecting foppish airs, George clasped Anne Crofts in his arms.

"My chuck, it's been so long!"

"George!"

"I'll never go away again," he said.

And over his shoulder a moment later, he grinned at Sir John Crofts who, weeping, watched them.

"These clothes I bought myself, sir," George said.

They were married that afternoon in the Church of St. Basil of Stornaway, Rugby Town. Anne was ravishing in a gown of white-and-marigold sarsenet all trimmed with long black bugles and topped by a wide supportassed ruff; and she carried a lace fan too, a city touch. All that she had produced seemingly from nowhere, yet it fitted her.

"I knew you would come back," she said simply. "You promised me."

It was not so much the gown itself as the fact of her frankness about it that startled George Fitzwilliam.

"Oh, I'm shameless," she said, then hung her head, blushing.

The very next day George rode over to Weddell Lodge to see about buying some land.

23

You Never Know Your Wife

HE HAD BELIEVED THAT HE KNEW ANNE as well as anybody on this earth. As children, wading in brooks, climbing trees, popping the popinjay, playing wild-mare or last-in-Hell or hoodman-blind, at Milton as well as here at Okeland, they had made no try to conceal or discolor their fondness for one another. They were remote cousins, and as such were permitted an intimacy that abroad or even in urban England would have been deemed iniquitous. For some years now they had been aware of one another's physical attractions. Their kisses were fiery, their trembling not that of embarrassment, and if it had not been for George's long absence in the Americas and in Spain doubtless they would have been in bed together before this, since George had been eager to marry her not only because he longed for an ordered and more quiet life but also because he wanted her body. Yet, knowing her so well, he had not supposed that marriage itself would bring many surprises. It did.

Anne Crofts had been one person. The wife of George Fitzwilliam was another.

Disconcerted, he yet was not dismayed; the changes weren't basic. If undeniably there was a certain officiousness about Anne's mannner in the house and garden, after dark she had slipped none of her ardor. Aunt Helen and Aunt Sylvia—long before made patient by circumstances—and a somewhat bewildered Sir John, were the principal sufferers from the new forwardness. George himself would be absent from the house most of the daylight hours, traveling to Rugby or to Northampton in search of fodder or supplies, or to Weddell Lodge in search of fellowship, or else riding around the land he had bought, supervising its drainage and its enclosure.

Anne's chief demands were windows and finery. Neither, he supposed, should have startled him. Everybody wanted windows today; and if she was a shade peremptory in the way she ordered them put in, and if she hired workers without first consulting etiher her father or her husband, who would have to pay them, it was a fault easily forgiven.

The clothes she had always craved. Nothing could be more natural. She had been cooped up here for many years, far from a city, many miles from the court. A few times when the queen was on a progress in the summer, the great and glittering procession had passed through part of Northamptonshire, but Anne herself had never been presented and, worse, had never been vouchsafed a chance to note the clothes and bijouterie of those who were. Sir John was no cheeseparer, but neither was he wealthy. What peacock plumes Anne could get before her marriage she'd made fullest use of. More than once George recalled to mind the time he'd dined here on his first visit to Sheffield and the ravishing blue and yellow costume she wore, snatching the breath out of him. On that occasion he had brought her from London a bright red silk stomacher, in which she gloried.

The Plymouth shops were by no means so well stocked as those of London, and what they had in the way of expensive clothing for women was largely Spanish— being in fact the loot of pirates, whether French, Dutch, or local— and therefore dull. *Male* Spanish attire tended to brightness, and George had done himself reasonably well along those lines before his departure for Okeland. George had at the same time bought so many ruffs and rabatines, kirtles and half-kirtles, bolts of velvet and lengths of reticella lace, that he found it necessary to buy an ass upon which to load them. Though some of these articles were for Sir John and the two maiden aunts, most, understandably, he gave to Anne. He was astonished not by her delight, which he'd expected, but by the gravity and continuing joy with which she treated them. It sometimes seemed as though these objects had become not a mere addition to her wardrobe but veritably a career in themselves. Though hers was a busy life as mistress of Okeland, still she found many hours to spend making gowns and petticoats and capes—or directing her aunts and tiring-women as *they* made them—and trimming them, altering them, most of all putting them on and taking them off. She was not flippant about this, nor even girlish. She showed none of the affectations of a flirt. She didn't pirouette; she did not make mock curtsies, or simper, or smirk; and though sometimes she would solemnly climb and then descend the staircase, studying the hang of the material on either side as she did so, or sweep back and forth across the garden, she could never be said to *strut*.

When by chance a stuffs pedlar did find his way to Okeland—there were those who, greatly daring, specialized in off-highway routes—Anne would hold him up half the day, haggling. And she'd buy without any preliminary conference with her husband, only demanding of him the price when that had been agreed upon.

"Thou must think I'm made of money," he'd grumble, but he always paid.

In truth, from the beginning he began to worry about gold, though he made no mention of this. Terence Weddell had been more than fair when he sold the land, which surely was worth what George paid for it, but George, who had spent much on clothes in Plymouth, now that he was out in the country, striving to improve the manor house and farm

132

alike, was appalled at the prices of things. Sugar twenty shillings a pound! Salt three bushels for sixpence! Beer eighteen shillings a hogshead! Laborers one and three a day! He had been told that this was yet another reason why Spain must be restrained in the New World. The sea of gold and silver that at little cost to herself she pumped out of America and into Europe to support her wars was like the pit Abaddon guards, having no bottom. No other nation possessed anything like such a treasury. So, prices went up. And up.

George assumed that this was true, and that it made sense. He had always previously been a part of some large household, where a duly appointed official handled the purse, and as long as you didn't steal you had no reason to trouble yourself about money. It was different at Okeland.

Anne suddenly had become concerned about her complexion, an excellent one, and the preparations she bought —ceruse, madder, ocher, rose water, cherry water, brazil, cochineal—were costly. George had never seen so many bottles, jugs, jars. Anne did not dye her hair—George would not have permitted it—but she spent hours goffering and brushing it.

Inevitably the question came:

"Why can't we go to London for a visit?"

"What for?"

"To see the city. I haven't been there since I was a chick."

"Thou'lt always be a chick to me."

"Go to! What's London like now?"

"Just the same. Dirtier, that's all. Noisier."

"And John Hawkins hath a house there too? We could put up in it. Thou'rt still his man, I suppose?"

"Well . . ."

The truth is, George didn't know. Nobody knew. Progress was a desirable thing, no doubt, but there were times when a man could not help sighing for the days he had never known, the feudal days when everybody was sure of his own place no matter how lowly, no matter how high. Was George still the servant of John Hawkins? There had been no contract, not even a verbal agreement. Certainly George, though not of nature sympathetic with this merchant, must forever feel *morally* obligated to him. More, there were moments as George counted his money and cast up his accounts, shaking his head, when he wondered whether he had done the right thing, from a worldly point of view, by moving to the country. Being away from a base gave one a wobbly feeling, even a brush of nausea.

133

"We could go to court," Anne pursued.

"The court moves around—Nonesuch, Hampton, Windsor, Whitehall, Greenwich."

"We could go after it. Thy friend Lord Burghley could present me to the queen."

It was not like Anne to natter like this. She never reveled in clack. Her persistence this night was unsettling.

"My friend Lord Burghley," George ventured, "is a very busy man."

He swiveled his eyes toward her, where she lay. The arrow-slit had been widened and paned by her orders and another window had been built into the east wall, so that their chamber was well sprinkled with starshine. Anne looked lovely. On her back, she had her hands clasped behind her head and was gazing in thought at a ceiling she could scarcely see.

For no reason, and naughtily, George tried to imagine what Aunt Sylvia would look like in that position. It was not kind. He'd encountered Aunt Sylvia in the garden only that afternoon and had paused politely to chat and admire her needlework. He scarcely knew the small dry quick-cackling woman, there being times when he could not with confidence distinguish her from her quick-cackling dry small sister, Helen.

"Tell me, why hast thou never married?" he had asked Sylvia Crofts.

She might have been expected to slap his face, or to snub him, or burst into tears. She did none of these things, only went on stitching, her bone-white fingers agile.

"Because my father could not raise a dowry," she had replied. "And of course I wouldn't mate below my station."

"Of course. I'll warrant thou hadst many an offer?"

"I had—some."

"And thou really wanted to?"

She had looked up suddenly, smiling at him. (She must have been beautiful as a girl, he thought.)

"Doesn't every woman?"

"I suppose so."

"At first you're afraid. Then you get frantic. And after a while you become afraid again. But by that time it's too late anyway."

She returned to her work, and George, bumbling an apology, had gone away.

Helen and Sylvia ... There but for the grace of God went Anne as well.

"Besides," he said to his wife, "why shouldst thou wish to meet the queen?"

"In order to look at her, of course."

"A cat can do that."

"It would mean more to me than to a cat."

"She, uh, she's not as fair as they say. That's a sort of figure of speech, about her beauty."

"I wasn't thinking about her face. I was thinking of what she'd have on."

"And besides, a presentation would cost a great deal of money."

"Well, we're rich, aren't we?"

He winced.

Anne was no babbler; she could be called laconic. At dinner, even when there were visitors, she listened well but seldom said a word beyond what etiquette called for. When George, having ridden in from the fields, would pause before dismounting to watch her fondly through one of the new windows as she plied embroidery or dipped candles or combed flax or bundled herbs with her aunts, he was put in mind of a couple of starlings, twittering with excitement, on either side of a staid, pensive swallow.

The only time Anne talked much was at night, like this.

"And money's not all," he went on cautiously.

"Thou fearest the city? But why? The indictment was killed, about that Italian."

"It was. But there are still dons in London, though the ambassador's not there. And they don't like what happened at Nombre de Dios. They say no alliance till they've been recompensed. And this at a time when the queen's majesty ogles Philip."

"Thou wert never a signer of that adventure!"

"On paper, no. In fact, yes. They know that. They know that I was awarded a lay and two extra shares beside. And if they see me they'll cause me to be nabbed, and the crown lawyers will make me disgorge every liard of it. Nay, chuck, 'tis better that I remain quiet for a while, till the wind veers to another direction."

"But—thou'rt no pirate!"

"That depends upon who points at me."

"And if thy business commands thee to—"

"Not business. Politics."

"Then I think that thy politics are stupid!"

"Don't call them *my* politics," he grumbled, and rolled over and pretended to go to sleep.

135

But she was whispering into the space between his shoulder blades. She was promising to talk no more—tonight.

Oh, she'd not nag! But from time to time, very casually, she would toss out some mention of "When I bow to the queen—" or "When we go to London—" She never puffed this. She simply sought to let George know that she had not forgotten.

24

Don't Go Near the Water

W HAT REALLY ASTOUNDED GEORGE was to learn that Anne was jealous.

He knew little enough about love in its romantic aspects. Most of his adult life in England, brief enough, had been spent amid a mercantile atmosphere, where the figures written in ink were more important than those wrapped in a busk and silk and sarsenet. He had been much abroad; but his page days in the household of his aunt had been given over largely to lessons in fencing, dancing, languages, and the anfractuosities of court etiquette, while his more recent memories were bleak: the France of song he had never known, and Spain to him was no land of moonlight, balconies, a tossed rose, but rather cockroaches and wine that had gone sour.

In consequence he could have been matter-of-fact, lacking in the decorative details of courtship. He seldom penned a sonnet. He could strum a lute well enough, and dearly loved to join in any glee; but most of the ballads he knew were of a bawdy sort, to be sung around a campfire—provided that the vinegarish Captain Drake was not within earshot. Chrétien de Troyes was no more than a name to him, and he had always thought that the rhymed activities of Lancelot and Guinevere, Tristram and Iseult, Aucassin and Nicolette, were just plain silly. From what little he did know of conventional, traditional, poetical amorousness, Eleanor of Aquitaine's code and so forth, he saw that jealousy loomed in it as a large fact; yet to George jealousy could only be an emotion degrading to the one who felt it and an insult to the person who was its butt.

In ordinary circumstances it would have infuriated him to learn that his wife was jealous. But he knew that this was not a usual, earthy case. Anne did not hold in doubt her spouse's fidelity. Granted, there was another woman in

136

her mind, one she feared, dreaded, and was fascinated by; but it was one who was unattainable, and who could not seduce, in a carnal sense, George Fitzwilliam or any man: Mary Stuart, queen of Scotland and the Isles.

Anne blanched and gasped, putting her hand over her heart, whenever she thought of the prisoner of Sheffield.

A woman could lie beside a man each night, a woman could have him in a cell, yet lose him. Anne knew this. Her instinct had told her. Familiarity breeds contempt, and the untasted will ever tease. A man might be of this world, eminently sensible, hardheaded forsooth, independent—yet a dream could lead him around by the nose. For dreams are exceedingly strong, at the same time being as hard to struggle against as smoke from a fire. There it was! Her helplessness! She could have done battle with a dame on the next estate. Against a princess locked in a tower far away she was lost.

George did not deride this reasoning. Rather, he sympathized. Though it was unfair to the Stuart, he refrained from any use of her name except sometimes in a slip of the tongue, treating Mary, by implication, as though she had been his partner in some vile affair of the past.

It made him feel mean, small.

In only one matter connected with the imprisoned queen did he refuse to give way. This was the tear-shaped ruby he carried in his left ear. He had few enough gauds, and what he had he wore only on special occasions; but the ruby was in his ear morning, noon, and night, as though he feared to take it out, as though he thought its removal even for an instant might destroy some spell. Anne did not fail to notice this, though she made no comment.

Knightly vows, as everyone knew, were holdovers, ludicrous relics, storybook nonsense. And yet, though he would never have admitted it, George had sworn to himself when he fastened the gem into place that it would remain there as long as he lived. He didn't know why. Certainly Mary Stuart had not asked or even suggested it. "Wear it sometimes and think of this poor caged bird," was all she had said.

More than once he wondered what he would say if Anne asked him to take the earring off. She never did.

Autumn over, winter in, he was at home more of the time, as they all were. Once the weather had become harsh the duties to be done were largely of a womanish nature, and Anne and the maidens were quite capable of taking care of them. Nevertheless George and Sir John did their part, if somewhat clumsily. The work was not simply su-

137

pervisory, for the servants at Okeland expected their betters to toil beside them. George never before had been a member of so poor a household, and he was amused to find himself carving beechen spoons and platters, fitting and riveting the bottoms of horn mugs and plugging the leaks in jacks, plaiting osiers and reeds into baskets and weirs, sharpening scythes, shaping new ash or willow teeth for the harrows and hardening these in the fire, fashioning ox-bows, yokes, forks, racks, rack-staves. . . .

There were mornings, not many, when George waved aside these trivia and called for his horse, frankly announcing that he would ride over to Weddell Lodge for a chat with Terence.

Though he did not look upon this as a scandalization, Sir John disapproved of the visits. This was not because of their effect upon the neighbors but because of their possible effect upon his son-in-law's soul.

"The man's a papist, I tell thee!"

"He could be."

"Oh, he communicates now and then. Maybe once every third or fourth week. But he only does that to save himself the fine."

"Who can blame him? Ten golden guineas each month would be a strain on anybody's purse. And they say it will be raised."

"But I tell thee he's a papist at heart!"

George would shrug, for he could see no profit at any time in arguing about religion.

"I'm not calling on his heart," he would reply.

Surely Anne guessed who it was her husband and their neighbor would talk about. But she made no comment.

Anne might have been relieved but more likely would have been puzzled and further worried had she listened, hidden, to one of those conversations. After the first few, the name of Mary Stuart seldom was spoken. As in the larger world of which it could have been called a microcosm, at Weddell Lodge the Scottish queen was in many minds but few mouths.

In part this reticence, at least at Weddell, might have been brought about by fear of the captive's welfare, her very life forsooth, since her position was parlous. In Scotland the son she had scarcely seen, her only child still little more than a baby, had been proclaimed king, but he was a pawn in the hands of her enemies. The last stronghold to fly her flag, Edinburgh Castle, had recently fallen, thanks to English help; and what friends she had were scattered and presently impotent, without organization. France, out of favor with the English queen and torn by civil war, no longer could even bluster about the treatment of Mary Stuart. Her latest suitor, Norfolk, had been beheaded for his activities in her behalf. The Spain to which she had transferred her hopes muttered sympathetically but was too eager to placate Elizabeth and get a hands-off promise in the Netherlands to raise its voice for the imprisoned princess.

In the Scroll Tower at Sheffield, frowned upon by the hills of Hallamshire, feeding and in caressive tones talking to her pets, Mary Stuart might well fear that the world had forgotten her.

Or—the silence at the lodge could have meant conspiracy. This thought troubled George through the winter and spring, and as a drowsy summer set in. Was Terence Weddell involved in one of the plots to free Mary of Scotland? With his otherwise morbid craving for obscurity he was, beyond a tittle of doubt, a link in the secret Catholic chain that crisscrossed England. George would have deduced this even without his experience among those harried people. Was he more? Was he one of those fervent young men who had dedicated their lives and fortunes to the cause of a liberated Mary Stuart? George hoped not. For all the allure of this woman, George could see that her forced release could only mean catastrophe to England. Sheffield was a strong place, and George was sure that Lord Shrewsbury had orders to cut his prisoner's throat at the first threat of attack; but even assuming that some one of these groups of harebrained youngsters did succeed in bringing off such a feat, where would Mary be taken or sent? Certainly not back over the border. Unless she came accompanied by an English army the Scots would have her throat squeezed within half a day; the enemies she had made there simply couldn't afford to let her live, for Mary, though a kind friend, was relentless as a foe, and she had a long memory. France might take her, but only to immure her in some nunnery, loading her with empty honors and leaving her to rot without any touch of that which she still somehow clung to at Sheffield—hope. Spain was far away, and the Narrow Seas between were at all times crowded with rapacious Huguenots made mad by the remembrance of St. Bartholomew's Day, fanatical Puritans from the south of England, and the even more fanatical Dutch rebels, the Beggars of the Sea, to whom the only good Catholic was a dead Catholic.

No, any plot to rescue the beauty in the Scroll Tower

could only have for its aim the seating of her upon a throne that from the papal point of view she had always been entitled to: the throne of England. That involved, necessarily, the killing of Elizabeth. It involved the invasion of the realm by some foreign force. It meant civil war—possibly, even probably, a whole series of civil wars, a semi-permanent state of strife such as had torn England from end to end in the bitter days when the Yorkists and Lancastrians grappled.

This troubled George's mind, but he made no mention of it. Neither he nor Terence Weddell ever referred to religion. When they met again, George had thanked him briefly though feelingly for the escape arrangements of two years before; that was all. Whatever his inner fervor, Terence must have seen that George Fitzwilliam was not a man whose beliefs could be swayed. There was an understanding between these two, the stronger since it had never been voiced. Several times when George came riding for a visit Terence Weddell in greeting him had hinted that the hour was not propitious; and George, sensing the presence of somebody underneath the staircase—all but *smelling* a priest—would excuse himself.

They needed one another, these two, yet they fumbled for a topic of talk. Religion was taboo. Terence had no interest in the land; and George's early eager prate of turfing, marling, denshiring, left him cold. Nor was he concerned with the problem of how to get workers from the village to tend the enclosures near the manor house, for indeed he seemed rather wishful of keeping such men away.

At last, there in the very middle of England, so far from any port, they settled upon navigation.

Had Anne overheard some of the talk at Weddell Lodge on a given afternoon, it most likely would have been about how to say a compass, how to feed the needle with a lodestone, why kennings and a rutter were treacherous in shoal water—and of course useless off soundings—and whether a Jacob's staff could be relied upon for getting the Mercator height.

Weddell loved geography but despised mariners, and except for a few Channel crossings he had never been to sea. Yet he was interested in George's New World travel and asked him questions about the action of the winds and sea currents, the nature of the strands along the Main and among the Indies, even the routine of a vessel under sail.

Once George chuckled. Of a sunny summer afternoon, following a chat, he was lolling toward the door.

140

"Two salts, eh? We arrange it all—a hundred miles from blue water!"

Terence—short, slight, jointy, with a birdlike jerkiness about him as he walked—waved his arms.

"Why not? *Somebody* has to study the sea. The mariners never will. They're too lazy, or too stupid, or maybe they're so busy picking weevils out of their biscuits or lice out of their hair that they can't find time to look around them. For hundreds of years they've been cruising in search of fish, and they never even noticed that there was another world just beyond the horizon. Or if they did notice it they forgot to mention it when they came home. Seamen are the most unimaginative men in all this world. They think of nobody else. They put down no observations. They keep no records."

"Most of 'em can't write."

"Most of 'em can't think, either. And yet they are in charge of protecting this isle. They are given a free hand, willy-nilly, in the task of doubling the size of the earth. Sailors! Sailors! I tell thee, Fitzwilliam, we simply can't leave the sea to such as them!"

George had paused in the doorway, and he watched a man who had just ridden up the avenue of lime trees and who was dismounting.

"You had best not say that to your visitor."

"Eh? Um-m. Who is he, d'ye suppose?"

"His name," George answered, "is Francis Drake."

25

Sailor on Horseback

WEDDELL LODGE WAS THE ONLY HOUSE George knew in which the entertaining was done in the library. Terence Weddell must have been near thirty, yet he was a bachelor, and a bachelor, moreover, of exceedingly studious tastes: a library was his natural habitat. The lodge boasted no gallery; it did have a solar, of course a screens, and a dining hall—it could hardly be called a great-hall—but the library was its hub.

Windows were fashionable; they permitted those inside to look out. But windows also permitted those outside to look in. Weddell Lodge was new, its mortar scarcely dry, and while it could have been that the windows of its library had been built high only to prevent a student's attention from wandering, as Terence averred, it could also have been to provide protection against the peering of some casual passer or some new arrival. George as a guest had been but clandestine, but it was safe to assume that his predecessors had been and his successors would be both clandestine *and* ecclesiastical.

In any event, Drake, when he was ushered into that library after George had introduced him to Terence Weddell, clearly was relieved to see the high windows.

This was not the tyrant George had known. The mouth that had been a steel trap twitched, and the eyes, once damn-you, warily moved back and forth. For all his psalm-singing background, Francis Drake, as George well knew, was inordinately fond of finery. He would not prink before his betters, nor yet before the members of his crew, but among friends or alone in his cabin he was as polychromatic as a pigeon's neck. He loved to wear a chain around his neck, a silver cabasset, a scabbard that was studded with rhinestones. Today it was not so. His doublet was the color of rust, his canions were black, his basehose unlocked, his bonnet a steeple, and the spurs he wore on one-hued boots were iron. His very beard, longer than usual, did not flare with the old strident red, stabbing like an accusatory finger, but shrank against his chest. Here was a man who strove to seem commonplace. Now and then he would look over his shoulder; he had been more at home in the steamy jungles of Panama than he was here in the middle of his own native land.

Noting this uneasiness, Terence refrained from a frank study and talked trippingly of minor things. It was Drake himself who broke this.

"Master Weddell, it was not to discuss the weather that I came."

"Oh?"

"Fitzwilliam here will tell you that skimble-skamble's not my fare. Said I well?"

"I fear that you have me in the lurch, captain."

"Master Weddell, it is my plan to venture into far seas, again, in search of—well, trade."

"So soon?" cried George.

"Oh, I'm still in disfavor, granted. That's why I travel with no staff, no retinue. That's why I ask you now, my gentles, if you will refrain from any reference to Francis Drake when you speak with neighbors—"

He looked from one to the other, and when each had silently assented, being in no way astonished by this request, he went on.

142

"The situation will change. And meanwhile, preparation's the watchword, eh? Why shouldn't an enterprise be making up? We may wait a month, we may wait a year or more, but whenever word does come we'll be off like an arrow from the bow."

"To where?" George asked.

Drake seemed not to have heard that question. He addressed himself to Terence.

"The money's pledged. And the vessels. All that remains is to get the right man. Master Weddell, you have translated Pigafetta's *First Circumnavigation of the Globe?*"

"Oh, yes. There's a copy right behind your head, captain, if you care to check something."

"And you are the author of *Paths Across the Ocean Sea?*"

"A small thing. Its success amazed us all. I mean to rewrite it some day, smooth it out."

"You studied at Mortlake under Dr. Dee, and you helped Humphrey Gilbert write his *Discourse to Prove a Passage by the Northwest to Cataia?*"

"Only as an adviser. Technical clarification. Sir Humphrey needs no one to teach him how to write."

"Master Weddell, will you sail with me on my new enterprise?"

"No."

"Eh?"

"Forgive the abruptness, captain, but may I remind you that you haven't even told us where you're going."

"No matter now. Probably Alexandria."

"You could cape-hop that. Anyway there must be almost as many pilots in the Mediterranean as there are ships."

" 'Tis possible we might go—elsewhere."

"Calais would be too far for me. Four times have I crossed the Channel, and I was sick as a dog each time."

"Let be! Three-quarters of my men are sick the first week out! You'd not be called upon to work the ship, only to be as you were with Humphrey Gilbert—an adviser."

The host shook his head as he simulated regret.

"Captain, I fear that all my voyaging will be as it's been in the past, right here in this room, among these books."

"You'd have a share, just like one of the adventurers! Man, you'd make your fortune!"

"It could be that I don't care to make a fortune."

Drake had risen. The pose of humbleness was gone; the old arrogance flowed back. He was being refused.

"This is flying against God's very will!"

"Captain, you must permit me to judge of that myself."

The departure was strained. On his entrance Captain Drake had announced that he was in the shire as much to call upon George Fitzwilliam as to call upon Terence Weddell, so that it had been a case of well-met; and he declined a mug of wine in order to ride off with George, who had been about to go anyway. Terence, contrite, strove to help him mount, but Drake shook him off angrily, abruptly, like a dog shaking off water.

Drake would have done well to accept that assistance; he needed it. George, who had watched the man dismount and thought he never saw a clumsier performance, did not dare to watch the mounting. Neither, as they rode toward Okeland through the dusk, did George dare to look sideways at his companion, who dug knees into an unoffending beast and gripped the reins like a drowning man. This no doubt was the farthest Francis Drake ever had been from the sea; and to give him credit, he made no pretense of equestrian skill. Nevertheless, George was glad that they didn't pass anybody he knew.

Drake fairly quivered.

"The man's a fool! I tell you he's a fool!"

" 'Tis a privilege some claim."

A thought struck Francis Drake, and he reined.

"Maybe he didn't hear my name aright? Maybe he doesn't know who I am?"

"He knows who you are," George said.

They resumed their way, Drake seething.

Nobody who was acquainted with him could have felt amazement to learn that Francis Drake was plotting another foray. If his nation wouldn't go to war with Spain he would do so alone. Already, as a result of those *recuas* outside of Nombre de Dios, he was richer than any of his relatives or friends ever had dreamt of being—the extent of the captain's own dream was beyond estimate—yet that he might retire, settle down, cease to rove, was unthinkable. Nor would a place like Ireland, with its petty picking, hold him long. Ireland was for the buzzards; an eagle would try America.

That he risked seizure of all his loot by being in England while he was still under a cloud would not have fazed this peppery small man, who, for all his fulminations against dice and cards, was a gambler to the core. He knew that the queen's favor could not be counted upon to shine long in any one direction, the exigencies of politics and her own temperament being what they were, and like a good mariner he wished his vessel to be caulked and stocked, and all atauto, so that when tide and wind permitted he could pop out of port and scuttle over the horizon beyond the reach of law, giving Queen Elizabeth no chance to change her mind.

"I said that I came to see you as well, Fitzwilliam. I am sure that you'll not be the dunce your friend is."

George said nothing. He was praying that Francis Drake wouldn't fall off his horse.

"I'll have eight vessels, mayhap nine. Will you command one?"

"As a—*captain?*"

Easygoing, amiable George was stung this time. He wouldn't make a move to draw, for his companion merited no such move; but rage was like a gag in his throat.

"Why not? You'd have a sailing master assigned to you, of course. And gentlemen have captained vessels ere this."

"Will you name one?"

They had reached Okeland, and Drake worked his feet out of the stirrups, dropped the reins, grasped the pommel, and otherwise prepared to dismount.

"We will speak of this later," he said.

"We will not," said George Fitzwilliam.

They had a small supper served in the solar, for supper at Okeland customarily was not formal. The staff ate in the kitchen and was called in only for evening prayers. Anne shone in silver and blue, but the visitor paid her scant attention, concentrating on her father, whose opinion of church law he found well-bottomed.

Miffed by the talk in the lane, Francis Drake ignored his one-time secretary. Toward the close of the meal, however, he swung excitedly upon George.

"See here, Fitzwilliam, your father-in-law hath just told me that Terence Weddell is under suspicion of being a Roman Catholic."

"I have heard so," George murmured.

"You should have told me!"

"Why?"

"I'm lucky that he turned down my offer!"

Knowing the importance that this man put upon reading, erudition, George was mildly astonished.

"You think that his devotion to the Virgin Mary would cause his hand to wobble when he drew a rhumb line?"

"I think that I want no taint of antichrist upon our voyage!"

"To—Alexandria?"

"To anywhere! Nor do we need such fancy fripperies of learning. The Lord will guide us."

"A good astrolabe too," George muttered as he made breadcrumbs, "wouldn't do any harm."

Whether she had trained herself to it during the long wait for a wedding or whether it was instinctual, Anne could do what so few wives can: she could refrain from asking questions. Her curiosity piqued, she would be watchful but silent. She'd get what she sought, if she got it at all, obliquely, fortuitously, in haphazard snatches. All things, she believed, or at any rate almost all things, come to her who waits long enough—and keeps her ears open. What George wanted to tell her he would tell, and when he didn't want to tell her she would learn gradually, by indirection.

You don't spur a willing horse; you don't goad a willing ass. Even in a matter so close to her heart as that of Mary Stuart she could make mumness her rule. Questions hurled at her husband might have barbs in them of which she herself knew nothing; they might set up wounds that festered, causing him to snarl and snap.

The case of the rejected admiral was different. Anne had heard of Francis Drake—who hadn't, since Nombre de Dios?—but his presence did not impress her, he being anything but her mind's picture of a hero, a patriot. His somewhat elephantine attempts at gallantry when first he met her disgusted even so secluded a woman as Anne, who, if she hadn't been to court, at least possessed the innate ease of her class. But soon, as abruptly as the turning-off of a beer tap, he had swung from her to her father in whom he saw a kindred spirit, and throughout the supper these two chattered, magpie-like, of candles and liturgy, baptism by immersion, the sinfulness of certain vestments, and the heinous custom of crawling to the altar on Easter eve to kiss the paschal lamb. The discourtesy—she saw of the guest during the meal only the back of his head and the back of his left shoulder—did not unsettle her; indeed, it was something of a relief. But Anne was quick to notice too the coolness between Francis Drake and her husband, and when they got to bed that night she asked him about this, though not immediately.

"Why did ever he seek to enlist Master Weddell, such a quiet gentle, so far from seeming a corsair?"

"He loves learning because he lacks it. Like every man who's never had Latin he sees something magical in it. He thinks that a given word only becomes potent when it is

146

in print. Actually Terence might have helped him a little, if he plans to sail to far parts."

"Does he?"

"His secrecy would suggest it. Alexandria's ridiculous. He only said that because it was the first name that swam into his head."

"And—thee?"

"He offered me the captaincy of one of his vessels. Me—a captain!"

"I'm sure thou'dst make a very good captain, sweeting."

"I might make a good scullery boy too, once I got used to it."

After a while, as though in exploration:

"Thou hast no love for Francis Drake?"

"I hate him. And he hates me."

"Why?"

"I don't know. Some men are born that way, to be enemies—like the lion and the unicorn. Captain Drake and I shared a small space for long hot months. We fought side by side and suffered together. I've saved his life, as he has mine; and I'd do it over again, and I think so would he. Yet I hate him. I could put it rationally. I could cry down city chuffs who view the world in terms of shillings and pence—and also stolen golden ducats. I could wince when I see such an one representing this country in other lands. I could say that no man who quotes the Bible as if he had written it himself, who can't read without moving his lips, and not much even that way, and who sits so badly in saddle—no man like that's the man for me. But there is more to it, chuck."

"I'm sure there is. Drake's a good mariner?"

"I've never seen a better, and I doubt that I ever will. Oh, his is a dirty business, but he does it damn' well. He can look at what to thee or me would be nothing more than sky and water, and within seconds he can tell where the ship is, which way it's going and how fast, what the day will be like, and how much longer the voyage will last—and tell it more accurately than Terence Weddell with all his books. He knows the sea as a baby knows its mother. He might have been born there."

They were lying naked, for the night was hot, and as he said "born" he placed a hand, very gently, on Anne's belly, which was big.

"And thou'dst have him go back to sea?"

"No—no. It pains me to cede this, chuck, but sometimes it seems that perhaps over the long course, Francis

147

Drake, for all his vulgarity, may prove to be a good thing for England."

"But you wouldn't go with him, even if he offered you a secretaryship? You prefer manure to roving?"

He had not taken away his hand. He paused, not from dearth of words for reply but in search of the best arrangement.

"I know my place," he said at last, slowly, thoughtfully, without anger, if without any exhilaration either. "And my place is here."

26

Go Away, Galahad

WAS FARMING, then, preferable to roving? George thought so. Certainly it was less monotonous. Even the months spent in Spanish cells counting cockroaches to keep madness off, in retrospect were not as dreary as the months at sea—the endless march of waves, the blazing sun, tar bubbling in the seams of the deck, timbers creaking as they had creaked last week and the week before and the week before that, the taste of salted food, and always inescapably everywhere the stink of bilge. Okeland by contrast offered something different every hour—from dawn, when the world lay sodden with dew, to sundown, when the birds fussed themselves to rest while creeping shadows sponged the slopes. The light changed, the color changed, and the odors. Moreover, and most important, things *grew*. George watched them, bemused. For he moved about his property, as about that of Sir John Crofts, directing the work on the spot, not from the manor house, believing that the best manure is the foot of the master.

Sir John, especially after the birth of Janet, the delight of his life, was glad to leave most of the supervision to his son-in-law, though he was full of advice. Their talk at meals, Anne complained, was crops and costs, costs and crops.

Costs indeed made up a grim topic. Northamptonshire was mostly champian, and Sir John's field had been devoted in large part to grain, very little to pasturage. After his first summer, that of 1574, George estimated that they had averaged less than eighteen bushels of wheat per acre, twenty-six of barley, thirty-three of oats and beans. With such fertile earth, with such good rainfall, this was poor. He had heard that in the Low Countries, where the

148

farmers used not only animal but human dung, putting even nail parings and hair clippings into the earth, the yield was much better.

The price of wool, like the price of beef, was going up. Most of the land George had bought from Terence Weddell he put into pasturage. He bought some swine and even some bees, for he was mindful of the old ryhme:

> *"He that hath both sheep, swine and hive,*
> *Sleep he, wake he, he may thrive."*

Yet he didn't thrive. It would take time, he got to know. One year, two years, wouldn't be enough. Laborers were hard to get, for many of them were making for the cities of the south, where the work was regular—and easier. The hands he could hire were lazy, and they demanded a crushing wage. Things bought outside, such as clothing and glass, were expensive.

He even worked after supper, reading whilst yet there was light, or sometimes after dark, by candle—tallow candles, not wax, for wax cost too much. He was accumulating a library—in no way comparable to that at Weddell Lodge but suited' to his own needs. His shelf held Fitzherbert's *Husbandry*, Thomas Tusser's *Five Hundred Good Points of Husbandry*, Reginald Scott's *A Perfect Platform for a Hop Garden*, Thomas Hill's *The Profitable Art of Gardening* and his *A Profitable Instruction of the Perfect Ordering of Bees*, as well as Heresbach's *Four Books of Husbandry*, as translated by Barnaby Googe; and he would pore over Mascall on pruning as a more romantic-minded man might pore over Ovid.

These and other authorities, he noted, exalted agricultural methods in the Low Countries. It was from Zealand or perhaps Brabant that there had come the practice, eagerly embraced by Sir John Crofts, of planting turnips out in the fields, thus providing fodder on less land than was required for hay.

George waxed curious about the Low Countries, which he had never visited, and one night he expressed a wish to go there.

"Praise be," was Anne's quick comment. "We can travel by way of London."

He frowned, though he turned away so that she could not see it. London, London! Sometimes it seemed to be all she could talk about: and George hated the place, as he hated the court wherever it was.

149

Occasionally he would try to explain this feeling to Anne, but she was infatuated, not open to reason. Lately, discouraged, he had ceased to splutter.

It was unsettling to reflect that since the birth of Janet and even more since that of little George, he and his wife had been seeing less of one another than they had been wont to do before he first went to the Indies. An enlarged Okeland was no palace, but it called for constant cleaning, and they could not afford a full staff of maids. Nor did George skimp his duties outside. Conscientious, he rode forth every day and personally supervised all the labor in the fields. In consequence, he was not often with Anne. Their talks in bed at night were liable to interruption from one of the cradles. Sometimes after supper they would play maw or little primero; but neither had much stomach for cards, and dice was not proper for a lady.

The cider press was the place where they did most of their talking. There were good apples at Okeland, and George had figured that cider for the maids and the field hands came almost fifteen per cent cheaper than beer, so they made a great deal of it. In the life of the farm, responsibilities were carefully given out; but it had never been ruled whether the making of cider was by right a part of the mistress' work or a part of the master's, and since they both enjoyed it they both did it. George of course had seen to the gathering of the fruit in the first place, as Anne would see to the storage of the cider, but in the actual pressing and jugging they worked together. Though they didn't dally, these were pleasant times.

"They say an ambassador's an honest man sent abroad to lie for his country," George told her at one of these sessions. "If that's all there was to it, all right. Nobody *has* to be an ambassador. But the way things are now, practically everybody who has any connection at all with the court *has* to do at least a little lying—and maybe it's getting to be more all the time. I don't know why this is, but I don't like it."

"Truly, sweetard, thou dost not think of *thyself* as a liar?"

"Sometimes I almost do. It could sneak into a man, that habit. Sometimes I get afraid that I might be lying without even knowing it."

"Would that be lying, then?"

He had no answer to this, but turned the press and watched the juice flow, sniffing its cleanness, his ear cocked to its gurgle.

"Besides, it could be that thou'rt too harsh on the court.

150

I'll reserve my own decision. When thou hast taken me there I'll make up my mind, when I can see for myself."

That was the way it always ended, on that note.

And that was why George sighed to himself, turning away, when Anne announced her intention of going to the Low Countries with him—by way of London.

He was by no means sure that such a visit could be arranged for himself alone, even if he could afford it. The Dutch and Flemings were in a more or less permanent state of revolt against their Spanish masters; half of their cities were besieged, while the countryside was overrun by soldiers. So Whitehall, being additionally moved by the fact that the Belgian provinces were hotbeds of English Catholic exiles, would issue no passport for travel there unless the applicant showed good cause. In such a matter it would be necessary to go to no less a person than the queen's first secretary. This was no longer Lord Burghley, "her majesty's housekeeper." There had been changes in high government. John Hawkins was treasurer of the royal navy now, in the place of his brother-in-law, Benjamin Gonson, and as a result he would be more often than ever in London. Burghley had been raised to lord treasurer of the realm. The queen's first secretary, succeeding Burghley, was Sir Francis Walsingham, about whom George knew nothing.

While he pondered this problem—should he write to Hawkins asking for his influence in getting a passport—a letter came from Walsingham himself.

It asked George, in effect ordered him, to appear before the personage "alone and unattended, and in the most inconspicuous manner that shall be convenient," for conference upon "something that appertaineth to the welfare of the realm."

What could that be? Certainly not turnips. George sensed the queen of Scots again.

The stipulation "alone and unattended . . . inconspicuous" irked him as sneaky, but at the same time it suggested that Spain was still in the ascendant at the English court, which in turn meant that Francis Drake's latest sea venture would remain motionless for the present. Also against such specific wording Anne had no recourse, although it caused her a great effort to contain her annoyance at not being permitted to accompany her husband to London.

In March of 1575, a scant week after he had received this letter, he set forth.

He called first upon Hawkins—a somewhat strained visit, since neither knew what attitude to take toward the other.

151

Was the enterprise at Okeland to be looked upon as a diversion, a hobby? Was George still Hawkins' man? George had refused a personal appeal on the part of Hawkins' cousin Drake to take a captaincy in the forthcoming expedition, in which Hawkins, beyond all doubt, was interested. The older man was nettled by this. Nevertheless John Hawkins was helpful, telling George, if somewhat guardedly, whatever he knew about Sir Francis Walsingham.

This man, moderately wealthy, had traveled much on the Continent and was thought of as Italianate, though his religious views were puritanical and extremely stringent. He could speak half a dozen languages, and had read everything. He had no private life: he was all work, an unremitting conscience, a drive that never slowed. Undoubtedly it was about Mary Stuart that he wished to see George. Walsingham had never met Mary Stuart, but he had extreme ideas regarding her.

"He mislikes her?"

"He hates her. He calls her the bosom viper. More than any other man I know, more even than my Lord Burghley, he subscribes to that motto—how doth it go?—'Vita Mariae—uh—' "

"Vita Mariae mors Elizabethae; vita Elizabethae mors Mariae."

"That's it."

Soon afterward, having been admitted by a side door, George stood in the presence of the first secretary himself, Walsingham, the new master of all English spies.

And George shuddered.

Here was a man who might have had vinegar in his mouth instead of spit. He was lank and long, though as George saw when he rose behind the table, not actually tall; he was slabsided, angular. His mouth was an abrupt slit, without color. His cheek and brow were cretaceous, his eyes dark hollows of disapproval. Over those eyes, as if he feared that they might betray him, habitually he kept his lids half-lowered. This implied no sleepiness! Those heavy creased lids which never quivered, suggested rather an extra awareness, a hidden feline alertness. Velvet-muscled, this man was at all times ready to pounce. He was dressed in black, as though he had been a gentleman executioner. Not the least frightening thing about him was his voice. It was hollow, though neither deep nor notably loud, and was compounded of echoes, as though it came out of a cave.

Acidulous, saturnine, he could have been expected to

152

give forth only harsh words; yet the first thing he said to George was praise.

"My Lord Burghley hath spoken highly of you. Your probity, your energy, your wit."

Astounded, George sat down. He swallowed.

"So too my lord of Shrewsbury, who writes that you have twice talked with his charge, and that she thinks right well of you."

This was an even greater jolt. At the same time, it flustered George, who felt his face go hot.

Walsingham leaned back a little, though not in relaxation. It was impossible to think of this man as ever being relaxed, as it was impossible to picture him playing tennis or riding to hounds or even, like Burghley, raising roses. He steepled his bone-thin fingers. His eyes were all but closed.

"Would you tell me about her, please, Master Fitzwilliam?"

This graveled George, who sat up straight. Never mind the nature of Mary Stuart's opinion of him! What Walsingham wanted was a catalogue of her weaknesses.

Cautiously he asked: "What is it you wish to know?"

"What sort of person is this schemer?"

"Why, very lovely to look at."

"So I've been told," Walsingham said dryly. "But what hath that to do with the policy of the queen's government toward her?"

"I should think it might have a great deal. *I* am not the first secretary, sir, but if I was I would surely take Mary Stuart's beauty into account. 'Tis worth a thousand pikemen."

"Um-m. What I seek is less sensational."

"Sir, when I met this lady I was stricken with bewilderment. I was dazzled."

Now the eyes came open, almost with a leathery rustling sound like that of a bat's wings.

"And has it affected your judgment, this bedazzlement?"

George shrugged.

"So it has been with other messengers," Walsingham went on. "They come back yammering of that exquisite mouth, those soul-searching eyes. Bah! Even Burghley, who's not susceptible to Satan's wiles every day, I can tell you—even he babbles a bit when he recalls to mind her smile. This is not what I seek."

George had averted his head, not because he blushed any longer, nor yet from fear of Walsingham's gaze, but only in order to control his anger.

"Perhaps if your worship would ask specific questions—"

"Very well."

153

For some time then they were businesslike, and George was as informative as might be, never hesitating; but in time there came the question that all along had been inevitable, hanging over him.

"Master Fitzwilliam, you would seem to have this woman's confidence. There are not many such men we can trust. Can we trust you? If in the very name of the queen's highness you should be asked to take a message to Sheffield Castle—a message, I mean, that might bring out the murderousness that's in the prisoner—"

He paused.

George cleared his throat.

"If the queen's highness commanded, I should of course obey."

"'Tis not a matter of mere obedience," Walsingham pointed out impatiently. *"How* would you deliver that message? Would the Stuart believe it?"

"Does your worship mean a message calculated to enmesh her in some plot against the life of the queen's highness?"

"Yes."

"Concocting such a plot, falsely?"

"Why not?"

George rose. He walked back and forth a little, his left hand gripping the hilt of his sword.

"Sir," he said at last, "chivalry to some may mean only dragons and entranced maidens; it is a clumsy word nowadays—that I realize. But could not any healthy man gag at the thought of tricking a prisoner in order that she might be slain?"

"Not tricking her, sirrah! She needs none! Simply offering her a chance to hire an assassin, that's all."

"Your worship is sure?"

"I am. But then, I lack chivalry. Which may clarify my vision. These foes I fight for the safety of the queen, these papists, d'ye think that they know anything about knight-errantry, Fitzwilliam? When Lord Moray was slaughtered as he rode through Edinburgh, was it face to face or from behind a screen? And what about William of Orange? Did *he* have a chance to draw and defend himself when King Philip's creature shot him? And—God save the mark!—Coligny?"

George said nothing.

"I tell you it's their own weapon—to be taken as long as the fanatic who wields it can be promised eternal bliss. Murder the right person, a person picked by the pope, and

Heaven's gates will be swung wide for you. D'ye believe that, Fitzwilliam?"

Still George was silent.

"Oh, I was in Paris the night of St. Bartholomew—and all the beastly days and nights that followed. I was her majesty's ambassador there, and I tell ye, Fitzwilliam, I saw such savagery as made me ashamed to call myself man. Every group that whooped past my windows had at least a leg to display, or a hand, usually a hacked-off head. Some of them waved chunks of skin, as brave as battle flags. They didn't only kill, they tore to pieces. The pavement was clobbered with blood. The Seine was so choked with bodies that it backed up over the embankment."

He too had risen now, and he leaned over the table, waggling a long lean schoolmasterish forefinger.

"And did their spiritual leader, their so-called Holy Father in Rome, did he reproach them for butchery? No! He *lauded* them! He struck a medal in honor of that glorious event!"

He sat down.

"And you would fight fair, Fitzwilliam, with people like that?"

"I— I am not informed on matters of dogma and high politics, your worship. I have never looked upon God as a member of any faction. And I fear I would make a poor messenger."

"Eh? No matter. We have no call for your services now anyway. You may go."

But as George started away: "Nay, a moment!"

He shuffled some papers, and lifted a letter.

"Near you in Northampton there lives a squire named Weddell?"

"Aye."

"We've been told that he too takes orders from the Vatican. Is that true?"

"I have heard it said so. I don't know for sure."

"You mean you won't tell?"

"I mean I don't know. I only know what neighbors say."

Walsingham turned aside. The tops of his cheeks had been touched with hectic red, but now they faded. His eyes had flared, but now he half-closed them, banking their fire.

"No matter," he said again. "You may go."

"A favor first, your worship?"

"What is it?"

"I'd visit the Low Countries."

155

"Why?"

"To study their methods of growing corn."

"Umph! To study at Douai, like enough!"

"Are you implying that—?"

"I'm implying nothing, save that I don't like Galahads. Your petition's denied. No passport. And now goodbye, Master Fitzwilliam. The door is right behind you."

27
Touch Not My Friend

THE SUN ROSE AND THE SUN SET, and if the days didn't march to music neither did they drag. There was always work to be done. One from the great world, visiting this part of Northampton, might have found it dull; but nobody at Okeland did.

They were not idle. Only a year after little George, Elizabeth was born. (George at first had thought to name her Mary, but decided against this without having mouthed it.) The local laborers, whey-faced under their rye-straw hats, and with sinews that might have been made of paper, demanded and eventually got a higher rate of pay. Aunt Helen died one night, very quietly. George contracted to breed a rag of colts. Sir John ailed. In the cornfields, fumiter, burdocks, nettles, and darnel flourished, despite George's cursingest efforts. The household gave up white bread when the price of wheat rose, but a drop in the price of barley and rye more than offset this. When winter came again and wages were not so high, George decided, he would, ungratefully, take down that park in which he had hidden after killing Salvo—it was part of the property he had bought from Terence Weddell—and, after raking out the leaves for compost, would cut the trees for fuel.

Okeland was not forgotten. In the chancellories of Europe the plotters and counterplotters, the counter-counterplotters as well, might have lost the name of George Fitzwilliam; but the queen's tax collectors did not. The mummers, mimes, and morris dancers, the beggars, itinerant tinkers, pedlars, avoided Okeland as a box from which few coins could be extracted; but Francis Drake remembered that address.

Twice the Plymouth skipper caused letters to be written to George, asking for his services. Each time in reply George wrote a felicitous "no."

On his visit to George and to Terence, Drake had concealed his identity. According to some reports he was in Ireland, according to others, dead. It was much the same to those who lived near Okeland. Drake had penetrated that county and returned from it without once being pointed out—a circumstance that might have miffed him.

With George it was otherwise. Nothing was known locally of his visits to the prisoner of Sheffield, but his record of enterprise under Hawkins and under Drake was public property. A man who had traveled to the New World was a sight even in Plymouth, even in London; in Northamptonshire he was unique. More, a squire who had visited in Devon came back with the story of George's freeing of the New Spain prisoners, and since it was not possible to let out the whole truth about this the tale was wonderfully embroidered. By these rustics, then, George was hailed as a hero who had bubbled the king of Spain. They never tired of asking him about this and connected exploits. "Is it true that he has horns and his teeth are black?" "These savages in the wilderness ... Is it true that they don't wear *no* clothes *at all?*" "Master Fitzwilliam, sir, would you be good enough to tell Tim here about the time you whipped all them dons at San Juan de Ulua, if I'm pronouncing that right?"

It would never do to greet such demands with a snort. George after all was dependent upon his neighbors' good will for many things: sociability, credit, transport for his crops, the seasonal supply of labor. No matter how weary of the questions he might get he could not afford to turn away from them.

"Is it true, your worship," a clod once asked him in the taproom of The Plow at Kettering, "that the streets of the Spanish cities in America are really paved with gold?"

"I'm afraid I never saw any like that."

"But the ones you did see, what were they paved with? Only pearls?"

"Mud, as I remember it," George replied. "Mostly mud."

The puritans George had met were simple, or they were uncouth, or both. He wouldn't have told his father-in-law this, but it was true. An exception, the only one he knew, was Sir Francis Walsingham. He often thought about this man, shivering as he did so. He had told Terence about Walsingham's question concerning him.

"It was but a letter he plucked from among others. But he knew where you lived, even before he looked at it."

Terence had nodded somberly.

"Thanks, my friend. Yes, we know about Walsingham.

157

We've been watching him for some time. He's no fool! Not that Burghley is either. But Burghley's a dutiful steward, whereas Walsingham is a flame."

"Do you think he means to get you into trouble?"

"Well, I'll leave for a while, before it can come. Could I ask you to act as caretaker here for a year or so? Of course there'd be a fee, and you could market the crops, such as they are."

"Never mind the fee—"

"I do mind. And you should."

"—but where would you go?"

"The Low Countries." He had smiled a small thorny smile. "But not to study their manuring. Bruges, Louvain, Douai. No, I'm not a priest, nor will I become one. But I have friends there, you understand."

"But you can't leave for the Low Countries without a passport, and if I couldn't get one how could you?"

"How? Why, I'll order it made for me. We have a printing press in London, you know. A very good one. And we have penmen who can sign Francis Walsingham's name better than he can."

The caretaker's fee was too much—paid in advance as it had been—and George was determined, if ever he could get that money together again, that he'd repay it when Terence came back. Going through the house now and then was a simple task. From time to time George would borrow an armful of books, as Terence had begged him. ("It keeps a book alive to be read," he had said.) And the produce of the garden, the orchards, the hay fields, more than paid George for his time and trouble.

The truth is, the two farms should have been made into one, since Weddell was by now almost surrounded by Okeland. Economy called for a merger. Some day, George decided, if it was possible, he would buy up the rest of Terence's property and combine these farms. Two houses of course would not be needed. Weddell Lodge, though the smaller, was the better built, and George had made up his mind to tear down Okeland, keep the name, and rebuild around the lodge, though not, to be sure, while Sir John lived.

All, he reflected sternly, would call for cash. And he had no cash, nor any immediate prospect of it.

The combined farms, the superimposed and rebuilt manor house—these could be classed with castles in Spain. He had best think right now of how to pay for the cows he had come to Rugby to buy. If he could only talk old Copplewait into—

His worriment was broken as he dismounted before the George and Dragon, for the door of that inn flew open and he was swept into a scene of wild excitement.

Those who first came out came backward, yet moving very fast, in full scamper, while they waved their arms, jabbering. Each held a dagger.

"God-a-mercy!"

"Mind him there!"

"Kill him! Kill the Moor!"

These were countrymen, not boys, but they looked like children when the one they fled from burst forth.

He was enormous. And his skin was black—not a dark brown, but black. His head was bare, his feet as well. His ruff was torn. His face gleamed with sweat, while his eyes rolled white, the size of tennis balls. No sword or poniard had been strapped about his red-doubleted waist, but in each hand he grasped a cudgel-like stick, the leg of a stool he had pulled apart.

"Throw something at his shins! Hit his shins!"

"Get a pitchfork, somebody!"

The giant paused, not panting like the others but blinking in the glare of the sun after the taproom's gloom. For all his bulk, there was something feline about him: his feet were spread wide, and he was ready to jump in any direction with deadly speed. He was a bull, an elephant, tormented past endurance by gadflies. George, who had never before seen him in anything but a loincloth, marveled that he did not split his clothes.

"Here's Master Fitzwilliam! Will you draw, sir? Oh, skewer him!"

"Nonsense," George said sharply.

"Eh?"

Two men came out of the inn, bent low in a crouch. Between them they carried, like a battering-ram, a long rusty-headed pike. They were about to rush the Negro and run him right through the back; but though he could not have heard them, he sensed them, jungle beast that he was, and he spun around, raising both huge hands, both cudgels. The men dropped the pike and fled back into the taproom.

The giant turned again, his mouth working, eyes rolling. Curiously crunched sounds came from his throat. He verged on panic and could think only to smash, to kill. All men were his enemies.

George started forward.

159

"Mind him, Master Fitzwilliam! He—"

"Go to, bum!"

George did not draw, nor did he make any sort of sudden movement.

A few feet from the wild man he stopped, smiling a mite, and in a low caressive voice as though calling a kitten he spoke one word, a name.

"Diego—"

The black dropped both stool-legs. He sprang forward, and threw his arms around George, and rubbed his thick rubbery nose against George's.

"*Señor!*"

Most of what he said was in his own Cimarron tongue or else in badly fractured Spanish, so that even George did not understand it; and of course it meant nothing at all to the scared countrymen. George and Diego, however, from experience could communicate by hand language and by tone of voice, and when at last they separated, each was laughing and weeping at the same time.

That his guide to the back door of Nombre de Dios was in England, George did not find extraordinary; for Francis Drake, whether out of a liking for the Cimarron or because it tickled his vanity to have so large and colorful a body servant (George believed it to be the latter) had brought him from Panama. That he was in the middle of Northamptonshire surpassed all understanding—just at first. Diego, it might be assumed, even if he was allowed ashore at all, would hardly have gone more than a few hundred feet from the edge of the sea of his own accord. He must, then, have been sent. There must be a letter.

George asked—and there was. Diego, who had forgotten it, now fetched it forth from somewhere under that straining doublet. George thrust it into his purse. It would be from Drake, of course. Knowing his fondness for Diego, Drake had sought to lure George back by this means. Which meant that the new venture must be making up again.

George was at once angry and flattered, but more immediately he was concerned about his companion. He soon had the story, as best Diego could tell it. Diego had not been turned loose upon the English hinterland alone. A sailor had gone with him, to keep him from toppling off his horse, to guide him to Okeland, to cause him to wear a riding mask and a wide-brimmed low-pulled bonnet as a screen against prying passers. After several days of travel, somewhere near at hand—Coventry? Leamington?—this companion had vanished. It might have been drunkenness, a fight, or ordinary desertion. Whatever the reason, a bewildered, frightened Diego, knowing that he was near the place where Señor Fitzwilliam lived, and in any event afraid to stay still, had floundered on. Somehow he had found his way into the taproom of the George and Dragon, Rugby, where, his fragmentary, recently acquired English having left him like his guide, he tried in vain to solicit information from the gathered clods, most of whom should have been out in the fields at that hour anyway. Flabbergasted at first, soon they had thought to make sport of him. Whereupon, an overtried Diego had gone berserker.

"I see. *Gracias.* Wait here a moment."

A thundercloud, George turned upon the others. He drew.

Half the population of the village was there by this time, crowding the narrow high street, but George addressed himself only to those who had tumbled out of the tavern. He swished his rapier, and they stepped back a bit.

"*So,* my fine bawcocks! Applause for ye! Because his words didn't come well and because his skin was dark you minded you could prick him like a chained bear, eh? You thought you'd play the dogs—aye, a part well chosen!—and you'd harry him with snaps and growls, never getting too near, and never having had to put up your tuppence to the keeper of the garden, is that it? Ballocks! You met a *man* this time, God rot ye!"

He swished the sword again, and again they stepped back, for it had a razor's edge and was very bright and long. He jerked his head to indicate Diego, who stood behind him now.

"Tosspots, pisspots, you were temerarious! You picked on a friend of mine!"

Diego grinned, all teeth. He didn't understand a word of it, but he was pleased to learn that his beloved *el señor* Fitzwilliam here in his own land was a leader, a chief, even as Diego himself had been in Darien.

"He tells me that somebody took his horse away but didn't walk it. I'll have that beast walked—aye, and head-rubbed and its gear tightened. Then it shall be brought before this door and held until my friend and guest is ready to mount again.

"He tells me," George went on, slowly, ominously, "that somebody bobbed his bung. That will be returned too, mind ye, and instanter. And down to the last penny-piece in it, down to the last cog.

"He tells me that when he came here he was carrying his boots in his hand, for that they hurt his feet. And these too were filched, eh? Well, randyboys, these too will be straight-away brought back—but they'll be polished first so that a man can see his face in 'em. Do I make myself clear?"

He swished the sword yet again, and it glittered in the sun.

"For if this is not done, and done now, I'll flail the skin off some tobies around here."

He sheathed. He turned toward the beaming Diego, but turned back for a final shot.

"I'll do more than that. I'll loose *him* on you again!"

He threw an arm across Diego's shoulders and laughed.

"Come along, *amigo*. I'll buy you a beer."

28

Between Two Stools

THE SHADOW LOOMED, swelling, seeming to lean in men-ace away from the wall; then it collapsed like a struck tent; but it rose again, enormous, expanding, dark as Erebus.

"I think you should go," said Sir John.

"No," said Anne.

The shadow swayed from side to side, monstrously abob. It ebbed. It stretched, straining the oak beams above.

"And you, Aunt Sylvia?"

She had no opinion. Seamed, small, crushed by many years, she must have been fifty. Since the passing of her sister she had seldom spoken, and though she went on work-ing day after day with a birdlike doggedness, in truth she was but herself awaiting Death's embrace. Tonight, in addi-tion, she had been badly rattled by Diego, from whom she couldn't rip her gaze. She shook a dazed head, and when she spoke it was in a voice barely audible—a voice thread-thin, as though she suffered from thirst.

"You— You must do as you think best, George."

Sideways, sympathetically, George studied a guest who might have sprung from the primordial ooze. As happy as a puppy with a shoe, seated in a thronelike chair on the dais, beaming down upon the others, who had taken more com-fortable places below, Diego threw that restless shadow. A shadow distorted, a grotesque. In truth there was nothing restless about Diego himself; he could take no part in the talk, but he was having a wonderful time.

Was that a representation *in petto*, was it a symbol, of America—a glowering, huge, ever-changing shadow thrown on a wall by one who, seen from near at hand, was all amiability? George thought not; the picture was too pat. The New World, as he had reason to realize, was anything but insubstantial, a shadow. It was harsh; it could terrify. It repelled him, and he didn't want to go back to it.

Beggars cannot be choosers, men said. George was no beggar yet, but he was perilously close to the edge; he teetered on the verge of bankruptcy. On the table before him were two documents, and it was these that had brought about the discussion.

One was the message Diego had delivered. It was from Francis Drake. That some unnamed scribe had done the actual writing made no difference; the voice was that of Drake, clear, imperious. George knew well, none better, how Drake could fuss over a letter, causing his secretary to recast it many times. He had a sharp ear, an infallible memory, and he knew what he wanted. He could be tart too. On Captain Drake's ship you were not permitted to give such cries as "Devil take it!" or "God rot it!" or even the universal "Upon my shot!"—this last being taken by him, rightly or wrongly, as a euphemism for "Upon my soul!" which in the nature of it would be blasphemous. Looking down upon the letter, George smiled at the sight of an old admonition, written after Drake had warned him that farming and roving did not mix and that he who tried both might fail in both: "Between two stools the arse goeth to the ground."

Chuckling, he read this aloud.

"Sh-sh," said Anne, glancing at Aunt Sylvia; but that old woman, still under the spell of Diego's shadow, had not heard.

The other article on the table was the Okeland account book, which told a grim story. For a long time George had known that the money situation was bad, very bad; but seeing it on paper, looking at the figures themselves, somehow made it seem even worse.

This need not be a losing battle. Okeland was naturally rich, and not too far from the market. The new methods Sir John and George had introduced would eventually increase the size of the crop, the size of the herds too. But— time was required. And time was an intangible something that couldn't be whittled, condensed, or stored away for future use.

Disaster was not inevitable. Okeland *could* be made to pay. There was nothing about the tale the ledger told that couldn't be righted, and for good, by five hundred golden guineas. But—where could such a stupendous sum be raised? Every acre of Okeland-Weddell was mortgaged, as was the house itself. The furniture was negligible, Anne's jewels, like those of Aunt Sylvia, were modest. George's prize money from the Nombre de Dios venture, staggering though it had seemed at the time he brought it here, was all gone; nor did he have any inheritance to borrow against.

Five hundred guineas. It was a vast sum, twenty-five years ago all but unthinkable, while even today George didn't suppose that there were twenty men in the kingdom who could have raised it out of hand, instanter. His uncle, John Russell, earl of Bedford, was a man of wealth but a man too of many business affairs, and in person a niggard. John Hawkins had inherited much and made more, but like Uncle John he kept his money busy, and it was not likely that at a given time he could lay his hands on anything like five hundred guineas. Burghley? Here was no gambler, like the others, but a cautious adventurer, one who looked before he leapt financially, if indeed he ever leapt at all. Burghley would have a nest egg. But—would he lend this to George Fitzwilliam? Most assuredly if he did it would be with an understanding about future service. He would insist that George become his "man." And George didn't want to be anybody's man any more.

Should he consider his own private feelings? But it wasn't only that. Anne Crofts had not married a mountebank, nor yet a trained dog who at the word of command would sit up on its hind legs and beg. Her father, Sir John, the proper proprietor of Okeland, had given all he'd got and was too old to be expected to gain more, by whatever means. But George, the real master, should have other resources.

And he *did* have.

He stared at the letter.

"I would go," said Sir John.

"The waiting," George muttered. "The delays . . . the emptiness . . ."

"What's war but waiting? Three-quarters waiting and one quarter looking for something to eat."

"Perhaps I don't like war?"

"Perhaps I didn't either, but it's the only way for a young man to make money." He rapped bony, waxy knuckles against the letter on the table. "He agrees thou'lt not be called upon to be a common captain, and thou'lt have the old secretaryship back. Three whole lays of the ad-

164

venture, before an anchor's up! And it should be a richer one even than before. The Mediterranean—"

"He'll not go to the Mediterranean," George said curtly.

"Why not?"

"There's too much competition."

"He *said* Alexandria, that night he stopped here. Could he be meaning to go back to the West Indies or New Spain?"

"No, not that either. Not Francis Drake. The Spaniards are no sluggards. By this time every town along the Main and in New Spain and among the islands will be cannoned and ramparted and stocked with a garrison. It would need such a fleet as the queen's self could hardly raise, to force one of them now."

"The smaller places?"

"The smaller places are for smaller men."

"The Far Indies are not. But—clear around Africa?"

George shook his head.

"The Portuguese have plugged that hole."

"Where else, then? Where else *is* there to go?"

"There is the Southern Sea, on the other side."

Sir John stared at his son-in-law.

"But—nobody's ever *been* there, except Spaniards!"

"Nobody had ever been below the Line, until a few years ago. Men used to say that whoever tried it would be burned to a crisp."

George nodded to the bobbing Cimarron.

"*He's* been there. He's paddled his feet in it. I've only seen it from afar, myself. And so has Drake. But it's there; I can vouch for that."

"How could he ever get *to* it? The Spaniards cross the isthmus and build vessels on the other shore."

"Magellan didn't."

George dipped a forefinger into his wine and started to draw lines on the top of the table.

"This is the way it was explained to me by Terence Weddell, and also by Master Hawkins from time to time, and by Richard Grenville that night we had the banquet when I brought the Spanish prisoners back. Grenville's fascinated by the scheme. I think he's behind Drake as much as Hawkins is. Look, you both have heard of the symmetry of nature, of course?"

"Well, something," ventured Sir John.

Anne only nodded. She had raised her head and was looking at George.

"Well, here's America. A great land mass like this,

165

see? Here's Florida . . . and New Spain . . . and then it gets narrow, just north of the Line here, and that's Darien, between the two seas. That's where Nombre de Dios is, and Panama."

"Yes, I know," said Sir John.

"Then of course there's another land mass, since it is always that way—always balanced, necessarily. Here's the Main, and here's Brazilwood Land, and then the land of the Amazons . . . But it slopes in toward Tierra del Fuego, from what we hear. This southern mass is not as large as that of the north, and what's more the Line does not divide them evenly but leaves more to the north. True?"

"Aye . . ."

"Well now, the earth is round. And it turns. It spins. We all know that, always have. But mark ye, if there was so much more land in the northern half, the upper half, why, land being heavier than water, it would wobble on its axis, is that not right?"

"Um-m. It would seem so."

"It *is* so, undoubtedly. The men who know about these things say so, the men who have studied them."

"Your friend Weddell?"

"Yes. But also Mercator. And Ortelius, Phrysius, and Finaeus. And Dr. John Dee. And many another as well. They point out that by the law of the symmetry of nature there must be a counterbalancing land mass far to the south, to offset this difference. Is that clear?"

"Well . . ."

"They call this far place Terra Incognita, which means Unknown Land, or sometimes Terra Australis, the Land of the South. It is bleak and bare, bitterly cold."

"How dost thou know?"

"It has been seen. By one man only! By Master Magellan, who found a narrow strait or channel above Tierra del Fuego, which is to say the southern part of America. He sailed through the strait and into the Southern Sea. Why couldn't Drake do the same? I don't like the man, but he's a master mariner if ever there was one."

"The men wouldn't go!"

"He wouldn't tell 'em. He would not even tell me. That's why he lets fall this foolish talk about Alexandria."

"But— But even if he got there, what would he do?"

George's was a tight smile.

"A thousand miles of seacoast, all unfortified because no enemy ever had been in that sea, treasure ships without a cannon on 'em, cities to be picked like peaches from a tree

166

—oho, Captain Drake would know what to do! Have no fear of that!"

"He couldn't get back," Anne said suddenly.

"Why not?"

"Thou hast said that the strait is narrow, a thin place. Wouldn't the dons fortify it against Drake's return?"

"Why truly, that they would. But there might be other exits. Look—"

He wetted his finger again, and drew more lines.

"Since there is a passage between the two ocean seas at the southern extremity of America here, it follows that there ·must be one at the northern extremity as well. That's the way all nature is: balanced. It stands to reason."

"Has anyone ever found a northern passage?"

"Frobisher thinks he has. He's equipping right now for a deeper try. Humphrey Gilbert is interested in that route too, since it's surely there. And others. But it wouldn't attract Captain Drake, for it leads away from the Spaniards, and the Spaniards are the ones with the money. But look: Granted that the dons would block the Magellan channel against any return—for they are no fools and they can move mighty fast when it comes to protecting their wealth—still, what's to prevent Drake from sailing on up this coast, up through the Southern Sea along the far side of the northern part of America, until he reached the other entrance of the northern passage? It *must* be there."

Sir John Crofts's eyes were sparkling.

"To sail clear around half of the known world! God's bodikins! What I wouldn't give to do that, if I were younger!"

There was some silence after that. Diego was munching an apple. Aunt Sylvia had fallen asleep. Sir John, in the candlelight, *looked,* indeed, younger. George felt somewhat ashamed of himself for failing to share that enthusiasm, yet Anne, it developed, was of his way of thinking.

"It might be a deed of derring-do," Anne said at last, "but it sounds like a sinful waste of time—to go into somebody's house by the front door and out by the back, ending at the same place."

"But ending with your arms full of plate," George reminded her. "Francis Drake never forgets his owners."

"And how can you be sure that the back door won't be locked? Or, what if you couldn't find it? What would you do then?"

George shrugged.

167

"The earth is round," he repeated. "There is still the long way home. It's been done once. It could be done again."

He rose.

"I don't know," he said to nobody in particular. "I'll sleep on it."

He did not. He lay awake for a long while, on his back, silent, but knowing all the time that Anne, who didn't stir, was awake beside him. He thought of the steaming jungles of Darien, the snakes, the swamps, of the maddeningly endless squeak of ship's timbers, the swish of unseen bilge, the hours and days that seemed to have no end ... In the darkness he shivered. After a long while he slipped his arms around Anne, and held her very tight.

"The symmetry of nature," he whispered, trying to sound playful, though in truth he was badly frightened.

Later he flopped over on his belly, his favorite position for sleep. Indeed, he pretended to sleep, even essaying a small tentative snore, as he lay listening to the dear familiar nightsounds of Okeland. It was no use. Anne never was fooled by such a performance. And when she did speak at last it was quietly, evenly, with no preliminary inquiry about his state of slumber. She *knew* he was awake.

"Thou hast made up thy mind?"

"Yes, dear."

There was an absent-minded thudding of hooves from the stables, a chorus of frogs from the duck pond, and from the wood the song of a nightingale.

"Thou art going?" she said.

"Yes, dear."

29

Watch That Man

GEORGE'S FEARS OF POSTPONEMENT and senseless delay were justified: he was destined to stay, all summer, all autumn, in Plymouth. Nor was he kept very busy, though he had to be on hand. Drake knew his backers; his plans were well laid; and some time before George arrived the five vessels were equipped and fully victulated so that they could have sailed at once, save for two things—God and Queen Elizabeth.

The ships were *Pelican, Marigold, Elizabeth, Benedict* (a mere pinnace, for scouting purposes), and the fat storeship *Swan.* The last two had no guns, but *Elizabeth* and *Marigold* bristled with them. *Pelican,* the largest, was so cluttered with artillery that when you were aboard of her it was hard to move: seven stout demi-cannons on each side, a couple of falconets, and mounted forward two long sakers, four-pounders. This promised to be an interesting trade voyage!

First the wind and then majesty said "no"; when one would relent the other was obdurate. The mariners might wake in the morning to tumble up on deck and scan the sky, the sound, the wind ribands. They'd raise a cheer. And then—then—a courier from London would appear. The queen's highness had decided that the fleet must not sail.

Variable as the winds were, this monarch's disposition was more so; and nothing could be done except sit and wait, chafing at the consumption of hard-won rations. By the time Elizabeth Tudor had changed her mind yet again, graciously giving permission for the adventure to proceed, the weather too had yawed and the wind once more was from the south, pinning them to Plymouth.

George was comfortable enough as the guest of John Hawkins. He was not obliged to sleep aboard ship, though he was constantly on call and of course prohibited from leaving Plymouth. His temper was frayed by the delays, and he tended to be snappish; but he forgot this and everything else when he returned to the house in Kinterbury Street one afternoon to find Anne.

There was a fond, small smile on her face as she held out her arms.

"If thou hadst gone, I sought to know it. And if thou hadst not, then maybe I could comfort thee a little."

She was wearing something blue, and he wept for gladness at the sight.

"Oh, I love thee, my chuck!"

"Can I believe this?" she asked.

"Eh?"

"Hast thou not told me that lying's become a habit with thee?"

He released her, and stepped back, shocked. For he took the charge seriously. Anne was not a playful woman; levity had no part in her make-up. But now, repentant, she seized him.

"Nay, sweetard," she pleaded. "I spoke in jest."

As if to make up for his trip to London, George squired her all around Plymouth even accompanying her into the shops. She, in her turn, did him a world of good, just by being there. But when at long last he sailed, of a cold wet morning, December 13, 1577, her presence made departure

169

just that much harder to bear. Standing on the quay in a dismal drizzle, he clung to his wife.

At The Plow in Kettering there had been sundry who from time to time expressed to George their wonder that he, who could, was not sailing the great ocean sea. "Why?" he asked. "God-a-mercy, it gives a man the mulligrubs to be pent in a place like this," they would answer, "but out there you could be *free!*"

George would then guffaw. "Heed this," he'd reply, "there is no jail so close-confining as a ship afloat. You can't walk without lurching, and holding on to something, and stepping over somebody, and even then you can't walk more than a few feet in any one direction. You're never *alone.*"

They'd cry: "Now, is that true?"

"Heed this," George would go on, "if you sneeze at sea you joggle somebody's elbow, and if you spit you sully somebody's boot, that's how tight they pack you. You sleep, when you can, in a bunk made of boards that push against your shoulders on each side and make you bend your knees, and if you start up you bump your head. Even so, unless your birth's exalted, or your investment very, very large, you must needs share this Stygian slit, taking turns with some stranger whose bugs you also share—for there are always bugs, forsooth!"

Customarily that quieted them, but on one occasion a newcomer to the neighborhood had named another inducement:

"Yet at least you'd get away from politics, out there!"

This amused George Fitzwilliam, this memory. Get away from politics? Why, they were carrying Whitehall right along with them!

The riffraff of the forward castle, though ignorant almost beyond belief, knew when the west coast of Africa was raised that they were not bound for Alexandria. They were stupid men, but not stolid; and now they were uneasy.

The officers, hand-picked by Francis Drake, would do anything he told them to do. The gentlemen did not feel that way. The gentlemen never did believe the Alexandria story, but they had been led to suppose that this was in truth a voyage of trade and exploration. It was possible and even probable, they thought—though at first they were careful to keep this from the hands, who might panic—that the fleet would make its way into the Southern Sea. But the reason for this, they assumed, would be to plant factories on Terra Australis or in the Spice Islands. The Spanish possessions would not be molested.

170

These men got a shock when off Cape Blanco the admiral picked up a Portuguese vessel with some unpronounceable name, which he thereupon rechristened *Christopher*. True, he swapped the pinnace *Benedict* for this; but the small *Benedict* already had proved herself unseaworthy, and the skipper of the new vessel was not given a voice in the "bargain." More, among the Cape Verdes they halted and took over—without any pretense of giving something in return—a large Portuguese ship, *Mary*, bound for Brazil Land, together with her cargo of wines and, even more important, her pilot, the renowned Nuña da Silva.

These were plain acts of piracy, since England was no more at war with Portugal than she was with Spain. They had not even started in the direction of the New World. And the delight with which Drake greeted the short, dark, laconic, heavily bearded Da Silva, one of the few men acquainted with the South Atlantic, further troubled the gentlemen.

To make matters worse, Drake appeared to think that these gentlemen should help handle the ships. They did not like it.

There were not many of them: Thomas Doughty and his brother, John, who had known Drake in Ireland; John Winter, who was well connected and seethed with resentment because George Fitzwilliam was not obliged to command a vessel as he was; John Saracold and John Audley, who, though merchants by occupation, here represented certain investors and hence were classed with the gentles; John Thomas, the only person in the fleet besides George who could really speak Spanish.

The Doughtys were the worst. They simply couldn't keep their mouths shut.

So it was that, all tightness, with tempers bent, they started for the Line, making a course that should take them to Tierra del Fuego, south of Brazil Land.

It was a strain. With the exception of Da Silva, a very old man, none of them ever had crossed the Equator. Even those of education, like the Doughtys, like George, quailed at the thought, though they might keep a bold face before the mariners.

What made it worse was the weather. Fury they could face, these men bred in the north, but the doldrums they had not even heard of; and days in mid-Atlantic dragged with an agonizing slowness, piling up into weeks. The sky was the same, merciless. There were no jumping fish; there were no clouds; there was nothing. Heat waves shimmered above the decks, and nobody dared to touch metal. Not even the night brought relief for there wasn't a smitch of breeze, so that the men lay panting, wondering when this torture would cease.

Francis Drake, who never trusted anybody, and who knew or sensed the talk that was going about, used these days of no-motion to pass from one vessel to another in his brightly painted cock, inspecting, instructing, giving encouragement.

As for George, he wrote poetry to his wife.

George had a poor hand for verse—a hole in his training. Not since school had he done much with it, and he never had wooed Anne Crofts as he should have done. A triolet now and then maybe, or a roundelay. Nothing more. He was now aware of the ugly old phrase to the effect that you don't chase a horse you've already mounted; or, more mellifluously:

> *"Think ye, if Laura had been Petrarch's wife,*
> *He would have written sonnets all his life?"*

This George knew, and he didn't care. Anne might never have a chance to read what he was writing. He might tear it up; he might not get home. She had trouble with her reading anyway and in this case understandably would be loth to ask for help. But just at the time, so far away, it felt good to write it, like talking to her, the nearest thing.

This was in Drake's own cabin, a sumptuous one. The *Pelican* was still; nobody stirred. Sunlight reflected off the water smashed through the ports and against a ceiling of polished oak.

Absorbed in one of man's most absorbing sports, at first George did not hear the door open. When he did hear, and had looked up, it was with some difficulty that he repressed a frown. No man enjoys being disturbed when he is writing to the woman he loves, and George in particular disliked to be confronted with Thomas Doughty.

The man was saponaceous. His learning was genuine, his breeding (George had checked) undisputed. But he was subtle, a schemer, who seldom looked at the person he addressed. He was large, languid, light-bearded.

He threw himself into a chair, something he would never have dared to do if the admiral was present.

"Fitzwilliam, why doth Captain Drake never summon a council? Does he have some sort of commission or authorization from the queen's majesty herself that causes him to act like an unanswerable master here?"

172

For weeks Doughty had been probing the admiral's secretary for this information. Now he was essaying a new course, a direct approach calculated to jar loose some response.

George, however, made no reply. He himself did not know whether such a paper existed, though he doubted it. He did know—for the official correspondence was open to him—that the queen herself had a stake in this enterprise. But she would not acknowledge it; she was too shrewd to put such things on paper. If Drake succeeded she would share his profits. If he failed she'd disown him.

"You and I—Winter—Thomas—we should be called into consultation. We never are. Is this fleet going to Peru, Fitzwilliam? Will it harry the don?"

Still George did not answer. Nobody knew where they were going, nobody but the commander-in-chief. The instructions, which George had read, could be variously interpreted. Most admirals would have proceeded with care, calling a council as often as this was convenient, if only in order to protect themselves. Not Francis Drake. His arrogance, his refusal even to recognize the rights of any of the others, officers or gentlemen, had given rise to talk that he had a personal, private order from the queen; and if he had not confirmed this, neither had he denied it.

George sighed, and put his half-finished poem away in a blue envelope.

"I have not been told," he said.

"You're gentle. You're close to Drake. What do *you* think?"

George shrugged.

"Whatever I think must be my own affair," he said mildly.

"God's kidneys, man! Hast thou no heart!"

"Don't you 'thou' me!"

"Say, if we go to Peru we'll all be hanged for pirates!"

"It seems likely."

"It would take a miracle to save us!"

"I have seen Captain Drake perform miracles," said George. "This is not meant to be irreverent."

"You're Bedford's nephew, yet you let yourself be ordered about like a lackey. I don't understand it."

He had talked this way before, though never with such force.

"Are you *afraid* of Francis Drake?"

George, who sometimes wondered whether he was, only

173

smiled. He wished that he had been allowed to finish that verse.

"Because you should know right here and now, Fitz-william, that there are those of us who don't see why—"

He went on, and on. Doubtless it was all very mutinous, but the heat was intense and George was not disposed to listen. George was thinking of the weeping willow by the duck pond at Okeland, the nightingale, the boxwood hedge he had caused to be planted, the great-hall, the stables.

"—and nothing less than a direct written order from her own majesty—not from any minister, mind you!—could justify it. Don't you agree?"

George was thinking of the humming of bees, the stamp of horses in their dark stalls, a crackling fire. He was remembering how on warm nights he and Anne used to lie side by side, stark naked, starfished out, enjoying them-selves even during the time their bodies didn't touch.

"—and what's more, I'm not alone. I can tell you, Fitz-william, I've been among the men, and you can take my vow for it that—"

"You have certainly been among the men," said Francis Drake as he stepped into the cabin. "I've been there myself and I know what you told them. Get out of my cabin, Doughty."

When the visitor had gone, not shutting the door, Drake stared after him.

"I have been watching that man. We may have to try him."

George had no love for Thomas Doughty. Yet—Doughty was well born. And George instinctively took a side opposite that of the "new men," as typified here by the admiral. George frowned at the open door.

"Because he's a gentleman?"

"Because he is in my way," said Francis Drake.

30

A Question for the Courts of Love

THAT SPAT MIGHT HAVE CLEARED THE AIR, for a breeze sprang up, and there was a whole series of thundershowers, which helped to fill the casks but were hard on the navigators, making even Nuña da Silva unsure of himself. They struck every night, yet it was certain that they drifted, off course and probably too far north.

The men, who didn't mark these navigational hazards,

were cheered. Not only was it cooler, but flying fishes began to appear and were easily caught. They made good eating. Also, there were birds.

The pelicans in particular fascinated George.

"They sleep up there, with their wings spread out," Da Silva said in his spaced English. "Then if they get a down-current of air and begin to approach the water, it wakes them. They hate water. It is their natural enemy. So they open their eyes and flap their wings and fly high again, and then they go back to sleep."

"Sounds like a pleasant life."

One morning the *Mary* was missed, with all its wine and its company, including Thomas Doughty. Doughty was military commander of the expedition, and his duties took him to each of the vessels in turn. However, the *Mary* turned up, unobtrusively, a few days later.

April 5 they raised land, which almost immediately was wiped from sight by the worst fog any of them ever had known. For six days they stumbled here and there, afraid of breakers, losing touch with one another, for this was a lee shore and leadsmen kept reporting that the water shoaled.

Da Silva had an explanation. The Indians who lived here, he said, were so cruelly treated by his own compatriots, the Portuguese, that they had made a pact with certain storm gods, pagan gods, to keep ships away. Whenever they sighted sail, he said, they would go to the beach and pick up a handful of sand and toss this into the air as a signal to the gods, who would then keep their part of the agreement and produce fog.

(George could not decide whether Da Silva really meant what he said or whether he was amusing himself. Anyway he was a skillful pilot. That they survived the first terrible week—a pampero, Da Silva called it—was largely due to his efforts.)

"I don't believe that," Francis Drake told his secretary. "The reason for the storm is Thomas Doughty. He's been conjuring."

George made no comment. It was true that both of the Doughtys, loose-mouthed men, more than once had boasted of supernatural powers. Yet George believed that in this case there was at work something more substantial than spells, incantations, pricked images.

It could have been meaningful that when at last the pampero subsided and they counted bowsprits, the only vessel missing—they had to comb the coast four days for her—was the *Christopher,* presently carrying Thomas Doughty.

175

All the vessels needed scraping. This would call for a halt, when the right place was found. Boot-topping—shifting all guns and stores to one side of a vessel so that her other side was partly exposed, scraping this, and then reversing the process—would not be advisable with vessels as beamy as these and in seas so uncertain. They would have to find a beach. This made every delay a possible disaster: the Magellan Strait, if it could be traversed at all could be traversed only in the southern summer—January, February, March—and if that season was missed they could not possibly hole up in some convenient cove for a year. This was not the Gulf of Darien, this bleak stony strand.

Thanks to their foul bottoms, they crawled; and their pace slowed even more when the admiral ordered them to keep a close formation lest once again a ship be lost.

Twice while coasting they sighted Indians, who were not giants as had been reported. One group of Indians was overtouchy and shot from the shore, killing two Englishmen. The others were friendly, if shy, and none wore any clothes.

Dragging along as a wounded animal drags itself on its belly, the ships made an anchorage at a place they called Port Desire—just before they were hit by a second pampero.

Da Silva told them that never had he known two such storms off this coast within so short a time. There must be witchcraft at work, he avowed.

"Aye," muttered Francis Drake.

Again they were scattered, not only *Christopher* but even *Pelican* being blown out to sea. It was more than ten days before the fleet could be reassembled.

Luck is luck; but this was not natural.

They put in at a place they called Seal Bay after the large herds of seals they found there. None of them ever had seen this animal, which they found so ludicrous that while they laughed they permitted hundreds to get away, seeking refuge in the sea. Hundreds of others they clubbed to death. The slaughter was horrid, messy, and very malodorous, but the meat of these beasts was good, especially the pups, and the hides were of service.

They left Seal Bay June 3, and that night *Christopher* disappeared again, both of the Doughtys being aboard. They found her two days later, and since nothing could be proved against captain or master, much less against the Doughtys, Francis Drake passed it off with a grim nod. He did, however, have the *Christopher* stripped of her metal and turned adrift, saying that she was no more than a trouble-maker.

176

The name of this, the first of the vessels they had seized, might have had some significance, George thought. She presumably was so called in honor of Christopher Hatton, a young man with a stake in this enterprise—as George, who kept the accounts, could testify. It was about this time too—in fact in Seal Bay—that the admiral, having vouchsafed no reason, formally rechristened the *Pelican* the *Golden Hind,* that being Hatton's hereditary device. This Christopher Hatton was not yet a major power at court, but he was a coming man. Burghley and Walsingham, though likewise investors in this enterprise, were older, warier. As for the other backers: Leicester could not be expected to do more than hold what he had; Humphrey Gilbert was in the savage, inconclusive, heartbreaking war of the Low Countries, while his half-brother, Walter Raleigh, was in the even worse war—from any courtier's point of view—of Ireland. But Christopher Hatton stayed at home, a remarkably handsome man, whose dancing the queen had praised. Already he was Captain of the Guard, a position of glitter, and at the time the expedition left Plymouth the rumor was that he'd soon be knighted. A man to be watched. Francis Drake was looking ahead.

June 20 they limped into the best bay they had yet seen. It was perfect for careening purposes, being perhaps a mile wide, two miles long, and everywhere a good four fathoms. The hills that hemmed it in were glum and rocky, but there were no boulders near the sea. The water was clear and cold, and it swarmed with fish. There could be no excuse here for the master of any ship to let her drag her anchor and be blown outside, for the hills blocked high winds, as a low sandy island blocked the mouth of the bay.

Nautically neat, spiritually the spot depressed. There was scant vegetation, only some dry, brittle, juiceless grass and so few trees that at last they broke up *Mary* for firewood. The hills glowered. The sky glowered. They never did see the sun.

It was the belief of all those who had taken part in the navigation, including George Fitzwilliam, that they were now in Tierra del Fuego, and so could expect only worse weather as they went farther south, even when summer had come back to those regions. It was also their opinion that this must be the very Port St. Julian marked on Magellan's chart, the haven where he had paused to refit. Magellan had done more. He had put down a mutiny here—if it really was Port St. Julian—and with some ceremony had executed two men. There were those among the ma-

177

riners who claimed to have discovered the ruins of the gallows—unlikely, after more than fifty years in that wet country, but the rumor had its effect.

It was hardly to be expected that Francis Drake would fail to take advantage of this. The hot gospeler might look upon all actors as limbs of Satan, but he himself had a high sense of drama.

At first everything was work. Drake caused all three remaining vessels—their flyboat, like the *Mary*, had been broken up for firewood—to be hauled ashore, demasted, and overtipped. Anywhere else in the world it would have been poor policy thus to ground all ships at once; but the chance of an enemy pinning them in this remote spot was slim, and the admiral wished to leave no means of escape until he had spoken.

Even George, who did not get around among the men, knew that the situation was serious. Unless something radical was done the gentlemen would revolt. They might be followed by many of the mariners. They'd seize the first vessel put into commission again, and they would sail for England, crying piracy. Drake and even George could see this making up. But George didn't know what to do about it. Drake did.

George was more than ever in the admiral's cabin these days, and that for several reasons. He was keeping a diary for the admiral, and at the same time compiling a more formal record of the voyage, this too to be ostensibly Drake's. He was teaching Drake Spanish. Also George enjoyed the company of Diego, who was not notably happy in his role of valet to a man who wouldn't permit him to go naked. Diego never had been able to do much with his English, and George was the only person with whom he could chat.

There was yet another reason. "You're never *alone!*" George had been wont to tell the customers of The Plow. "You never get a chance to *think,* at sea!" Yet the secretary of a personage traveling in such state as Francis Drake, whose cabin was sacrosanct, did get a little privacy now and then. It was in the admiral's cabin, the only possible place, that George Fitzwilliam was wont, from time to time, to work upon that sonnet sequence for Anne.

All the same, it was not like living in the country; and once they were aground at Port St. Julian, and the vessels careened for cleaning, George put on his boots and indulged himself in a great luxury—a walk.

He went alone. He wanted to think.

178

Here was no Dorsetshire. The bleakness of the land all but shrieked. The very ground was harsh, unresponsive, a dirty grayish-brown. Low liver-colored clouds scuttled past, for the wind, a wet one, never paused; but there were no trees to toss their branches, no shrubs to bob and bow. Not only was there no hint of sun: this dreary landscape looked as though the sun never *had* shone upon it and never *would*, having, like God, forgotten it.

George trudged on, preoccupied with a problem that once had been sung by Bailleul, Mauléon, and the ineffable Chrétien de Troyes, and debated by Eleanor of Aquitaine, Marie of Champagne, and other ladies in the Provençal courts. But George was not interested in its historical significance, only in its immediate validity—if valid it was.

The question was: Can a man love two women at the same time?

George believed that a man could, because he believed that he did.

Okeland's chatelaine and the Strange Guest were two different persons, and why should it not be possible and even advisable to love them in two different ways? Was love indivisible? If it were split, would not each part flourish?

He loved Anne for what she was: his wife, his favorite companion. He loved Mary Stuart for what she represented. Was this weak and irresponsible, this attitude? Men laughed at chivalry, but was it, after all, dead? Was it even dying? Didn't it still make a great difference in the souls of men, even such men as denied its existence? Did a person have to wear shining armor, did he have to prance in the tiltyard, in order to know what chivalry meant? George thought not. He believed that a man might be a farmer and still have Galahad's own spirit. Not all the tortures of the Inquisition could have wrung from George any thought of a physical infidelity to Anne, yet at the same time he would always hold in his heart an image of the lovely pale prisoner at Sheffield.

But he would not mention this at home. He sometimes wondered how much physical fidelity—on the part of their husbands—meant to most women? Perhaps it was largely a male idea. Anyway it was best to be quiet about it.

Bemused, he touched the ruby in his right ear as he walked.

A flake of snow like a tiny wet rag hurled hard at him and struck his face. Then there was another, and another. Almost immediately, as though at a signal, the snow

179

ceased. The wind fell off. George crested a small rise and came into sight of sea and camp alike.

He saw instantly that something was wrong.

31
This Man Must Die

T HE THREE VESSELS, looking like great fish out of water, lay deserted along the beach. Nor were any of the tents occupied or any of the guns guarded. There were no fires. The men, in small arm-waving, gesticulating groups, strewn across the improvised bowling green, were looking toward the *Golden Hind.* The admiral was not among them—he was always easy to spot afar because of his polychromatic clothes. Either he had ordered them to assemble on the green (which was anything but green) or else, more ominously, *they* had ordered *him* to appear there.

Either way, it spelled trouble. George started to run down to the ships.

Francis Drake was in his cabin, which was crazily aslant in this high-and-dry vessel. He was troubled about something, and mumbling to himself. George he greeted with a glad nod; but it was upon the valet, faithful Diego, that most of his preparation fell. It quickly became clear that whatever he was rehearsing in his mind, whatever it was that caused his lips to move, this man Drake was engrossed not in thoughts of what he should *do* when he faced a hundred and fifty men, but in thoughts of what he should *wear.*

It was another of his contradictions that though he might denounce the pomps and vanities of this wicked world, still he maintained a wardrobe any king could envy. When Drake conducted prayers on deck, as he did every morning and again every evening, sometimes he told the hands that a humble and contrite heart was the greatest offering anyone could make to his Creator. Yet he ate off gold plate; he had musicians to play for him—he who couldn't even whistle the simplest air!— and he strutted in satin and silk. Had anyone found the temerity to tax him with this, and had Drake condescended to answer, that answer probably would have been that though it scraped his soul so to shine he believed he owed it to the queen's majesty, whose arm he was, whose hand. He often spoke of the queen that way, as though he was doing her a personal favor. It was one of the reasons—it and his own bland as-

180

sumption that he was above any council—that gave rise to the rumor that this man did actually have a commission from Elizabeth Tudor.

Now he examined the doublets, the hose, the bonnets, the capes—fussing, clucking his tongue—holding some of them against himself or at arm's length up to the light. He brushed, smoothed, lifted off lint, fretted, and commanded Diego to work with comb and needle and goffering-iron. He polished. He laid the pieces of apparel side by side, sometimes many of them, shifting and changing them as though they were flowers he arranged in a vase.

At last a military costume was chosen: this would screen the splendor of his breast with steel. In part he made up for that coverage by selecting a doublet with parti-colored puffed silk sleeves. He wore a white wired ruff, a morion, tooled leather gauntlets, canions slashed black and red, black base hose, scarlet leather half-boots. He was brave. The breast- and back-plates, like the morion, were brilliantly burnished. The breast-plate was fitted with a tapul, in the Spanish fashion. He fussed about this.

When he was ready to appear he sent his trumpeter, young John Brewer, to announce him. He took a last look at himself in the mirror, not an easy task in that slanted place.

"You'll attend me, Fitzwilliam."

"Aye."

Drake looked around, saw the desk, went to it, opened a drawer.

"I need a piece of paper . . ."

He took the first thing that came to hand, not looking at it, and crammed it beneath his breastplate, on the left side.

"Very well."

The day was, for that place, bright. Body armor was not usual among the English, even at court, and Francis Drake had all eyes before he even took his stance atop a small barrel of wine.

He started mildly, protesting that he had no natural eloquence such as was given to some, nor yet any training in rhetoric, being but a plain honest Englishman.

This the men liked and cheered.

Then Drake drew a long breath—and plunged into the most moving speech that George Fitzwilliam ever had heard. George had lived close to this man for a long while and supposed he knew all his talents, but this speech was astounding.

Drake at first pointed to none, neither friend nor foe, but treated them all as though they were equally guilty. He made it plain that thereafter no one was above manual service on any ship under his command, and he would listen to no wrangles about birth or precedence.

". . . for I must have the gentlemen to haul and draw with the mariners, and the mariners with the gentlemen . . . nothing else will do."

Neither should there be any further talk, even among themselves, about a council. *He* was the council, all there would ever be. He represented her gracious majesty the queen, who had given him no instruction to seek advice. No matter what others had done! Any who opposed him now were opposing their own lawful monarch, and he'd know how to handle them.

Easily, even scornfully, he announced that he was removing all officers from their posts. They would be restored when they had done his bidding.

Was that clear?

Nobody said anything.

Drake pointed to Thomas Doughty, as though indicating a snake against whom they should protect themselves. This man, he made it known, was a traitor and a spy, and the voyage could not go on with him. In addition, Doughty was a practitioner of witchcraft, who would have doomed them all. Drake then commanded—he didn't *ask*, he com-manded—that the man be tried, here and now. They must choose a jury amongst themselves. He, Francis Drake, agent of her highness Elizabeth, queen of England, would pass sentence. He would await their decision in his cabin; and he adjured them not to take too long about it, for the law could prove impatient.

His authorization? Did anyone question it? Well, no man might expect him to pass around a paper the queen herself had handed him. Such a paper was not for the vulgar. Yet, if they cared to hear it—

He reached under his breastplate, on the left side, the side of the heart. He drew out a blue envelope, and from this, reverently, took a piece of paper, which he unfolded.

"Know ye by these presents, that my trusted and truly-beloved servant, Francis Drake, Esquire—"

It was polysyllabic, and it was all-embracing, for it made him a little king over here at the other end of the world.

The admiral was touchy about his lack of education, and there were few, perhaps there were not any, who knew that he could not really read. If in the audience there had been some such they surely assumed that he had learned this testament by memory, as indeed he had. Only George Fitzwilliam knew that what Drake looked at as he spoke

182

was a sonnet intended for Anne of Okeland.

When the admiral finished there were tears in his eyes, and truly most of the men were weeping too. The admiral kissed the place where the signature would have been if there had been a signature, thus making them all feel, stingingly, the presence of a woman who was in fact very far away. He refolded the paper and put it back into its blue envelope. He started to stuff this under his breastplate on the left side, from whence he had taken it; but impulsively—it appeared—he changed his mind. He went to George and thrust the envelope into his hands.

"This is too precious a paper, it is too sacred a document, to be subjected to the push and jostle of a crowd," he said in a voice the farthest hand could hear. "Master Fitzwilliam, you will return it to my cabin, and wait for me there."

George saw the trick, but he had no choice. If he remained on the bowling green it was probable that he'd be picked as a juror. And it was unlikely that he would vote for the conviction of a gently born person on the evidence at hand. For as one of twelve, George would have dared— and surely none of the others would have dared—to stand out against the admiral.

With a sob Drake said: "Guard this as though it were your own baby. Now, go."

George was to be eliminated. He bowed his head in grave acknowledgment, took the envelope, and went back to the *Golden Hind,* where he rejoined Diego, who was putting away the rejected garments. George helped him.

"What they doing out there?"

"A little thing called murder. But they're doing it legally."

"Señor?"

"Never mind."

Part of the proceedings—when they were finished with the wardrobe—they watched from the deck. A jury was empaneled, a certain amount of evidence was heard, and another speech was made. Then the admiral returned to his ship.

"I hope that the absence of that particular paper from our desk didn't inconvenience you, Fitzwilliam," he said while Diego was unstrapping his armor.

"That's all right," George answered.

"It was part of the work of the Lord," Francis Drake pointed out. "And now, if you two will leave me for a while—"

He was getting down on his knees as they went out.

183

He called them back a little later and made known that he would remain in the cabin.

"I must not do anything to influence their decision," he said.

Two hours and fifty-four minutes later the men on the beach sent a committee to notify the admiral that Thomas Doughty had been duly tried by a jury, which had found him guilty as charged. What was the wish of the queen's representative?

"Death," said Francis Drake.

32

Diego Was Bewildered

AUGUST 17 THEY SAILED from that abode of gloom and on the 24th they arrived at the eastern mouth of the passage between the seas. The men were to call this—though never within the admiral's hearing—the Tunnel to Hell.

It is notable that this name was applied *afterward*, for the Hell was not the strait but its western end. Magellan Strait itself they found a not unpleasant place. The first few days it was wide, and if the hills on either side were stark there were sometimes fires and once they saw a few Indians fishing. The second afternoon they stopped at an island they called Penguin Island after the curious bird they found there in great numbers. The penguin walked upright, and it appeared to wag its absurd stubs of wings only for comic effect, as a jester his bauble. It had no feathers, only a thick black and white down, like that of a gosling. It was slow, and easily slaughtered. In that one afternoon the mariners estimated that they had clubbed to death two thousand —the smallest being about ten pounds in weight—yet the beach was still black with them.

Two days later they rounded a bend and the strait narrowed at some points to not more than a mile and a half across.

It made for silence, that closeness, and the men had time to reflect upon what had happened to Thomas Doughty.

They had to proceed with caution; they always hove-to at night. Still, the strait was passed through in sixteen days.

They came out into the great, the fabled South Sea—and were hit by what could only have been the wrath of God. For a month the water was mad, the air in a frenzy. Spray stung them like the studs on a scourge. They shortened so much canvas that by the third day and for all the rest of that terrible time they were being driven under bare sticks.

It was the *direction* in which they were driven that frightened them. The wind was north-northwest, and they were helpless before it, three cockleshells implacably pushed south. This was the end of the world, down here. The only thing below them was Terra Incognita Australis, upon the spikes of which they might at any moment be pounded to pieces.

Marigold vanished one night. They never did learn what had happened to her.

Drake had prepared a stone monument for the western end of the Magellan Strait, meaning with this to claim all that country for Queen Elizabeth. He never had a chance to erect it. Even after *Golden Hind* and *Elizabeth* had staggered back to the place from whence they had emerged, the weather still was so bad that this ceremony had to be postponed. Another storm struck them. *Golden Hind* rode out this second blow, but *Elizabeth* took refuge in the strait and was never seen again. They waited for more than a week, keeping watch. At last they set a northern course. The fleet of five that a year ago had sailed out of Plymouth now was one. The men, who had numbered more than a hundred and sixty, were less than eighty.

The weather cleared, and the wind steadied, blowing clean from the south, so that they fairly bowled along. The health of the crew, badly strained in those weeks of storm, waxed better every day. Other than ships and fighting men, the only thing they lacked was water. They had wine, but they craved water, which proved to be hard to come by in this wild country where the rivers sank into the sand before they could reach the sea.

They lost their master gunner, Great Nele, a Dane—as distinguished from Little Nele, who was a Fleming—on one of their attempts to fill the casks. It was at an island named Mocha, and the landing party was attacked by Indians. Great Nele was killed without linger, an arrow through his breast. The giant Diego, struck in the side of the neck, was whirled completely around and slammed against George, who half-hauled and half-carried him back to the boat, where he fainted from loss of blood as George clucked over him like a mother. The admiral himself was hit in the face, just beneath the right eye. They were lucky to get away.

Again, near La Serena, a party of Spanish horse captured one of their number, a lad named John Minivy, who was slow about getting back to the boat. The Spaniards cut off

185

Minivy's head and paraded it on the end of a pike up and down the beach until sunset, when they carried it away. The admiral sent a party ashore after dark to bury the headless corpse.

In neither of these cases did they get a drop of water.

It would seem that the incident near La Serena was not reported overland, for when they arrived at Valparaiso they astounded everybody, and took over the one vessel there, a coaster named *Capitana*, with the greatest of ease.

In the *Capitana* were 1,770 jars of wine, a large number of cedar boards, and 24,000 pesos of gold from Valdivia. They took it all, including the vessel itself. However, one seaman had escaped and swum ashore to give the alarm, so that when they looted the village they did not get much.

They sailed December 6.

From December 22 to January 19, as George duly noted in Francis Drake's diary, they watered, wooded, and generally recovered at Salada Bay. They brought up from below and mounted several brass culverins. They also brought up the parts of a pinnace, which was assembled and launched. Their chief purpose in putting in at Salada Bay, however, and their only purpose in remaining there so long, was the hope of being rejoined by either *Marigold* or *Elizabeth*. But nothing like this happened.

They resumed their northward course.

At Tarapaca, in an unlocked storehouse, they found two men asleep with three thousand pesos of silver just brought down from Potosi on llamas. These llamas were the funniest beasts yet: bushy things with long skinny necks, an expression of perpetual astonishment on their faces. Also in the storehouse was a large quantity of *charquí*, beef that had been cut into long thin strips and dried in the sun. They took it and later ate it, as they did the llamas.

February 5 they dropped in at Arica, where they seized thirty-seven bars of silver, five hundred pesos in silver coins, and three hundred jars of wine. Always wine!

Callao, the port of Lima, was a sleepy little place, though the harbor was crowded with ships. These were small ships, all of them empty. The governor made a great ado about pursuit, but Drake shook him off.

It was at Callao that they heard about the *Cacafuego.*

Cacafuego was not her real name, Heaven forbid. Spanish is a language that cultivates its obscenity to such an extent as to make much of it untranslatable. "Spitfire" was as near as George could get, and nobody thought that amusing. The Spaniards were indefatigable nicknamers, and

186

since each vessel should have a formal title, preferably religious, it was expected that each should also have a playful one. Columbus' *Niña* was properly the *Santa Clara*, while his flagship, *Santa Maria*, more often was called by the men *La Gallega*. The *Cacafuego's* real name was *Nuestra Señora de la Concepción*.

This ship, privately owned, bound for Panama, was said to bulge with treasure. For more than two weeks they stalked her, passing smaller prizes, and late in the afternoon of March 1, on a flat sea, they raised her. Before full darkness—what resistance could she make without so much as a pistol on board?—they took her.

Though there had been no fighting, the confusion was great. Mariners were whooping with joy after a glimpse of the treasures below. Passengers and officers of the Spanish ship were pleading for their lives.

Amid all the commotion there were two men who were silent, below deck on the *Golden Hind*. George Fitzwilliam, who would be responsible for the classification, evaluation, and stowage of all those immense riches, took no part in the celebration, for Diego was dying.

That Cimarron was a bewildered man. He had been struck by an arrow shot by some red man he never saw; this was graspable: Diego's whole life had been a fight. But the later part of that life—the years in England and Ireland as Drake's valet, the months at sea—were beyond his understanding. Nor could he love his master, though he conscientiously tried to do so; for he had been a chief, a sort of king, among his own people, and he was not attuned to act as lackey. Drake had tired of him, for though Diego was picturesque he was also stupid. It had been tacitly agreed that if Diego survived the Mocha wound, and if *Golden Hind* should go anywhere near Panama, he might be put ashore and given a chance to seek out his own savage hillpeople. Perhaps that was why Diego had lasted so long. He had been very sturdy, and he took a long time dying.

His friend George Fitzwilliam was with him. Nobody thought of these two, the excitement being so great. The shouts and stamping, the thud of money chests, came faintly from above.

George had tried to persuade the Cimarron to think about the welfare of his soul, the future life; but Diego shook a feeble head. The savage had been converted to Christianity largely because of politeness—it had seemed to mean so much to the admiral!—and he never had made any try to survey its mysteries. He knew now that he was about to

187

die and that he would not see his own people again, and his eyes begged George not to spend the last precious hours talking about transfiguration and things like that. So George had fallen silent.

The hilarity on deck continued until almost dawn. Diego did not. "*Hasta luego,*" he whispered at last, a little after midnight. His eyes rolled up, and he was done.

The men sang up above, and they talked exultantly of the things that they would do when they got home, as they passed jacks of rum back and forth. For they were very happy: the voyage had been made.

But George Fitzwilliam, down below, wept by the side of his dead friend's hammock.

33
Hangover and Hard Work

IT WAS A GODLIKE OCCUPATION—or so some men would have esteemed it—to sit in judgment over such a mass of treasure: to count and recount, stack and restack, the 1,300-odd bars of silver, to seal the fourteen huge chests after attesting to the weight of their contents, to class according to size the pearls, nuggets, opals, diamonds, rubies, and to pile the plate in great, glowing, exact stacks. It was also tiring. The air below deck was fetid; the light was poor. They had run out of wax candles, and George had only tallow ones. The realization that if he desired he could mount these in priceless gem-studded candlesticks did not in any way lessen their stink or the strain that they caused his eyes.

The admiral positively forbade that the performance of George's other routine duties, the keeping of the diary and the teaching of Spanish, be conducted on deck, where George might get some fresh air. Drake's reason, it could be supposed, was reluctance to let the hands see that somebody else did his writing or that he needed instruction in anything at all.

However, he prized George; and he was not a cruel man, so he promised readily enough to throw George's way whatever outside chores might present themselves. This was why they called George from the counting-house when a bark was sighted moving south.

She was slow, and looked heavy, and she hugged the shore.

After a few days in the company of the *Cacafuego*—

188

days of hangover and hard work—they had turned that vessel loose, together with her crew and passengers, though with very little of her original rich cargo. They had not then made a course for the Gulf of Panama, as no doubt the Spaniards would expect them to do, but instead had headed for the coast of Nicaragua, which they raised March 16. They could hardly hope to gain more riches. Their concern now was to get away.

Drake ordered around the pinnace and put George in charge. Then he went back to his cabin.

Four hours later George confronted him there.

"She's a coaster. Belongs to a man named Rodrigo Tello. She wouldn't be of any use to us."

"Gold?"

"None. No silver either."

"We don't have room for any more silver anyway."

"No pearls, no plate."

"What *is* she carrying? She looks crank in the bows."

"She's out of a place called Nicola, on the Rio de Pamar, and she's headed for Panama with a cargo of lard."

"Ugh!"

"Also sarsaparilla. That might be good for the men."

"All right. But don't be long about it."

"Also a large supply of honey and of dried maize."

"Bah! Is that all?"

"That's all in the hold, sir. But in the cabin—"

"What about the cabin? We don't need any prisoners."

"These two might interest you; they come from Acapulco."

"Um-m. I know all I need to know about that port. I'd like to burn the shipping there, to prevent it from chasing us across the sea, but the officers of the *Cacafuego* said it's too strong."

"Aye. These two men were waiting there for a new governor of the Philippines to come up from Panama, but it seems that this personage—his name by the way, is Don Gonzalo Ronquillo—has elected to sail directly from Panama, so these two are on their way—"

Drake sprang to his feet.

"You mean they're—*pilots?*"

George nodded, grinning.

"The best in this part of the world. Alonso Sanchez Colchero and Martin de Aquirre, complete with charts."

Francis Drake rolled his eyes up and threw out his arms.

"Prayers! We must thank God for this!"

"A good idea," George agreed. "But it's near sundown,

189

and we don't want those pilots to drift out of sight, now do we?"

In his triple capacity—historian, interpreter, navigator—George sat in at each of the conferences that followed. He was an admirer of Nuña da Silva—that caustic, cantankerous old Portugee who had been sent ashore with the *Cacafuego*, being of no use in this ocean. And he found Colchero and De Aquirre of the same class: men learned and at the same time practical, and stubbornly independent. Spain and Portugal for many years had striven to keep their sea lore to themselves. De Aquirre and Colchero, like Da Silva, belonged to a privileged group: artists who were at the same time adepts, holders of secrets, nautical high priests. Theirs was a knowledge that properly should have been universal, and they knew this. They might serve an enemy of their country, but they could not be forced. Drake was anxious to have one or both of them accompany the expedition west, and he offered large cash sums, also privileged positions in England afterward. Baffled by their bland refusal, furious because he couldn't get his way, he turned to threats, and blustered in such a manner as to disgust his secretary, who had never before seen him so wild, so vulgar. Colchero and De Aquirre remained unmoved.

Yet these pilots were not mum, especially with George in whom they recognized a kindred spirit. And all their maps, charts, and rutters or coast-books, together with their sealed sailing directions, were legitimate loot, to be held for reference. When at last, after several days of abuse, these inflexible men were put aboard of a Panama-bound coaster, hailed for that very purpose, the officers of *Golden Hind* had a much better idea of where they were and how they might get out.

It would not be the part of wisdom to spread sail for the other side of the South Sea at this time, since such a voyage would mean arrival in the Spice Islands at the height of the typhoon season. Several months should be allowed to elapse. Here was an opportunity to search the coast of California for the western end of that interoceanic passage, the other end of which Frobisher already had found—or thought he had found. This was a project close to George Fitzwilliam's heart, though the admiral seemed indifferent. As George had told Sir John Crofts, Drake never was interested in any enterprise that led *away from* the Spaniards and their accumulated gold, his lodestone. Nevertheless, and since there was no other way of passing the weeks, they turned north.

First, almost as though absent-mindedly, they took the town of Guatulco, Guatemala. It was a miserable, flea-bitten place and George could see no reason for molesting it, since they didn't even need wood or water. They picked up no shipping, neither did they get any news. Most of the inhabitants had decamped, and the few they captured—government officials who had refused to fly—stolidly resisted all questioning, howsoever streaked with threat. Drake was red with rage and indignation.

The mariners remained three days in Guatulco, and it was not likely that any of them ever would boast to his grandchildren about this feat-at-arms. The sole reason for it that George could see—and George was outspoken in his dislike of the deed, further irritating the admiral—was its effect upon the hands who had been waxing restless. Things, in truth, had come *too* easily: there had been no fighting, and the men yearned for violence as they might have yearned for women. So they were permitted to sack the town.

Poor grubby sunbaked little Guatulco! They all but pulled it to pieces. Though they already had too much and though it wasn't very good, being somewhat sour, they took all the wine that they could find. Though they had no use for the bell from the church tower, and the labor was considerable, they unhitched and carried it off—only to throw it overboard a few days later. The church itself, easily the most pretentious building in town, they ransacked. They slashed the paintings and the altar cloth, and spat upon them. They splintered each saint's image. Using a maul, they battered the crucifix, and with this same tool they cracked the altar stone. One wag donned the chasuble, in which he paraded, now and then blowing his nose upon it. He was loudly cheered.

George, sickened by this exhibition, appealed to the admiral; but Francis Drake was curt, cold, and refused to interfere.

"They need the exercise," he said cynically.

California was a disappointment, as were the Californians —a glum unresponsive pack of beggars, drooping, dirty, not at all like the savages of Patagonia.

Though the mariners lived in such close quarters, and though they were farther from home than ever before, discipline was not relaxed: the admiral saw to that. Yet George himself, in the privacy of the cabin, and now that Diego was gone, became increasingly critical of the chief. Thus, when after only a few weeks of scouting the California coast the admiral gave orders to make about in search of a haven,

191

George noisily remonstrated. George knew he couldn't win—for by this time Francis Drake thought himself infallible—but he believed that he should at least put himself on record as having been opposed to turning away from the first chance anybody had known to seek out the far end of Frobisher's passage; and when Drake suggested that he write into the record that the swing-around had been forced upon them by snow and adverse winds, George flatly refused.

"I had to do that sort of thing when I was a diplomat. Not now."

"You know, of course, that I can have some scribe rewrite the thing? Scribes are cheap."

"They always have been."

"You should think about when we get back."

"*If* we get back."

"That's a harsh word, Master Fitzwilliam."

"One of the harshest in the language. A truly *laconic* word. You've heard the story of the laconic reply?"

Guardedly: "Well . . ."

George went ahead all the same.

"Old Philip of Macedonia, the father of Alexander the Great, was a very fierce fighter. He didn't care for quarter. Once he was trying to bully the people of Laconia with an army at their borders. 'If I enter Laconia you shall all be exterminated,' he wrote. And they replied with that one famous word: 'If.' That's what we mean when they say that a thing is 'laconic.' "

Sensitive as he was about classical references, Drake could appreciate this story; and he came as near as he was ever likely to come to smiling. Nevertheless they continued south. Drake had no intention of getting beyond the range of the Spanish charts simply for the sake of a possible alley among the icebergs.

They found a fine bay, guarded on the north by a long rocky point, and there they remained for some weeks, refitting, careening. There was a great deal of fog, also many seals. They were comfortable there, but the labor took a long time. In order that the *Golden Hind* might be beached for scraping, every scrap of water, wine, food, and treasure had to be hauled out of her, also all the guns; and afterward, of course, it all had to be put back.

They broke up for firewood a small vessel they'd brought from Guatulco, having scarcely enough hands left to man *Golden Hind* herself.

They left the magnificent bay July 23, 1579.

None of them questioned the existence of Frobisher's north-

192

west passage, but only George had been eager to seek it out for the sake of science. The others, after long exposure to tropical suns and at the first touch of chill, were glad to hear a southing order for the Moluccas, sometimes called the Spice Islands.

The trip was long, hot and uneventful, the wind being with them all the way, the seas smooth. They saw no other vessel, and only faintly glimpsed a few flat scorched atolls.

The sultan of Ternate was a grumpy man, very fat, with a disagreeable expression. George would not have trusted him as far as he could spit, but Francis Drake appeared avid for some sort of contract or treaty, and they arranged at last to buy, with silver, six tons of cloves.

Repairing always, patching, scraping, laboriously holding themselves together, they built a fort on a place they called Crab Island; and there they lived, somehow, for a little while.

They did not seek new scenes; rather they avoided them. The men were weak, worn, and they had very little powder left.

George figured out—from the investments, the number of individual lays, including two of his own, and the value by his own estimate of the treasure, minus the pay of the crew —that *if* they got back (that laconic word again!) the voyage would prove to have paid about 4,700 per cent.

Already they had done what the maddest men never dreamed of. What if they had passed the land of Lochac? What if they did miss Ophir? They couldn't conceivably carry anything more.

They were wary. They tiptoed, avoiding all passers.

The night of January 9, 1580, far from any inhabited place, they struck a reef. Wind and seas were driving them farther on. They prayed, and some swore. Wildly they dumped cannons, also three tons of cloves. Then the wind fell off, the sea subsided, and *Golden Hind* slithered back into deep water.

March 26 they set a course for the Cape of Good Hope. By the end of June they were back in the Atlantic.

September 26, 1580, they sailed into Plymouth Sound.

For months they had been as furtive as thieves, hailing no sail; for they were no longer armed, and they were very weak, slow too, their bottom being slubbered over with barnacles, their hold crammed with metal.

Any pirate could have snapped them up, the greatest prize in history.

Even when they entered the English Channel they re-

193

mained coy. Yet the boat they encountered as they started into Plymouth Sound was no enemy. She was small, fat, clumsy, capacious: a fisher.

"Ahoy!"

"Ahoy yourself! What ship is that?"

Drake made no answer, being too eager to ask his own questions. With hands cupped, he called:

"Does the queen's majesty still live?"

"The—The queen?"

"Queen Elizabeth, dolt! She's alive?"

"Why shouldn't she be?"

Drake exhaled and leaned against the rail, relieved. That was all he needed to know. He never had sweated or trembled like this in battle. He was as weak as a baby, and could scarcely stand.

But another thought struck him, and his hands went to his mouth again, while to his face came the frown so many men had learned to fear.

"Tell me, what's Devonshire coming to when men make sail with nets on the Lord's day? You should hang your heads in shame!"

Those in the crumster were puzzled.

"This ain't the Sabbath, if your worship please."

"Don't call it that!"

("Sabbath" Captain Drake scorned as Jewish, while "Sunday" he believed to be of classical origin.)

"Well, it ain't the Lord's day either, then."

"Why, you fools! This is the twenty-fifth of September."

"No, sir. It's the twenty-sixth, and it's a Monday."

They might have gone on for some time this way, had not George intervened.

"The man's right, sir. We went around the world from east to west, and when we crossed the one hundred and eightieth meridian of longitude, a day dropped out of the calendar. That was last year, September 2, by my calculations. I told you at the time, sir, but you tut-tutted it."

"And—this is truly—"

"Monday, September 26, sir."

"Blessings be! I do not have to come back to England and see men setting forth on the Lord's day. Call the hands together, Fitzwilliam. We'll have a service."

"Aye, aye, sir."

"But first get them to grease the anchor cables. And I want my plum-colored doublet laid out, and the dark blue velvet bonnet. You understand?"

"Aye, aye, sir."

194

34

Home Is the Hero

IF THE OYSTER COULD BE DEFINED as a fish built like a nut, Sir Laurence Godden might be called a man built like an apple. He was round; he was red, yet cool; he gleamed. He had taken some time to ripen, and might also take a long while rotting, for he would do this only in spots at first. He was bland, but he could be mildly acidulous. He even had, in the middle of an otherwise bald head, a stiff uptwisted fillup of hair that suggested a stem.

He smiled soapily.

"You must find it very tame here now, Master Fitzwilliam?"

George shrugged, a movement made supple by practice. Sir Laurence—attended by three other neighbors, each appropriately obsequious—was first cousin and political secretary to the earl; and since he would not call at Okeland merely to congratulate Sir John on the return of his son-in-law, and since he had already hinted at a soon-to-occur vacancy in Parliament, there seemed no shadow of doubt that he was feeling out Anne's father for the post. Now that George was back, Sir John had both the time and the money to go to Parliament, something that for years he had dearly wished to do. George summoned a deprecatory grin.

"Oh, not so tame," he murmured.

It was good to be rich. George had noted the change right away. More caps and bonnets were lifted to him—and lifted higher. From the lowest laborer grumbling over his wage, which had never before been half so high, to the very earl himself who had sent his own kinsman, the attitude of others was different. Even his wife, though never a natterer, was hushed in his presence if others were about. Just now, for instance, though she bent over her embroidery at the far end of the great-hall, a picture of ladylike industry, George had no doubt that she heard every word.

Sir John Crofts leaned forward.

"But—Wentworth?"

Peter Wentworth of Lillingstone-Lovell might be a hard man to dislodge. He was a rabid puritan, eloquent, troublesome, tiresome, tart. A champion, and surely fearless, he sometimes embarrassed his fellow members of the House of Commons by the stridency of his speech, as he nettled his

195

neighbors here in sleepy Northampton by the fervor of his religious views.

"We hope to persuade Wentworth to resign on the ground of ill health."

"Why, the man's as strong as an ox!"

Sir Laurence still smiled, but his gooseberry eyes had gone opaque.

"There are, uh, ways of doing this," he said.

He finished his brandy and smacked his lips. It was good French brandy, though not so good as they should have had in their new circumstances, George reflected. George hoped to lay down a truly great cellar.

"It would in part depend," Sir Laurence continued, "on what substitute we had. If this was a man who'd have the confidence of every gentleman in the district, a man of outstanding integrity and ability, why, Peter Wentworth might be ousted. And we think we have found such a man. That's the reason we have come here this afternoon."

He turned full upon George.

"Master Fitzwilliam, would you consent to stand for the seat?"

The slow hum of an Okeland afternoon did not for an instant cease, but George's breathing did. There had been no hint of this, no clue previously given by the visitors.

Sir Laurence when he spoke for his cousin did not look for a refusal. He stared fixedly at George.

George had to think fast. If he refused the offer or even appeared to pause, he would incur the displeasure of the shire's hereditary nobleman, a displeasure that could mean shillings and pence, privileges too. On the other hand, if he accepted, it would break Sir John's heart.

Anne's hands as she leaned over the embroidery frame had ceased to move. Her maids, no doubt so instructed, worked on without a whisper. Anne's breath, George was sure, was caught up like his own. Her father, blinkless, had not yet fully realized what it was Sir Laurence said.

George smiled a little. He fished a letter from his purse. It had come by royal messenger that morning, and George had not intended to tell of it until he was ready to depart for London. But here was an emergency.

"I am most deeply touched." He was urbane, resuming his Madrid manner. "But when the queen's majesty speaks, even though it be through one of her ministers, a good subject's days are not his own. I have been summoned to London, sir, by Master Secretary Walsingham."

"Ah?"

196

"He urges haste, in the name of his august mistress. It could be that all they wish is mine own account of the late circumnavigation," went on George, who knew that they ardently desired to get their hands on the diary he had kept for Francis Drake. "On the other hand, it may be their wish to send me somewhere on a mission. I must hold myself open for such an assignment. His lordship your cousin, sir, I am sure will understand."

"Um ... Yes. In that case ... Well."

With the stirrup cup—it was served in glasses and deeply impressed the visitors—they were more relaxed, talking amiably. Anne and Aunt Sylvia came out and curtseyed. It was all very nicely done. Sir John had recovered and was the good host again, though it was George who helped Sir Laurence into saddle.

"Aye, tame, I should think," Sir Laurence wheezed. "I could certainly think it would seem so, after all you've been through."

As George had expected, the moment the men were gone Anne pounced upon him, demanding that she be taken to London too. This, curtly, he refused. The argument was suspended at supper, largely out of respect for Sir John Crofts, but it was renewed as soon as they were in their bedchamber.

Anne did not even pause long enough to praise him for having won the offer of a seat. All she could think of was London, and she actually *scolded* him—she who in ordinary circumstances was careful to keep her voice down—for having failed to tell her about that letter from Francis Walsingham.

She brushed aside his cavil that he might not be able to attend her for more than a few hours once the city was reached, and that she, having no relatives there, would be unguarded.

"I'm unguarded here!"

"Save for thy father, a steward, two assistant stewards, two gardeners, and four field hands, besides the women."

"Pooh!"

"Also, London's a much more perilous place than Northampton."

"Pooh!"

He pointed out that he might be sent away immediately, even somewhere abroad. He was a public figure now. He was available.

"But thou'lt see the queen, at least?"

"It seems likely."

"Then why shouldn't I?"

"Because thou hast not been commanded to appear. 'Tis not the custom to drop in on an anointed monarch as though she was a neighbor in the country. She—Well, she's not much to look at anyway."

"Not like the French woman at Sheffield, I take it?"

It was the first mention of Mary Stuart since George's return, and it came explosively—a shock. He had kept his ears open to little avail: England appeared to have forgotten "the strange guest" although George sensed that she was, as the saying went, in every man's mind, in no man's mouth.

Anne must have been overwrought to let slip that name. It was dark, and he could not see her.

But he could see, by the side of the bed where it rested on a stool, the December 1577-September 1588 diary of Francis Drake. A scrupulously honest narrative, signed at several of the more telling places by the admiral himself—for he could write his name, though with difficulty—it would be found to differ in sundry important respects from the official version of the voyage as compounded of the carefully pruned reports of the admiral and his officers. In the hands of Spanish spies it could be a bombshell. Spain and England were still, on paper, at peace; and Spain had a strong claim for the recovery of the loot, a claim that it might be hard to deny before the world *if* it was bolstered by such a document as this. The treasure was immense, and undoubtedly Elizabeth and her ministers would do everything possible to keep it in England, among themselves. But they wouldn't risk war—or at least the queen wouldn't, Burghley wouldn't, or Walsingham. The diary assuredly should have been sent to Whitehall by messenger immediately after the *Golden Hind* had dropped anchor at Plymouth. That this had not been done, that in the excitement George Fitzwilliam had been permitted to slip away with it under his arm, surely must have brought about a shrill scolding; and George suspected that Captain Drake, hero though he was, had had his ears boxed. The summons of that morning had been peremptory. George was to prepare himself instanter and was directed to wait only for one thing: the arrival, soon after the messenger, of a band of men-at-arms. Nothing else should delay him. He had not told Anne of this.

Now she stirred.

"But *why?*" she whispered fiercely. "Why should one piece of paper be permitted to stand against the word of many men?"

" 'Tis more than one piece of paper. There's hundreds there."

"Well then, why should hundreds?"

"Because, my sweet, there are so many men who believe that ink can't lie. This is absurd, but they do. Their fellow men they might not credit, even in chorus—well, *especially* in chorus—but if it's writ on paper, they think, it simply must be true."

"Nonsense! Now if you'd only—"

"Sh-sh-sh!"

George had felt no fear of a thief while he slept, for the window was too high to be entered from the back of a horse, even if the rider stood in saddle, as once George had done; and though many things had lately been planted in the garden there was no vine set to climb this particular wall. The only way to enter the room he shared with his wife was through that in which her father bedded, and Sir John was a light sleeper.

But Sir John was not asleep now. The sobbing was so low, so slight, that they barely heard it. No doubt Sir John had supposed *them* asleep, and even so he was holding in his grief as best he could, being ashamed of himself.

It was an eerie sound, that sobbing. Utterly still, they lay for a long while listening to it. Parliament had meant a lot to Sir John Crofts.

35

All of Impulse

ANNE WAS SILENT ALL THE NEXT DAY, and it was a silence that perturbed her husband. Though he had many things to look after, having been home for such a short time, George did not venture far from the house, for he was conscious of the diary in the bedroom. He wished that the soldiers would come and he could be on his way. The sooner he went the sooner he'd get back, and the sooner he got back the better. There were preparations for winter that clamored to catch his attention. There were, too, neighbors who pressed invitations upon him: they were eager to hear the tale of the voyage from his own lips. There was Terence Weddell, who had returned from the Continent. Most of all, there was that never-failing wonder to be enjoyed: his wife.

So he fretted. And when no men came he announced angrily that he would depart at dawn, alone.

Anne made no comment at supper, nor yet later in bed. This in itself was odd, a disturbing circumstance. George did not sleep well that night.

The morning was different. It was all sparkle and nip, with smoke columns, straight-stripped, standing without wobble against a cobalt sky, a morning so still and clear that your throat caught at the feel of it against your face and you half believed you could hear God breathe.

George bussed his wife. He noted with some concern that she wore a brown cheverel dress, short in the skirt, a hat that matched, no ruff but a simple white fall, and shoes, as though she too were about to depart. Did she mean to be prepared, in case he changed his mind and asked her to go with him? Was she, who so seldom wept, intent upon trying tears? Would she storm?

Nothing happened. She only smiled up at him, bidding him to ride with care.

He bowed before Aunt Sylvia, shook hands with Sir John, and said a grateful farewell to the servants, every one of whom was out to Godspeed him.

Carefully he worked the diary, the sheets of which had been bound between stiff leather boards, into the right saddlebag.

He mounted, waved, and was off:

> *"Come away, come sweet love!*
> *The golden morning breaks.*
> *All the earth, and all the air,*
> *Of love and pleasure speaks."*

Just before he reached the edge of the small wood he must rim before he came to the Crossed Keys, he turned in saddle. This was the highest point of land for many miles around.

There were not many in the group before the door of Okeland now, and he was disheartened to see that Anne no longer was there. Of course she had many household duties, but he had hoped that she would remain for that final wave.

But it didn't matter, he told himself.

He tried the lay again:

> *"Come away, come sweet love!*
> *Do not in vain adorn*
> *Beauty's grace that should rise*
> *Like to the naked morn—"*

It was no use. Even with a lute he would have been in poor voice. Perhaps the wood by his side depressed him. It was the same in which he had hidden after skewering Antonio Salvo, and the fright that he felt that early evening sometimes would come back to him, chilling his blood. He owned that wood now, having bought it from Weddell, and for years he had meant to cut it down, to use the land for pasture, enclosing it. Farmers, he supposed, like housewives, always had things they *planned* to do. If ever by chance they did get them all done they wouldn't be housewives any longer—or farmers.

The wood was at his east, so that it blocked the early sun, making the track dark. A breeze moved through it, stirring the leaves—still on the trees but sered at the edges—so that they whispered together, a susurrant sound.

As by instinct, George's hand went to the right saddlebag, just forward of his knee. Once the hand was there, he consciously used it, undoing the flap, half-withdrawing the diary, patting this, carefully replacing it.

He was worried about Anne. He'd been churlish. Should he turn back, even now? No. If there was to be trouble on this trip—and he felt in his bones that there would be—he should take it alone, not dragging in his wife.

Perhaps he should have waited for the men-at-arms? Then he might have brought Anne who could have one of her women with her, probably Helen, her favorite.

But—turn back before all those servants?

To his right, fields fell away to the west, bright with dew, an opalescent sheen. But to the left was the wood, its leaves sibilant, shadows close-packed. Queerly, as his steed paced past, George had the conviction that he was being watched from that wood. He could see nothing there and he could hear nothing but the furtive conference of leaves, yet he loosed the sword in his scabbard and once again he felt for and assured himself of the safety of the diary.

Clear at last of the shadow of the wood, and about to get upon the Market Harborough road—no highway, but better than the track he presently followed—he heaved a sigh of relief. For he no longer felt that he was being watched.

Surely, at least, there was nobody in the Crossed Keys. That shabby inn had been closed for more than two years, he had heard, though from its look it might have slumbered for twenty. How could any building in so short a time get to look so desolate? It had fallen apart bit by weary bit, crumbling to the soft sponginess of rot.

Even decay can fascinate. George reined, shaking his head. He had no fondness for the Crossed Keys, but he felt impelled to pay it the tribute of a sigh. Slowly he rode around

201

it. And slowly he went away, shaking his head again, along the route to Biggleswade.

He had gone no more than a mile from the inn when he rounded a curve to find himself confronted by two men. They were mounted, facing him; and so narrow was the way that they blocked it. One held a drawn sword, a very long one. The other held a pistol, which he pointed at George.

"Here it is," George muttered, almost pleased to see that his presentiment had been well based.

He came to a halt, perforce.

"What the Devil do *you* want?" he cried.

In the course of his travels, as in the course of many hours spent riding over the fields, George Fitzwilliam's face had come to look as though it had been stained with walnut juice, and there was little that sun and dust and rain could do to it now. Nevertheless he had not even thought of undertaking a journey without his loo or half-mask. He no longer needed this, as when he'd just come out of a Spanish prison; but it remained a habit, as also perhaps a mark, an outward sign, of his gentility.

The men who confronted him also were masked, but their masks were large and long, covering the whole face: all George could see was eyes.

Their clothes, he was quick to note, were not cut in Spanish fashion. Moreover, the one who held the sword, and who now spoke, had no trace of Spanish accent. Foreigners, George supposed, would attract too much attention out here in the country. King Philip's spy-master in London, whoever he was, controlled a large purse, and he could afford the service of natives.

"Get down," the swordsman said.

So that was it? They wanted the horse, not George himself? They knew what was in the right-hand saddlebag?

For a wild instant George cursed his servants. They had all been there to bid him farewell, true, but it was the previous night that he'd disclosed his plan to start for London at dawn, and one of them could have slipped this snippet of news to somebody who lurked out of doors. However, that wouldn't account for this accoster's knowledge that the diary was in a saddlebag. Until just before he mounted, George had meant to stuff the thing under his doublet.

He'd been seen, then. And a message had been flashed, somehow, to these skulkers.

The wood! Some member of the band who had climbed a tree, and who was possessed of sharp eyesight, could have

overlooked the scene before the Okeland Manor door, drawing his own conclusions. These conclusions such a man
might well have verified when George, riding past the wood,
had taken another peek at the diary. And he could have
signaled this information to the men who now confronted
George.

George didn't stir, but continued to regard the two coldly,
his lip curled. As in Nombre de Dios, he reckoned, arrogance was the best policy.

They looked formidable. George had little knowledge of
mounted swordplay, as the man who addressed him might
have. The other, the one with the pistol, seemed less sure
of himself. The pistol was heavy: he held it in both hands.
The barrel was made of iron, very thick, very wide, a
small cannon. The match was lighted, burning well in the
crisp morning air, while the striker was drawn back. The
man's forefinger was on the trigger.

They were fallible, those machines, and this one did not
faze George. At least half the time they failed to fire. At
best they wouldn't shoot more than a few yards. At worst,
what with their huge touchholes, they were likely to flare
back into the face of the man who held them—a possibility
of which this particular scoundrel seemed well aware.
George believed that the pistol was shown largely in the
hope of intimidating him, and that the man with the drawn
sword was capable of dealing with this situation by himself. Even so, George would have wheeled and galloped
back toward Okeland, except for two things.

His mare, Alberta, was fresh but not fast, whereas these
robbers were extremely well mounted; and since there was
a third one back in the wood it could be assumed that part
of the beauty of their plan lay in the fact that this man
could cut off George's retreat.

At that very moment George heard hoofbeats behind him.

"I said 'dismount.' "

"Why, so you did," George agreed.

Alberta was a willing beast, but as she was no racer
neither was she a hunter. He did not know how she might re-
spond if he rode her across fields. In any event, he must not
let himself be struck from behind. That approaching horseman sounded very close, back there. George turned.

He saw Anne. She smiled radiantly; and she was followed on an ass, by Helen her maid, and two large hampers
of clothing.

"Stop there!" George yelled.

She had seen the men now, and she no longer smiled. She

203

reined to a halt, obedient. Helen too stopped. Probably they were out of the range of the pistol, but he couldn't be sure.

It had been his thought to draw sword and charge, but the presence of his wife changed that. A madheaded scheme anyway, he nodded thoughtfully, grimly. He started to dismount.

His foot slipped in the stirrup. Alberta, always a twitchy steed, shied. And the pistoleer fired.

Whether the man, like Alberta, had acted from nervousness, or whether he truly thought that George was about to resist, made no difference. That shot for an instant obliterated the rest of the world. A mass of gray-white smoke filled the air, which was made acrid with the smell of gunpowder. George felt as though he had been hit in the chest with a pike. He went backward, over Alberta's rump, to the ground.

The mare reared, screaming, made panicky by the shot.

Stunned, but retaining his senses, George scrambled to his feet. He drew sword and slapped Alberta's flank with the flat.

"Away, girl! *Away!"*

The mare wheeled, jumped a hedge, bolted across a hayfield.

And the robbers did just what George had hoped that they would do. They went after Alberta.

George brushed himself. He did not sheath. He made a brief bow to his wife. He rather admired her daring and ingenuity, for it was clear that she thought that if she surprised him from behind, dressed for travel, and packed and attended, he would let her come along rather than go back to the manor house and face all those servants. But of course he couldn't let this admiration show. A lesson was called for.

"Well met, my dear. This markes me more than ever determined that thou'lt not go with me until proper preparations can be made. We'll return now, and I'll wait for the escort, as I should have done in the first place."

"Art—Art thou all right?"

"I'm jarred, no more. Here, let me go first. There's another of these rascals back in the wood—if that shot hasn't frightened him away."

"But—Alberta! The diary!"

"Alberta will find her way back to the stables. Everybody around here knows her. As for the diary, I hid that in another place while I rode around the old Crossed Keys. An impulse."

He lugged the thing out from under his doublet. That

204

doublet was ripped, a little to the right of the breastbone, and the stiff leather cover had been gashed by lead.

"A *lucky* impulse," George amended. "Now let's get back."

The queen's men-at-arms arrived at Okeland the next morning; and three days after that in London, George delivered the diary to Sir Francis Walsingham.

He wondered if he would ever hear of that diary again—if anybody ever would. He doubted it. The thing would be lost to history, alas. The queen's majesty, though she had but lately learned of the existence of the diary and its whereabouts, had been in closet for many long hours and even days with Francis Drake, whom she knighted. She would have sopped up details, descriptions, figures; and she had the memory of an elephant. Already she knew everything that George had written; the diary itself could give her no news. Her only interest in it was to see it destroyed—to see this with her own royal eyes—lest it fall into the hands of the Spaniards and be of incalculable value to them in a lawsuit to recover the treasure. She must protect her investment. She might be doing it at that very moment.

In his mind's eye George could picture her: her accipitrine face lit by the red flames, she leaned over a fire in one of the remoter chambers at Hampton Court or Nonesuch, gloating, as with her own hand she fed the diary, page by torn page, to oblivion. She would probably stir the ashes afterward; she wanted to be sure of her money.

Well, that was high politics, George supposed. He shrugged. After all, he had done *his* part.

36

How Many Women?

GEORGE'S WRISTS RESTED upon his knees. Exasperated, he waggled his hands, so that the reflection of the gemmery in his ring flecked the ceiling.

"But—why *me*? With all the well-mounted men you have at your command, why pick one who hates this service?"

"There are various reasons," replied Sir Frances Walsingham, who, long and dour, drably dressed, fitted that lugubrious place. "One is that you have done it several times. You know the way."

"So would a professional courier."

"A professional courier would expect to be paid. Not so you."

"Why not?"

"Look at the money you've made! It puts you into a different class. The queen's highness likes to have her errands run by men who can pay their way."

"I see."

"There are inconveniences about being rich, as you will learn."

"I think I am learning it."

"And there are other reasons. You will be well received, for Shrewsbury likes you and so doth Mary Stuart."

Fatuously, George was thrilled. His heart skipped like that of some smitten boy, and his mouth went dry.

"Then too, you have been away, and so you're not involved in Shrewsbury's domestic wrangles."

"Eh?"

"You see? You've never even heard of the strife with his wife! But everybody else in England has. Their feud may yet affect governmental policy. I'd like a report on this, too."

"You would?"

"The queen's majesty would."

"Oh? She's interested in such petty matters?"

"Master Fitzwilliam, when the premier peer of the realm and its richest countess—who happen also to be host to the world's most embarrassing visitor—when *they* call one another names it is not a petty matter: it is an affair of state."

"I see."

"There is yet another reason why you'll make the ideal messenger just now, Master Fitzwilliam. You are one of the Argonauts. You've been near to the captain who is being called the master thief of the unknown world. You have a tale to tell and all the world wishes to hear it."

Miserably: "I know."

Walsingham looked like a man who looks older than he is. It was a characteristic he had in common with Lord Burghley, who, however, could never have known youth, and might almost have been born with a long beard and a wrinkled brow. Walsingham harrumphed, sourly eyeing his protégé.

"Thus you have an entertainment value, like some fine poet."

"Sing for my supper, eh?"

"It could be called that. To select an Argonaut is subtly flattering. It is like sending Shrewsbury a brace of gerfalcons or a prime stallion. Except that *you* can keep your eyes open."

"And you want me to tell my story to Mary Stuart? Damn it, man, I've just told it to one queen!"

He had indeed spent most of the morning in a private chamber with her majesty of England, who asked him many questions about the circumnavigation, questions that hit like pellets. He could still see her thin small face as she leaned toward him, intent upon his words, her small dark cold eyes not unlike the eyes of a snake, bloodless lips, knife-edged nose, waxy oval mustard-colored freckles, stringy reddish hair. He still could hear the squeak of her querulous voice.

Walsingham frowned. For all his scorn of the bright and gay, at heart he was the perfect courtier and it smarted him to hear an anointed monarch lightly named. He harrumphed again, this time with a note of disapproval.

"Not unless she asks for it. She may know nothing about the trip around the world. She gets only what Shrewsbury elects to feed her, and this he might have thought to withhold. For Mary has connived in secret messages with the king of Spain. She would make him her heir. She'd send him her son, the king of Scotland, whose title she does not recognize. Her French cousins have all but repudiated her, so she casts her lot with Spain. A desperate thing to do."

"She's a desperate woman."

"Perhaps not desperate enough. It could be that Shrewsbury guards her *too* carefully. It could be that she should be given more rope."

"To hang herself with?"

"What else?"

The man was shameless, as he was implacable. He had been trying for years to get Mary Stuart legally killed, and he would continue to try, using any means at hand. He made no bones about this, for he esteemed it a patriotic duty, a duty as well to his puritanical God. Whatever else he might be, Francis Walsingham was no hypocrite: he was so powerful that he could afford to be honest.

"You ask me to help you betray a prisoner? You ask me to rig some trap into which an unsuspecting woman will stumble, just because she has expressed a fondness for my company?"

"No. There are limits to what any man can be commanded."

"It gladdens me to hear you concede that."

"What I *do* expect you to do is examine the situation at Sheffield Castle. See what precautions are taken against the French woman's escape. They may be overrigorous. See what state of health she's in, and what state of mind too. The place may be too strong. We may have to move her."

207

"And what card would you play for that? The queen?"

Sarcasm never had an effect upon this saturnine man.

"I expect you to deliver me a report on the conditions of her captivity."

"Oh, she's a captive now? I had thought she was still a guest."

"We have official reports, of course. But they lack certain details. And I know of no man better equipped to carry out this task than you, Master Fitzwilliam. I cannot sympathize with your softness toward an unscrupulous conspirator, but I have nothing but applause for your integrity."

"Why, thank you!"

"If you don't wish to accept this commission at my hands, I can of course arrange to have the queen herself ask you. That would be a command, then."

George sighed. He waggled his hands again, and again those flecks of colored light rioted across the ceiling.

"All right," he said. "Now, could you be more specific? Just what lies am I expected to tell this time?"

George brought a bolt of sarsenet, a roll of whipped reticella lace, and sundry sweetmeats, such as sugar sops and eringo, to Anne and Aunt Sylvia; but he was reluctant to talk about the trip. Oh, yes, he had seen the queen. For a long while? Too long. What did she look like? Oh, about the same—maybe a little skinnier, a little more shrewish. What was she wearing? To tell the truth, he had not noticed, excepting that it was something blue.

None of this was very satisfactory, and silence fitted down like a lid on Okeland after Anne had asked him outright where he was being sent this time.

"Oh, north."

"To see whom?"

"Why," he answered carelessly, "the other queen."

She looked at him a moment, then turned sharply and went back to the kitchens.

He felt sorry for her. Like everybody else—everybody who hadn't met her—Anne thought of Mary Stuart as a schemer of no conscience, to face whom was fatal for any man, for she ruined them simply in order to feed her own lascivious delight. Anne could not be expected to know how gentle and sweet the Scottish queen was, how thoughtful, how kind. True, she had been brought up in the rottenest court in Christendom, the court of France, but that did not necessarily make *her* rotten. If only she could be taken out of that great gloomy pile and allowed to move about, smiling that inimitable smile of hers! But—she had *too* much charm. She was too lovely. They were afraid of her, so they kept her locked up.

Anne was a woman, and she took it like a woman, personally. He didn't blame her, but in this one matter he avoided her. He hated to see her suffer.

No doubt Anne, like everybody else, believed that the trouble between the Shrewsburys—a widely discussed tiff, George had learned—could be pointed back to Mary of Scotland, who had led the nobleman astray. This was nonsense. Dry, cautious George Talbot, sixth earl of Shrewsbury, was not one to be led astray by anybody, least of all by someone under his own roof: he took his responsibilities much too seriously. And Mary of Scotland took her royal position too seriously to be guilty, even absently, of flirtation. Why, she was the most *un*flirtatious woman imaginable! Anybody who knew her knew that; just as anyone who knew Bess of Hardwick, old Hatchet-Face, would know that she'd cause trouble in Heaven itself, if ever she got there.

George was glad when the time came to ride north.

Anne permitted herself to be kissed, but there was nothing more than that. For a fleet moment George thought of digging out those sonnets, which he had never mentioned to her; but he passed this plan, being too shy.

Aunt Sylvia, who was very old, and Sir John, who was both old and ailing, might not have noticed that there was anything wrong; but certainly the servants did.

Dumpy inside, George rode first to Weddell Manor, which was on his way anyway. It would be good to see Terence again, after so long. But Terence wasn't there, and the stupid retainers appeared to have no notion of where he was or when he would come back. Sylvestre the short, the bass-voiced, was not there either. Nobody seemed to know what had happened to Sylvestre. George nodded, and went on.

It was a morning of glint and flare, colored like a huge pearl, chill yet dry. After a while, as he rode north, his spirits revived. For—this was England. Where else was there a country so clean, so pleasant to the eye? He began to hum, and then to sing:

> *"God save our gracious sovereign,*
> *Elizabeth by name,*
> *That long unto our comfort*
> *She may both rule and reign."*

Well, he subscribed to that sentiment. Elizabeth Tudor was truly the sovereign, and he would fight for her title at any time, no matter what he thought of the lady herself. She was

England, as this was England around him. That he went to call on another queen did not make him a traitor. And as for Anne . . .

Somewhere in Derbyshire, when it was getting late and he should have begun to think about an inn, three glass balls bounded out before his path.

It was odd, he thought as he reined. He had not passed so much as a wattle-and-thatch hut for some time. But here were these glass balls.

One was bright green, one blue, the other the yellow of buttercups, a frivolous color.

They had come out of the wood on his left, where stealthy shadows congregated now.

He dismounted and picked the things up. It so happened that he had to relieve himself anyway, so he turned to the left and walked a little way into the wood.

Immediately he came upon a glade, where the sun still shone. There were eight or nine men there, most of them hunkered down on their heels, all of them ragged. There was a small fire, which he had not sniffed because the wind was adverse.

A large man, a veritable Goliath of Gath, bearded like a Visigoth, hair everywhere, and no doubt lousy as well, held an exquisite Toledo rapier, a sword any duke might have envied. With the flat of it, viciously he slapped the bare back of a smallish, hunched man, who was whimpering under the chastisement. The welts appeared long and red, angry. The other men watched.

Here was a band of ruffians, George assumed, and they had their own discipline, their rules, their convictions, and punishment. Ordinarily he would have turned away.

But that was a memorable piece of steel. How had the rascal got it?

"You could put that to better use," George said coldly.

Absorbed until that moment, none of them had seen him. Now they gasped, their jaws dropping. The humped small one, flat on the ground, only went on moaning; but the giant who held the rapier whirled upon George.

"God's cullions! Who art thou?"

It was much to be thou'ed by such slime, yet George remained equable.

"It was made for a gentleman," he pointed out. "It should be used in a gentlemanly fashion. That's good steel, you clod."

Breathing heavily, as much from astonishment as from his recent exertions, the giant regarded George for a long minute. George of course wore his loo. His bonnet was bright, but no aigrette fastened it. The rings on his fingers were covered with thin red leather gauntlets. The gaze of the giant instantly centered upon the ruby in the lobe of George's left ear.

"Um-m," he said.

Inwardly George boiled. Who was this blob of ordure that dared look upon an earring Mary Queen of Scots once had owned?

George should have bowed and backed away; it was none of his affair; but that stare infuriated him. It was as though the filthy fellow actually had reached out and laid a hand upon Mary Stuart. It was sacrilege!

"A better use for it, popinjay? Mayhap thou'rt right. A better use for it might be to run it through thy guts."

"Good," said George. "Why don't you try?"

He drew.

37
Artists in the Moonlight

THE LIGHT WAS GOOD, though it would not remain so, The ground was level and dry, and moreover it was uncluttered. The fire, with a pot hanging from a tripod, was off to one side of this clearing. The beaten man had crawled or been dragged away from the center; and the others, all eyes, had simply shuffled back a bit.

The hairy man, the big one, stared. He was not fazed, only flabbergasted; he had not expected defiance. For he was, evidently, an upright-man: a chief or crownless king of the underworld of the road. Such complete ruffians had absolute command over their own gangs of nips and foists, dummerers, Abraham-men, hookers, fraters, what-not. Such a personage stayed undisputed among his followers. He had all power of punishment, even to life and death. This he kept, of course, only because he was so strong, so violent, and desperate. Already marked, probably branded as a thief, so that the next time he was napped it would mean a noose, he had nothing to lose but his life. And he would brook no wisp of disagreement; he couldn't afford it.

The upright-man, an utter outlaw, always was a brute, though sometimes he was a cunning brute.

This one was different from most, not in the manner of ferocity but because of his weapon. A cudgel would have

211

been more usual, or if a sword, then a heavy old-fashioned broadsword. A rapier in the hand of such a ruffian was like a bracelet around the neck of a bull.

Yet this Visigoth at least knew how to hold it. After his first eye-popping amazement he smiled—a rather mean, side-slanted smile. He started toward George.

He did not move like a fencer—right foot forward, left arm back, the point threatening. Instead he *strolled,* superbly confident, while he swished the blade before him as though he would knock the heads off daisies.

George retreated.

It has been said that the best fencer in the world would not be afraid to face the second-best fencer, but he might well be afraid to face the fifth- or sixth-best. However many treatises might be written, or diagrams drawn, however many lectures might be given about the punta riversa, the stoccata, the incartata, the volte, all the rest of it, there remained the fact that swordplay was dangerous even for the adept. You never knew what might happen. You never could be sure what the other man might do; and the scantier his training, the greater this uncertainty.

George retreated a little farther.

Scornfully, Goliath fell into guard position. He cut high for the head. George ducked, and half-lunged, pinking the right kneecap.

The upright-man bellowed. It must have been hideously painful, like being touched with a red-hot poker. It would not cripple him, but it caused him to pause for a moment.

Then George went in.

George would have preferred a feeling-out period, would have liked to wait for the other to attack. But what with the falling light and the possibility of interference if the upright-man shouted for it—George could have been tripped—he deemed it best to get the business over with right away.

He feinted high, then feinted low. Then he slipped under the Visigoth's guard and touched the right forearm, drawing blood. He menaced the eyes, steadily advancing. The giant, bewildered, fell back.

George held his blade in the high line, circling the point. The giant fell farther back. George dropped his guard suddenly, and went in low—to slap with the flat the pricked kneecap. There was another screech of pain.

George moved ahead, not smiling, making no unneeded motion. He had scant respect for bravado. Flourishes were for fencers who didn't know better; George was not performing for the benefit of spectators. His object was to win.

212

This bout should be an easy one, but he would not relax until it had been finished.

Had he dared, the giant would have turned, would have run away. As it was, he retreated until his back was against a tree at the edge of the glade. There, trapped, his eyes enormous, face wet with sweat, he perforce paused. He lowered his point.

George took this for surrender. Disgusted, he turned away.

"You may keep your sword," he muttered.

It might have been the intake of breath from those who watched, or perhaps the prompting of his own protective instinct. Whatever it was, without conscious reasoning he threw himself flat. And the Visigoth, who had been about to run him through as his back was turned, stumbled over him, cutting only air.

George leapt to his feet.

"Now you may *not* keep your sword!"

Their positions were reversed, and George again had the length of the glade in which to pursue. He did this, never giving the upright-man a chance to make a stand, while he pinked him in three places and sliced a chunk of skin from the right shoulder.

It was too much. The ruffian, whimpering in fright, dropped his rapier and ran into the wood.

George sheathed. He looked around. Save for the beaten man, who lay face down, they were all staring at him, wondering who he was.

He jerked his head to indicate the darkening wood.

"Will he come back?"

They chinned an emphatic no. The upright-man should have stood his ground. Once he had shown the white feather he need hope for no further obedience—unless he got control of another such group elsewhere. Meanwhile, the men who regarded George Fitzwilliam were leaderless, and they looked a little lost.

George smiled at them.

He went to where the stumpy small man lay, and gravely he studied a back that might have been a mass of raw beef. There was, oddly, something familiar about this man, who lay, his face buried in the grass, semiconscious, sometimes moaning a little. But George had no acquaintances among strolling players, and the hideously slashed back and the failing light did not encourage a close inspection. He shook his head.

"Better do something. Anybody got butter?"

Some one tittered. In the half-darkness George could not see which it was.

"Anybody got any French brandy?" a voice asked. "Anybody got any peahen cooked in Burgundy? Anybody got any marchpane?"

George grinned.

"Well, what about bear grease?"

"I have that," said the man next to him. "I'll take care of him."

"Good. Give him these again, when he recovers."

George put the three glass balls on the ground before the lashed man.

"A juggler, eh?"

"Aye, your worship. And a good one."

"But I take it not good enough to please old Fusty-Whiskers, the personage who has just departed? He dropped his tossers, and Fusty-Whiskers kicked them aside and started to lam him, eh?"

"Aye. He was often that way. Impulsive."

They spoke of the upright-man as though he were dead. As far as they were concerned he was.

George ambled over to the pot.

"Smells good. What is it?"

"Cony."

"Smells more like chicken."

"It's cony. You can't catch chickens running wild in the wood."

"You can catch 'em running tame in a farmyard, after dark."

"Cony. Would your honor like to try some?"

"Supernaculum!"

"Again, please, sir?"

"Go to! What I meant was that it would be a delight. Thanks."

They served him in the upright-man's bowl, a silver one: all the rest were treen. They seated him upon the upright-man's stool.

"Excellent chicken," he pronounced.

He stretched his legs, wiped his mouth, and contentedly belched.

"Come now," he said. "You have been kind to this wayfarer. But I must give you good even, if I'm to get to Whittington before midnight."

"The Cock and Pyenot?"

"Aye."

"That's full of fleas, your honor."

214

"Oh? I had not heard so. I've never slept there, but it's only a few miles from the place where I mean to go, and—"

"Why not spend the night here, sir? There's God's plenty of water"—and indeed before this George had heard the important pitter of a brook near at hand—"and we could have berries for breakfast and perhaps more of that, uh, cony."

George paused. The night was mild, and he had ridden hard.

"Mighty Mitch won't come back," another said, clearly referring to the upright-man. "You could use his blankets. They're cleaner'n the ones at the Cock and Pyenot."

This, following the offer of the stool and the silver bowl, had about it a suggestion of investment in the robes of some abdicated king; and George was wary about getting involved with strangers. Nevertheless these men were quiet, not ruffianly, though surely in rags; and they seemed sincere, being grateful. Before George could make up his mind, an old man spoke. He was the oldest of them all, and the most dignified.

"If your worship will loiter here we'd be pleased to regale you with an exhibition of our art."

George swallowed, uncertain whether he had heard aright. "You—Well then, you are artists?"

"Oh, truly, sir! You didn't take us for vagabonds, did you?"

"No, no! Of course not!"

"Most of us have played in London. Or at least *near* London. Southwark. I myself have been a member of the earl of Leicester's company."

"Have you, now?"

"Yet too much of the city, you see, sir, it cramps the free spirit. A player can't go on giving of his best every morning and every afternoon unless he make contact with the people—the everyday people, I mean, the *working* people, the *common* people."

"Yes, I can see that that might be so."

The old man clapped his hands and called an order, and they unpacked their baggage, with extraordinary results. They must have planned to spend most nights in barns or stables rather than in the open air, for they had pitifully few camping utensils. But they did have many cloaks and robes, crowns and scepters, spangles, musical instruments, hoops—all of them, at least in the light of an emergent moon, looking very rich indeed, very brave.

It was startling. These ragamuffins, clad in false finery, glittering, were skilled. They danced, they played, they tumbled. Two put on a truly hilarious burlesque wrestling match: they had George roaring with laughter. The wee juggler with his glass balls was excused from performing tonight, though George again and again was assured that he was brilliant, a true artist.

The old man himself was the most impressive. Radiantly robed, his chin high, he spoke one of George's favorites:

> *"The rugged Pyrrhus, he whose sable arms,*
> *Black as his purpose, did the night resemble*
> *When he lay couched in the ominous horse—"*

The old man's beard gleamed white in the moonlight. He had a resonant baritone, and he rolled the accents—yet not mouthing them, for they never tangled in his teeth.

> *"But, as we often see, against some storm,*
> *A silence in the heavens, the rack stand still,*
> *The bold winds speechless and the orb below*
> *As hush as death, anon the dreadful thunder*
> *Did rend the region—"*

It was magnificent. It was English. The old man's face, as he looked up, was lit with glory. The syllables rang.

> *"Out, out, thou strumpet, Fortune! All you gods*
> *In general synod, take away her power;*
> *Break all the spokes and fellies from her wheel,*
> *And bowl the round nave down the hill of heaven,*
> *As low as to the fiends!"*

George was weeping long before the end; they all wept, though the others must have heard it before. George wrung the old man's hand.

"God's mercy! I wish I could do that!"

"Thank you kindly, sir." The old man himself was weeping. "To the performer, praise is salt."

This was too solemn a note on which to end the evening, so at George's request they passed him the lyre, which was in tolerably good tune. There were also a recorder and a lysarden, and every one of the men had a good voice and knew all the airs.

When he unsaddled and rubbed down his horse—he did not permit any of the artists to do this for him—George had fetched out of a saddlebag a flask of brandy, which he now

216

passed around. It wasn't much, but they did not need much
to fight the gathering chill.

They sang then. They sang "Kiss Me, Alice, Let Me Go"
and "Green Sleeves," and "Never Weather-Beaten Sail," and
many another popular one. They did it well, too. If a fussy
old owl was the only creature to hear, it made no difference
there under the moon. And when at last they rolled up in
their blankets or rags on a bed of plucked moss, they were
sleepy and happy.

"You have never been members of the queen's own company, any of you?" George asked in the darkness.

"Oh, no, sir," several whispered.

"I have been approached," the old man said. "I have
taken it into consideration. Perhaps I should have accepted,
if only to be able to say that I had."

"I see. But then none of you has ever performed before
a queen?"

"Why, no, your worship."

"Tomorrow," George promised, "you will do so."

38

The Gilt Was Wearing Thin

HE HAD SPOKEN TOO SOON. The players could not get to
Sheffield the next day if they had to go by foot.

"If we'd had a horse we'd've et it," one of them pointed
out.

So George rode ahead, the agreement being that they
would present themselves at the gate the following morning.
This would give George a chance to prepare Lord Shrewsbury.

Though the weather was mild, the sight of the castle
struck a chill to George's breast. Rain better suited Sheffield;
sunshine seemed afraid to fall on those gray walls. It was
the most *relentless* building George ever had seen. That
scummy moat could have been Styx; the guard, in chat with
a slattern from the village, many-headed Cerberus and his
mistress Hecate; whilst those who plodded back and forth
across the draw suggested the Erinyes. George looked up,
half expecting to see carved in the stone above the gateway
the words of the Italian poet: *Lasciate ogni speranza voi
ch'entrate*—All hope abandon, ye who enter here.

As each time before, he skipped when he passed under a
portcullis that dangled like some Damoclean sword; yet his

mien when he demanded entrance was supercilious. He would not even consent to see John Bateman the secretary, but insisted that he be taken instanter to my lord of Shrewsbury himself. And this was done.

Shrewsbury's eyes darted back and forth, and his voice was more fretful than ever, but his manners remained fine and it was with warmth that he greeted George Fitzwilliam, rising to shake George's hand, calling for wine. Bateman he waved away.

Shrewsbury, since Norfolk's execution the premier peer of the realm, held most of his properties in the north of England, far from any seaport. He had not been an investor in the voyage of circumnavigation: this George knew. All the same, and like everybody else in England, noble or common, he was fascinated by the affair. He would have many questions to ask. Pent in this dreary grand place, laden with responsibilities, aware that men were sniggering behind his back about his effort to divorce his wife, he had been highly unhappy; and he looked upon George with relief. He even started to talk about Drake before the arrival of the wine.

"Um, to be sure, aye," murmured George, looking away.

He had a pearl of great price here, and he knew it. Sing for his supper, forsooth? Why, he'd sing for more than that!

"The man himself I'm unacquainted with, of course. One of that Plymouth crowd, and clearly a pusher. They do say that the queen's highness bestowed the accolade upon him by reason of these monumental robberies. Oh, I cry your pardon, Master Fitzwilliam!"

George smiled.

"Not a bit. I call them robberies too."

He sipped his wine, a full-bodied red Beaune, very good.

"So I wondered if perhaps you—"

"Forgive me, my lord, but were it not meet that the queen's concern come first?"

"You have some word from her majesty?"

"Only indirectly. I saw her, last week. I talked long with her, as I shall tell you anon. But just now—it was Master Secretary Walsingham's suggestion, as you can see in his letter—if you can promise me an audience—"

"Surely! I'll write right now!"

He did so, with an almost undignified haste, his hand shaking.

"Oh, she'll consent! She hasn't had a visitor in four months! And she always did like you, Master Fitzwilliam."

218

"If she consents, I take it that I might be permitted to wear my sword on that occasion?"

"Well ... After all, we do know you well by this time, eh? Ha, ha! Aye, I think we could make that small privilege."

"Gramercy."

But George, who knew he had a good thing, would not be rushed. He had been bored by that business, three years of ennui, yet it was as though he were the only man ever to reach the moon and return to tell his tale. From the lousiest oaf who loafed outside of The Plow, up to her royal majesty Elizabeth, by grace of God queen of England and Ireland, queen of France, etc., they hung on his every word.

"There's another matter, my lord. Or rather, an extension of the first. Master Secretary Walsingham gave me to understand that it was his wish—so far of course as this concurred with your own convenience, my lord—that Scotland's grace should be amused in some manner, or diverted."

"Frank Walsingham said that?"

It bumped George to hear the lank vinegarish secretary called "Frank." But he was dogged. If he was to tell a lie at all, it might as well be a big one.

"Nay, I know not his reason. Something devious, no doubt."

"No doubt," darkly.

"And it was because of this that I brought a troupe of players."

If he had said that he brought a coopful of tigers Shrewsbury could not have been more astounded.

"Players! Good God, man, you mean that the queen lent you her own?"

"Oh, no. Not those."

"Leicester's, then?"

"Not his either. No, these have no sponsor, and they, uh, they really have no name. But talent they do have, as my lord will see tomorrow morning when they come knocking at the gate."

"But— But look here, Fitzwilliam, unlicensed players are forbidden by law!"

"So many things are forbidden by law, my lord."

"But such men are rated as vagabonds, criminals. I can't allow them inside my castle."

"Not even to entertain Scotland's monarch? Not even to please Sir Francis Walsingham? Oh, the lady's your charge, sir, and you are to be the judge of her security, but doesn't that include her bodily well-being? It would be most embarrassing if she died. Everyone would say that she had been assassinated. Now—couldn't a circus be called a health measure?"

He spread his hands.

"After all, the outer bailey is large, and the portcullis could be lowered, the bridge raised. Your own soldiers, your own townspeople—what have you to fear from a handful of mummers?"

In any other circumstances, he was sure, he would not have won his petition. As it was, Shrewsbury agreed only with many complicated qualifications. But he did agree.

Then, and not until then, George told his tale. It was interrupted only once, and then by a messenger from Mary Stuart's own apartments in the Scroll Tower. Shrewsbury read the note with impatience, then shoved it aside.

"Scotland pleads her stomach. She's abed. But she sends a greeting to you, sir, and will receive you tomorrow morning at eleven. Now, as to the time when you went ashore at—"

"Forgive me, my lord, but did you tell her anything about the players?"

"No, no. Now if—"

"Good. Then I shall break these news to her."

He did so next morning on the ground floor of the Scroll Tower, which was as dim as ever. He had kept the earl of Shrewsbury's own valet de chambre busy for more than three hours the previous evening, after the besought tale had been finished at last, and he looked his best, well rested, the dust of the journey wiped away.

He knew the same sensations that he had felt the first time he entered this chamber: tightening of the throat, airiness of the knees and feet, inability to turn his head, or even to swerve his eyes. Though he could not see her distinctly, when first he came in, she caught him as before; and she held him.

"We are happy to greet you again, Master Fitzwilliam."

It was the same voice, limpid, not chill, not caressive either, the voice of a fond faithful friend. Yet . . . something was different.

"So much has happened in the world since last we met, Master Fitzwilliam. But none of it happened to me. I simply stay here. So I have nothing to tell you. But surely *you* have something to tell *me?*"

He did not believe that she was hinting for the tale of the circumnavigation, of which it was unlikely that she had heard; and in any event, George had promised Shrewsbury not to mention this.

"Immediately, ma'am. Aye. Not of the past."

"Who cares for the past, sirrah? Rise, rise."

It was not until he got to his feet that he had a real look at her.

She had much declined. She would always be beautiful, and her voice was a young woman's; but the years of confinement had taken their toll. The face was pasty, and even its delicate heart-shape was somewhat marred by flabbiness under the chin. The eyes remained enigmatic, and George couldn't even have named their color, though he knew that they were dark; but the hair was much thinner than it had been, and he suspected that it was braced and laced with switches, and possibly touched with dye. The gown was very long, so that George was not vouchsafed a glimpse of the ankles, which he had heard were swollen now with dropsy. The gown itself was in good condition, but the draperies over Mary Stuart's head, her royal hangings, had faded; and the gilt was wearing off, for now George could scarcely read those curious words: *En ma fin est mon commencement.*

These things did not matter. She was Mary Stuart. That was all he needed to know, or cared to.

Shrewsbury and only three gentlemen were ranged behind George, though the guards at the door were four. The master of the household, that same aged man George had seen twice before, was impeccably dressed, and his air was one of distinction, but he no longer had a sword at his side. Behind the throne, where there should have been scores, there were but eight attendants, male and female alike.

George noted that young Anthony Babington was not one of these, and he asked about him.

"He has inherited," Queen Mary replied. "He has an estate in Northumberland, near Chartley."

"He would do well to stay there," put in the host. "He's a fanatic, that lad."

"My lord Shrewsbury always fears ardor, in any form," Mary said with a small thorny smile. "He dreaded that one of his too-ready men-at-arms would cut down poor little Tonino. So he sent him away. Tonino had no right to such fervor."

Shrewsbury muttered something, but did not otherwise speak.

Queen Mary asked about Terence. There was not much that George could tell her, for he had not seen Terence Weddell in more than three years, and the rumors of the countryside were hazy.

She understood, and gave him a chance to change the subject.

"You mentioned some *immediate* news, Master Fitzwilliam?"

"Ma'am, 'tis of a frivolous nature."

"And who is Scotland to be above frivolity? Pray proceed."

"Ma'am, there is a company of strolling players clamoring for admittance, and my lord of Shrewsbury has agreed that they may be permitted to give their show in the lower bailey this afternoon, provided that your majesty will consent to honor it with her presence."

Tears leapt to her eyes, and she clapped her hands in joy and amazement. It had been so long!

George too wept, nor did he seek to conceal this, for he continued to look straight at her, which was something like staring at the sun.

"You are kind," she whispered at last, after swallowing. "I'll consent to see this on two conditions."

"And they are, ma'am?"

"First, that my servants also be permitted to watch."

" 'Tis granted in advance. My lord of Shrewsbury already promised that."

He heard the earl behind him gasp, but there was no interposition.

Mary Stuart reached out to touch George's forearm.

"The other condition, Master Fitzwilliam, is that you stay by my side and help me to laugh and to cheer."

"Majesty!"

He dropped to both knees, passionately kissing the hand. For a moment he could not trust himself to move.

"Methinks there may be more than one Anthony Babington," muttered the earl of Shrewsbury.

39

"The Show Is Over!"

THAT FALSE ST. MARTIN'S SUMMER WAS GONE. Winter had its foot inside the door. Clouds loured. The air smelled of rain, or even snow. The sky rumbled.

None of this damped the spirits of the visitors, who might have been unaware of it, so great was the excitement. Lord Shrewsbury could shake his head at ardor, fervor; but he had a townful of it beyond his moat. When word sped that a company of players was to hold forth in the outer bailey, old and young, weak and strong, came from every direction. The bridge was black with them.

Each as he entered was searched. This precaution, like the posting of so many guards—every one of the thirty soldiers was on duty, while each member of the castle staff of more than forty had been assigned to sentry duty— seemed to George unnecessary. There was after all nobody to impress, save only George himself, and he could not believe that he meant so much. Was the earl *twitchy?* And had his state of high nerves communicated itself to his retainers? Here was an edgy situation.

Yet it could not be denied that Mary Stuart, when she threw herself on the mercy of her cousin Elizabeth, had a record of swift movement, quick thinking, disguise, and escape. Her brilliant exit from water-girt Lochleven Castle showed that she was most marvelously hard to hold. More, she was designed to turn young men's heads; this too she had proved, and many times. She needed but to smile, no matter where the place, and some featherbrained but athletic champion would plead for the privilege of risking life and limb, braving the rack, the pilliwinks, the gallows itself, in her service, however illicit. It made her a woman to be watched, in every sense of the word.

Also, not only the man who sought by any wile to rescue her, but also the man who sought to slay her, must be forstalled. As she had the gift of plunging some into lunatic love, so also she could drench the souls of others with a hate as black and bitter as gall. This was especially true in recent years, what with the mounting anger against Spain, the rise of the puritan party, the machinations of Catholic seminarists. George had seen how the mere mention of Mary Stuart's name could send such a temperate soldier as Sir John Crofts into a spasm of rage. If to thousands the lady was persecuted Purity, to thousands of others she was Jezebel, Lucifer's lieutenant, Antichrist himself, to be stamped out at all costs. These men too, like the Babingtons, were unaccountable yet cunning.

So all were examined before being admitted, and passed one by one. They took this in good part, each patiently awaiting his turn.

They had three good reasons, besides natural willingness to drop work for any holiday.

First, there were the players. The profession being in disrepute, Sheffieldians never had seen mummers of any sort, and many may never even have seen acrobats or listened to a minstrel.

Then there was a queen. She had been twelve years in captivity now, ten of them here in Sheffield; yet few of the residents had viewed her. When their business took them to the castle, it was only to the outer bailey, a semipublic yard in which Mary was not allowed. On the rare occasions when she rode forth for a canter in the park—Shrewsbury's own jealously policed enclave—that outer bailey first was cleared; and in any event she would be so hedged by soldiery as to be scarcely glimpsed by the nimblest. All sorts of stories—it was but human—were told about her. Actually seeing her would be like catching sight of a myth, or having a fairy story come true.

Finally, there was his lordship. He was not a "popular" earl, and knew no obligation to show himself in public. Though he could not be called an absentee landlord, there being scarcely a day when he was not at either the castle or the nearby lodge—he had not been to London or indeed more than a few miles from his estates since Mary Stuart like an Old Man of the Sea had been fastened upon his back —still he was aloof, remote, preoccupied with personal affairs, a conscientious housekeeper but not one to mix. He had been especially reserved of recent months, since the break with his countess, the red-headed Bess of Hardwick, who was cordially disliked in the town. And this too added to the eagerness to see him again, for the people dearly loved a marital spat in high places, and they would study their earl, speculating on how he was "taking it."

It was little enough they learned from his appearance that afternoon. George Talbot, sixth earl of Shrewsbury, wore clothes that befitted his station—a lilac doublet of silk, purple canions with blue-gray slashes, white gauntlets, a scarlet velvet bonnet, even his Garter—but his face might have been congealed in some colorless paste for all the emotion it showed. He was cool, correct. He never pointed, never raised his voice. The people were disappointed.

They were not disappointed in the queen.

A fanfare—it must have been her first in many years— announced her. When she came under the archway between the two courts her step was light. She had pleaded illness only the previous day, and even now she was supported by her handsome distinguished master of the household and a lady-in-waiting, both of them persons she towered over; yet she all but skipped.

224

A cheer went up. She paused, lifting a tiny white hand. Then she smiled; and they were hers.

There might have been eight hundred persons in the outer bailey, all crowded against the walls. There were no other spectators, for the ramparts above, like the towertops and arrowslits and windows, had been cleared. George noted that about a quarter of the persons went to their knees, and some began to cross themselves; but nobody reproved them.

Mary Stuart did not sag, anywhere. Her hair was caught under a blue caul embroidered with gold and surmounted by a red cloth, yellow-plumed cap. A tight-fitting blue bertha covered her bosom. Her stomacher—it was one of the new French V-shaped ones—was scarlet. Her petticoat was purple, her kirtle black. There was a crucifix hung by a chain around her neck, and from her waist was suspended a mirror; but she did not touch these.

She stood a long moment, as more and more persons fell to their knees.

You can dress a dummy in glittering garb, but a dummy cannot turn its head, and neither can it speak. Mary Stuart was every inch a queen, trained to such scenes as this; and even the men who stood closest to her did not see any sign that while with majestic mien she surveyed those before her she was carrying on a conversation with George Fitzwilliam.

"You have a message?"

"Ma'am, only my own."

"And—that?"

George paused. His ostensible mission—to give Scotland an account of his adventures—he had already promised Shrewsbury not to mention. What the queen's secretary really sought—more detailed information about Shrewsbury's precautions, should Mary of Scotland be given less freedom, or more—George could not divulge. But he could warn her!

Now he bowed. Like her, he spoke without seeming to move his mouth. He was not as adroit in this as was the queen; but then, fewer were watching him, and even to those he was turned sidewise.

"Perchance there are too many Babingtons?"

"He hasn't pounced."

"He will. He or somebody like him. I fear for your life, ma'am."

"I don't. When every night you lie down wondering whether you'll ever get up again, then you cease to fear. All I dread is that they may do it in the dark, with a dagger, before I can make my peace with God. For years I have dreaded this. I must hold myself prepared."

"To escape, ma'am?"

"Prepared to appear before the Heavenly Throne was what I meant."

More and more of the spectators were dropping to their knees. The queen stood there, a superb figure of a woman, slowly turning her head, acknowledging this obeisance, talking all the time from a corner of her mouth.

"Your warning then, sirrah?"

George whispered: "I have carried messages for your highness, and this might give me the right to point out that if only you would refuse to countenance plotters—"

"Not beat against the barred window? Have you ever lived in a cage, Master Fitzwilliam?"

"Ma'am, I have met Francis Walsingham. You haven't. He hates you."

"For that I forgive him. But I tell you—"

She saw Shrewsbury take a step toward her. She crooked her arm at George.

"Would you help me?" she asked. "I don't walk well, these days."

It had been planned that the queen of Scots should go directly from the outer bailey to a throne that had been set out for her. It was not veritably a throne, only a large X-chair set upon a small square dias, cushioned with velvet. There was no overhang.

She would have none of this. The soldiers waited, and those who immediately flanked her tried to push her, if apologetically, toward the X-chair; but she shook her head. These people had come to see her, and see her they should. Though it caused her pain—as George, who held her arm, could know—she insisted upon circling the yard, smiling here, waving there, nodding. She accepted none of the gifts offered—this had been agreed upon in advance—and several times she refused to lay hands on a diseased petitioner, but she demurred so graciously that all were charmed.

George glanced sideways at Lord Shrewsbury. He was impassive. He must have been troubled inside. It was plain why Shrewsbury was reluctant to expose his prisoner. If he allowed Mary Stuart to smile as she was smiling now, Queen Elizabeth wouldn't have a friend left in Sheffield. Additionally, Shrewsbury was vexed about the circuit, a violation of orders. But he said nothing. There was a halberdier on either side of him; and these men stood erect, statues, their weapons upright before them, razor-edges out.

226

The master of the household made some ado about arranging the cushions, but Mary Stuart brushed him away and sat down, thanking George.

After seating her, George knelt, his heart beating fast, for he knew the value of every split-second here.

"I tell you this," she went on, as smoothly as though their talk never had been broken, "that I'll heed no harebrained scheme."

His head of course was bowed, but he could be sure that Mary Stuart spoke smilingly, for the benefit of others, as though she said something gracious, formal, courtly.

"It must be real," she pursued. "I'll slip through no smashed door. When I leave this prison, Master Fitzwilliam —if ever I do—it will be as queen of England."

He swallowed.

"Then Elizabeth Tudor would be dead, ma'am?"

"She is not likely," in a silken whisper, "to step from that throne and invite me to take her place—now, is she?"

"Ma'am, if—"

In a louder voice: "Nay, rise, rise, Master Fitzwilliam, and stand here, so that we can enjoy this performance together."

She waved to her right side, and he went there. How many men would have been willing to die for the privilege? The dais was small, and by standing off it and by bending a little toward the queen he would keep his head lower than hers, yet at the same time virtually lean on the arm of the chair.

She smiled at him, very close.

Then, facing the populace, she smiled again, and all but laughed. She clapped her hands.

"Let the show begin," she cried.

As though it had picked up a signal the sky was split with lightning, and there was a crash of thunder. Nobody looked up.

A morris dance was first.

A few times during this past hour George Fitzwilliam had felt misgivings about these players and about the impulse that had caused him to bring them here. After all, they *were* a rabble. But when he saw Mary Stuart's delight his fears evaporated. Even if the players were poor the queen would enjoy them.

They were not poor. The morris dance went off well, and then there were some instrumental pieces, and a minstrel with a lute sang several lays. They were light airs, those lays, and amusing, though perhaps in deference to the presence of royalty they were not bawdy. Yet the crowd liked them. And

227

Mary Stuart, who could hardly have understood every word, clapped with enthusiasm.

"He's an angel," she cried to George.

"A rather mangy one, ma'am."

"You're too fussy!"

The burlesque wrestlers, clowns, were extraordinarily funny. Mary, queen of Scotland and the Isles, laughed so hard that she had to hold her sides, leaning back, while tears streamed down her cheek. As for George, he almost collapsed over the arm of her chair.

On the other hand, the old man's recital was not the high point of the programs, as it had been in the moonlight. The old man was superb, true:

> *"But if the gods themselves did see her then*
> *When he saw Pyrrhus make malicious sport*
> *In mincing with his sword her husband's limbs—"*

He missed no nuance; his frenzy was flawless; yet it was patent that he would win but moderate applause. George supposed this was but natural. What was Pyrrhus to these louts? And what Hecuba?

> *"The instant burst of clamor that she made,*
> *Unless all things mortal move them not at all,*
> *Would have made milch the burning eyes of heaven,*
> *And passion in the gods."*

Shrewsbury, a halberdier on either side of him, was much too concerned with the temper of the crowd to catch any classical reference. As for Mary Stuart, her hearing disappointed George. Though she did not throw the old man a purse—this too had been forbidden—she did lean forward to applaud him. She knew that it had been art, but her ear for English was not yet trained to the point where it could seize upon the magnificence of those lines. She was of course kind, but she would have preferred to have the burlesque wrestlers back.

The sky spoke again, and it grew dark in the court.

Each of the other performers had been ambulatory, favoring the queen but with trained persistence moving around the courtyard, facing now this way and now that, as they worked. The next one, the juggler, confronted the queen and the queen alone, being, it would appear, spellbound.

This juggler did not even see George Fitzwilliam. But

228

George saw him—saw his face for the first time—and it was all George could do to keep from crying out.

The juggler was small, with enormously broad shoulders, not a hunchback but suggestive of that. His was extremely dark hair.

He was Sylvestre, Terrence Weddell's valet.

Had this been planned? Had the glass balls, the beating, been arranged as George rode that lonesome road? Did those mummers know that he was on his way to Sheffield, that he would surely gain admittance to the castle?

It was a wild thought, but that was a wild moment.

Should he call to Lord Shrewsbury? Should he stop the show? Terence Weddell was a sincere Catholic, and it stood to reason that his valet was the same. Sylvestre might in addition be rabid, a fanatic. Would he go to any lengths in order to get into the presence of Mary Queen of Scots? Why else was he here? Was there some frenzied hysterical plot to seize her, take her away? It would have been futile, and would mean much killing. Should George speak?

If Sylvestre was a designer he was maladroit. He could hardly hold his glass balls, much less toss them into the air, he was so fastened to the sight of the queen. He moved a step toward her.

Shrewsbury said something to a halberdier, who raised his weapon.

Sylvestre did not see this. He moved another step toward Mary Stuart.

George started forward, meaning to get between them. He feared that the dwarf might try to kiss Mary's feet or embrace her ankles. No physical contact with the players or anybody in the audience was to be permitted: this was part of the contract.

Sylvestre broke into a run. Now he was saying something, babbling something rather. Nobody could make out what it was.

He put one hand under his parti-colored shirt. He might have been replacing the balls. George at least knew that he was not reaching for a weapon.

Lord Shrewsbury spoke again.

The thing that was thrown caught Sylvestre underneath his raised left arm. It was heavy and exceedingly sharp. It all but cut the little man in half. It spun him around, and he fell on the pavement, splattering George's base-hose with blood.

"You—might—have—waited," George sobbed.

He stepped directly before the dead figure, to shield it from the sight of Mary Queen of Scots.

George Talbot, earl of Shrewsbury, raised both arms, and the soldiers began to close in, shoving the crowd toward the main gate, obliquing their pikes to do so.

"The show is over," Lord Shrewsbury cried. "You must all go home. The show is over."

It began to rain.

40

Good-by, This World

HIS WIFE WAS PREGNANT, his father-in-law in dubious health, so George should have hurried home; but curiosity in part, though even more, to give him credit, an urgent sense of fear for the safety of his friend, prompted him to stop a few miles away at Weddell Lodge. Maybe Terence would be home now. Or if he wasn't, his absence could be taken as a hint of guilt.

The parklike approach of Weddell Lodge, its townhousey appearance, originally had puzzled George. Now he knew that Terence preferred to have his visitors obliged to dismount at the gate, some distance away, and open this for themselves. It never was attended, even in the daytime. The gate was noisy, heavy, clumsy, and its opening, and the sub-. sequent remounting, would give the dog or one of the inhabitants of the house some warning of approach. At least, nobody could dash up to the door.

It was late when George arrived, yet there was a light in the library. Terence had a visitor?

George did not open the gate, but climbed over it, leaving his horse outside, a beast much too tired to wander. He walked up the avenue of lime trees and was within a few feet of the door before the dog in back heard or smelled him and began to bark furiously, fighting its chain.

Instantly the light in the library went out.

A moment later the door was opened a few inches, and a cocked pistol appeared, the muzzle toward George.

"Don't come nearer, but explain yourself."

"Tut, tut," said George. "Such rudeness to an old companion!"

"George!"

After these two had embraced, and while Terence was relighting the candles, they nattered on like a couple of girls, for the reunion was good. But seriousness came soon, George introducing it. He told Terence about Sylvestre.

He did not try to trap his friend. He asked no preliminary questions, but plunged right into the tale.

Terence was touched. Tears rolled down his face and his mouth quivered, while the knuckles of his pressed-together hands went white.

"He left me almost a year ago. You weren't back yet. I begged him to stay, but the call of the road was too strong. He went to London—or said he was going there. I gave him money, much more than the wage I owed him, and I got him a let-pass to protect him on the way. He said he knew where he could get a place with a troupe of players. I haven't heard from him since."

"That had been his occupation before?"

Terence nodded.

"Aye. It was on the road that I met him. He was sick of the life then, and we fell to talking, so that I learned he was of my own faith. That makes a difference, you know. It's a bond."

"I can believe it."

"Sylvestre was very devout. It's important to think of that, in this traffic. He was not intelligent, but he was strong, he was faithful. Thank God he never did have to endure the rack, but I had to take the possibility into consideration when I trusted him."

Yes, thought George, *I* am hailed as a hero, while *you* all the while risked torture and death. *I* had a few touchy times, but *you* walked the edge of a cliff every day all day, year after year. *I* stood a chance of wearing out my finger-nails counting money, or choking on a biscuit weevil, or being bored to death, but *you* might at any time have your joints pulled open one by one, and your testacles clipped, your guts yanked out, your head cut off.

But he said nothing of this. Neither did he mention the priest who must have been hiding under the stair, where, George hoped, being an old hand at that sort of thing, he wasn't too uncomfortable. The less George knew the better. There was always the possibility that they might some day take *him* to London Tower, and lay him on La Gehenna, that ingenious table machine of little cranks and pulleys, and stretch him until he screamed—by the hour. He preferred to be as ignorant as possible.

"Why did he go back to the road?"

Terence shrugged, shaking a sad head.

"Had it in his blood, I suppose. He was forever fetching

231

out those ridiculous glass balls, until I simply couldn't pretend any longer to be interested. He craved a real audience. A different audience every time. I paid him well and never beat him. I was fond of him. And he got a great spiritual satisfaction from being able to help me in my, well, 'calling.' But still—he went away."

"Will his death bring the bailiffs?"

"I don't see why. He wouldn't have spoken to his companions about me, lest he slip some reference to what went on here. And you say that he was killed instantly?"

"Oh, instantly. He didn't know what hit him."

"Wasn't there any sort of trial or inquiry?"

"Yes, but it didn't last long. Sylvestre was already buried by that time—just outside the castle grounds, only a few hours after it happened. There was a hearing, and the soldier made a statement; but after all, the order had been heard by hundreds—and it was given by the high steward of England, lord lieutenant of the county, and a man who was acting in defense of what I suppose could be listed as the queen's own property. Not much to be done there, eh? The other players were paid and dismissed. They'll talk, of course, but who believes what a strolling player says?"

Terence looked into the fire, again shaking his head.

"The oddest part," he whispered, "is that poor Sylvestre should be accused of trying to murder her."

"*I* believed that he was about to throw himself at her feet," George said, "and so did most of the others, and it was certainly proved afterward that he had no weapon. But Lord Shrewsbury thought otherwise. And the official record will bear him out."

"He worshipped that woman," Terence whispered. "He adored her as though she was a saint. She *was*, to him. He was always getting me to tell about the time I was one of her pages, and when you were here he'd hide outside the door by the hour in the hope that you'd talk about her too. That miniature you brought me: he all but groveled before that, as if it was an icon."

"But the law says that he tried to kill her."

In the screens again, before the door, George picked up the pistol. He noted that it wasn't loaded, and put it aside.

"You should certainly get another dog," he said in a feeble try at jocularity.

"Yes."

George put a hand upon his shoulder.

"Because I don't want thee to be napped. Thou'rt a good neighbor, and I'd mislike to lose thee."

232

"Thanks," Terence muttered.

There were lights too in the Okeland windows, which alarmed George, for it was near to midnight. He cursed himself for having broken the trip, and spurred his tired horse.

There was some stir in the stables, and he went there first, surprising a groom.

"What?"

"Thank the Lord you're back, sir. Sir John's very ill."

"And you're going for a leech?"

"For a minister, sir. To Rugby."

"H-m-m. He's that bad?"

"He'll not last the night."

"Wait here. I'll go instead. But I'd speak with my wife first. Saddle Alberta for me, and rub this one down."

With death itself George had been long familiar, and it held no horrors for him. Sir John was old and had been failing. It was the effect upon his wife that George was most concerned about, his wife and the child she carried.

Nevertheless the sight of Sir John was a shock. George had been gone only five days, but it might have been five years. The knight's face was as colorless as the pillowcase behind it. It was seamed like an old rock, and might have been sanded. The eyes, only half open, were lusterless, glazed. The upper lip sometimes twitched; yet this was the only sign of life, and without it George would have said that the man was already gone.

They were all there: Anne with the baby in her lap; Aunt Sylvia, herself more than half dead; the house servants, hushed, frightened. It was clear that they had some time since given up hope of communicating with Sir John.

He showed no sign that he recognized George, who spoke to him. The lip did not twitch again for a while.

"The last thing he said," Anne whispered, "he asked for a priest."

"He knows how bad it is, then?"

"He knows all right."

By "priest" Sir John had meant a minister of the state church, the Church of England. In London such a person might have been called a pastor, since tending his flock would be more apparent in that crowded place. In the smaller seaports, with their puritanical sects, which favored extemporizing, and long sermons, he would have been called a preacher. To Sir John Crofts he was still a priest.

The country in general, at least the hinterland, was not

233

well provided in this respect. The church was a new thing, only recently established, or, as some insisted, restored; and the authority of the bishops differed from place to place, from time to time as well, which made for confusion. Discipline was lax, standards uncertain. Elizabeth Tudor, a puny woman at best, nearing fifty, and still, despite her flirtations, determinedly unwed, might at any time die—or be killed. In that event the "strange guest" at Sheffield almost certainly would ascend to the throne, and the old religion would be more or less forcibly reinstated. It was a prospect that didn't please young men who might otherwise have been ecclesiastically inclined. And so, as the older ministers died off there were few to take their places.

Conditions in this part of Northampton were especially bad. The nearest Anglican divine, so far as George knew, was at Rugby, several hours ride each way over abominable roads, and he was a "sporting" minister, unrestrained, utterly unreliable.

"I have sent for Gates."

George shook his head.

"I stopped that. It would take all the rest of the night to get Gates here. *If* he could be found and *if* he was sober."

"But what—"

"Maybe I can find a nearer one."

Lest he never see his father-in-law alive again, though he would be gone but a short while, George knelt by the side of the bed and said a prayer. Sir John's hand moved a little. Then George went out.

He made no try for silence this time when he rode up the avenue of lime trees to the door of Weddell Lodge, and a mystified Terence was waiting for him in the library. George explained.

"Wouldn't that be fraud?"

"I'm not asking that he be given extreme unction. Just that he see a man in black standing there, praying for him. If he *can* see any longer. Aren't they allowed to do that, as a simple act of compassion?"

"I'll ask him. Wait here."

A few minutes later the priest entered the library. He was young, a mere beardless boy, yet he was thoughtful, ascetic of appearance, an aristocrat, and, more important, a man of common sense, a man of good will. George liked him instantly, and trusted him. He wore clerical garb, but his head had not been shaved. He was introduced simply as Father Smith, though his real name, George guessed, might have been a noble one.

234

He was crisp, asking few questions, listening attentively to the answers.

"I realize that there is a certain amount of risk involved, and for the benefit of a man who isn't of your faith," George said impatiently. "I'll answer for my wife, but of course the servants will see you. But as far as your cassock's concerned, it could be an Anglican one—"

The priest smiled.

"It was once," he murmured.

"—and if only you remember not to cross yourself—"

"Master Fitzwilliam, you misunderstand. It is not the danger of arrest and death that I fear, but rather the danger of craving these things too warmly."

"Eh?"

"That my work will be cut short by the public hangman I don't doubt. But it's my duty to put off that day as long as possible, so that I can serve my communicants. They taught us at the seminary, Master Fitzwilliam, that a craving for martyrdom is something that should be suppressed."

"I see. And—you don't think my father-in-law's worth the risk?"

"I didn't say that. Any man who is about to die, no matter what his faith, deserves the services of such as I. But I've got to think of the good of the greater number. In this case I believe we are all right. I was to move out of here tonight anyway."

"In a little while," Terence put in. "That's why you see us up so late, George. The horses are already saddled."

"If I got away before dawn, and you were waiting for me, d'ye think we could make it to where we're going before there was traffic on the road?"

"We could if we pushed."

"Good. You won't go into the house with us, since you're already suspect?"

"No," said Terence. "I'll wait at the edge of that little wood on the rise toward Biggleswade."

The priest nodded. He pulled on a hood, designed to protect his head from the night air. He unlooped the crucifix from around his neck and kissed it, and put it into a pocket.

"Your wife's father may be able to see better than you suppose, and after all it's *his* spiritual welfare that we're thinking of, eh?"

Okeland must have seemed small and mean by comparison with some of the houses this young priest had visited, had indeed been raised in, but his manner, George was sure, would have been the same in any place—palace or shep-

235

herd's hut. Wall hangings, coronas of candles, teakwood chests, meant nothing to him. Neither did those who stood about, any one of whom could have betrayed him. He scarcely nodded to Anne and to Aunt Sylvia, and it could be that he never even saw the servants. He went right to the bed. He knelt.

There was no need to lie, none to practice deceit. If nobody was told that here was a Jesuit missionary from the Continent, neither was anybody told that here was an Anglican minister. His name was not mentioned, nor did George call him "Father," while he himself remembered not to make the sign of the cross, nor yet to rattle his rosary beads. He talked in a low steady vibrant voice, in English, sometimes with his head bowed, his eyes closed, praying, at other times directly addressing Sir John, whose face was so close to his own. The words were measured, but without pattern, of a consolatory nature. They were generalized, not particular, having to do with the goodness of God, Christ our Redeemer, the forgiveness of sins, and such. There was about them nothing set or sectarian. Whether the knight was aware of this talk they were never to know. A few times the lips twitched.

Death came early, and very quietly. There was no stiffening of the limbs, no throat rattle, and the eyes remained the same, half open, expressionless.

How the priest sensed it, would be hard to tell. He looked up, stared hard at Sir John for a moment, then took from his purse a small mirror, which he held before the knight's open mouth. He sighed a little, put the mirror away, and crossed Sir John's arms on his breast. Then he went on with his prayer.

The others got down on their knees and prayed with him, and afterward Anne and Aunt Sylvia found that they could weep again.

The priest refused all refreshment, but he was glad to have George ride a little way with him, to the wood, since he did not know this shire, never having seen it in daylight.

"Thank you, Father," George said. "Here's a purse for your poor. And thank *thee* too, Terence, my true friend."

They nodded, then rode rapidly away, for the sky to the east was lightening.

"My God, I hope they aren't caught," George whispered.

Aunt Sylvia and the steward and Anne's tiring-women from time to time after that, circuitously—for they wouldn't dare to be direct in such a matter, George being the master of the household now—strove to learn from him where he

236

had found that charming priest who attended Sir John at his death. He only shook his head in reply.

Anne never asked him at all. Perhaps she was afraid to learn.

41

Memento Mori

THE DAY THE NEWS CAME that they had killed the queen of Scots church bells were rung and bonfires built, while laborers ran in from the fields, glad of an excuse to take a holiday.

Yet the deed was not unexpected.

At first the government had juggled this monarch as the late Sylvestre might have juggled one of his balls, hustling her from Carlyle Castle to Lowther, to Bolton, to Tutbury, a glum place, from whence she was shipped to Wingfield Manor, a rather pleasant one. But soon they moved her back to Tutbury, and when the northern earls rose in revolt in 1569 her guards took Queen Mary farther south, lest she be freed. She spent some time at Coventry. After the rebellion had been quashed she was shifted to Tutbury again, then Chatsworth. From Chatsworth, November 28, 1570, while George Fitzwilliam still lay in a Spanish prison, they had moved her to Sheffield, where she was to remain for fourteen crushingly unhappy years.

All this time, and while her friends in France systematically robbed her of her dowry, her household was whittled down, her living allowance reduced. Thanks to my lord of Shrewsbury, a kind man, she was not publicly humiliated; but she was not allowed the exercise she needed, so that her health failed.

Toward the end this rigor was abated for a few weeks in the summer, when she was permitted to go to Buxton to take the waters, or to Chatsworth or Worksop or Wingfield, Shrewsbury properties; but Sheffield remained her real jail.

Plot after rescue plot, exploded, could not be traced to her. Besides, many might sympathize with her wish to break that odious prison, for wasn't it any captive's instinct to escape? It would be different if she could be proved to have plotted against the life of Queen Elizabeth. To get her head —and Walsingham, like Cecil, was determined to get it— the ministers would find it necessary to tie her directly to

237

some such scheme. Meanwhile, as Walsingham had learned at least in part from George Fitzwilliam, her confinement was oversevere. Mary Stuart could no longer walk alone, and she had to be helped to mount—she who had been one of the great horsewomen of her time! who after the battle of Langside had ridden nineteen hours without pause!— so that no such display of suppleness as had marked the escape from Lochleven could be looked for again. That is, it would no longer be helpful to give her enough rope, since she didn't have the strength to hang herself.

Some new policy was called for. Shrewsbury was *too* efficient, *too* conscientious, and Walsingham, at long distance, started a campaign calculated to get him relieved.

Shrewsbury for years had been pleading for just that, yet when the time came he balked.

Mary had cost him money and infinite anxiety. She tied him down, preventing travel. Innocently enough, no doubt, she yet had been the means of bringing about his rift with his wife. But he was a stubborn man; he did not wish to let Mary go. He wouldn't confess failure.

In part this could be because in spite of himself Lord Shrewsbury had fallen in love with his charge. In part also it could be a matter of prestige. For all his wealth and high place, *politically* Shrewsbury was not a power. He was not "of the court," and no good at manipulation. When he came to grips with a master like Francis Walsingham his defeat was sure. It took time, but it was done. September 7, 1584, Shrewsbury was replaced by Lord Somers and Sir Ralph Sadler, who resigned a year later in protest against the way they were obliged to treat their ward, and were succeeded in turn by Sir Amyas Paulet, a hot gospeler, fiery of eye if toothless.

Now they were moving her again: Sheffield to Wingfield to Tutbury; then Wingfield again, Chartley, Tixall, back to Chartley; and at last Fotheringay, the end of the line.

George knew Fotheringay Castle, which was not far from Milton, his own ancestral seat. A royal property, though by no means as large or as strong as Sheffield, like Sheffield it was a depressing place. George had played there as a boy. Indeed, his older brother, Sir William Fitzwilliam, the present head of the family, once had been its castellan. George shuddered when he thought of Mary Stuart at Fotheringay.

Yet it was not there but at the next-to-the-last stop, the comparatively cheerful Chartley, that the trap had been sprung. George learned many of the details from Terence Weddell, who had been approached by the conspirators but because of the essential part that the killing of Queen Elizabeth must play in this plot had refused to join. Yet Terence was suspect. Even while he told George how it had happened he was packing his bags, a passport in his pocket.

"There was this brewer in the village. Mary's household was being allowed one hogshead of beer a week, on Saturday. A courier from the French embassy would call and hand over a message, which the brewer would give to one Thomas Phelippes, a professional forger in Walsingham's pay, who was living in the village under another name. It would be in cypher, but Phelippes knew the cypher. He'd copy the letter and give it back to the brewer, who would roll it up and stick it into the hollowed-out bung-stopper of the hogshead, which would be delivered next morning to the queen's apartments at Chartley. The old one, the empty, would be taken away, of course, and in the bung-stopper of that there'd be a message from Mary Stuart. Phelippes would copy this and then give it back to the brewer, who would give it to the ambassador's courier, who would give it to the ambassador, who would give it to Babington or to whomever it was addressed. They kept this up for months."

"Would that be young Anthony Babington?"

"Aye. He lives near there. Or did. He's like me, a harborer of priests, which is bad enough. But Babington wanted to go further—an invasion of the realm, an uprising of Catholics here, and a quick end to Elizabeth. Six young fools like himself had pledged themselves to kill Elizabeth. They were arrested with Babington, night before last, in St. James's Wood. They're in the Tower. And I'm for Douai."

He went to a window. It was late August, and the country drowsed, drenched in sunlight. He sighed.

"They'll expropriate, I'm sure. I'd make thee a deed, George, save that it might stir suspicion. You could buy in easier. It's a logical addition to your place. And there won't be any other bidders, not after the way you refused to stand for Parliament against Wentworth."

"I didn't do it for that reason."

"No, no!"

Terence was about to back away from the window, when something caught his eye, and he showed like a man whose heart had been snicked out.

"I waited too long. Look: two sheriff's men. I know from here."

They had come through the gate at the end of the lime-

239

tree avenue. They remounted, and started toward the house.

"Run for it!"

"How?"

"My horse out there! She's saddled!"

"That would get you into trouble."

"I could say you'd stolen it! No, wait! *Stroll* out! But first—"

Crouching, his shoulders high, bonnet low, he ran outside and leapt upon Alberta's back. He heard the sheriff's men hallo, but he kept going. He went around the manor house, across a meadow, over a ditch, past a wood. It was rough, but they stayed close behind him, as he could hear. Not until they were out on the Market Harborough road, eight miles from Weddell Lodge, did George look back. Then, seeming astonished by what he saw, he came to a halt.

"Why the Devil didn't you tell me you were sheriff's men?" he demanded. "I was there to collect a debt, and I thought you were some of his damned papist friends, so I ran."

That such a hero should fly so readily might have been hard to believe, but the sheriff's men were short of time.

"Where is *he?*"

"Now how should I know?"

Master Fitzwilliam was owner of Okeland, son-in-law of the late Sir John Crofts, intimate of Sir Francis Drake, and locally vouched for by Peter Wentworth. It would not do to question him too hard. They wheeled and on tired horses raced back toward Weddell Lodge. They did not catch Terence. Terence never was seen in Northampton again.

Whether he had been involved, even if remotely, in that plot the exposure of which shook England, George did not learn. It was possible. For Anthony Babington had chosen to confess. "Why, for that lady, sir, I swear, I'd let myself be torn to pieces, limb from limb!" he had cried to George, some ten years ago, when he was a stripling of fourteen or fifteen, a page at Sheffield. "Let's hope you never have to," George had replied. The memory was ironic. Babington of Dethick and six other well-born young hotheads quite literally were torn limb from limb, after being hanged, one morning on Tyburn. The others all had said, "Damn your eyes, no!" whereas Babington had talked.

Mary Stuart, not knowing all this, was moved from Chartley to Tixall, ostensibly for an outing, and while she was away her apartments at Chartley were ransacked, the very paneling being ripped out, the very mattresses chopped, and all her letters and papers—also her cash—taken. Soon

240

after that she was moved to Fotheringay. They were almost ready.

She was tried, as all the world knew, by an extraordinary commission of peers and knights. She was allowed no lawyer, nor was she confronted with her accusers or permitted to see the letters that were used in evidence against her.

There was Babington's confession, a telling instrument. There were statements by her two secretaries, Curle, a Scot, and the Frenchman, Nau. Nobody could be sure that the secretaries had not been tortured—the authorities insisted that Babington had not—but it was certain at least that they were led to the small low-ceiled chamber in London Tower where the rack was kept, and the workings of this apparatus explained to them. That was sometimes enough. Nau and Curle did not appear in person at the trial. No witness did.

Mary, without a friend there, defended herself magnificently. But she was convicted. She was sentenced to die.

It was weeks, it was more than three months, before Queen Elizabeth could find courage to sign the death warrant of her cousin and rival, a woman she never had met. When this had been done the rest followed quickly, for the ministers could not run the risk that Elizabeth might change her mind yet again. Mary Stuart was executed in the greathall at Fotheringay the morning of February 8, 1587.

That was why the church bells rang.

A midland farmer, troubled about dung and fumiter, about the corn being inned, the sarclers paid, is unlikely to hear "inside" stories of statecraft. George had been told by Terence the reason for the Babington Plot's exposure. He was to hear details of the death of Mary Stuart from a man he never saw.

It was at the Plow one early spring afternoon, and George had stopped not because he craved company—the contrary was true—but because he was thirsty. He never did reach the common room. Just outside the door, a hand raised to the latch, he stopped, overhearing through an open window the voice of a stranger.

"Aye, I was there. All the time. I was in the service of Lord Huntingdon, and I was just off the platform, so close that a couple of drops of blood got splashed onto my jerkin. I can tell you they scrubbed that, afterward! They wouldn't let any get away!"

He cleared his throat, then coughed a little.

"Oh? You'd hear about this? Well—"

There was a splash and a gurgle. It was clear even to George outside that the speaker, scarcely six weeks after the

241

event, had become a past-master of pauses, an expert at hesitation, who could cast a most marvelously rueful glance at his mug.

He took up the tale, a moment later, in practiced terms.

"They had this platform, I'd say about twelve feet each way, made of wood, and it was maybe two feet high, and covered with black cloth. That was at the end of the greathall, where the fireplace was. Three sides of it they had a small low railing, and that was covered with this same black cloth. On the fourth side were a couple of steps. That was all I saw when I first came in, except that there was a fire in the fireplace, but it was chilly there just the same.

"Well, they lined us up around all four sides, and we were supposed to stand facing *out*—I mean, away from the platform—but naturally we had plenty of chance to look over our shoulders."

"What'd you carry?"

"Halberds. But we never had to use 'em. And we could rest the butts on the floor—I mean, we never had to hold 'em obliqued, which can make your arms mighty tired."

"Go on."

"I was wondering if—"

"Here."

"Thankee. Well, I'd been standing there a little when the soldier next to me, name of Hal Garth, he pushed me and told me to look around, and I did, and there was the executioners. It gave me a jump. I'd never seen or heard 'em come in. They must have walked like cats. They were both dressed in tight black, with white aprons."

"Like butchers?"

"Yes, like butchers. Which of course they were, really. One had an axe, and it was a big one, though the shaft was short. You wouldn't have wanted to cut down a tree with it. Heavy. That was the chief executioner, and Hal Garth whispered to me that his name was Bulle. I don't know that for a fact; it's just what Hal told me. They both had black masks over their faces."

George Fitzwilliam's hand fell to his side, but he did not otherwise move. That lady! That kind lovely lady! He bowed his head.

"So then the lords started coming in. Never saw so many. Might have been Parliament, except that they didn't have any place to sit. They just stood there. There was a crowd outside too. You could hear 'em, but you couldn't see 'em, the windows were too high."

"No place to sit down at *all?*"

242

"Only for her. There was a stool on the platform. Then there was the block itself, but nobody'd want to sit on *that,* ha-ha! Could I have— Ah, thankee."

The gurgle again.

"There was more on the platform next time I looked. One was Lord Shrewsbury. I knew him. And another I heard afterward was Lord Kent. Then there was a preacher, come from Peterborough, dean of the cathedral there."

"They didn't allow her a Roman priest?"

"No. She asked for one. I heard it. But 'they said no. Then there was another man there; I guess he was the sheriff. He was all in black. But he didn't do anything, just stood there. He had a white stick in his hand. And when *she* came in I couldn't see her at first because just then the sergeant was standing right there. But I could *hear* her, and I could tell two or three people were helping her to walk."

"She weeping?"

"Never a tear! No, she sat as quiet as could be. In black. That's what I saw when I got a chance to turn my head. But she had a white ruff and a long white veil from the top of her cap, like a bride at a wedding. She was holding a cross in both hands, in front of her. Then another man come up, I don't know who he was, but he unrolled a piece of paper and he read out of it for a long time. Lawyer stuff. I couldn't make any sense out of it."

"The death sentence," somebody offered.

"That must have been what it was. I was watching Mary at the time. She'd put the cross down into her lap, but she didn't seem to be listening much, and when he was all through—the man who'd been reading—and we'd all yelled 'God save the queen,' why, then she took the cross up again, and she asked once more if she couldn't please have a priest, but they said no. Well then, my Lord Shrewsbury said to her 'Ma'am, you hear what we are commanded to do?' And she just nodded, as if he had no more than said it was a nice day—which it wasn't. She just said 'You must do your duty.' And then she got up. She had two women on the platform with her now, and they had to help her, but once she got up she shooed them away and stood there by herself. And she made a speech. I don't know ... I suppose I should have listened to it more. It was in English, and it wasn't very long, something about her being an anointed queen that had never planned to kill anybody anywhere at any time. That was the gist of it anyway."

A pause. A plash. A long wet sigh of contentment.

"After that this man from Peterborough started to pray at

243

her, and everybody repeated what he said, but she wouldn't listen. She got down on her knees and started to pray all by herself. *He* was praying in English, in a loud voice, but *she* was praying in something else, I guess it was Latin, very quiet. That went on for some time. Then the executioner went over to her and started to take a chain from off her neck, because he said that that was his by right, which as you know they always are. But she said no. She said he'd be paid properly—the money was all laid out—and she'd promised that chain to somebody else. They pulled back and forth a little while, but finally Bulle gave up. But he didn't like it. So he began taking off her dress and her ruff, which would have got in the way of the axe. But she stopped him. 'Let me do this,' she said. 'I understand it better than you,' she said. But she couldn't seem to raise her arms high enough—rheumatism, I suppose—and those two women had to help her again. *They* were weeping like fountains, but Mary Stuart herself didn't let go a tear. I'll swear to that. I'd have seen it if she had.

"Anyway these two women, they did manage to get the dress off, and there she was in bright red underwear. No, you couldn't see much skin. But everything was very clean and neat, I'll say that.

"Then these women, they tied a fancy lace kerchief around her eyes, and she sat down and picked up that cross again, and said 'All right.' She must have thought Bulle would do the job sideways, the way I hear they do it in France, only they use a sword there. He went to her, him and his assistant, and they helped her over to the block— she couldn't see then because of that bandage around her eyes—and she got to her knees there. But even then she didn't put her head down. She didn't seem to think she was supposed to. Bulle had to do that for her."

George thought: Yes, Mary Stuart was not accustomed to stooping.

"He did a bad job. Maybe he was nervous. The first time he hit her he hit her over the right ear. She made a little groan-sound, but she didn't move. And he hit her again, this time getting in a pretty fair one across the neck, though even then it didn't quite take the whole head off, the way it should. But it must have killed her. But he had to hit her a third time afore he could get the head free. Then everybody yelled 'God save the queen,' and Bulle he got out his platter and reached down to pick up the head to show it, the way he's expected to. But he took hold of it by the hair—and that all came off! See? She was as bald as an

244

egg, and she'd been wearing a wig!"

He laughed; but nobody else laughed.

"Well, he carried this around to each window, holding it up, and there was blood running over the sides and down both of his arms. You could hear everybody out there yelling 'God save the queen' and then— Look: I wonder if I could—"

"Here—"

"Aye. It was the second one that splashed the blood on me. Right here, aye. My, how they scrubbed it! But that's the very spot. You want to put your hand there? Well, now, how much would you—"

George went away, for he feared that if he entered the taproom he might kill that man.

Grief had scant chance to coast. There was a message from Hawkins waiting for him. It said to report in Plymouth immediately. It was not a request but a command. The Spaniards were coming.

42

"If It's a Fight You Want—"

No MAN HAD EVER SEEN a sight like this. A nation, complete with brass and banners, rose out of the dawn. On right, on left, as well as ahead, the horizon was studded with sails that gleamed in the early light; and though already there were more vessels than George Fitzwilliam had supposed to exist in the world, others, perversely, were appearing all the time.

The noises they made were multitudinous, and seemed everywhere. Trumpets greeted the day; and the roll of drums, changing the watch, was as ubiquitous as thunder—and almost as loud. Stern lanterns were being doused, twitching out as did the stars in an oily green sky, and doubtless there were shouts exchanged from vessel to vessel, but these were not to be distinguished aboard the ketch *Anne*. Bells rang; sea and sky alike, in every direction, seemed to be filled with the clang of bells.

For a moment George feared that he had somehow stumbled into the very middle of the Spanish fleet. And indeed, if he didn't put about, that's where, in a matter of minutes, he might be. Yet he stood like a man spellbound, paralyzed.

More and more of them loomed into sight. They were perfectly spaced, mathematically exact, military in the precision with which they moved, beautifully handled. They formed an enormous crescent, the tips of which, on either side, could scarcely be seen, they were so far away.

Right between those tips was the tiny six-gun *Anne;* and it was headed for the center. It drifted, mainsail flapping like a lame duck. Nobody even held the tiller, which swung back and forth, for the helmsman, like everybody else aboard, stood stunned by the sight of the Armada.

More and more sails appeared, as the last of the stars went away and the moon faded. The hulls too could be seen now. They were huge. There were some pinnaces or dispatch boats, and perhaps twenty caravels, but the greatest number of the vessels, the overwhelming majority, were high-sided and many-decked, built with enormous castles fore and aft. At least a dozen, all near the center of the line, were twice as big as any vessel those aboard the ketch ever had seen.

It is small wonder that they doubted their eyes.

The reds and pastels lent by a lightening sky weren't needed by this fleet. The vessels themselves were streaked with gilt, their bows carved and painted, their aftercastles a miracle of fretwork. Few sails, even the smallest, but bore some sort of device. Most of those sails, all the biggest ones, showed a colossal red cross, the Crusaders' cross, testifying that this was designed as a holy war rather than a mean expedition of conquest, avarice. Also there were, literally, thousands of silken streamers, banners, oriflammes, ensigns, pennants, and pennoncels, some of them many yards long, all sewn with threads of white, yellow, orange, crimson, azure, green.

For George it was agony to tear his gaze away.

"Hard larboard! Grommets, break out that spritsail! And two bonnets on the course!"

The spell was split. They were mariners once more, not children peering at a fairy-story pageant. Yet—they would never be the same again.

This was somewhere between the Lizard and Guernsey, at the very entrance of the English Channel. The Spanish ships, as well they might, were closing their ranks. Now there was a call for nearness, whatever the danger of collision. The maneuver was complicated, albeit exquisitely performed, and it would take time; yet somebody had noted the little scouting vessel and had gone to the trouble of sending a pinnace after her. The farther up the channel the Spaniards got before the fleet at Plymouth came swarming out, the harder it would be to stop them from making contact with their invasion forces in the Low Countries.

"Put on the last bonnet! And hoist that topper!"

"We're being chased, sir," said young Cornelius van Doorn.

"So it would seem."

Fishermen in those waters say that in fine summer weather —this was July 19—the wind customarily "goes around with the sun." It will blow from the north at night, edging toward northeast as the dawn spreads. By noon it would come clear around and be blowing from the south. In the afternoon it would be from the southwest. There is usually a lull at sundown, they say, but when the wind picks up again, after dark it is once more from the north.

It was ahead of schedule this morning. Though none of the body of the sun yet had shown, the wind was blowing from the southeast. The ketch's new course was north, and it was moving fast. But the pinnace was fast too. George watched her. Foam creamed at her bows, and she had cracked on everything but the cook's shirt. She was gaining on them.

"Master gunner!"

"Sir?"

"Load that saker in the stern. And do you, Doorn, rig the whipstaff to get the helmsman out of the way of the kick."

Doorn was extremely young, still in his teens, but he was a veteran of these troubled waters, being one of that company of nautical rebels who called themselves the Beggars of the Sea. As such, his life was forfeit if the Spaniards caught him. Recently he'd had a close shave. The *Anne,* then called the *Kabbeljaw,* had been surprised by a patrol boat near Flushing. The skipper and most of the crew had been killed when they resisted, and only Doorn—the mate then as he was now—and a few hands were left. He fully expected death, probably a prolonged one. The chance arrival of one of the earl of Cumberland's private pirate vessels alone had saved him. The ketch had been brought into Plymouth, where George Fitzwilliam, who had been on the lookout for some small fast vessel, bought her from Cumberland's agents and renamed and refitted her, retaining of the crew only the mate, young Doorn.

George had no dislike of Dutchmen, but for his present purpose he thought them too passionate in their hatred of Spaniards to be counted upon to keep their heads. Doorn, however, he did hire for his knowledge of the sailing points of this ketch.

The Nombre de Dios expedition, like the voyage of circum-

247

navigation, had been, on paper at least, a mercantile adventure. This was war now, real war, and George had not the slightest objection to taking an active command at sea—indeed, he had insisted upon it. He was not only captain and owner of the *Anne;* he was also her sailing master.

The dons, who always moved slowly—King Philip was famous for his *pie de plomo,* his foot of lead—had taken a long while to come. For years this invasion had been threatened, as the Spaniards were barbed by the behavior of just such swashbucklers as Francis Drake—*Sir* Francis Drake now—and his cousin John Hawkins. Philip didn't want to do it, for he had more than he could handle with the rebellious Low Countries, the recently snatched Portugal, and the New World; but he saw no alternative.

Don't wait for them to come—break them before they get started! was the Hawkins-Drake counsel. Hit 'em at home! But Queen Elizabeth preferred to keep her ships near her own shores, where she could control them. The army, under Leicester, was pitifully unprepared, a joke. If ever the crack Spanish troops did come pouring ashore there would be no stopping them. It was up to the navy to prevent that. After much wrangling and political maneuvering, the war party had prevailed at least enough to get the queen to consent to an off-balance blow. That had been the previous year, 1587, when George was called to Plymouth to assist in the preparations. After months of outfitting, victualing, restocking, recruiting, the actual thrust was something of a lark. With George commanding a small bark he had bought for the occasion—he was to sell her later at a profit—they had met with no mentionable resistance when they sailed into the harbor at Cadiz, chief supply port for the fleet that was being assembled at Lisbon, the greatest fleet in the history of mankind. They burned as many of the storeships as they could reach—more than ten thousand tons, plus cargo—and there and along the coast in the form of supply vessels meant to converge upon Cadiz, they seized vast amounts of dried fruit from Andalusia, olive oil, flour, wine, salt, gunpowder, pike staves, breastplates. The venture had been commissioned "to prevent or withstand such enterprises as might be attempted against her Highness' realm or dominions," but the men called it "singeing King Philip's beard." It was reckoned that this raid—if so massive a movement could be called a raid—had set back by a full year the invasion of England.

It had set it back; it had not killed it. The Spaniards,

though dismayed, were not discouraged. They started all over again, assembling another enormous fleet.

Drake pleaded to be permitted to smash that one too, in its place of birth, as he had done before. The queen's chief objection to war was known to be its expense; and Drake pointed out that by taking the fight to the enemy, *his* way of waging war, the institution actually could be made to show a profit. It was of no avail. Elizabeth was frightened by this time, and the ships were commanded not to stir from the Channel.

So there was the long and tedious task of keeping the narrow seas, holding warships and men in readiness, with wages and supplies furnished on a weekly basis and never liberal. It was the kind of work George did well and hated. He got home very little that winter.

"I thought you'd have more time to spend here, once you were rich," Anne said.

"I thought so too. But it seems we were wrong. It seems that the more money a man has the more time he is expected to give to the public service—free."

"I might as well be a mariner's wife."

"Aye. But it can't last forever."

Remembering this, he eyed the Armada, which was making up-Channel on a course about northeast by east; and he admired the seamanship. The ketch's course, almost due north, was taking it away from that glorious sight. The pinnace, pressing on every inch of canvas, was creeping up.

George shook his head. He knew what van Doorn was thinking. Doorn would have turned to fight. That's the way they were, those Dutchmen: emotional. But as George saw it, it was his duty to get to Plymouth with the news of the arrival of the Armada, not to turn aside for a duel. He saw no shame in running away; there would be plenty of time for fighting later.

George did, however, consent to tell his reason for loading the stern gun.

"They're touchy. They have old-fashioned ideas. The captain of that craft, if we fire at him—even if we don't reach him (and we probably won't)—he'll feel himself in honor bound to fire back four or five times. He believes that the admiral's watching him, but he'd do it anyway."

He pointed to the pinnace, where they could see in the light of the rising sun a glint of brass far forward.

"He'll fire from the bow, and every time he does there'll be a recoil. And every recoil will slow him a bit. Oh, not much! But inches could count in a chase like this, I think. If the fleet's bound up in Plymouth Sound, England's lost!"

The gunner worked out the tompion, a plug that had been placed into the muzzle of this small brass stern saker for the purpose of keeping out spray and sea water. He mopped the inside, which proved to be perfectly dry. He weighed powder, and cut a ball. He loaded, rammed home the wadding, and goosed the touchhole with a wire, having first fastened a strip of tin around that part of the gun so that the loosened powder wouldn't be whuffed away. He stepped back and picked up a match that one of his mates had lighted. He regarded the pinnace.

"I don't think it will," he muttered.

"Fire anyway," said George.

Timing it for a rise of the stern, the gunner put the match to the touchhole. Though they were firing back into a following wind, there was very little flare. The powder burned briskly, almost with a *poof*, and the gun went off.

They saw the plash. It had been only a few yards short of the pinnace, and perfectly in line.

"A bigger charge?" George suggested.

"Wouldn't be safe," the gunner said. "I used all I dared that time, more'n I should've."

"They're loading, back there!" van Doorn cried.

The bit of brass at the pinnace's bow coughed and a round white-gray cloud of smoke came out of it, tumbling over and over as the wind took it toward *Anne*. When it enveloped them for a moment it was streaked and thin. Before this time they had seen the ball hit, woefully short. But still the pinnace gained on them.

"Better load it again," said George, troubled.

The helmsman, the only man in the ketch who was facing forward, let out a great yell. He pointed exultantly.

Those aboard the pinnace had of course all been facing forward—and the pinnace put about.

The chase was ended.

For somebody else had got in with the news before George could do so, and now from out of Plymouth Sound under the shadow of Mount Edgecombe, around Rame Head, English ships were being painfully warped—Lord Howard's, the queen's, John Hawkins', Martin Frobisher's, Francis Drake's.

Here were not gaudy galleons. They showed no gilt, blew no trumpets. No banners streamed from their mastheads. They were pygmies compared with the giants from Spain; but they were handsomely gunned, as they were vigorously manned, and ready for anything. They made a course due east, meaning to close with the Spanish flank.

"Yonkers aloft! Put her over! Smart there! Take in that spritsail! And, master gunner—"

"Aye, aye, sir"

"Load everything!"

"Aye, aye!"

"Our course is due east," George Fitzwilliam told his mate. He dropped a hand on the lad's shoulder. "And if it's a fight you're yearning for, *mijnheer,* I think you are going to get it."

43

Conclave of the Besmudged

FOR TWO WEEKS he had not taken off his clothes, and if he had slept at all it was in snatches, so that when the order was flown for him to report immediately aboard the flagship, he cursed with a bitterness that bubbled out of his heart. Dizzy, perhaps made lightheaded by the cannonading, he went so far as to shake a fist at the *Ark Royal,* where the admiral was. Nevertheless he prepared to obey.

Those preparations were not elaborate. When he had sailed from Plymouth it was for the purpose of making a two-day scouting cruise, and he had with him no other clothes than those he wore, encrusted now with dirt and un-burned gunpowder: "Cudgel me and you'd bat out enough to fire another broadside," he had said only that morning. Neither could he wash. As there was no gunpowder left so was there precious little water, and what there was—there being no beer at all—must be saved for drinking purposes. George's beard was black, as was his face. He had lost his bonnet. His hose was ripped, his boots scuffed and scorched. His mouth tasted like a blacksmith's bib.

"You're in command," he muttered to Cornelius van Doorn.

"Aye, aye, sir."

The Dutcher too had a face as black as any Senegam-bian's, so that he crickled when he smiled or even spoke—the red eyes and the tear-washed skin around them, together with the extruded wet lips, touched up that negroid appear-ance. He too had lost his bonnet; but his hair, determinedly yellow, was finer than George's and had not caught so much grit.

This was his first command, and he was very serious about it.

It was not the ketch *Anne*. The second night of the running battle, when the Spanish fleet, still keeping its formation, was assembled in the tricky waters off Portland, the *Anne* had stumbled upon a caravel that was dragging its anchor. Without grappling hooks or boarding nets, they had swarmed all over her in a matter of minutes, and that for two reasons: her skipper and more than half of the crew of forty-odd were violently sick from some kind of food poisoning, and the others, confused, had been so busy trying to cut the cable of the offending anchor and to make about that they did not realize how far from formation they were. It was a great stroke of luck. The caravel, *San Juan de la Purificación*, commonly called *El Chico*, was a well-found vessel, in no way damaged, carrying two extra suits of sails, a chest of gold and silver coins for pay purposes, and a large supply of provisions and gunpowder, both of which would command fabulous prices anywhere along the south shore of England just then. By the rules of warfare, cargo and caravel alike went to George as a private adventurer. It would be a tidy fortune, and almost any other skipper would have headed for shore to take advantage of it. George never even considered this course. Instead he stripped his own *Anne* of his six guns, her provisions, and all her canvas save a small topsail, and loaded her—overloaded her, rather—with Spaniards, whom he told to find their way to shore as best they could, praying meanwhile that they would not be murdered when they got there. He retained only a handful of powderboys.

He liked the *Anne*—she was smart—but she was too small. He hoped that she would survive, somehow. He couldn't worry; there was too much to do.

This feat he had supposed would pass unnoticed, but he was mistaken. It was several days before he could be sure that any English ship he neared wouldn't open fire on him, but the word at last had been spread, and instead of being cannonaded when she hove into sight *El Chico* was cheered. And George, who already had the distinction of having discharged the first shot in this greatest of sea fights since Lepanto, now had the added distinction of being the only man to board an enemy vessel.

For it had been a standoff fight, contrary to all the rules of sea warfare. The Spaniards had the best soldiers in the world, and if they could ever come to grips with the enemy, as they hoped to do, the result would not be in doubt. But the English were nimble, and they were alert. *Fight the ships!* was the Hawkins-Drake dictum.

252

Those ships were fast. When they moved in together for the first time, the morning of the 21st—it was a Sunday but for once Francis Drake didn't seem to mind—it was not in battle spread-formation, Mediterranean style, but as a single line, one following the other. The Spaniards, bracing themselves, could hardly believe their eyes, and when the first vessel had wheeled, fired a broadside, and fallen off, and the second had done the same, and the third, the Spaniards had given a great cheer, for they thought, poor fools, that their enemy was in retreat! It must have bewildered them when the English returned almost immediately to do the same thing over again, in reverse. And then do it again. And again.

After all, why *should* they close? Why should they risk an embrace almost certain to crush them, for they were like dogs yapping and snapping around a chained bear—for all their show of ferocity, careful not to get too close.

Spanish soldiers lined the rails, six deep, their helmets gleaming, pikes or swords in their hands, tears in their eyes as they screamed to the heretic dogs to stand up and fight like men. But the heretic dogs only fired their cannons and fell back, reloading for the next run. Never had so much gunpowder been burned as in these past two weeks. Yet they begged for more. They would have paid anything for powder with which to finish the fight. It was not to be. Fortunately the don too was out of the stuff, so that now, battered, reeling, the winds denying him any chance of a return to the sands of Gravelines, he could only continue to run.

This was in the North Sea somewhere off Tynemouth, at the end of that five-hundred-mile fray.

As his cock was being brought around, George studied the Armada. Its course, he reckoned, was northwest by west. Their own course for the past half hour had been almost due west. They planned to put in somewhere, maybe the Firth of Forth. They had perforce broken off the pursuit.

Close-up, as he had so many times seen it, the Armada at that moment no doubt presented a pitiful sight. She had been mauled—spars shot away, anchors lost, rudders damaged, scarcely a hull that hadn't been holed. Her sails were shredded, coming apart. Always slow, now she could barely move: she staggered like a man in the last stages of exhaustion.

From where George stood at the head of the Jacob's ladder she seemed glorious still. The wrecked rigging, the severed lines, did not show, and the sails looked whole, full-bellied, their red crosses defiant in the light of the setting sun.

Those Spaniards were brave men. Their world was dead around them; they had been passed by, for they represented a way of life that already was gone. Yet when they died, when their fond foolish ideas of chivalry at last were exploded, something of Romance would expire at the same time, as something had done last year when the men at Fotheringay hacked off the head of Mary Stuart.

George Fitzwilliam knew that. He was too weary to be sure of much else, but he did know that.

"Have we got a man left who can still row?" he asked.

He was too tired to ponder the purpose of the call. It could hardly be a council. Why a council? There was no question of tactics. The only thing they could do was limp to the nearest port and get something to drink. Besides, by no means all of the captains were being summoned, in fact only a few.

"Here we are, sir. Should I help you?"

William Howard, earl of Effingham, lord high admiral of England, was tall, lank, slabsided, blunt. He was that rarity, an aristocratic mariner. He might have been spotted anywhere as a seafaring man. He held his position because of his birth; but though an accomplished courtier when he condescended to be, he preferred the poop deck to an armchair in some palace; and though he could hardly be expected to have the nautical knowledge of his vice-admiral, Drake, or his rear-admiral, John Hawkins, yet he was nobody's fool.

"Ah, Beeston . . . and Hawkins . . . and our old pirate friend Martin Frobisher . . . come aboard, sirs, come aboard!"

He had a voice that might have been caked with chalk.

"Captain Fitzwilliam, sir! You're most welcome!"

It was jolting to be greeted thus, right in the waist, by a man who, like all the rest of them, resembled an African slave. For though my lord had retained his bonnet and his sash of authority as the queen's personal representative on the sea, and also his fine long Spanish rapier, he was as shabby as any, and his face too had been blackened with smoke.

Even a Howard, George marveled, can get dirty.

He led them to the poop.

There were drummers, rigid at attention, and a couple of trumpeters who sounded a fanfare. There was a clump of officers and gentlemen-adventurers: they all looked alike.

"What's this mean?" George whispered to his old master.

"Don't you know? Didn't they tell you?"

254

"If they did I didn't hear it. My ears have been ringing so—"

He broke off, for he had seen a friend. Despite the charred clothes, the charcoal face, there could be no mistaking him.

"*Terence!*"

"Sh-sh! Thou'rt part of a ceremony. And that's not my name here." But he squeezed George's elbow, trying to turn him. "It's good to see thee and know that thou hast survived."

"I thought thou'd gone to the Continent!"

"I came back when I heard of the Spanish fleet. I—I'm going to take holy orders at Douai, George. Next time thou seest me, and pray God it be soon, I'll be in priest's garb. But I couldn't let them invade England—and me sitting off to one side."

He pushed George forward, toward the center of the deck.

"There, they called thy name," he whispered. "Good luck!"

George stumbled toward Lord Howard, who stood with bare sword. It was not until then that George realized what was happening. Here was an investiture! a field-of-battle accolade, the finest kind!

"Well, I'll be damned," he muttered as he went to one knee.

The blow on his shoulder was no formal tap. It was sound and firm, even harsh, a man's greeting. It rocked him, clearing his head.

"*Rise, Sir George!*"

Then Lord Howard, beaming, thrust the sword beneath his left arm and shook George by the hand.

And George, a little out of breath, rejoined John Hawkins, who had just become Sir John Hawkins. Terence, perhaps not trusting himself to control his emotions, had disappeared. Hawkins was watching Martin Frobisher, George Beeston and Roger Townsend become knights. George was watching the red sails of the Armada as they slid away.

Yes, something had died. . . .

But something too had been born.

"This, uh, this'll be confirmed by the queen?"

"Oh, aye. At a big function in London. A splendid court affair."

"Good," said George. "I'll bring my wife."

www.ingramcontent.com/pod-product-compliance
Lightning Source LLC
Chambersburg PA
CBHW020750250626
47155CB00003B/1007